P9-DBP-690

Kemptville And District
Home Support Inc.
P.O. Box 1192
Kemptville, Ontario KoG 1Jo

Hornet's Nest

ALSO BY PATRICIA CORNWELL

A Time for Remembering

Postmortem

Body of Evidence

All That Remains

Cruel and Unusual

The Body Farm

From Potter's Field

Cause of Death

Patricia Cornwell

Hornet's Nest

G. P. PUTNAM'S SONS

New York

G. P. Putnam's Sons
Publishers Since 1838
200 Madison Avenue
New York, NY 10016

Copyright © 1996 by Cornwell Enterprises, Inc.
All rights reserved. This book, or parts thereof,
may not be reproduced in any form without permission.
Published simultaneously in Canada

Library of Congress Cataloging-in-Publication Data

Cornwell, Patricia Daniels.
Hornet's nest / Patricia Cornwell.
p.   cm.
ISBN 0-399-14228-2 (acid-free)
I. Title.
PS3553.0692H6   1997   96-32085   CIP
813.5'4—dc20

Printed in the United States of America
1   3   5   7   9   10   8   6   4   2

This book is printed on acid-free paper. ∞

Book design by Marysarah Quinn

To Cops

Chapter One

That morning, summer sulked and gathered darkly over Charlotte, and heat shimmered on pavement. Traffic teemed, people pushing forward to promise as they drove through new construction, and the past was bulldozed away. The USBank Corporate Center soared sixty stories above downtown, topped by a crown that looked like organ pipes playing a hymn to the god of money. This was a city of ambition and change. It had grown so fast, it could not always find its own streets. Like a boy in puberty, it was rapidly unfolding and clumsy at times, and a little too full of what its original settlers had called pride.

The city and its county were named for Princess Charlotte Sophia of Mecklenburg-Strelitz before she became George III's queen. The Germans, who wanted the same freedoms the Scotch-Irish did, were one thing. The English were another. When Lord Cornwallis decided to come to town in 1780 and occupied what became known as the Queen City, he was met with such hostility by these stubborn Presbyterians that he dubbed Charlotte "the hornet's nest of America." Two centuries later, the swarming symbol was the official seal of the city and its NBA basketball team and the police department that protected all.

It was the white whirling dervish against midnight blue that Deputy Chief Virginia West wore on the shoulders of her crisp white uniform shirt with all its brass. Most cops, frankly, had not a clue as to what the symbol meant. Some thought it was a tornado, a white owl, a beard. Others were certain it had to do with sports events in the coliseum or the new two-hundred-and-thirty-million-dollar stadium that hovered downtown like an alien spacecraft. But West had been stung more than once and knew exactly what the hornet's nest was about. It was what awaited her when she drove to work and read *The Charlotte Observer* every morning. Violence swarmed, and everybody talked at once. This Monday, she was in a dark angry mood, ready to really stir things up.

The city police department recently had relocated to the new pearly concrete complex known as the Law Enforcement Center, or LEC, in the heart of downtown on Trade Street, the very road British oppressors long ago had followed into town. Construction in the area seemed endless, as if change were a virus taking over West's life. Parking at the LEC remained a mess, and she had not completely moved into her office yet. There were plenty of mud puddles and dust, and her unmarked car was new and a striking uniform blue that sent her to the carwash at least three times a week.

When she reached the reserved parking spaces in front of the LEC, she couldn't believe it. Occupying her spot was a drug dealer's set of chrome mags and parrot-green iridescent paint, a Suzuki, which she knew people flipped over in more ways than one.

"Goddamn it!" She looked around, as if she might recognize the person who had dared this perpetration.

Other cops were pulling in and out, and transporting prisoners in this constantly moving department of sixteen hundred police and unsworn support. For a moment, West sat and scanned, teased by the aroma of the Bojangles bacon and egg biscuit that by now was cold. Settling on a fifteen-minute slot in front of sparkling glass doors, she parked and climbed out, doing the best she could with briefcase, pocketbook, files, newspapers, breakfast, a large coffee.

She slammed her door shut with a hip as the dude she was looking for emerged from the building. He was jailing, jeans at low tide in that cool lockup look of six inches of pastel undershorts showing. The fashion statement got started in jail when inmates had their belts confiscated so they wouldn't hang themselves or someone else. The trend had crossed over every racial and socioeconomic line until half of the city's pants were falling off. West did not understand it. She left her car right where it was, fought with her armload as the dude mumbled good morning, trotting past.

"Brewster!" Her voice halted him like a pointed gun. "What the hell you think you're doing parking in my space!"

He grinned, flashing rings and a fake Rolex as he swept arms open wide, the pistol beneath his jacket peeking out. "Look around. Tell me what you see. Not one damn parking place in all of Charlotte."

"That's why important people like me are assigned one," she said to this detective she supervised as she tossed him her keys. "Bring them back when you've moved my car," she ordered.

West was forty-two, a woman who still turned heads and had never been married to anything beyond what she thought she was here on earth to do. She had deep red hair, a little unattended and longer than she liked it, her eyes dark and quick, and a serious body that she did not deserve, for she did nothing to maintain curves and straightness in the right places. She wore her uniform in a way that made other women want one, but that was not why she chose police blues over plain clothes. She supervised more than three hundred wiseass investigators like Ronald Brewster who needed every reminder of law and order West could muster.

Cops greeted her on her way in. She turned right, headed to offices where Chief Judy Hammer decided everything that mattered in law enforcement in this hundred-mile area of almost six million people. West loved her boss but right now didn't like her. West knew why she had been called in early for a meeting, and it was a situation beyond reason or her control. This was insane. She walked into Hammer's outer office, where Captain Fred Horgess was talking on the phone. He held his hand over the receiver and shook his head in a *there's nothing I can do* way to West as she walked up to the dark wooden door, where Hammer's name was announced brightly in brass.

"It's not good," he warned with a shrug.

"Why is it I didn't need you to tell me that?" West irritably said.

Balancing her burdens, she knocked with the toe of her Bates hi-gloss black shoe and nudged up the door handle with a knee, coffee almost spilling but caught in time. Inside, Hammer sat behind her overwhelmed desk, surrounded by framed photographs of children and grandbabies, her mission statement, *Prevent the Next Crime*, on the wall behind her. She was early fifties, in a smart houndstooth business suit, her telephone line buzzing relentlessly, but she had more important matters on her mind at the moment.

West dumped her load on one chair and sat in another one near the brass Winged Victory award the International Association of Chiefs of Police had presented to Hammer last year. She had never bothered to get a stand or give it an honored place. In fact, the trophy, which was three feet high, continued to occupy the same square of carpet next to her desk, as if waiting for a ride to someplace better. Judy Hammer won such things because she wasn't motivated by them. West removed the lid off her coffee, and steam wafted up.

"I already know what this is about," she said, "and you know what I think."

Hammer gestured to silence her. She leaned forward, folding her hands on top of her desk. "Virginia, at long last I have gotten the support of city council, the city manager, the mayor," she started to say.

"And every one of them, including you, is wrong," West said, stirring cream and sugar into her coffee. "I can't believe you've talked them into this, and I can tell you right now, they're going to find some way to screw it up because they don't really want it to happen. You shouldn't want it to happen, either. It's a damn conflict of interest for a police reporter to become a volunteer cop and go out on the street with us."

Paper crackled as West unwrapped a greasy Bojangles biscuit that Hammer would never raise to her lips, not even back in the old days when she was underweight and on her feet all day long, working the jail, juvenile division, crime analysis, records, inspections, auto theft, all those exciting assignments women got back in the days when they weren't allowed in patrol. She did not believe in fat.

"I mean, come on!" West said after a bite. "The last *Observer* cop reporter screwed us so bad you sued the newspaper."

Hammer did not like to think about Weinstein, the worthless wonder, a criminal, really, whose M.O. was to walk into the duty captain's office or the investigative division when no one was around. He stole reports right off desks, printers, and fax machines. This collaborative behavior culminated in his writing a front-page Sunday profile about Hammer, claiming she commandeered the police helicopter for personal use. She ordered off-duty cops to chauffeur her and do domestic jobs around her house. When her daughter was picked up for drunk driving, Hammer had the charges fixed. None of it was true. She did not even have a daughter.

Hammer got up, clearly frustrated and disturbed by the mess the world was in. She looked out a window, hands in the pockets of her skirt, her back to West.

"*The Charlotte Observer*, the city, think we don't understand them or care," she started her evangelism again. "And I know they don't understand us. Or care."

West crumpled breakfast trash, and scored two points in disgust. "All the *Observer* cares about is winning another Pulitzer Prize," she said.

Hammer turned around, as serious as West had ever seen her.

"I had lunch with the new publisher yesterday. First time any of us have had a civilized conversation with anyone from there in a decade, at least. A miracle." She began her habitual pacing, gesturing with passion. She loved her mission in life. "We really want to try this. Could it blow up in our faces? Absolutely." She paused. "But what if it worked? Andy Brazil . . ."

"Who?" West scowled.

"Very, very determined," Hammer went on, "completed our academy for volunteers, highest marks we've ever had. Impressed the hell out of the instructors. Does that mean he won't burn us, Virginia? No, no. But what I'm not going to have is this young reporter out there screwing up an investigation, getting the wrong view of what we do. He's not going to be lied to, stonewalled, hit on, hurt."

West put her head in her hands, groaning. Hammer returned to her desk and sat.

"If this goes well," the chief went on, "think how good it could be for the department, for community policing here and around the world. How many times have I heard you say, 'If only every citizen could ride just one night with us'?"

"I'll never say it again." West meant it.

Hammer leaned over her desk, pointing her finger at a deputy chief she admired and sometimes wanted to shake for thinking too small. "I want you out on the street again," she ordered. "With Andy Brazil. Give him a dose he won't forget."

"Goddamn it, Judy!" West exclaimed. "Don't do this to me. I'm up to my ears decentralizing investigations. The street crime unit's all screwed up, two of my captains out. Goode and I can't agree on anything, as usual . . ."

Hammer wasn't listening. She put on reading glasses and began reviewing a memo. "Set it up today," she said.

Andy Brazil ran hard and fast. He blew out loudly, checking the time on his Casio watch as he sprinted around the Davidson College track, in the small town of the same name, north of the big city. It was here he had grown up and gone to school on tennis and academic scholarships. He had lived at the college all his life, really, in a dilapidated frame house on Main Street, across from a cemetery that, like the recently turned co-ed school, was older than the Civil War.

Until several years ago, his mother had worked in the college food service, and Brazil had grown up on the campus, watching rich kids and Rhodes scholars on their way in a hurry. Even when he was about to graduate magna cum laude, some of his classmates, usually the cheerleaders, thought he was a townie. They flirted with him as he ladled eggs and grits on their plates. They were always startled in a dense sort of way when he trotted past in a hallway, loaded with books and afraid of being late to class.

Brazil had never felt he belonged here or anywhere, really. It was as if he watched people through a pane of glass. He could not touch others no matter how hard he tried, and they could not touch him, unless they were mentors. He had been falling in love with teachers, coaches, ministers, campus security, administrators, deans, doctors, nurses since he could remember. They were accepting, even appreciative, of his unusual reflections and solitary peregrinations, and the writings he shyly shared when he visited after hours, usually bearing limeades from the M&M soda shop or cookies from his mother's kitchen. Brazil, simply put, was a writer, a scribe of life and all in it. He had accepted his calling with humility and a brave heart.

It was too early for anybody else to be out this morning except a faculty wife whose lumpy shape would never be transformed by anything but death, and two other women in baggy sweats breathlessly complaining about the husbands who made it possible for them to be walking while most of the world worked. Brazil wore a *Charlotte Observer* tee shirt and shorts, and looked younger than twenty-two. He was handsome and fierce, with cheekbones high, hair streaked blond, body firm and athletically splendid. He did not seem aware of how others reacted to the sight of him, or perhaps it didn't matter. Mostly, his attention was elsewhere.

Brazil had been writing ever since he could, and when he had looked for a job after graduating from Davidson, he had promised *Observer* publisher Richard Panesa that if Panesa would give Brazil a chance, the newspaper would not be sorry. Panesa had hired him as a *TV Week* clerk, updating TV shows and movie blurbs. Brazil hated typing in programming updates for something he did not even watch. He did not like the other clerks or his hypertensive, overweight editor. Other than a promised cover story one of these days, there was no future for Brazil, and he began going to the newsroom at four in the morning so he could have all of the updates completed by noon.

The rest of the day he would roam desk to desk, begging for garbage-picking stories the seasoned reporters wanted to duck. There were always plenty of those. The business desk tossed him the scoop on Ingersoll-Rand's newest air compressor. Brazil got to cover the *Ebony* fashion show when it came to town, and the stamp collectors, and the world championship backgammon tournament at the Radisson Hotel. He interviewed wrestler Rick Flair with his long platinum hair when he was the celebrity guest at the Boy Scout convention. Brazil covered the Coca-Cola 600, interviewing spectators drinking beer while stock cars blasted past.

He turned in a hundred hours' overtime five months in a row, writing more stories than most of Panesa's reporters. Panesa held a meeting, gathering the executive editor, managing editor, and features editor behind closed doors to discuss the idea of making Brazil a reporter when his first six months were up. Panesa couldn't wait to see Brazil's reaction, knowing he would be thrilled beyond belief when Panesa offered him general assignment. Brazil wasn't.

Brazil had already applied to the Charlotte Police Department's academy for volunteers. He had passed the background check, and was enrolled in the class that was to start the following spring. In the meantime, his plan was to carry on with his usual boring job with the TV magazine because the hours were flexible. Upon graduation, Brazil hoped the publisher would give him the police beat, and Brazil would do his job for the paper and keep up his volunteer hours at the same time. He would write the most informed and insightful police stories the city had ever seen. If the *Observer* wouldn't go along with this, Brazil would find a news organization that would, or he would become a cop. No matter how anybody looked at it, Andy Brazil would not be told no.

The morning was hot and steamy, and sweat was streaming as he began his sixth mile, looking at graceful antebellum buildings of ivy and brick, at the Chambers classroom building with its dome, and the indoor tennis center where he had battled other college students as if losing meant death. He had spent his life fighting for the right to move ahead eighteen miles, along I-77, to South Tryon Street, in the heart of the city, where he could write for a living. He remembered when he first started driving to Charlotte when he was sixteen, when the skyline was simple, downtown a place to go. Now it seemed an overachieving stone and glass empire that kept growing. He wasn't sure he liked it much anymore. He wasn't sure it liked him, either.

Mile eight, he dropped in the grass and began plunging into push-ups. Arms were strong and sculpted, with veins that gracefully fed his strength. Hair on wet skin was gold, his face red. He rolled over on his back and breathed good air, enjoying the afterglow. Slowly, he sat up, stretching, easing himself into the vertical position that meant getting on with it.

Andy Brazil trotted back to his twenty-five-year-old black BMW 2002 parked on the street. It was waxed, and shellacked with Armor All, the original blue and white emblem on the hood worn off forever ago and lovingly retouched with model paint. The car had almost a hundred and twenty thousand miles on it, and something broke about once a month, but Brazil could fix anything. Inside, the interior was saddle leather, and there was a new police scanner and a two-way radio. He wasn't due on his beat until four, but he rolled into his very own spot at noon. He was the *Observer*'s police reporter and got to park in a special spot near the door, so he could take off in a hurry when trouble blew.

The instant he entered the lobby, he smelled newsprint and ink the way a creature smells blood. The scent excited him like police lights and sirens, and he was happy because the guard in the console didn't make him sign in anymore. Brazil took the escalator, trotting up moving metal stairs, as if he were late somewhere. People were statues coming down the other side. They glanced curiously at him. Everyone in the *Observer* newsroom knew who Brazil was, and he had no friends.

The newsroom was big and drab, filled with the sounds of keys clicking, phones ringing, and printers grabbing fast-breaking stories off the wire. Reporters were intense in front of computer screens, flipping through notepads with the paper's name on cardboard covers. They walked around, and the woman who covered local politics was running out the door after a scoop. Brazil still could not believe he was a player in this important, heady world, where words could change destinies and the way people thought. He thrived on drama, perhaps because he had been fed it since birth, although not generally in a good way.

His new desk was in the metro section, just beyond the glass-enclosed office of the publisher, Panesa, whom Brazil liked and was desperate to impress. Panesa was a handsome man, with silver-blond hair, and a lean look that had not become less striking as he had skated beyond forty. The publisher stood tall and straight in fine suits dark blue or black, and wore cologne. Brazil thought Panesa wise but had no reason to know it yet.

Each Sunday, Panesa had a column in the Sunday paper, and women in the greater Charlotte area wrote fan letters and secretly wondered what Richard Panesa was like in bed, or at least Brazil imagined this was so. Panesa was in a meeting when Brazil sat behind his desk and covertly glanced into the publisher's transparent kingdom as Brazil tried to look busy opening notepads, drawers, glancing at old printouts of long-published stories. It did not escape

Panesa's notice that his boyish, intense police reporter had arrived four hours early his first day on his new beat. Panesa was not surprised.

The first item on Brazil's agenda was that Tommy Axel had left another 7-Eleven rose on Brazil's desk. It had the sad, unhealthy complexion of the people who shopped in establishments that sold dark red, tightly furled passion at the counter for a dollar ninety-eight. It was still wrapped in clear plastic, and Axel had stuck it inside a Snapple bottle filled with water. Axel was the music critic, and Brazil knew he was watching this very minute from not very far away, in features. Brazil slid a cardboard box out from under his desk.

He had not finished moving in, not that the task was especially formidable. But he had been assigned nothing yet and had finished the first draft of a self-assigned piece on what it had been like to go through the volunteer police academy. He could add and cut and polish only so many times and was terrified by the thought of sitting in the newsroom with nothing to do. He had made it a habit to scan all six editions of the newspaper from wooden spools near the city directories. He often read the bulletin board, checked his empty mailbox, and had been meticulous and deliberately slow in moving his professional possessions the very short distance of forty-five feet.

This included a Rolodex with few meaningful phone numbers, for how to reach television networks and various shows, and stamp collectors or Rick Flair, was of little importance now. Brazil had plenty of notepads, pens, pencils, copies of his stories, city maps, and almost all of it could fit in the briefcase he had found on sale at Belk department store when he had been hired. It was glossy burgundy leather with brass clasps, and he felt very proud when he gripped it.

He had no photographs to arrange on his desk, for he was an only child and had no pets. It entered his mind that he might call his house to check on things. When Brazil had returned from the track to shower and change, his mother had been doing the usual, sleeping on the couch in the living room, TV loudly tuned in to a soap opera she would not remember later. Mrs. Brazil watched life every day on Channel 7 and could not describe a single plot. Television was her only connection to humans, unless she counted the relationship with her son.

Half an hour after Brazil appeared in the newsroom, the telephone rang on his desk, startling him. He snatched it up, pulse trotting ahead as he glanced around, wondering who knew he worked here.

"Andy Brazil," he said very professionally.

The heavy breathing was recognizable, the voice of the same pervert who had been calling for months. Brazil could hear her lying on her bed, sofa, fainting couch, wherever she got the job done.

"In my hand," the pervert said in her low, creepy tone. "Got it. Sliding in, out like a trombone . . ."

Brazil dropped the receiver into its cradle and shot Axel an accusing glance, but Axel was talking to the food critic. This was the first time in Brazil's life that he had ever gotten obscene phone calls. The only other situation to come even close was when he was blasting his BMW at the Wash & Shine in nearby Cornelius one day and a pasty-faced creep in a yellow VW bug pulled up and asked him if he wanted to earn twenty dollars.

Brazil's first thought was he was being offered a job washing the guy's car since Brazil was doing such a fine job on his own. This had been wrong. Brazil had turned the high pressure wand on the guy for free. He had memorized the creep's plate number and still had it in his wallet, waiting for the day when he could get him locked up. What the man in the VW bug had proposed was a crime against nature, an ancient North Carolina law no one could interpret. But what he had wanted in exchange for his cash had been clear. Brazil could not fathom why anyone would want to do such a thing to a stranger. He wouldn't even drink out of the same bottle with most people he knew.

Brazil was not naive, but his sexual experiences at Davidson had been more incomplete than those of his roommate, this he knew. The last semester of his senior year, Brazil had spent most nights in the men's room inside Chambers. There was a perfectly comfortable couch in there, and while his roommate slept with a girlfriend, Brazil slept with books. No one was the wiser, except the custodians, who routinely saw Brazil coming out of, not going into, the building around six o'clock every morning as he headed back to the second floor of the condemned building he and his roommate shared on Main Street. Certainly, Brazil had his own small private space in this dump, but walls were very thin and it was difficult to concentrate when Jennifer and Todd were active. Brazil could hear every word, everything they did.

Brazil dated Sophie, from San Diego, on and off during college. He did not fall in love with her, and this made her desire uncontrollable. It more or less ruined her Davidson career. First she lost weight. When that didn't work, she gained it. She took up smoking, and quit, got mononucleosis and got better, went to a therapist and told him all about it. None of this turned out to be the aphrodisiac Sophie had hoped, and their sophomore year she stabilized and slept with her piano teacher during Christmas break. She confessed her sin to Brazil. She and Brazil started making out in her Saab and her dorm room. Sophie was experienced, rich, and pre-med. She was more than willing to patiently explain anatomical realities, and he was open to research he really did not need.

At one P.M., Brazil had just logged onto his computer and gone into his basket to retrieve his police academy story, when his editor sat next to him. Ed Packer was at least sixty, with fly-away white hair and distant gray eyes. He wore bad ties haphazardly knotted, sleeves shoved up. At one point he must have been fat. His pants were huge, and he was always jamming a hand inside his waistband, tucking in his shirttail all around, as he was doing right now. Brazil gave him his attention.

"Looks like tonight's the night," Packer said as he tucked.

Brazil knew exactly what his editor meant and punched the air in triumph, as if he'd just won the U.S. Open.

"Yes!" he exclaimed.

Packer couldn't help but look at what was on the computer screen. It grabbed his interest, and he slipped glasses out of his shirt pocket.

"Sort of a first-person account of my going through the academy," Brazil said, new and nervous about pleasing. "I know it wasn't assigned, but . . ."

Packer really liked what he was reading and tapped the screen with a knuckle. "This graf's your lead. I'd move it up."

"Right. Right." Brazil was excited as he cut the paragraph and pasted it higher.

Packer rolled his chair closer, nudging him out of the way to read more. He started scrolling through what was a very long story. It would have to be a Sunday feature, and he wondered when the hell Brazil wrote it. For the past two months, Brazil had worked days and gone to the police academy at night. Did the kid ever sleep? Packer had never seen anything like it. In a way, Brazil unnerved him, made him feel inadequate and old. Packer remembered how exciting journalism was when he was Brazil's age and the world filled him with wonder.

"I just got off the phone with Deputy Chief Virginia West," he said to his protégé as he read. "Head of investigations . . ."

"So who am I riding with?" Brazil interrupted, so eager to ride with the police, he couldn't contain himself.

"You're to meet West at four this afternoon, in her office, will ride with her until midnight."

Brazil had just been screwed and couldn't believe it. He stared at his editor, who had just failed the only thing Brazil had ever expected of him.

"No way I'm being babysat, censored by the brass!" Brazil exclaimed and didn't care who heard. "I didn't go to their damn academy to . . ."

Packer didn't care who heard for a different reason. He had been a complaint department for the past thirty years, here and at home, and his attention span tended to flicker in and out as he mentally drove through different cells, picking up garbled snippets of different conversations. He suddenly recalled what his wife had said at breakfast about stopping for dog food on the way home. He remembered he had to take his wife's puppy to the veterinarian at three for some sort of shot, then Packer had a doctor's appointment after that.

"Don't you understand?" Brazil went on. "They're just handling me. They're just trying to use me for PR!"

Packer got up. He towered wearily over Brazil like a weathered tree gathering more shadow the older it grows.

"What can I say?" Packer said, and his shirt was untucked again. "We've never done this before. It's what the cops, the city, are offering. You'll have to sign a waiver. Take notes. No pictures. No videotapes. Do what you're told. I don't want you getting shot out there."

"Well, I've got to go back home to change into my uniform," Brazil decided.

Packer walked off, hitching up his pants, heading to the men's room. Brazil slumped back in his chair and looked up at the ceiling as if the only stock he owned had just crashed. Panesa watched him through glass, interested in how he was going to turn this around, and convinced he would. Systems analyst Brenda Bond blatantly glared at him from a nearby computer she was fixing. Brazil never paid her any mind. She was repulsive to him, thin and pale, with coarse black hair. She was hateful and jealous, and certain she was smarter than Brazil and all because computer experts and scientists were like that. He imagined Brenda Bond spending her life on the Internet inside chat rooms, because who would have her?

Sighing, Brazil got up from his chair. Panesa watched Brazil pick up an ugly red rose in a Snapple bottle, and the publisher smiled. Panesa and his wife had desperately wanted a son, and after five daughters it was either move to a larger home, become Catholic or Mormon, or practice safe sex. Instead, they had gotten divorced. He could not imagine what it must be like to have a son like Andy Brazil. Brazil was striking to look at, and sensitive, and though all the results weren't in, the biggest talent ever to walk through Panesa's door.

Tommy Axel was typing a big review of a new k.d. lang album that he was listening to on earphones. He was a goofball, sort of a Matt Dillon who wasn't famous and never would be, Brazil thought. He walked up to Axel's desk and clunked the rose next to the keyboard as Axel boogied in his Star Trek tee shirt. Surprised, Axel pushed the earphones down around his neck, faint, thin music leaking out. Axel's face was smitten. This was the One for him. He had known it since he was six, somehow had a premonition that a divine creature like this would overlap orbits with his when the planets were aligned.

"Axel," Brazil's heavenly voice sounded like a thunderclap, "no more flowers."

Axel stared at his lovely rose as Brazil stalked off. Brazil didn't mean it, Axel was certain, as he watched Brazil. Axel was grateful for his desk. He scooted his chair in closer and crossed his legs, aching for the blond god walking with purpose out of the newsroom. Axel wondered where he was going. Brazil carried his briefcase as if he wasn't coming back. Axel had Brazil's home phone number because he had looked it up in the book. Brazil didn't live in the city, sort of out in the sticks, and Axel didn't quite understand it.

Of course, Brazil probably didn't make twenty thousand dollars a year, but he had a *bad* car. Axel drove a Ford Escort that wasn't new. The paint job was beginning to remind him of Keith Richards's face. There was no CD player and the *Observer* wouldn't buy him one, and he planned to remind everyone there of that someday when he landed a job with *Rolling Stone*. Axel was thirty-two. He had been married once, for exactly a year, when he and his wife looked at each other during a candlelight dinner, their relationship the mystery of all time, she from one planet, he from another.

They, the aliens, agreeably left for new frontiers where no person had gone before. It had nothing to do with his habit of picking up groupies at concerts after Meatloaf, Gloria Estefan, Michael Bolton, had worked them into a lather. Axel would get a few quotes. He'd put the boys and their winking lighted shoes, shaved heads, dreadlocks, and body piercing, in the newspaper. They called Axel, excited, wanting extra copies, eight-by-ten photographs, follow-up interviews, concert tickets, backstage passes. One thing usually led to another.

While Axel was thinking about Brazil, Brazil was not thinking about him. Brazil was in his BMW and trying to calculate when he might need gas next since neither that gauge nor the speedometer had worked in more than forty thousand miles. BMW parts on a scale this grand were, in his mind, aviation instrumentation and simply beyond his means. This was not good for one who drove too fast and did not enjoy being stranded on a roadside waiting for the next non–serial killer to offer a ride to the nearest gas station.

His mother was still snoring in front of the TV. Brazil had learned to walk through his decaying home and the family life it represented without seeing any of it. He headed straight to his small bedroom, unlocked the door, and shut it behind him. He turned on a boom box, but not too loud, and let Joan Osborne envelop him as he went into his closet. Putting on his uniform was a ritual, and he did not see how he could ever get tired of it.

First, he always laid it out on the bed and indulged himself, just looking for a moment, not quite believing someone had given him permission to wear such a glorious thing. His Charlotte uniform was midnight blue, creased and new with a bright white hornet's nest that seemed in motion, like a white twister, on each shoulder patch. He always put socks on first, black cotton, and these had not come from the city. Next he carefully pulled on summer trousers that were hot no matter how light the material, a subtle stripe down each leg.

The shirt was his favorite because of the patches and everything else that he would pin on. He worked his arms through the short sleeves, began buttoning in the mirror, all the way up to his chin, and clipped on the tie. Next was his name plate and whistle. To the heavy black leather belt he attached the holder with its Mag-Lite and his pager, saving room for the radio he would check out at the LEC. His soft Hi-Tec boots weren't patent leather like the military type he had seen most of his life, but more like high-top athletic shoes. He could run in these if the need ever arose, and he hoped it would. He did not wear a hat because Chief Hammer did not believe in them.

Brazil inspected himself in the mirror to make sure all was perfect. He headed back downtown with the windows and sunroof open and propped his arm up whenever he could because he enjoyed the reaction of drivers in the next lane when they saw his patch. People suddenly slowed down. They let him pass when the light turned green. Someone asked him directions. A man spat, eyes filled with resentment Brazil did not deserve, for he had done nothing to him. Two teenaged boys in a truck began making fun of him, and he stared straight ahead and drove, as if none of this was new. He had been a cop forever.

The LEC was several blocks from the newspaper, and Brazil knew the way as if he were going home. He pulled into the parking deck for visitors and tucked his BMW in a press slot, angling it the way he always did so people didn't hit his doors. He got out and followed polished hallways to the duty captain's office, because he had no idea where the investigative division was or if he could just stroll in without asking permission. In the academy, his time had been spent in a classroom, the radio room, or out on a street learning how to direct traffic and work nonreportable accidents. He did not know his way around this four-story complex, and stood in a doorway, suddenly shy in a uniform that did not include gun, baton, pepper spray, or anything helpful.

"Excuse me," he announced himself.

The duty captain was big and old at his desk, and going through pages of mug shots with a sergeant. They ignored him. For a moment Brazil watched Channel 3 television reporter Brent Webb, perched over the press baskets, going through reports, stealing whatever he wanted. It was amazing. Brazil watched the asshole tuck the reports into his zip-up briefcase, where no other journalist in the city would ever see them, as if it were perfectly acceptable for him to cheat Brazil and everyone trying to report the news. Brazil stared at Webb, then at this sergeant and captain who did not seem to care what crimes were committed in plain view.

"Excuse me," Brazil tried again, louder.

He walked in, rudely ignored by cops who had hated the paper so long they no longer remembered why.

"I need to find Deputy Chief West's office." Brazil would not be ignored.

The duty captain lifted another plastic-sheathed page of hard-boiled mugs up to the light. The sergeant turned his back to Brazil. Webb stopped what he was doing, his smile amused, maybe even mocking as he looked Brazil up and down, assessing this unfamiliar guy playing dress-up. Brazil had seen Webb enough on television to recognize him anywhere and had heard a lot about him, too. Other reporters called Webb *The Scoop*, for reasons Brazil had just witnessed.

"So how do you like being a volunteer?" Webb was condescending and had no idea who Brazil was.

"Which way to investigations," Brazil replied, as if it were an order, his eyes piercing.

Webb nodded. "Up the stairs, can't miss it."

Webb studied the way Brazil was dressed and started laughing, as did the sergeant and duty captain. Brazil helped himself to the TV reporter's briefcase and pulled out a handful of purloined offense reports. Brazil smoothed and shuffled them. He perused and stacked them neatly, taking his time, while everyone watched and Webb's face turned red.

"Believe Chief Hammer might like to see *The Scoop* in action." Brazil smiled at him.

Brazil's boots were quiet as he walked off.

Chapter Two

Patrol was the largest division of the Charlotte Police Department, but investigations was the most treacherous, it was Virginia West's belief. Citizens followed burglaries, rapes, and homicides with fearful eyes. They complained when violent offenders weren't instantly snatched off the street, as if the Rapture had come. West's phone had not stopped ringing all day.

The trouble started three weeks ago when Jay Rule, a businessman from Orlando, arrived in the Queen City for a textile meeting. Hours after Rule left the airport in a rental Maxima, the car was found abandoned in a dark, overgrown vacant lot off South College Street, in the heart of downtown. The interior bell was dinging its complaint that the driver's door was open and headlights on. A briefcase and overnight bag had been gone through in the backseat. Cash, jewelry, portable phone, pager, and no one was quite sure what else, were gone.

Jay Rule, thirty-three, was shot five times in the head with a .45

caliber pistol loaded with a high-velocity, extremely destructive hollowpoint ammunition called Silvertips. His body was dragged fifteen feet into kudzu, his pants and undershorts pulled down to his knees, his genital area spray-painted bright orange in the shape of a large hourglass. No one, including the FBI, had ever seen anything like this. Then the following week, it happened again.

The second homicide was less than two blocks from the first, just off West Trade Street, behind the Cadillac Grill, which wasn't open at night, because of crime. Jeff Calley, forty-two, was a Baptist minister visiting Charlotte from Knoxville, Tennessee. His mission in the city was simple. He was moving his failing mother into a nursing home called The Pines and staying in the Hyatt while he did so. He never checked in. Late that night, his rental Jetta was found, driver's door open, bell dinging, same modus operandi.

Week three, the nightmare repeated itself when fifty-two-year-old Cary Luby visited from Atlanta. West was discussing his case over the phone when Brazil appeared in her doorway. West did not notice him. She was too busy shuffling through large, gory scene photographs as she continued arguing with an assistant district attorney.

"That's not correct, I don't know where you got that, okay? He was shot multiple times in the head, contact. A .45 loaded with Silvertips . . . Yeah, yeah, exactly. All within several blocks of each other." She was beginning to get annoyed. "Jesus Christ. Of course I've got people down there undercover, hookers, pimps, trolling, hanging out, whatever it takes. What do you think?"

She switched the phone to her other hand, wondering why she ever wore earrings, and irritated that anyone might question her ability to do her job. Checking her watch, she looked through more photographs, pausing at one that clearly showed the painted hourglass, which was rather much a solid orange figure eight. The base was over the genitals, the top over the belly. It was weird. The A.D.A. continued asking questions about the crime scene, and West's patience was deteriorating. So far, this day had been shit.

"Just like the others," she told him emphatically. "Everything.

Wallet, watch, wedding band." She listened. "No. No. Not credit cards, anything with the victim's name. . . . Why? Because the killer's smart, that's why." She sighed, her head beginning to throb. "Jesus friggin' Christ. That's my point, John. If we're talking *carjacking*, then why wasn't his rental Thunderbird taken? *Not a single car has been.*"

She swiveled around in her chair and almost dropped the phone when she saw the young male volunteer cop standing in her doorway, writing as fast as he could in a reporter's notepad. The son of a bitch was looking around West's office, taking down every confidential word being said about the most sensational, scariest murders the city had ever known. So far, sensitive details had been kept out of the press as political pressure gathered and darkened and swarmed.

"Gotta go," West abruptly said.

She slammed down the receiver, hanging up on the A.D.A. She pinned Brazil with her eyes.

"Shut the door," she said in a quiet, hard way that would have terrified anyone who worked for her or was about to get arrested.

Brazil was unflinching as he got closer to the desk. He was not about to be intimidated by this big-shot bureaucrat who had sold him down the river. He dropped Webb's stolen offense reports in front of her.

"What do you think you're doing?" West demanded.

"I'm Andy Brazil with the *Observer*," he said with cool politeness. "Webb's swiping reports out of the press basket. In the off chance you might care. And I'm going to need to check out a radio. I was supposed to meet you at four."

"And what? Eavesdrop?" West shoved back her chair, got up. "Looks to me like you already got your story."

"I'm going to need a radio," Brazil reminded her again, for he couldn't imagine being out on the street and not having a lifeline to the dispatchers.

"No you're not. Trust me," West promised him.

She angrily stuffed files into her briefcase and snapped it shut.

She grabbed her pocketbook and stalked out. Brazil was on her heels.

"You've got your nerve," she went on furiously, as if she had been mad at this young man in uniform all of her life. "Just like every other asshole out there. Give 'em a little, want more. Can't trust anybody."

West wasn't at all what Brazil had expected. He didn't know why he'd assumed the deputy chief would be overweight and over-bearing, flat-chested, with a square, masculine face, and over-processed hair. But no. She was maybe five-six, five-seven, with dark red hair barely brushing her collar, and very good bones. She was almost handsome, and buxom, and not the least bit fat, but he didn't care and would never be interested. She was unkind and un-attractive to him.

West shoved open glass doors leading into the parking lot. She dug into her pocketbook, heading to her unmarked Crown Victoria.

"I told everyone what a bad idea this was. Would they listen?" She fumbled with keys.

"Would you?" Brazil demanded.

West paused, looking at him. She yanked open the door, and Brazil blocked it.

"It might be nice if I got a fair trial." He shoved his notepad at her, flipping through scribbles he had made while West was on the phone. "I was describing your office and you," he announced much like the A.D.A. West had just been talking to on the phone.

She didn't have to skim much to know she'd made a wrong as-sumption. She sighed, stepping back, looking volunteer officer Brazil up and down, wondering how it could be possible that a re-porter was dressed like this. What had policing come to? Hammer had lost her mind. Brazil should be arrested for impersonating an officer, that was the reality of things.

"Where do you live?" West asked him.

"Davidson."

This was good. At least the next hour and a half would be spent in the commute. West might even be able to stretch it out. The longer she could keep him off the street, the better. She almost smiled as she climbed into her car.

"We'll go there first so you can change clothes," she gruffly said.

For a while, they did not speak as scanner lights blinked, and dispatchers and cops cut in and out on the radio like Rollerbladers. The Mobile Data Terminal (MDT) beeped as it logged calls and displayed addresses and messages on its computer screen. West and Brazil drove through the city as rush hour peaked. It looked like it might rain. Brazil was staring out his window. He felt stupid and mistreated as he took off his police tie and unbuttoned his collar.

"How long you been with the *Observer?*" West asked him, and she felt a tug around her chest, as if her bulletproof vest were rubbing her wrong, except she wasn't wearing one. She felt a little sorry for this ride-along.

"A year," Brazil answered, hateful toward Deputy Chief West and wondering if she were going to let him ride with her again.

"How come I've never heard of you before now?" she asked.

"I didn't get the police beat until I finished the academy. That was the deal."

"What deal?"

"My deal." Brazil continued to stare sullenly out the window.

West tried to change lanes but the jerk next to her wasn't cooperative. She gestured angrily back at him. "Same as you, drone!" She stopped at a red light and looked at Brazil. "What do you mean, *deal?*"

"I wanted the cop shop, told them I'd make it worth their while."

"What's that supposed to mean?"

"I want to know cops. So I can write about them. I want to get it straight."

West didn't believe him. Reporters always said shit like that, lied with pretty tongues, no different than people in general, really. She drove on, got out a cigarette, and lit it.

"If you're so curious about us, how come you didn't become a cop for real?" she challenged him.

"I'm a writer," Brazil said simply, as if this were his race, his religion, or family name.

"And we all know cops can't write." West blew out smoke. "Can't even read unless there's pictures."

"*There are* pictures."

She threw up her hands and laughed. "See?"

Brazil was silent.

"So why do you live way the hell in Davidson?" she asked.

"I went to school there."

"I guess you must be smart."

"I get by," he told her.

The gleaming Crown Victoria turned onto Main Street, which was what its name suggested in this charming college town. Homes were genteel, white frame and brick, with ivy and sprawling porches and swings. West had grown up outside of Charlotte, too, but heading in a different direction, where there wasn't much but red clay and fathomless farmland. She couldn't have afforded to go to a college like Davidson and doubted her SATs would have impressed anybody in a positive way. Brazil's college was sort of like Princeton and other places West had only read about.

"While we're on the subject," she said, "I don't remember any police stories by you."

"This is my first day on the beat."

She couldn't suppress her growing dismay over what she had been saddled with this night. A dog barked and began chasing her car. Suddenly, it was raining hard.

"So what'd you do for a year?" she investigated further.

"The TV magazine," Brazil added to his resume. "A lot of overtime, a lot of stories nobody wanted." He pointed, releasing his shoulder harness. "It's that one."

"You don't take your seatbelt off until I've stopped the car. Rule number one." West pulled into a rutted, unpaved driveway.

"Why are you making me change clothes? I have a right . . ." Brazil finally spoke his mind.

"People wearing what you got on get killed out here," West cut him off. "Rule number two. You don't have a right. Not with me. I don't want anyone thinking you're a cop. I don't want anyone thinking you're my partner. I don't want to be doing this, got it?"

Brazil's house hadn't been painted in too long to tell the color. Maybe it had been pale yellow once, maybe eggshell or white. Mostly now it was gray and flaking and peeling, like a sad old woman with a skin condition. An ancient, rusting white Cadillac was parked in the drive, and West decided that whoever lived here didn't have taste, money, or time for repairs and yard work. Brazil angrily pushed open the car door, gathering his belongings as he got out, and halfway tempted to tell this deputy chief to get the hell out of here and not come back. But his BMW was still in Charlotte, so that might pose a problem. He bent over, peering inside at her.

"My dad was a cop." He slammed the door shut.

West was typical brass, typical anybody who had power, Brazil fumed as he strode up the walk. She didn't give a shit about helping somebody else get started. Women could be the worst, as if they didn't want anybody else to do well because no one was nice to them when they were coming along, or maybe so they could pay everybody back, persecute innocent guys who'd never even met them, whatever. Brazil imagined West at the net, a perfect lob waiting for his lethal overhead smash. He could ace her, too.

He unlocked the front door of the house he had lived in all his life. Inside, he unbuttoned his uniform shirt and looked around, suddenly conscious of a dim, depressing living room of cheap furniture and stained wall-to-wall carpet. Dirty ashtrays and dishes were wherever somebody had forgotten them last, and gospel music swelled as George Beverly Shea scratched *How Great Thou Art* for the millionth time. Brazil went to the old hi-fi and impatiently switched it off.

"Mom?" he called out.

He began tidying up, following a mess into a slovenly old kitchen where milk, V8 juice, and cottage cheese had been left out by someone who had made no effort to clean up or hide the empty fifth of Bowman's cheap vodka on top of the trash. Brazil picked up dishes and soaked them in hot sudsy water. Frustrated, he yanked out his shirttail and unbuckled his belt. He looked down at his name tag, shiny and bright. He fingered the whistle on its chain. For an instant, his eyes were filled with a sadness he could not name.

"Mom?" he called out again. "Where are you?"

Brazil walked into the hallway, and with a key that no one else had a copy of, he unlocked a door that opened onto the small room where he lived. It was tidy and organized, with a computer on a Formica-topped desk, and dozens of tennis trophies and plaques and other athletic awards on shelves, furniture, and walls. There were hundreds of books in this complicated person's simple, unassuming space. He carefully hung up his uniform and grabbed khakis and a denim shirt off hangers. On the back of the door was a scarred leather bomber jacket that was old and extra large and looked like it might have come from some earlier time. He put it on even though it was warm out.

"Mom!" Brazil yelled.

The light was flashing on the answering machine by his bed, and he hit the play button. The first message was from the newspaper credit union, and he impatiently hit the button again, then three more times, skipping past hang-ups. The last message was from Axel. He was playing guitar, singing Hootie & the Blowfish.

"I only wanna be with you . . . Yo! Andy, it's Axel-don't-axe-me. Maybe dinner? How 'bout Jack Straw's . . . ?"

Brazil impatiently cut off the recording as the phone rang. This time the caller was live and creepy, and breathing into the phone as the pervert had sex with Brazil in mind, again without asking.

"I'm holding youuu so haarrrddd, and you're touching me with your tongue, sliiiidiiing . . ." she breathed in a low tone that reminded Brazil of psycho shows he sometimes had watched as a child.

"You're sick." He slammed the receiver back into its cradle.

He stood in the mirror over his dresser and began brushing hair out of his eyes. It was really bugging him, getting too long, streaks from the sun catching light. He had always worn his hair one of two ways, short or not as short. He was tucking an obstinate strand behind an ear when suddenly the reflection of his mother boiled up from behind, an obese, raging drunk, attacking.

"Where have you been?" his mother screamed as she tried to backhand her son across the face.

Brazil raised an arm, warding off the blow just in time. He wheeled around, grabbing his mother by both wrists, firmly but gently. This was a tired old drama, an endless rerun of a painful play.

"Easy, easy, easy," he said as he led his besotted mother to the bed and sat her down.

Muriel Brazil began to cry, rocking, slurring her words. "Don't go. Don't leave me, Andy. Please, oh pleeeassse."

Brazil glanced at his watch. He looked furtively at the window, afraid West might somehow see through shut blinds and know the wretched secret of his entire life.

"Mom, I'm going to get your medicine, okay?" he said. "You watch TV and go to bed. I'll be home soon."

It wasn't okay. Mrs. Brazil wailed, rocking, screaming hell on earth. "Sorry, sorry, sorry! Don't know what's wrong with me. Andyeeee!"

West did not hear all of this, but she heard enough because she had opened car windows to smoke. She was suspicious that Brazil lived with a girlfriend and they were having a fight. West shook her head, flicking a butt out onto the weed-choked, eroded drive. Why would anyone move in with another human being right after college, after all those years of roommates? For what? She asked no questions of Brazil as they drove away. Whatever this reporter might have to say to explain his life, she didn't want to hear it. They headed back to the city, the lighted skyline an ambitious monument to banking and girls not allowed. This wasn't an original thought. She heard Hammer complain about it every day.

West would drive her chief through the city, and Hammer would look out, poking her finger and talking about those businessmen behind tall walls of glass who decided what went into the paper and what crimes got solved and who became the next mayor. Hammer would rail on about Fortune 500 yahoos who didn't live anywhere near here and determined whether the police needed a bicycle squad or laptops or different pistols. Rich men had decided to change the uniforms years ago and to merge the city police with the Mecklenburg County Police. Every decision was unimaginative and based on economics, according to Hammer.

West believed every bit of it as she and Brazil cruised past the huge, new stadium where David Copperfield was making magic and parking decks were jammed with thousands of cars. Brazil was oddly subdued, and not writing down a word. West looked curiously at him as the police scanner rudely announced this modern city's primitive crimes, and the radio softly played Elton John.

"Any unit in the area," a dispatcher said. "B&E in progress, four hundred block East Trade Street."

West floored it and flipped on lights. She whelped the siren, gunning past other cars. "That's us," she said, snapping up the mike.

Brazil got interested.

"Unit 700," West said over the air.

The dispatcher wasn't expecting a deputy chief to respond and sounded somewhat startled and confused.

"What unit?" the dispatcher inquired.

"700," replied West. "In the nine hundred block. I'll take the B&E in progress."

"Ten-four, 700!"

The radio broadcast the call. Other cars responded as West cut in and out of traffic. Brazil was staring at her with new interest. Maybe this wasn't going to be so bad after all.

"Since when do deputy chiefs answer calls?" he said to her.

"Since I got stuck with you."

The projects on East Trade were cement barracks subsidized by the government and exploited by criminals who did deals in the dark and got their women to lie when the cops showed up. Breaking and entering around here, it had been West's experience, usually meant someone was pissed off. Most of the time, this was a girlfriend calling in a complaint on an apartment where her man was hiding and had enough outstanding warrants to be locked up twenty times.

"You stay in the car," West ordered her ride-along as she parked behind two cruisers.

"No way." Brazil grabbed the door handle. "I didn't go to all this trouble to sit in the car everywhere we go. Besides, it isn't safe to be out here alone."

West didn't comment as she scanned buildings with windows lighted and dark. She studied parking lots filled with drug dealer cars and didn't see a soul.

"Then stay behind me, keep your mouth shut, and do what you're told," she told him as she got out.

The plan was pretty simple. Two officers would take the front of the apartment, on the first floor, and West and Brazil would go around back to make sure no one tried to flee through that door. Brazil's heart was pounding and he was sweating beneath his leather jacket as they walked in the thick darkness beneath sagging clotheslines in one of the city's war zones. West scanned windows and unsnapped her holster as she quietly got on the radio.

"No lights on," she said over the air. "Closing in."

She drew her pistol. Brazil was inches behind her and wished he were in front, as furtive officers they could not see closed in on a unit scarred by graffiti. Trash was everywhere, caught on rusting fences and in the trees, and the cops drew their guns as they reached the door.

One of them spoke into his radio, giving West, their leader, an update. "We got the front."

"Police!" his partner threatened.

Brazil was concerned about the uneven terrain, and clotheslines hanging low enough to choke someone, and broken glass everywhere in the tar-black night. He was afraid West might hurt herself and turned on his Mag-Lite, illuminating her in a huge circle of light. Her sneaking silhouette with drawn pistol was bigger than God.

"Turn that fucking thing off!" she whipped around and hissed at him.

Charlotte police caught no one on that call. West and Brazil were in a bad mood as they rode and the radio chattered. She could have gotten shot. Thank God her officers hadn't seen what this idiot reporter had done. She couldn't wait to give Hammer a piece of her mind and was halfway tempted to call her boss at home. West needed something to give her a boost and pulled into the Starvin Marvin on South Tryon Street. Before she had shifted the car into park, Brazil was pulling up his door handle.

"You ever heard of looking before you leap?" she asked, like a severe schoolteacher.

Brazil gave her an indignant, disgusted look as he undid his seatbelt. "I can't wait to write about you," he threatened.

"Look." West nodded at the store, at the plate glass in front, at customers prowling inside and making purchases. "Pretend you're a cop. That should be easy for you. So you get out of your cop car? Don't check? Walk in on a robbery in progress? And guess what?" She climbed out and stared inside at him. "You're dead." She slammed the door shut.

Brazil watched Deputy Chief West walk into the convenience store. He started to make notes, gave up, and leaned back in the seat. He did not understand what was happening. It bothered him a lot that she did not want him around, even though he was convinced he didn't give a rat's ass. No wonder she wasn't married. Who would want to live with somebody like that? Brazil already knew that if he were ever successful, he wouldn't be mean to people new at life. It was heartless and said everything about West's true character.

She made him pay for his own coffee. It cost a dollar and fifteen cents, and she hadn't bothered to ask him how he drank it, which wasn't with Irish cream and twenty packs of sugar. Brazil could barely swallow it but did the best he could as they resumed patrolling. She was smoking again. They began to cruise a downtown street, where prostitutes clutching washcloths strolled languidly along the sidewalk, following them with luminous, empty eyes.

"What are the washcloths for?" Brazil asked.

"What do you expect? Finger bowls? It's a messy profession," West remarked.

He shot her another look.

"No matter what kind of car I drive, they know I'm here," she went on, flicking an ash out the window.

"Really?" he asked. "I guess the same ones have been out here, what, fifteen years, then? And they remember you. Imagine that."

"You know, this isn't how you make points," West warned.

He was looking out and thoughtful when he said, "Don't you miss it?"

West watched the ladies of the night and didn't want to answer him. "Can you tell which are men?"

"That one, maybe."

Brazil stared at a big, ugly hooker in a vinyl miniskirt, her tight black top stretched over opera breasts. Her come-hither walk was slow and bulging as she stared hate into the cop car.

"Nope. She's real," West let Brazil know, and not adding that the hooker was also an undercover cop, wired, armed, and married with a kid. "The men have good legs," she went on. "Anatomically correct perfect fake breasts. No hips. You get close, which I don't recommend, they shave."

Brazil was quiet.

"Guess you didn't learn all this working for the TV magazine," she added.

He could feel her glancing at him, as if she had something else on her mind.

"So, you drive that Cadillac with shark fins?" she finally got around to it.

He continued looking out at the trade show along the street, trying to tell women from men.

"In your driveway," West went on. "Doesn't look like something you'd drive."

"It isn't," Brazil said.

"Gotcha." West sucked on the cigarette and flicked another ash into the wind. "You don't live alone."

He continued staring out his window. "I have an old BMW 2002. It was my dad's. He got it used and fixed it up, could fix anything."

They passed a silver rental Lincoln. West noticed it because the man inside had the interior light on and looked lost. He was talking on his portable phone, and casting about in this bad part of town. He turned off on Mint Street. Brazil was still looking out at dangerous people looking back at them when West got interested in the Toyota directly ahead, its side window knocked out, the license plate hanging by a coat hanger. There were two young males inside. The driver was watching her in the rearview mirror.

"What you wanna bet we got a stolen car ahead," West announced.

She typed the plate number into the MDT. It began to beep as if she'd just won at slot machines. She read the display and flipped on flashing blue and red lights. The Toyota blasted ahead of them.

"Shit!" West exclaimed.

Now she was in a high-speed pursuit, trying to be a race driver and balance a cigarette and coffee and snatch up the mike, all at the same time. Brazil didn't know what to do to help. He was having the adventure of his life.

"700!" West's voice went up as she yelled into the mike. "I'm in pursuit!"

"Go ahead, 700," the radio came back. "You have the air."

"I'm north on Pine, turning left on Seventh, give you a description in a second."

Brazil could scarcely contain himself. Why didn't she pass, cut the car off. The Toyota was just a V6. How fast could it go?

"Hit the siren!" West shouted at him as the engine strained.

Brazil didn't have this course in the volunteer academy. Unfastening his seatbelt, he groped around under the dash, the steering column, West's knees, and was practically in her lap when he found a button that felt promising. He pressed it as they roared down the street. The trunk loudly popped up. West's car rocked into a dip as they sped after the Toyota, and crime-scene equipment, a raincoat, a bubble light, flares spilled out, scattering over pavement. West couldn't believe it as she stared into the rearview mirror at her career bouncing away in the afterburn. Brazil was very quiet as police lights were turned off. They slowed, crawled off the road, and stopped. West looked at her ride-along.

"Sorry," Brazil said.

Chapter Three

West answered nothing more for an hour and twenty-five minutes, as she and Brazil inched their way along the street, collecting police gear that had jumped out of the trunk. The bubble light was shattered blue plastic. Flares were crushed paper cases leaking a dangerous composition. A Polaroid crime-scene camera would capture nothing anymore. The raincoat was miles away, snagged on the undercarriage of a station wagon, touching the exhaust pipe and soon to catch on fire.

West and Brazil drove and stopped, picked up, and drove again. This went on without conversation. West was so angry she did not dare speak. So far, two patrol units had cruised past. There was no doubt in the deputy chief's mind that the entire four-to-midnight shift knew exactly what had happened and probably thought it was West who had hit the switch because she hadn't been in a pursuit in this life. Before tonight she had been respected. She had been admired by the troops. She stole a hateful glance at Brazil, who had recovered a jumper cable and was neatly coiling and tucking it beside the spare tire, which was the only thing that hadn't flown out, because it was bolted down.

"Look," Brazil suddenly spoke, staring at her beneath a street-light. "I didn't do it on purpose. What more do you want me to say?"

West got back in the car. Brazil halfway wondered if she might drive off without him, and just leave him out here to be murdered by drug dealers or hookers who were really men. Maybe the consequences were occurring to West, too. She waited for him to climb in. He shut the door and pulled the seatbelt across his chest. The scanner hadn't stopped, and he was hoping they'd go on something else quick so he could redeem himself.

"I have no reason to have a detailed knowledge of your car," Brazil said in a quiet, reasonable tone. "The Crown Vic I got to drive during the academy was older than this. The trunk opened from the outside. And we don't get to use sirens . . ."

She shoved the car in gear and drove. "I know all that. I'm not blaming you. You didn't do it on purpose. Enough already," she said.

She decided to try another part of town, off Remus Road near the dog pound. Nothing would be going on there. Her assumption would have been accurate, were it not for an old drunk woman who decided to start screaming on the lawn of the Mount Moriah Primitive Baptist Church, near the Greyhound bus station and the Presto Grill. West heard the call over the scanner and had no choice but to back up the responding unit. She and Brazil were maybe four blocks away.

"This shouldn't be anything and we're going to make sure we keep it that way," West pointedly told Brazil as she sped up and took a right on Lancaster.

The one-story church was yellow brick with gaudy colored glass windows all lit up and nobody home, the patchy lawn littered with beer bottles near the JESUS CALLS sign in front. An old woman was screaming and crying hysterically and trying to pull away from two uniformed cops. Brazil and West got out of their car, heading to the problem. When the patrolmen saw the deputy chief in all her brass, they didn't know what to make of it and got exceedingly nervous.

"What we got?" West asked when she got to them.

The woman screamed and had no teeth. Brazil could not understand a note she was wailing.

"Drunk and disorderly," said a cop whose nameplate read *Smith.* "We've picked her up before."

The woman was in her sixties, at least, and Brazil could not take his eyes off her. She was drunk and writhing in the harsh glare of a streetlight near the sign of a church she probably did not attend. She was dressed in a faded green Hornets sweatshirt and dirty jeans, her belly swollen, her breasts wind socks on a flat day, arms and legs sticks with spiderwebs of long dark hair.

Brazil's mother used to make scenes outside the house, but not anymore. He remembered a night long ago when he drove home from the Harris-Teeter grocery to find his mother out in front of the house. She was yelling and chopping down the picket fence as a patrol car pulled up. Brazil tried to stop her and stay out of the way of the axe. The Davidson policeman knew everyone in town and didn't lock up Brazil's mother for disturbing the peace or being drunk in public, even though he had justification.

West was checking the old woman's cuffed wrists in back as blue and red lights strobed and her wailing went on, pierced by pain. West shot the officers a hot, angry look.

"Where's the key?" she demanded. "These are way too tight."

Smith had been around since primitive times and reminded West of jaded, unhappy old cops who ended up working private security for corporations. West held out her hand, and he gave her the tiny metal key. West worked it into the cuffs, springing them open. The woman instantly calmed down as cruel steel disappeared. She tenderly rubbed deep angry red impressions on her wrists, and West admonished the troops.

"You can't do that," she continued to shame them. "You're hurting her."

West asked the woman to hold up drooping arms so West could pat her down, and it entered West's mind that she ought to grab a pair of gloves. But she didn't have a box in her car because she wasn't supposed to need things like that anymore, and, in truth, the woman had been put through enough indignity. West did not like searching people, never had, and she remembered in the old days finding unfortunate surprises like bird claw fetishes, feces, used condoms, and erections. She thought of rookie days, of fishing cold slimy Spam out of Chicken Wing's pocket right before he socked her with his one arm. This old lady had nothing but a black comb, and a key on a shoelace around her neck.

Her name was Ella Joneston, and she was very quiet as the police lady cuffed her again. The steel was cold but didn't have the teeth it did a minute ago when the sons-a-bitches *snaked* her. She knew exactly what it was they wrapped around her wrists in back where she couldn't see, and it bit and bit without relief, venom spreading through her, making her shake as she screamed. Her heart swelled up big, beating against her ribs, and would have broken had that blue car with the nice lady not pulled up.

Ella Joneston had always known that death was when your heart broke. Hers had come close many times, going back to when she was twelve and boys in the projects knocked her down right after she'd washed her hair. They did things she never would speak of, and she'd gone home and picked dirt and bits of leaves out of braids and washed off while nobody asked. The police lady was sweet, and there was someone in plain clothes there to help her, a clean-looking boy with a kind face. A detective, Ella reckoned. They took each of her arms, like she was going to Easter Sunday and dressed in something fine.

"Why you out here drinking like this?" The lady in uniform meant business but she wasn't harmful.

Ella wasn't sure where *out here* was. She didn't have a way to get places. So she couldn't be far from her apartment in Earle Village, where she had been sitting in front of the TV when the phone had rung earlier this evening. It was her daughter with the awful news about Efrim, Ella's fourteen-year-old grandson, who was in the hospital. Efrim had been shot several times this morning. Everyone supposed the white doctors tried all they could, but Efrim had always been stubborn. The memory brought fresh hot tears to Ella's eyes.

Ella told the lady cop and the detective all about it as they situated her into the back of a police car with a partition to make sure Ella couldn't hurt anyone. Ella mapped out Efrim's entire short life, going back to when Ella held him in her arms right after Lorna birthed him. He was always trouble, like his father. Efrim started dancing when he was two. He used to act big beneath the streetlight out front, with those other boys and all their money.

"I'm going to get your seatbelt on," the blond detective said, snapping her in and smelling like apples and spices.

The old woman reeked of stale bad hygiene and booze, triggering more images for Brazil. His hands were shaking slightly and not as facile as usual. He didn't understand what the woman was muttering and gumming and crying about, and every breath smelled like the inside of a Dumpster in the heat. West wasn't helping a bit now, standing back and watching, making Brazil do the dirty work. His fingers brushed the old woman's neck and he was startled by how smooth and warm it was.

"You're going to be all right." Brazil kept saying what couldn't possibly be true.

West was not naive. She knew patrol was a problem. How could it not be with Deputy Chief Goode heading it? That beat cops might be a little too rough or simply unprofessional in general wasn't a shock, but West couldn't stomach it. She approached the two patrolmen, both older and miserable in their jobs. She got in

Smith's face and remembered being a sergeant and putting up with dead wood like him. As far as she was concerned, he was so low on the food chain, she wouldn't slop hogs with him.

"Don't let me *ever* see or hear of anything like this again," West said in that low tone that Brazil found scary.

West was close enough to see stubble that looked like sand, and a firestorm of broken blood vessels caused by what Smith did when he wasn't in a patrol car. His eyes were lifeless on hers, for his building had been vacant for years.

"We're out here to help, not hurt," West whispered. "Remember? That goes for you, too," she added to his partner.

Neither cop had any idea about the boy riding with the deputy chief this night, and they sat inside the cruiser with its hornet's nest on the doors, watching the midnight-blue Crown Victoria leave. Their prisoner in back was quietly snoring.

"Maybe Deputy Chief Virgin finally found a boyfriend," said Smith as he peeled open two sticks of Big Red gum.

"Yeah," said the other cop, "when she gets tired of Romper Room, I'll show her what she's missing with the big dogs."

They laughed, pulling out. Moments later, the scanner announced more bad news.

"Thirteen-hundred block Beatties Ford Road," it said. "Report of an ambulance held hostage by a subject with a knife."

"Glad we're tied up on a call," Smith said, smacking a mouthful of cinnamon.

It was West's bad luck that Jerome Swan had not experienced a pleasant evening. It had begun at a fuzzy hour before the sun had gone down in this rundown part of the city. West had no reason to be aware of the nip joint in the area known as the Basin, off Tryon Street, very close to the dog pound, where she had been heading for quite some time now. So when the call went out, she was trapped, really. Two marked units got there first, and then Captain Jennings arrived with his ride-along, City Councilman Hugh Bledsoe.

"Shit," West said when they rolled up on the scene. "Fuck."

She parked on the side of the narrow, dark street.

"You see that tall man right there getting out of the car, the one in the suit? You know who that is?"

Brazil reached for the door handle, then thought better of it.

"I know exactly who it is," he said. "Huge Bedsore."

West shot him a surprised look. It was true the cops had a pet name for their city councilman, but she wasn't clear on how Brazil knew about it.

"Not one peep out of you," West warned as she opened her door. "Stay out of the way." She got out. "And don't touch anything."

The ambulance was rumbling, and parked in the middle of the street with the tailgate open wide, light spilling out as red and blue flashed and strobed from cop cars. The men had convened near a rear tire to come up with a plan. West followed around to the back to assess the problem for herself, Brazil right behind her and dying to get in front. Swan was inside, as far back as he could get, wielding a pair of surgical scissors, his eyes bloody egg yolks filled with fury when the woman cop in the white shirt filled his vision.

He had knots on his head and was bleeding from the fight he had gotten into at the nip joint where he had been gambling and drinking Night Train Express fortified wine. When he was put in the ambulance, it was one of those times when he decided he really didn't feel like going anywhere just that second. Whenever this happened, Swan seized the environment. In this case, he grabbed the closest dangerous object he could and yelled to the paramedics that he had AIDS and was going to cut every one of them. They jumped out and got the cops, all of them men except for that one with the big tits peering in at him like she might do something.

West saw the problem plainly. The subject was holding down the lock to a side door that led out to the street, and the only way to get to him was for someone to climb inside the ambulance. This didn't require much of a plan. West went around to confer with the committee of officers still gathered by the same tire.

"I'm going to divert him," she said as Bledsoe stared at her as if he'd never seen a woman in uniform. "The minute he takes his hand off the door, you guys grab him," she made sure they understood.

She got closer to the open back of the ambulance and made a face, waving a hand before her eyes.

"Who used pepper spray?" she called out.

"Even that didn't stop him," one of the cops let her know.

Next thing Brazil knew, West had climbed inside the ambulance and picked up an aluminum stretcher to use as a shield. She did this easily, and her lips moved. Swan didn't like whatever it was she was communicating to him. His eyes were on hers, arteries bulging in his neck as he twitched and challenged her with looks and utterances. She was halfway inside when he lunged. Swan was sucked out as if he opened the door of an airplane. Brazil went around to check and found him facedown on the street being cuffed by all those men with a plan. City Councilman Bledsoe watched, hands in his pockets. His eyes followed West as she walked back to her car. Then he stared at Brazil.

"Come here," Bledsoe said to him.

Brazil cast a furtive glance in West's direction, certain he might get left alone out on this dark, unfriendly road. He was mindful that West had ordered him not to talk to anyone.

"You're the ride-along," Bledsoe stated as he got closer.

"I don't know if I'm *the* ride-along," Brazil answered.

He was just trying to be modest, but the councilman took it the wrong way. He thought the kid was being a smartass.

"Guess Superwoman there just gave you a good story, huh?" The councilman nodded his head toward West, who was getting back into her car.

Brazil was beginning to panic. "I've got to go," he said.

Bledsoe had a goatee and liked gloss gel. He was the minister of the Baptist church on Jeremiah Avenue. Strobing police lights flashed in his glasses as he stared at Brazil and mopped his neck with a handkerchief.

"Let me just tell you one thing," he went on, getting unctuous. "The city of Charlotte doesn't need people coming out here and being insensitive to humanity and poverty and crime. Even this man here is not to be ridiculed or laughed at."

Swan was being led away, dazed. He had been minding his own business in the nip joint one minute and was sucked up by aliens the next. Bledsoe swept a hand over the lighted skyline in the distance, rising and sparkling like a kingdom.

"Why don't you write about that?" The councilman said it as if he wanted Brazil to start taking notes, so he did. "Look at all the good, the accomplishments. Look at how we've grown. Voted the most attractive city to live in nationwide, third largest banking center in the country, with an appreciation of the arts. People are in line to move here. But no. Oh no." He tapped Brazil's shoulder. "I'll wake up in the morning to another depressing story. An ambulance hijacked by a man with a knife. News intended to strike fear in the hearts of citizens."

West started pulling out and Brazil broke into a run, as if he were about to miss the school bus. Bledsoe looked surprised and annoyed for he hadn't finished talking, and West knew it was no accident that the councilman just happened to be out tonight while Andy Brazil, the experiment in community policing, was riding. Bledsoe would find his way into a story and impress his constituents this reelection year with how diligent and caring he was. CITY COUNCILMAN TAKES TIME TO RIDE WITH POLICE. She could see the headline now. Opening the glove box, she rummaged for a roll of Tums.

She stopped the car so Brazil could climb in. He wasn't even breathing hard and had just sprinted a good fifty yards. Reminders like that made West want to smoke.

"I told you not to talk to anyone," she said, lighting up.

"What was I supposed to do?" He was indignant. "You walked off without me and he got in my face."

They passed more impoverished houses, most of them boarded up and not lived in anymore. Brazil was staring at West, thinking about Bledsoe calling her *superwoman*.

"They made a mistake promoting you," Brazil said. "That was really something, what you did back there."

West had been good at this once. Taking the sergeant's exam had been the first step toward paperwork and political correctness. If Hammer hadn't come to town, West was fairly certain she would have looked for something else.

"So tell me," Brazil was saying.

"Tell you what?" West asked, blowing out a stream of smoke.

"What did you say to him?" Brazil wanted to know.

"Say to who?"

"You know, the guy in the ambulance."

"Can't tell you."

"Come on. You said something that really pissed him off," Brazil insisted.

"Nope." West flicked an ash out the window.

"Oh, come on. What?"

"I didn't say anything."

"Yes you did."

"I called him a pussy," she finally confessed. "And you can't print that."

"You're right," Brazil told her.

Chapter Four

The downtown skyline was huge around a terrible crime scene, minutes past ten P.M. Police were tense and sweating, their flashlights probing a parking lot behind an abandoned building, and an area overgrown with weeds where the black rental Lincoln had been abandoned. The driver's door was open, headlights burning, interior bell dinging a feeble warning that was too late. Detective Brewster had been called in from home and was standing near the Lincoln, talking on his portable phone. He was dressed in jeans and an old Izod shirt, his badge and a Smith & Wesson .40 caliber pistol and extra magazines clipped to his belt.

"Looks like we got another one," he said to his in-transit boss.

"Can you give me a ten-thirteen?" West's voice sounded over the phone.

"Ten-thirteen's still clear." Brewster looked around. "But not for long. What's your ten-twenty?"

"Dilworth. Heading your way on forty-nine. E.O.T. Ten-fifteen."

Brazil had learned how to talk on the radio in the academy and understood codes and why Brewster and West were talking in them. Something very bad had gone down, and they didn't want anyone else, a reporter, for example, monitoring what they were saying. Basically, Brewster had let West know that the scene was still clear of people who shouldn't be there, but not for long. West was en route and would arrive in less than fifteen minutes.

West reached for the portable phone she had plugged into the cigarette lighter. She was on red alert, driving fast as she dialed a number. Her conversation with Chief Hammer was brief.

West shot Brazil a severe look. "Do everything you're told," she said. "This is serious."

By the time they reached the crime scene, reporters had gathered in the night, all poised as Brazil's peers tried to get close to a terrible tragedy. Webb held a microphone, talking into a camera, his pretty face sincere and full of sorrow.

"No identification of the victim who, like the first three shot to death very close to here, was driving a rental car," Webb taped for the eleven o'clock news.

West and Brazil were quiet and determined as they made their way through. They avoided microphones jabbed their way, cameras rolling in their faces as they ducked and dodged and hurried. Questions flew all around them as if some fast-breaking news bomb had gone off, and Brazil was terrified. He was acutely self-conscious and embarrassed in a way he did not understand.

"Now you know what it's like," West said to him under her breath.

Bright yellow crime scene tape stretched from woods to a streetlight. Big black block letters flowed across it, repeating the warning CAUTION CRIME SCENE DO NOT ENTER. It barred reporters and the curious from the Lincoln and the senseless death beyond it. Just inside it was an ambulance with engine rumbling, cops and detectives everywhere with flashlights. Video-tape was running, flashguns going off, and crime-scene technicians were preparing the car to be hauled into headquarters for processing.

Brazil was so busy taking everything in and worrying about how close he was going to be allowed to get that he did not notice Chief Hammer until he walked into her.

"Sorry," Brazil muttered to the older woman in a suit.

Hammer was distressed and immediately began conferring with West. Brazil took in the short graying hair softly framing the pretty, sharp face, and the short stature and trim figure. He had never met the chief, but he suddenly recognized her from television and photographs he had seen. Brazil was awed, openly staring. He could get a terrible crush on this woman. West turned and pointed at him as if he were a dog.

"Stay," she commanded.

Brazil had expected as much but wasn't happy about it. He started to protest, but no one was interested. Hammer and West ducked under the tape, and a cop gave Brazil a warning look should he think about following. Brazil watched West and Hammer stop to investigate something on the old, cracked pavement. Bloody drag marks glistened in the beam of West's flashlight, and based on the small, smeared puddle just inches from the open car door, she thought she knew what had happened.

"He was shot right here," she told Hammer. "And he fell." She pointed to the puddle. "That's where his head hit. He was dragged by his feet."

Blood was beginning to coagulate, and Hammer could feel the heat of the throbbing lights and the night and the horror. She could smell death. Her nose had learned to pick it up the first year she was a cop. Blood broke down fast, got runny around the edges and thick inside, and the odor was weirdly sweet and putrid at the same time. The trail led to a Gothic tangle of overgrown vines and pines, with a lot of weeds.

The victim looked middle-aged and had been dressed in a khaki suit wrinkled from travel when someone had ruined his head with gunshots. Pants and jockey shorts were down around fleshy knees, the familiar hourglass painted bright orange, leaves and other plant debris clinging to blood.

Dr. Wayne Odom had been the medical examiner in the greater Charlotte-Mecklenburg area for more than twenty years. He could tell that the spray-painting had occurred right where the body had been found, because a breeze had carried a faint orange mist up to the underside of nearby poplar leaves. Dr. Odom was reloading a camera with bloody gloved hands, and was fairly certain he was dealing with homosexual serial murders. He was a deacon at Northside Baptist Church and believed that an angry God was punishing America for its perversions.

"Damn it!" Hammer muttered as crime-scene technicians scoured the area for eivdence.

West was frustrated to the point of fear. "This is what? A hundred yards from the last one? I got people all over the place out here. Nobody saw anything. How can this happen?"

"We can't watch the street every second of the day," Hammer angrily said.

From a distance, Brazil watched a detective going through the victim's wallet. Brazil could only imagine what West and Hammer were seeing as he impatiently waited by West's car, taking notes. One thing he had learned while writing term papers was that even if he didn't have all the information, he could create a mood. He studied the back of the abandoned brick building, and decided it had been some sort of warehouse once. Every window was shattered, and an eerie dark emptiness stared out. The fire escape was solid rust and broken off halfway down.

Emergency lights were diluted and weird by the time they got to the thicket where everyone was gathered. Fireflies flickered around the dinging rental car, and Brazil could hear the sounds of far-off traffic. Paramedics were coming through, sweating in jumpsuits, and carrying a stretcher and a folded black body bag. Brazil craned his neck, writing furiously, as the paramedics reached the scene. They unfolded the stretcher's legs, and Hammer turned around when metal clacked. West and Brewster were studying the victim's driver's license. No one was interested in giving Brazil a quote.

"Carl Parsons," Brewster read from a driver's license. "Spartanburg, South Carolina. Forty-one years old. Cash gone, no jewelry if he had any."

"Where was he staying?" Hammer asked him.

"Looks like we got a confirmation number for the Hyatt near Southpark."

West crouched to see the world from a different angle. Parsons was half on his back and half on his side in a nest of bloody leaves, his eyes sleepy slits and dull. Dr. Odom inflicted yet one more indignity by inserting a long chemical thermometer up the rectum to get a core temperature. Whenever the medical examiner touched the body, more blood spilled from holes in the head. West knew that whoever was doing this had no plan to stop.

Brazil wasn't going to stop, no matter how much West got in his way. He had done all he could to capture visual details and mood, and now he was on the prowl. He happened to notice a new bright blue Mustang parked near an unmarked car, where a teenaged boy sat in the front seat with a detective Brazil had seen before, running around impersonating a drug dealer. Brazil took more notes as the teenager talked and paramedics zipped the body inside a pouch. Reporters, especially Webb, were obsessed with getting footage and photographs of the murdered man being carried away like a big black cocoon. No one but Brazil focused on the teenager climbing out of the detective's car and returning to his Mustang, in no hurry.

The top was down, and when Brazil headed toward the flashy car, the teenager's blood began to pound with excitement again. The nice-looking blond guy had a reporter's notepad in hand. Jeff Deedrick got out his Chap Stick and cranked the engine, trying to look cool as his hands shook.

"I'm with *The Charlotte Observer*," Brazil said, standing close to the driver's door. "I'd like to ask you a few questions."

Deedrick was going to be famous. He was seventeen but could pass for twenty-one unless he got carded. He would get all those girls who, before this night, had never paid him any mind.

"I guess it's all right," Deedrick reluctantly said, as if weary of all the attention.

Brazil climbed inside the Mustang, which was new and did not belong to Deedrick. Brazil could tell by the dainty blue lanyard keychain that matched the color of the car. Most guys too young to drink didn't have cellular phones, either, Brazil noted, unless they were drug dealers. He was willing to bet that the Mustang belonged to Deedrick's mother.

First Brazil got name, address, phone number, and repeated every syllable back to Deedrick to make certain all was correct. This he had learned the hard way. His first month on the job, he had gotten three *We Were Wrong*s in a row for insignificant, picayune errors relating to insignificant details, such as somebody *junior* versus somebody *the third*. This had resulted in an obituary about the son, versus the father. The son was having tax problems, and didn't mind the mistake. He had called Brazil, personally, to request that the paper leave well enough alone. But Packer wouldn't.

Perhaps Brazil's most embarrassing mistake, and one he preferred not to think about, was when he covered a loud, volatile community meeting about a controversial pet ordinance. He confused a place with a person, and persisted in referring to *Latta Park* this and *Miss Park* that. Jeff Deedrick, however, he had right, of this Brazil made sure. There would be no problems here. Brazil eyed the crime scene in the distance, as paramedics loaded the body into the ambulance.

"I admit I had a few, am driving along and know I'm not going to make it home," Deedrick kept talking, nervous and excited.

"Then you pulled back here to use the bathroom?" Brazil flipped a page, writing fast.

"Pulled in, and see this car with lights on, the door open and think someone else is taking a leak." Deedrick hesitated. He took off his baseball cap and put it on backward. "I wait, don't see no one. Now I'm getting curious, so I go on over and see him! Thank God I got a phone."

Deedrick's wide stare was fixed on nothing, and sweat was beading on his forehead and rolling from his armpits. At first he thought the guy was drunk, had dropped his pants to take a piss, and had passed out. Then Deedrick saw orange paint, and blood. He had never been so frightened in his life. He galloped back to his car, peeled out, and floored it the hell out of there. He pulled off under an overpass and peed. He called 911.

"My first thought?" Deedrick went on, a little more relaxed now. "It's not really happening. I mean, the little bell is ringing and ringing, all this blood, pants down around his knees. And I . . . Well, you know. His parts."

Brazil looked up at him. Deedrick was stuttering.

"What about them?" Brazil wanted to know.

"It's like they were spray-painted traffic cone orange. With this shape."

Deedrick was blushing as he outlined a figure-eight in the air.

Brazil handed him the notepad. "Can you draw it?" he asked.

Deedrick shakily drew an hourglass, to Brazil's amazement.

"Like a black widow spider," Brazil muttered as he watched West and Hammer duck under crime-scene tape, ready to leave.

Brazil ended the interview in one big hurry, conditioned by now to fear being left. He also had a question that Hammer and West needed to hear. He addressed the chief first, out of respect.

"Has the killer spray-painted all his victims with an hour-glass?" Brazil said earnestly and with excitement.

West went still, which was rare for her. She did not move. Brazil thought Hammer was the most overpowering person he had ever met. She waved him off with a *no comment* sort of gesture.

"I'll let you handle this," she said to West.

Hammer headed to shadows where her car was parked. West strode to her Ford without a word, and when Brazil got in and fastened up, they had nothing to say to each other. The scanner was active and it was getting very late. It was time to return Brazil to the parking deck so he could get in his own car and get the hell out of her hair. That was the way West felt about it. What a night.

They were riding back to the LEC at almost midnight, both of them keyed up and tense. West couldn't believe she had hand-delivered a reporter to that scene. She absolutely could not take it in. This had to be somebody else's life that was happening to West on a dimension where she had no control, and she was reminded of a time she would never admit to anyone, when she was a sopho-more at a very small, religious school in Bristol, Tennessee. The trouble began with Mildred.

Mildred was very big and all the other girls on her floor were afraid of her. But not West. She saw Mildred as an opportunity be-cause Mildred was from Miami. Mildred's parents had sent her to King College to get saved, and to straighten out. Mildred found someone in Kingsport who knew someone in Johnson City who had dealings with a guy at Eastman Kodak who sold pot. West and Mil-dred lit up one night on the tennis courts where no one could see anything except tiny orange coals glowing and fading by a net post on court two.

It was awful. West had never done anything this wicked, and

now she knew why. She lost control, belly laughing and telling out-landish stories while Mildred confessed she had been fat all her life and knew precisely what it felt like to be black and discriminated against. Mildred was something. The two of them sat out on red and green Laykold for hours, finally lying on their backs and star-ing up at stars and a moon that looked like a bright yellow swing swelling with the round shadow of promise. They talked about having babies. They drank Cokes, and ate whatever Mildred had in her pocketbook.

Mostly this was Nabs, Reese's Cups, Kit Kats, and things like that. God, how West hated to think about that wretched time. It was her luck that, in the end, marijuana made her paranoid. A cou-ple tokes into the third joint, she wanted to run as fast as she could, dive into her dorm room, punch in the lock, hide under the bed, and come back out in camouflage, a Tec-9 ready to go. When Mil-dred decided that West was physically attractive, the timing wasn't good.

West believed women were great. She'd loved every woman teacher and coach she'd ever known, as long as they were nice. But there were a couple of problems here. She had never really contem-plated the possibility of what Mildred's interest might mean about West, or West's family, or of West's possibilities in the afterlife. Plus, Mildred grabbed West no differently than a guy would. Mildred didn't even ask, and this was unfortunate, since West was in cam-ouflage, at least in her mind. West turned into the LEC parking deck for visitors.

"You can't do anything with that," West said to Brazil in an ac-cusing tone.

"With what?" Brazil asked in a measured voice.

"You know *what*. In the first place, you had no business talking to a witness," West said.

"That's what reporters do," he replied.

"In the second place, the hourglass is something only the killer knows. Got it? So you don't put that in the paper. Period."

"How can you say for a fact the killer's the only one who knows about it?" Brazil was about to lose his temper. "How do you know it won't trigger information from somebody out there?"

West raised her voice and wished she had never met Andy Brazil. "You do it, and the next homicide in this city's going to be you."

"Yours," he helped her out.

"That's it." West turned into the police deck. She was not going to have this squirt correct her grammar one more time. "You're dead."

"I believe you just threatened me." Brazil drew attention to it.

"Oh no. Not a threat," West said. "A promise." She jammed the car into park. "Find someone else to ride with." She was the maddest she'd ever been. "Where are you parked?"

Brazil yanked up the door handle in a murderous reply. "Well, guess what?" he said. "Fuck you."

He got out and slammed the door. He stalked off into the dark, early morning. He managed to write his stories in time for the city edition, and he pulled off I-77 on his way home and bought two tallboy Miller Lites. He managed to drink both as he drove very fast. Brazil had a frightening habit of pushing his car as far as it would go. Since his speedometer didn't work, he could only guess how fast he was going by the RPMs. He knew he was flying, going close to a hundred miles an hour, and it wasn't the first time he'd done this. Sometimes he wondered if he were trying to die.

At home, he checked on his mother. She was unconscious in bed, and snoring with her mouth open. Brazil leaned against the wall in the dark, the night-light a sad dim eye. He was depressed and frustrated. He thought about West and wondered why she was so heartless.

West walked into her own small house and tossed keys on her kitchen counter as Niles, her Abyssinian cat, appeared. Niles was on her heels, much like Brazil had been all day, and West flicked on her sound system and Elton John reminded her of the night. She hit another button, changing to Roy Orbison. She walked into the kitchen, popped open a beer, and felt maudlin and didn't know why. She went back into the living room and turned on the late-night news. It was all about the killing. She plopped on the couch at the same time Niles decided she should. He loved his owner and waited for his turn as the TV played bad news about a dreadful death in the city.

"Believed to be another out-of-town businessman simply in the wrong place at the wrong time," Webb said into the camera.

West was restless, worn out, and disgusted, all at the same time. She wasn't happy with Niles, either. He had climbed up her book-cases while she was out. She could always tell. How hard was it? He leapt up three shelves, just high enough to knock down bookends and a vase. As for the framed picture of West's father on the farm, well, what did Niles care about that? That cat. West hated him. She hated everyone.

"Come here, Sweetsy," she said.

Niles made his ribs rattle, knowing how much it pleased her. It worked every time. Niles wasn't stupid. He reached around and licked his hindquarters because he could. When he looked at the lady who kept him, he made sure his eyes were very blue and crossed. Owners fell for that, and predictably, she snatched him up and petted him. Niles was happy enough.

West wasn't. The next day when she got to work, Hammer was waiting for her deputy chief, and everybody seemed to know it. West left her Bojangles breakfast without even opening the bag. She dropped everything and hurried down the hall. West almost ran into Hammer's outer office and felt like giving Horgess the fin-ger. He very much enjoyed West's negative reaction to being sum-moned like this.

"Let me call her," Horgess said.

"Let me let you." West didn't disguise how surly she felt.

Horgess was young, and had shaved his head. Why? Soon he would dream of hair. He would lust after it. He would watch movies starring people with hair.

"She'll see you now," Horgess said, hanging up the phone.

"I'm sure." West gave him a sarcastic smile.

"For God's sake, Virginia," Hammer said the instant West walked in.

The chief was gripping the morning paper, shaking it, and pacing. Hammer didn't wear pants often, but today she was in them. Her suit was a deep royal blue, and she wore a red and white striped shirt and soft black leather shoes. West had to admit, her boss was stunning. Hammer could cover or show her legs without gender being an issue.

"Now what?" Hammer railed on. "Four businessmen four weeks in a row. Carjackings, in which the killer changes his mind, leaves the cars? Robberies? A weird hourglass symbol spray-painted on the victims' groins? Make and model, names, professions. Everything but the damn crime-scene photos right there for all the world to see!"

The headline was huge:

BLACK WIDOW KILLER CLAIMS FOURTH VICTIM

"What was I supposed to do?" West said.

"Keep him out of trouble."

"I'm not a babysitter."

"A businessman from Orlando, a salesman from Atlanta, a banker from South Carolina, a Baptist minister. From Tennessee. Welcome to our lovely city." Hammer tossed the paper on a couch. "What do we do?"

"Letting him ride wasn't my idea," West reminded her.

"What's done is done." Hammer sat behind her desk. She picked up the phone and dialed. "We can't get rid of him. Got any idea how that would look? On top of all the rest of it?" Her eyes glazed as the mayor's secretary answered. "Listen, Ruth, get him now. I don't care what he's doing." Hammer started drumming polished nails on the blotter.

West was in a worse mood when she left her boss's office. It wasn't fair. Life was hard enough, and she was beginning to wonder about Hammer. What did West know about her, anyway, except that she had come to Charlotte from Chicago, a huge city where people froze their asses off half the year and the mob had its way with public officials. Next thing, Hammer sailed here, that house-wife husband of hers tagging along.

Brazil wasn't pleased with his circumstances, either. He was punishing himself again this morning, pounding up bleacher steps in the stadium where the Davidson Wildcats lost every football game, even some they hadn't played, it seemed. He was going at it and didn't care if he had a heart attack or was sore tomorrow. Deputy Chief West was a lowlife cowboy and as insensitive as shit, and Chief Hammer wasn't at all what he had fantasized. Hammer could have at least smiled or glanced at him and made him feel welcome last night. Brazil headed back up the steps again, sweat leaving gray spots on cement.

Hammer wanted to hang up on the mayor. She had just about enough of his unimaginative way of solving problems.

"I understand the medical examiner believes these murders have a homosexual connection," he was saying over the phone.

"That's one opinion," Hammer answered. "The fact is that we don't know. All the victims were married with children."

"Exactly," he slyly said.

"For God's sake, Chuck, don't pile this on me so early in the morning." Hammer looked out the window and could almost see the bastard's office from where she sat.

"Point is, the theory is helpful," he went on in his South Carolina drawl.

Mayor Charles Search was from Charleston. He was Hammer's age and often considered what it might be like to bed her. If nothing else, it would remind her of things she seemed to have forgotten. Her place, for starters. If she wasn't married, he would swear she was a lesbian. He sat in his leather judge's chair, headset on, and doodled on a legal pad.

"The city, out-of-town businesses, won't be as bothered by this . . ." he was trying to say.

"Where are you so I can break your neck," Hammer said over the phone. "When was your lobotomy? I would have sent flowers."

"Judy." This doodle was really good. He focused on it, putting his glasses on. "Calm down. I know exactly what I'm doing."

"Of course you don't."

Maybe she was a lesbian, or bisexual anyway, with a grating Midwestern accent. He reached for a red pen, getting excited over his art. It was an atom with orbits of little molecules that looked weirdly like eggs. Birth. This was seminal.

To make matters ever so much worse this morning, West had to go to the morgue. North Carolina didn't have the best system, it was West's opinion. Some cases were taken care of locally, by Dr. Odom and the police forensic labs. Other bodies were sent to the chief medical examiner in Chapel Hill. Go figure. It was probably all about sports again. Hornets fans stayed in Charlotte, Tarheels got their lovely Y-incision in the big university town.

The Mecklenburg County Medical Examiner's office was on North College Street, across from the award-winning new public library. West was buzzed in at the glass entrance. She had to give the place credit. The building, which was the former Sears Garden Center, was brighter and more modern than most morgues, and had added another cold room the last time USAir had crashed another plane around here. It was a shame that North Carolina didn't seem inclined to hire a few more M.E.s for *the great state of Mecklenburg*, as some sour senators were inclined to disparage the state's fastest-growing, most progressive region.

There were only two forensic pathologists to handle more than a hundred homicides a year, and both of them were in the necropsy room when West arrived. The dead businessman didn't look any better now that Dr. Odom had started on him. Brewster was at the table, wearing a disposable plastic apron and gloves. He nodded at her as she tied a gown in back, because West didn't take chances. Dr. Odom was splashed with blood, and holding the scalpel like a pencil as he reflected back tissue. His patient had a lot of fat, which looked worse inside out.

The morgue assistant was a big man who was always sweating. He plugged an autopsy saw into the overhead cord reel, and started on the skull. This West could do without. The sound was worse than the dentist's drill, the bony smell, not to mention the idea, awful. West would not be murdered or turn up dead suspiciously in any form or fashion. She would not have this done to her naked body with people like Brewster looking on while clerks passed around her pictures and made comments.

"Contact wounds, entrances here behind the right ear." Dr. Odom pointed a bloody gloved finger, mostly for her benefit. "Large caliber. This is execution style."

"Exactly like the others," Brewster remarked.

"What about cartridge cases?" Dr. Odom asked.

"Forty-fives, Winchester, probably Silvertips," West replied, thinking about Brazil's article again and all that he had revealed. "Five each time. Perp doesn't bother picking them up, doesn't care. We need to get the FBI on this."

"Fucking press," Brewster said.

West had never been to Quantico. Her dream had always been to attend the FBI's National Academy, which was rather much the Oxford University of police training. But she'd been busy. Then she kept getting promoted. Finally, the only thing she was eligible for was executive training up there, for God's sake. That meant a bunch of big-bellied chiefs, assistant chiefs, and sheriffs, out on the firing range trying to make the transition from .38 specials to semi-automatic pistols. She'd heard the stories. All these guys blasting away, dumping brass into their hands, and taking the time to stuff it neatly in their pockets. Hammer offered to send West last year. Forget it. West didn't need to learn a thing from the FBI.

"I'd like to know what their profilers would have to say," West said.

"Forget it," Brewster said, chewing a toothpick and swiping Vicks up his nose.

Dr. Odom picked up a big sponge, and squeezed water over organs. He grabbed a tan rubber hose, and suctioned blood out of the chest cavity.

"He smells like he was drinking," said Brewster, who could no longer smell anything except childhood memories of colds.

"Maybe on the plane," Odom agreed. "What about those guys at Quantico?" He eyed Brewster, as if West had never brought up the subject.

"Busy as jumping beans," Brewster replied. "Like I said, forget it. They got what? Ten, eleven profilers and are about a thousand cases behind? Think the government's going to fund shit? Shit no. Too damn bad, too. 'Cause those profilers are damn good."

Brewster had applied to the FBI early on, but forget that, too. They weren't hiring, or maybe it had to do with the polygraph test he wasn't about to take. He sniffed more Vicks. God, he hated death. It was ugly and it stunk. It was a tattletale. Like this fellow's dick, for example. The guy looked like a balloon with this little knot, so all his air didn't get out.

West was angry, her face hard, as she stared at the fleshy nude body opened up from neck to navel, and blaze orange paint no amount of scrubbing would wash away. She thought of his wife and family. No human should ever have to come to such a grim place and be put through something like this, and she felt fresh anger toward Brazil.

She was waiting for him when he trotted out of the Knight-Ridder building, his notepad in hand as he headed to his car and a story. West, in uniform, climbed out of her unmarked Ford, and she strode toward Brazil like she might tackle him. She wished she could have bottled that dead smell and sprayed it in Brazil's face, and rubbed his nose in the reality West had to live with every day. Brazil was in a hurry and had a lot on his mind. A Honda was on fire in the Mental Health parking lot, according to the scanner. Possibly, it was nothing, but what if someone was in it? Brazil stopped. He was startled as West jabbed a finger into his breastbone.

"Hey!" He grabbed her wrist.

"So how's the Black Widow reporter today?" West coldly said. "I just came from the morgue, you know, where reality's laid out and carved up? Bet you've never been there. Maybe they'll let you watch someday. What a good story that would be, right? A man not old enough to be your daddy. Red hair, hundred and ninety-seven pounds. Guess what his hobby was."

Brazil released West's arm. He groped for words but didn't have any.

"Backgammon, photography. He wrote the newsletter for his church, wife's dying of cancer. They got two kids, one grown, other a freshman at UNC. Anything else you want to know about him? Or is Mr. Parsons nothing but a story to you? Little words on paper?"

Brazil was visibly shaken. He started walking off to his old BMW as the Honda in the Mental Health parking lot burned and he no longer cared. West wasn't going to let him off so easy. She grabbed his arm.

"Get your goddamn hands off me," Brazil said. He jerked his arm free, unlocked his car door, and got in.

"You screwed me, Andy," West told him.

Brazil cranked the engine and squealed out of the parking deck. West returned to the LEC and didn't go straight to investigations because she had a few of her own. She stopped off at the Records Room, where women in their own special uniforms ruled the world. West really had to court these girls, especially Wanda, who weighed somewhere between two-fifty and three hundred pounds and could type a hundred and five words a minute. If West needed a record or to send a missing-person report off to NCIC, Wanda was either a hero or hell on earth, depending on when she was fed last. West brought in a bucket of KFC once a month, and sometimes Girl Scout or Christmas cookies, depending on what was in season. West approached the counter and whistled at Wanda, who loved West. Wanda secretly wished she was a detective and worked for the deputy chief.

"Need your help," West said, and her police belt was making her lower back ache, as usual.

Wanda scowled at a name West had scribbled on a slip of paper. "Lord have mercy," she said, shaking her head. "If I don't remember that like it was yesterday."

West couldn't be certain, but thought Wanda had gained more weight. God help her. Wanda took up two lanes of traffic.

"You sit on down." Wanda pointed with her chin, as if she were Chinese. "I'll get the microfilm."

While Wanda's minions typed, stacked, and racked, West went through microfilm. She had her glasses on and was hurt by what she saw when she got to old articles about Brazil's father. His name, too, was Andrew, but people had called him Drew. He had been a cop here when West was a rookie. She had forgotten all about him and had never made the connection. Christ, but now that she was looking at it, the tragedy came back to her and somehow put Brazil's life in focus.

Drew Brazil was a thirty-six-year-old robbery detective when he made a traffic stop in an unmarked car. He was shot close range in the chest, and died instantly. West took a long time looking at articles, and staring at his picture. She headed upstairs to her division and pulled the case, which no one had looked at in a decade, because it had been exceptionally cleared, and the dirtbag was still on death row. Drew Brazil was handsome. In one photograph, he wore a leather bomber jacket that West had seen before.

The scene photographs clubbed her somewhere in her chest. He was dead in the street, on his back, staring up at the sun on a spring Sunday morning. The .45 caliber bullet had almost ripped his heart in half, and in autopsy photographs, Odom had two thick fingers through the hole to demonstrate. This was something young Andy Brazil need never see, and West had no intention of talking to him ever again.

Chapter Five

Brazil was looking up articles, too, in the *Observer* file room. It was amazing how little had been written about Virginia West over the years. He scrolled through small stories and black and white photographs taken back in a day when her hair was long and pinned up under her police hat. She had been the first female selected as rookie of the year, and this impressed him quite a lot.

The librarian was impressed, too. She peeked at Andy Brazil about every other second, her heart stumbling whenever he walked into her domain, which was fairly regularly. She'd never seen anyone research stories quite the way this young man did. It didn't matter what he was writing about, Brazil had to look something up or ask questions. It was especially gratifying when he spoke to her directly as she sat primly at her neat maple desk. She had been a public school librarian before taking this job after her husband had retired and was underfoot all the time. Her name was Mrs.

Booth. She was well past sixty and believed that Brazil was the most beautiful human being she had ever met. He was nice and gentle and always thanked her.

It shocked Brazil to read that West had been shot. He could not believe it. He scrolled faster, desperate for more details, but the lamebrain who had covered the incident had completely missed an opportunity for a huge 1-A story. Damn. The most that Brazil could pin down was that eleven years ago, when West was the first female homicide detective, she had gotten a tip from a snitch.

A subject West had been looking for was at the Presto Grill. By the time West and other police arrived, the subject was gone. Apparently, West answered another call in the same neighborhood, and the same subject was involved, only now he was really fried and irritable. He started firing the minute West rolled up. She killed him, but not before he winged her. Brazil was dying to ask her about it, in detail, but forget it. All he knew was that she took a bullet in the left shoulder, a flesh wound, a graze, really. Was the bullet as hot as he had heard? Did it cook surrounding tissue? How much did it hurt? Did she fall or bravely finish the gunfight, not even realize until she held out a hand and it had blood on it, like in the movies?

The next day Brazil drove to Shelby. Because of his tennis prowess, he had heard of this small, genteel town in Cleveland County, where Buck Archer, friend of Bobby Riggs, who had lost to Billie Jean King in the Battle of the Sexes, was from. Shelby High School was a well-kept brick complex, and home of the Lions, where students with money got ready for college in big cities like Chapel Hill and Raleigh. All around was farmland and cow towns with names like Boiling Springs and Lattimore. Brazil's BMW rumbled around to the tennis courts, where the boys' team was holding a summer camp. Kids were out with hoppers of chartreuse balls. They were whacking serves, overhead smashes, cross-court shots, in pain and sweating.

The coach was prowling the fence, clipboard in hand, dressed in long white Wimbledon pants, a white shirt, a shapeless hat, zinc oxide on his nose, and all of it out of fashion and old.

"Move your feet. Move! Move!" he called out to a boy who would never move anything fast. "I don't want to see those feet stop!"

The boy was overweight and wore glasses. He was squinting and hurting, and Brazil remembered the suffering inflicted by coaches and drills. But Brazil had always been good at everything he tried, and he felt pity for this kid and wished he could work with him for an hour and maybe cheer him up a little.

"Good shot," Brazil called out when the boy managed to scoop one up and push it over the net.

The boy, who did not play in the top six positions, missed the next shot, as he searched for his fan behind the green windscreen covering the fence. The coach stopped his tour, watching this blond, well-built young man heading toward him. He was probably looking for a job, but the coach didn't need anyone else for this camp, which was the most worthless crop in recent memory.

"Coach Wagon?" Brazil asked.

"Uh huh?" The old coach was curious, wondering how this stranger knew his name. Oh God. Maybe the kid had played on the team some years back and Wagon couldn't remember. That was happening more and more these days, and it had nothing to do with Johnnie Walker Red.

"I'm a reporter for *The Charlotte Observer*," Brazil was quick and proud to say. "I'm doing a story on a woman who played on your boys' team a long time ago."

Wagon might be deleting a lot of files these days, but he'd never forget Virginia West. Shelby High School had no women's team back in those days, and she was too good to ignore. What hell that had caused. At first, the state wouldn't hear of it. That kept her off the team her freshman year while Wagon battled the system on her behalf. Her sophomore year, she played third racket, and had the hardest flat serve for a girl that Wagon had ever seen, and a slice backhand that could go through hot bread and leave it standing. All the boys had crushes on her and tried to hit her with the ball whenever they could.

She never lost a match, not singles or doubles, in the three years she played tennis for Coach Wagon. There had been several stories about her in the *Shelby Star*, and the *Observer* when she blazed through spring matches, and the regionals. She had reached the quarterfinals of the state championship before Hap Core slaughtered her, thus ending her career as a male athlete. Brazil found the articles on microfilm after he got back to the newspaper. He rolled through more stories, like someone possessed, as he made copious notes.

The pervert was also possessed, but beyond that distinction, there were no similarities between her profile and Brazil's. The pervert was writhing in her chair in her dim den in her small house where she lived alone in Dilworth, not far from where Virginia West lived. The two were not acquainted. The pervert was in a La-Z-Boy brown vinyl recliner, footrest up, pants down, as she breathed hard. Information about her was not forthcoming, but the FBI would have profiled her as a white female between the ages of forty and seventy, since the female sex drive wasn't known to develop transmission problems as early as the male's. Indeed, profilers had noted that women got into overdrive about the same time they ran out of estrogen.

This was why Special Agent Gil Bird at Quantico, busy working on serial murders, would have pinned the female pervert's age at a reasonable forty or fifty, her biological clock a phantom-pain of time, ticking only in her imagination. Her periods were simply that, an end of sentence, a coda. It wasn't that she really wanted Brazil. She just thought she did. Her lust was far more complicated. Bird would have offered a possible scenario that might have explained it, had he been officially invited into the case.

Special Agent Bird would have accurately hypothesized that it was payback time. All those years the pervert was dissed, and not nominated for the homecoming court, and not worshiped, and not wanted. As a young woman, the pervert had worked in the cafeteria line at Gardner Webb, where basketball players, especially Ernie Presley, always grunted and pointed, as if she were as common as the greasy scrambled eggs and grits they desired. Andy Brazil would have treated her in precisely the same fashion. She did not have to know him to prove her case. At this stage in her frustrated life, she preferred to screw him in her own time, and in her own way.

Blinds were drawn, the television turned low and playing an old Spencer Tracy and Katharine Hepburn movie. The pervert was breathless as she whispered on the phone, drawing it out, enunciating slowly.

"Saw you driving. Shifting gears. Up and down in high gear . . ."

Her power over him was the most exciting thing she'd ever known in her nothing life. She could not contain it as she thought of his humiliation. She controlled him as completely as a fish in a tank, or a dog, or a car. Her heart was on a drum roll as she heard his confused silence over the line, and Hepburn walked into the bedroom, dressed in a satin robe. What incredible bones. The pervert hated her and would have switched channels, but she did not have a free hand.

"Screw yourself," Brazil's voice rewarded her with its presence. "You have my permission."

The pervert didn't need permission.

Packer scrolled through Brazil's latest and most masterful article.

"This is great stuff!" Packer was ecstatic about every word. "One hell of a job! *Wild, Wild West.* Love it!"

Packer got up from a chair pulled close. He tucked in his white shirt, his hand jumping around as if his pants were a puppet. His tie was red and black striped and not the least bit elegant.

"Ship it out. This runs one-A," Packer said.

"When?" Brazil was thrilled, because he had never been on the front page.

"Tomorrow," Packer let him know.

That night, Brazil worked his first traffic accident. He was in uniform, with clipboard in hand, the appropriate forms clamped in. This was a lot more complicated than the average person may have supposed, even if the damage was nonreportable, or less than five hundred dollars. It appeared that a woman in a Toyota Camry was traveling on Queens Road, while a man in a Honda Prelude was also traveling on Queens Road, in this unfortunate section of the city where two roads of the same name intersected with each other.

The pervert was nearby in her Aerovan, stalking and listening to the police scanner and Brazil's voice on it. She was working her own accident about to happen as this young police boy pointed and gestured, all in dark blue and shiny steel. She watched her prey as she rolled past flares sparking orange on pavement in the dark of night, crossing Queens as she traveled west on Queens.

Streets having the same name could be attributed to rapid hormonal growth, and was similar to naming a child after oneself no matter the gender or practicality, or whether the first three were christened the same, as in George Foreman and his own. Queens and Queens, Providence and Providence, Sardis and Sardis, the list went on, and Myra Purvis had never gotten it straight. She knew that if she turned off Queens Road West onto Queens Road East and then followed Queens Road to the Orthopedic Hospital, she could visit her brother.

She was doing this in her Camry when she got to that stretch she hated so much, somewhere near Edgehill Park, where it was dark, because the day was no longer helpful. Mrs. Purvis was the manager of the La Pez Mexican restaurant on Fenton Place. She had just gotten off work this busy Saturday night and was tired. None of it was her fault when Queens ran into Queens and the gray, hard-to-see Prelude ran into her.

"Ma'am, did you see the stop sign there?" The boy cop pointed.

Myra Purvis had reached her limit. She had turned seventy last February and didn't have to take this sort of shit anymore.

"Is it in Braille?" she smartly asked this whippersnapper in blue with a white tornado on his arms, reminding her of something she once used to mop her kitchen floor. What was the name of that? Genie in a Bottle? No. Lord, this happened a lot.

"I want to go to the hospital," that man in the Honda was complaining. "My neck hurts."

"Lying like a rug," Mrs. Purvis told the cop, wondering why he wasn't wearing any hardware beyond a whistle. What if he got in a shoot-out?

Deputy Chief West didn't often get out to cruise so she could check on her troops. But this night she had been in the mood. She floated along rough, dark streets in David One, listening to Brazil's voice on the scanner in her car.

"One subject requesting transport to Carolinas Medical Center," Brazil was saying.

West saw him in the distance, from the vantage of her midnight-blue car, but he was too busy to notice as he filled out a report. She circled the intersection as he worked hard, talking to subjects in barely damaged cars. Flares languished along the roadside, his grille lights silently strobing. His face was eerie in blue and red pulses, and he was smiling, and seemed to be helping an old biddy in a Camry. Brazil lifted his radio, talking into it.

He marked E.O.T. for End Of Tour and drove to the newspaper. Brazil had a ritual few people knew about, and he indulged himself in it after zipping through a small story on Charlotte's quirky traffic problems. He went up the escalator three moving steps at a time. The workers in the press room had gotten used to him long months before and didn't mind when he came into their off-limits area of huge machinery and deafening noise. He liked to watch some two hundred tons of paper fly along conveyor belts, heading to folders, destined for bundles and driveways, his byline on them.

Brazil stood in uniform and watched, not talking, overwhelmed by the power of it all. He was used to laboring on a term paper that took months and was read by maybe one person. Now he wrote something in days or even minutes, and millions of people followed every word. He could not comprehend it. He walked around, avoiding moving parts, wet ink, and tracks to trip on as the roar filled his ears like a tornado on this sixth night before the seventh day of his career's creation.

It was chilly out the next morning, Sunday, and sprinkling rain. West was building a high wooden fence around her yard on Elmhurst Road, in the old neighborhood of Dilworth. Her house was brick with white trim, and she had been fixing up the place since she'd bought it. This included her latest, most ambitious project, inspired, in part, by people driving through from South Boulevard, and pitching beer bottles and other trash in her yard.

West was wet as she hammered, with tool belt on. She held nails in her mouth and vented her spleen, as Denny Raines, an off-duty paramedic, opened her new gate and helped himself to her property. He was whistling, had jeans on, and was a big, handsome guy and no stranger to this industrious woman. She paid him no mind as she carefully measured a space between two boards.

"Anyone ever tell you you're anal-retentive?" he said.

She hammered, which was suggestive of what he felt like doing to her the first time they met, at a crime scene, when he could only suppose she had been called from home since she was in charge of investigations, and the victim was a businessman with the weird orange paint over his parts and bullets in his head. Raines took one look at the babe in brass and that was the end of his rainbow. She hammered, eating nails, in the rain.

"I was thinking about brunch," he said to her. "Maybe Chili's."

Raines approached from the rear and wrapped his arms around her. He kissed her neck, and found it wet and a little salty. West didn't smile or respond or take the nails out of her mouth. She hammered and didn't want to be bothered. He gave up and leaned against what she was building. He crossed his arms, and studied her as water dripped off the bill of his Panthers baseball cap.

"I take it you've seen the paper," he said.

He would bring that up, and she had no comment. She measured another space.

"This is an affirmative. Now I know a celebrity. Right there. This big on the front page." He exaggerated with his hands, as if the morning paper with West in it was ten feet tall. "Above the fold, too," he went on. "Good story. I'm impressed."

She measured and hammered.

"Truth is, I learned stuff even I didn't know. Like the part about high school. Shelby High. That you played on the boys' tennis team for Coach Wagon? Never lost a match? How 'bout that?"

He was more enchanted with her than ever, roaming her with his eyes and not getting charged a dime a minute. She was aware of this and feeling ripped off as she tasted metal and hammered.

"You got any idea what it does to a guy to see a good-looking woman in a tool belt?" He finally got to his fetish. "It's like when we roll up on a scene and you're in that goddamn uniform. And I start thinking thoughts I shouldn't, people bleeding to death. Right now I got it for you so bad I'm busting out of my jeans."

She slipped a nail from between her lips and looked at him, at his jeans. She rammed the hammer into her belt, and it was the only tool that was going to be intimate with her this day. On Sunday, without fail, they had brunch, drank mimosas, watched TV in her bed, and all he ever talked about was calls he had been on over the weekend, as if she didn't get enough blood and misery in her life. Raines was a doll, but boring.

"Go rescue somebody and leave me alone," she suggested to him.

His smile and playfulness fled as rain fell in a curtain from heaven. "What the hell did I do?" he complained.

Chapter Six

West stayed outside in the rain alone, hammering, measuring, and building her fence as if it were a symbol of what she felt about people and life. When her gate opened and shut again at three P.M., she assumed it was Raines trying again. She slammed another nail into wood and felt bad about the way she had treated him. He had meant no harm, and her mood had nothing to do with him, really.

Niles could have done with the same consideration. He was in the window over the kitchen sink, looking out at his owner in a flood. She was swinging something that looked like it might hurt Niles if he got in her way. Niles had been minding his own business earlier, walking in circles, kneading the covers, finding just the right warm spot to settle on his owner's chest. Next thing, he was an astronaut, a circus acrobat shot out of a cannon. It was just a darn good thing he could land on his feet. He stared through streaming water at someone entering the yard from the north. Niles, the watch cat, had never seen this person, not once in his ancient feline life.

Brazil was aware of a skinny cat watching him from a window as he trespassed and West hammered, calling out to someone named Raines.

"Look, I'm sorry, okay?" she was saying. "I'm in this mood."

Brazil carried three thick Sunday papers wrapped in a dry-cleaning bag he had found in his closet. "Apology accepted," he said.

West wheeled around and fixed him in her sights, hammer mid-swing. "What the hell are you doing here?" She was startled and taken aback and did her best to sound hateful.

"Who's Raines?" Brazil got closer, his tennis shoes getting soaked.

"None of your damn business." She started hammering as her heart did.

He was suddenly shy and tentative in the rain as he got closer. "I brought you some extra papers. Thought you might . . ."

"You didn't ask me." She hammered. "You didn't give me a warning. Like you have some right to investigate my life." She bent a nail and clumsily pried it out. "Ride around all night. The whole time you're a spy."

She stopped what she was doing to look at him. He was soaked and dejected, wanting her to be pleased. He had given her the best he knew.

"You got no fucking right!" she said.

"It's a good story." He was getting defensive. "You're a hero."

She went on, enraged and not certain why. "What hero? Who cares?"

"I told you I was going to write about you."

"Seems to me that was a threat." She turned back to her fence and hammered. "And I didn't believe you meant it."

"Why not?" He didn't understand any of this and didn't think it was fair.

"No one has before." She hammered again and stopped again, trying to stay mad but not doing a good job of it. "I wouldn't have thought I was all that interesting."

"What I did is good, Virginia," he said.

Brazil was vulnerable and trying not to be. He told himself that what this hammer-wielding deputy chief thought didn't matter in the least. West stood in the rain, the two of them looking at each other as Niles watched from his favorite window, tail twitching.

"I know about your father," West went on. "I know exactly what happened. Is that why you run around playing cop morning, noon, and night?"

Brazil was struggling with emotions he didn't want anyone to know about. West couldn't tell if he was angry or close to tears as she chipped away at him with her own investigation into his past.

"He's plainclothes," she said, "decides to pull a stolen vehicle. Number one violation. You don't do that in an unmarked car. And the asshole turns out to be a felon on the run, who points his gun close range. Last thing your father said was, 'Please God no,' but the fucker does it anyway. Blows a hole in your daddy's heart, dead before he hits the pavement. Your favorite newspaper made sure Detective Drew Brazil looked bad in the end. Screwed him. And now his son's out here doing the same thing."

Brazil sat on the swampy lawn, staring hard at her. "No, I'm not. That's not the point. And you're cruel."

West didn't often have such a powerful effect on guys. Raines never got this intense, not even when she broke it off with him, which she had done three times now. Usually, he got mad and stormed off, then ignored her as his phone didn't ring until he couldn't stand it anymore. Brazil she did not comprehend, but then she had never known a writer or any artist, really. She sat next to him, both of them in a grassy puddle and drenched. She tossed the hammer and it splashed when it landed, its violence spent for the day. She sighed as this young volunteer-cop-reporter stared at drops streaking past, his body rigid with rage and resentment.

"Tell me why," she said.

He wouldn't look at her. He would never speak to her again.

"I want to know," she persisted. "You could be a cop. You could be a reporter. But oh no. You got to be both? Huh?" She playfully punched his shoulder and got no response. "You still live with your mother, I got a feeling. How come? Nice-looking guy like you? No girlfriend, you don't date, I got that feeling, too. You gay? I got no problem with that, okay?"

Brazil got up.

"Live and let live, I always say," West went on from her puddle.

He gave her a piercing look, stalking off. "I'm not the one they call gay," he said in the rain.

This did not threaten West. She had heard it before. Women who went into policing, the military, professional sports, coaching, construction, or physical education were oriented toward same-sex relationships. Those who succeeded in any of these professions or owned businesses, or became doctors, lawyers, or bankers and did not paint their nails or play round-robin tennis in a league during office hours were also lesbians. It did not matter if one were married with children. It mattered not if one were dating a man. These were simply facades, a means of faking out family and friends.

The only absolute proof of heterosexuality was to do nothing quite as well as a man and be proud of it. West had been a known lesbian ever since she was promoted to sergeant. Certainly, the department was not without its gay women, but they were closeted and full of lies about boyfriends no one ever met. West could understand why people might assume she was living the same myth. Similar rumors even circulated about Hammer. All of it was pathetic, and West wished people would let their rivers flow as they would and get on with life.

She had decided long ago that many moral issues were really about threats. For example, when she had been growing up on the farm, people talked about the unmarried women missionaries who kept busy at Shelby Presbyterian Church, not far from Cleveland Feeds and the regional hospital. A number of these fine ladies had served together in exotic places, including the Congo, Brazil, Korea, and Bolivia. They came home on furlough or to retire, and lived together in the same dwelling. It never occurred to anyone West knew that these faithful ladies of the church had any interest beyond prayer and saving the poor.

The threat in West's formative years was to grow up a spinster, an old maid. West heard this more than once when she was better than the boys in most things and learned how to drive a tractor. Statistically, she would prove to be an old maid. Her parents still worried, and this was compounded by the nineties fear that she might be an old maid who was also inclined elsewhere. In all fairness, it wasn't that West couldn't understand women wanting each other. What she could not imagine was fighting with a woman.

It was bad enough with men, who slammed things around and didn't communicate. Women cried and screamed and were touchy about everything, especially when their hormones were a little wide and to the right. She could not imagine two lovers having PMS at the same time. Domestic violence would be inevitable, possibly escalating to homicide, especially if both were cops with guns.

After a light solitary dinner of leftover spicy chicken pizza, West sat in her recliner chair in front of the TV, watching the Atlanta Braves clobber the Florida Marlins. Niles was in her lap because it was his wish. His owner was at ease in police sweats, drinking a Miller Genuine Draft in the bottle and reading Brazil's article about herself because it really wasn't right to be so hard on the guy without taking a good look at what he had done. She laughed out loud again, paper rattling as she turned a page. Where the hell did he get all this stuff?

She was so caught up, she had forgotten to pet Niles for fourteen minutes, eleven seconds, and counting. He wasn't asleep, but merely pretending, biding his time to see how long this might go on that he might add it to her list of infractions. When she ran out of indulgences, there was that porcelain figurine on top of the bookcase. If she thought Niles couldn't jump up there, she had another think coming. Niles could trace his lineage back to Egypt, to pharaohs and pyramids, his skills ancient and largely untested. Someone hit a home run and West didn't notice as she laughed again and reached for the phone.

Brazil didn't hear it ring at first because he was in front of his computer, typing, possessed by whatever he was writing as Annie Lennox sang loudly from the boom box. His mother was in the kitchen, fixing herself a peanut-butter sandwich on Sunbeam white bread. She slurped another mouthful of cheap vodka from a plastic glass as the phone rang from the wall. She swayed, grabbing for the counter to steady herself, and got a drawer handle as two blue phones on the wall rang and rang. Silverware crashed to the floor, and Brazil jumped up from his chair as his mother managed to grab at her double-vision of the phone and bump it out of its cradle. It banged against the wall, dangling from a snarled cord. She lunged for it again, almost falling.

"What?" she slurred into the receiver.

"I was trying to reach Andy Brazil," West said over the line, after an uncertain pause.

"In his room going." Mrs. Brazil made drunken typing motions. "You know. Usual! Thinks he'll amount to Hemingway, something."

Mrs. Brazil did not notice her son in the doorway, stricken as she talked on in fractured, bleary words that could not possibly make sense to anyone. It was a house rule that she did not answer the phone. Either her son got it or the answering machine did. He watched in despair, helpless as she humiliated him yet again in life.

"Ginia West," Mrs. Brazil repeated as she finally noticed two of her sons coming toward her. He took the phone out of her hand.

West's intention had been merely to confess to Brazil that his story was rather wonderful and she appreciated it and didn't deserve it. She had not expected this impaired woman to answer, and now West knew it all. She didn't tell Brazil a thing other than that she was on her way. This was an order. West had dealt with all types in her years of police work and was undaunted by Mrs. Brazil, no matter how vile, how hateful and hostile the woman was when her son and West put her in bed and made her drink a lot of water. Mrs. Brazil passed out about five minutes after West helped her into the bathroom to pee.

West and Brazil went for a walk in darkness broken by an occasional lighted window from old Southern homes along Main Street. Rain was gentle like mist. He had nothing to say as they drew closer to the Davidson campus, which was quiet this time of year, even when various camps were in session. A security guard in his Cushman watched the couple pass, pleased that Andy Brazil might finally have a girlfriend. She was a lot older than him but still worth looking at, and if anyone needed a mother figure, that boy did.

The guard's name was Clyde Briddlewood, and he had headed the modest Davidson College security force since days when the only problem in the world was pranks and drunkenness. Then the school had let women in. It was a bad idea, and he had told everyone he could. Briddlewood had done his best to warn the preoccupied professors as they were hurrying to class, and he had alerted Sam Spencer, the president back then. No one listened. Now Briddlewood had a security force of eight people and three Cushmans. They had radios, guns, and drank coffee with local cops.

Briddlewood dipped Copenhagen snuff, spitting in a Styrofoam cup as Brazil and his girlfriend followed the brick walk toward the Presbyterian church. Briddlewood had always liked that boy and was sorry as heck he had to grow up. He remembered Brazil as a kid, always in a hurry somewhere with his Western Auto tennis racket and plastic bag of bald, dead tennis balls that he'd fished out of the trash or begged off the tennis coach. Brazil used to share his chewing gum and candy with Briddlewood, and this touched the security guard right down to his boots. The boy didn't have much and lived with a bad situation. True, Muriel Brazil wasn't hitting the sauce back then as bad as she did now, but her son had a lousy deal and everyone at Davidson knew it.

What Brazil didn't know was that a number of people who lived in the college community had plotted behind the scenes for years and had raised money from wealthy alumni, even dipping into their own wallets to make certain that when Brazil was college age, he was offered an opportunity to rise above his situation. Briddle-wood himself had put a few bucks in the pot when he didn't have much to spare, and lived in a small house far enough away from Lake Norman that he couldn't see the water but could at least watch the endless parade of trucks hauling boats along his dirt road. He spat again, silently rolling the Cushman closer to the church, keeping his eye on the couple, to make sure they were safe out here in the dark.

"What am I going to do with you?" West was saying to Brazil.

He had his pride and was in a humorless mood. "For the record, I don't need you to do a thing for me."

"Yeah you do. You got serious problems."

"And you don't," he said. "All you got in your life is an eccentric cat."

This surprised West. What else had he dug up about her? "How'd you know about Niles?" she wanted to know.

West was aware they were being stalked by some security guard in a Cushman. He was hanging back in shadows, certain West and Brazil couldn't see him creeping in the cover of boxwoods and magnolia trees. West couldn't imagine how boring that job must be.

"I have a lot in my life," she added.

"What a fantasy," Brazil said.

"You know what? You're a total waste of my time." She meant it.

They walked on, moving away from the campus and cutting through narrow roads where faculty lived in restored homes with cherished lawns and old trees. Brazil used to wander these lanes as a boy, fantasizing about people inside expensive homes, imagining important professors and their nice husbands and wives. Light filled their windows and seemed so warm back then, and sometimes draperies were open and he could see people moving inside, walking across the living room with a drink, sitting in a chair reading or at a desk working.

Brazil's loneliness was buried out of reach and unnamed. He did not know what to call the hollow hurt that started somewhere in his chest and pressed against his heart like two cold hands. He never cried when the hands pressed, but would tremble violently like a distressed flame when he thought he might lose his tennis match or when he didn't get an A. Brazil could not watch sad movies, and now and then beauty overwhelmed him, especially live music played by symphonies and string quartets.

West could feel rage building in Brazil as they walked. The mounting silence became oppressive as they passed lighted homes and dark thick trees armored in ivy and kudzu. She did not understand him and was beginning to suspect she'd made a big mistake thinking she could. So what if she'd worked hostage negotiation, homicides, and was experienced in talking people out of killing themselves or someone else? This didn't mean she was even remotely capable of helping a strange guy like Andy Brazil. In fact, she didn't have time.

"I want this killer," Brazil started in, talking louder than was necessary or wise. "Okay? I want him caught."

He was obsessed, as if what this killer was doing was personal. West had no intention of getting into his space on this. They walked on. Brazil suddenly kicked a rock with a fancy black and purple Nike leather tennis shoe that looked like something Agassi would endorse.

"What he does." Brazil kicked more rocks. "What do you think it must be like?" His voice got louder. "Driving somewhere in a strange city, tired, away from home, a lot on your mind. Getting lost, stopping to ask directions." Another rock skittered across blacktop. "Next thing, you're being led to some Godforsaken place, behind an abandoned building. A warehouse. A vacant lot."

West stopped walking. She was staring at him as he furiously stomped ahead, wheeled around.

"Hard cold steel against your head as you beg not to die!" he yelled as if the crime had happened to him. "As he blows your brains out anyway!"

West was frozen as she watched something she had never seen before this moment. Porch lights of nearby houses flipped on.

"He pulls your pants down and spray-paints this symbol! *How would you like to die that way?*"

More lights came on. Dogs barked. West went into her police mode without a conscious thought. She walked over to Brazil and firmly took his arm.

"Andy, you're disturbing the entire neighborhood." She spoke with quiet calm. "Let's go home."

Brazil stared defiantly at her. "I want to make a difference."

She nervously scanned their surroundings. "Believe me. You are."

More lights turned on, and someone had come out on his porch to see what crazy person had wandered into his quiet neighborhood. Briddlewood had fled in his Cushman minutes earlier.

"Which is why we need to go," West added, pulling Brazil along as they started walking back. "You want to help. Okay. Tell me what you have to contribute besides tantrums and words."

"Maybe we could plant something in one of my stories to trick him." He had an idea.

"I wish it were that simple," she said, and she meant it. "And you're assuming he reads the paper."

"I bet he does." Brazil wished she would have an open mind, as he flew through possibilities of what subliminal propaganda he might plant to ensnare this monster.

"The answer's no. We don't plant stories."

Brazil hopped ahead again, excited. "Together we could get him! I know it."

"What's this together stuff?" West said. "You're just a reporter. Hate to remind you of that fact."

"I'm a volunteer cop," he corrected her.

"Uh huh. The gunless wonder."

"You could give me shooting lessons," he then said. "My dad used to take me out to a dump in the country. . . ."

"He should have left you there," she said.

"We'd shoot cans with his .38."

"How old were you?" West asked when they were in Brazil's driveway.

"Starting when I was seven, I think." He had his hands in his pockets and was looking down as he walked, a streetlight lighting up his hair. "Seems like I was in the second grade."

"I mean, when he died," she gently said.

"Ten," he said. "I had just turned ten."

He stopped, and did not want West to leave. He didn't want to go in and face the way he lived.

"I don't have a gun," he told her.

"Thank you, Jesus," she said.

Chapter Seven

Days went by. West had no intention of furthering the cause of Andy Brazil. His problems were his own, and it was time he grew up. When the following Sunday rolled around and Raines was interested in brunch, she called Brazil because she was a certified firearms instructor. If he needed help, it was only fair that she offer. He said he could be ready in ten minutes. She told him that unless she flew the Concorde to Davidson, she would not be picking him up for at least an hour.

She drove her personal car for this, a Ford Explorer with dual airbags. It was a white sports utility vehicle with four-wheel drive that ate snow for a snack. She roared into his driveway at three P.M., and he was out the door before she could open hers. The obvious range would have been the one at the police academy, but this she could not do because volunteers were not allowed, nor were guests. West chose The Firing Line on Wilkinson Boulevard, just past Bob's Pawn Shop, and a number of trailer parks, the Oakden Motel, Country City USA, and Coyote Joe's.

Had they continued another block or two, West realized, they would have ended up in the parking lot of the Paper Doll Lounge. She had been in there before on fights. It was disgusting. Topless women were on the same block as gun and pawn shops, as if breasts and g-strings somehow belonged in the same category as used merchandise and weapons. West wondered if Brazil had ever visited a topless lounge and sat stiffly in a chair, his hands in a white-knuckle grip on armrests, as a naked woman rubbed against his inner legs, and got in his face.

Probably not, West decided. She had a feeling he was a foreigner who didn't speak the language, hadn't tried the food or seen the sights. How could this have happened? He didn't have girls after him in high school, in college? Or boys? She did not understand Andy Brazil as he foraged through shelves of ammunition inside the firing range shop, picking out Winchester 95 grain full metal jacket .380, Luger 115 grain ball nine-millimeter cartridges, and contemplated .45 automatic 230 grain, Federal Hi-Power, Hydra-Shok hollowpoints, and Super X 50 Centerfire that were too expensive for practice. He was going nuts. This was a candy shop, and West was buying.

Gunshots sounded like a war going on inside this range, where NRA rednecks worshiped their pistols and drug dealers with cash and leather hightops got better at killing. West and Brazil were loaded down with hearing protectors, safety glasses, and boxes of ammunition. She was a woman in jeans, carrying two pistol hard cases. Dangerous-looking men gave her hostile glances, not happy about her invading their club. Brazil was picking up danger signals as he surveyed his surroundings.

The men didn't seem to like him, either. He was suddenly conscious of being in Davidson tennis sweats and having tied a bandanna around his head to keep his hair out of his eyes. These guys all had guts and big shoulders, as if they worked out with forklifts and cases of beer. He had seen their trucks in the parking lot, some of them with six wheels, as if there were mountains and streams to climb and cross along I-74 and I-40. Brazil did not understand the tribe of Male he had grown up around in North Carolina.

It was beyond biology, genitals, hormones, or testosterone. Some of these guys had naked pinups on the mudflaps of their tractor trailers, and Brazil was frankly horrified. A guy saw a foxy woman with a body, and he wanted her protecting his radials from gravel? Not Brazil. He wanted her at the movies, the drive-through, and in candlelight.

He was using the staple gun, fastening another target to cardboard and attaching it to the frame in his lane. West, the instructor, was examining her pupil's latest target. The silhouette she held up had a tight spread of bullet holes in the center of the chest. She was amazed. She watched Brazil push cartridges into the magazine of a stainless steel Sig Sauer .380 pistol.

"You're dangerous," she let him know.

He gripped the small gun with both hands, in the position and stance his father had taught him in a life he scarcely recalled. Brazil's form wasn't bad, but it could be improved, and he fired one round after another. He dropped out the empty magazine and smacked in a new one. He fired nonstop, as if he couldn't shoot fast enough and would kill anybody else in life who hurt him. This would not do. West knew the reality of the street.

She reached for a button in his booth and held it in. The paper target suddenly came to life and screeched along the lane toward Brazil, as if it were going to attack him. Startled, Brazil shot wildly. BAM! BAM! BAM! Bullets slammed into the target's metal frame, into the back rubber wall, and then he was out of ammo. The target screeched to a stop, rocking from its cable in his face.

"Hey! What are you doing?" He turned to West, indignant and bewildered.

She did not answer at first as she pushed cartridges into black metal magazines. She smacked one into her big bad black .40 caliber Smith & Wesson semiautomatic, then looked at her student.

"You shoot too fast." She racked back the slide and it snapped forward. She aimed at her own target in her own lane. "You're out of ammo." She fired. BAM-BAM. "And out of luck." BAM-BAM.

She paused, and fired twice again. She set down her pistol and moved close to Brazil, taking the .380 from him, and opening the slide to make sure the gun was unloaded and safe. She pointed it down the lane, hands and arms locked, knees slightly bent, in the proper position and stance.

"Tap-tap and stop," she told him as she demonstrated. "Tap-tap and stop. You see what the other person's doing and adjust." She returned the .380 to him, butt first. "And don't slap the trigger. Take it home tonight and practice."

That night, Brazil stayed in his room and dry-fired West's .380 until he had a significant blister on his index finger. He aimed it at himself in the mirror, that he might get used to seeing a gun pointed at him. He did this with music playing and fantasies spinning, the deadly tiny black eye staring at his head, his heart, as he thought of his father, who had not drawn his gun. His father had not had time even to key his radio. Brazil's arms were beginning to tremble, and he had not eaten supper.

It was a few minutes past nine, and his mother had refused to eat earlier when he had offered to fix her a hamburger patty and a salad of fresh tomatoes and Vidalia onions, with oil and vinegar. More alert than usual, she was watching a sitcom, and in the same faded blue flannel robe and slippers she wore most of the time. He could not grasp how she could live the way she did, and had given up thinking he could change her or the life she hated. In high school he, her only child, had been the expert detective, rooting through the house and her Cadillac, seeking her hidden stashes of pills and liquor. Her resourcefulness was amazing. Once she had gone so far as to bury whisky in the yard beneath the rosebushes she used to prune when she still cared.

Muriel Brazil's greatest fear was to be present. She did not want to be here, and the nightmare of rehabilitation and AA meetings darkened her memory like the shadow of a monstrous bird flying over her and splaying its claws, ready to snatch her up and eat her alive. She did not want to feel. She would not sit in groups of people who had only first names and talked about the drunks they once were and binges they used to go on, and how wonderful it was to be sober. All spoke with the sincerity of contrite sinners after a religious experience.

Their new god was sobriety, and this god allowed plenty of cigarettes and black decaffeinated coffee. Exercise, drinking copious amounts of water, and talking regularly to one's sponsor were critical, and the god expected the recovering one to contact all he had ever offended and apologize. In other words, Mrs. Brazil was supposed to tell her son and those she worked around at Davidson that she was an alcoholic. She had tried this once on several of the students she supervised at the ARA Slater food service that catered the cafeteria in the new Commons building.

"I've been away a month at a treatment center," Mrs. Brazil told a junior named Heather, from Connecticut. "I'm an alcoholic."

Mrs. Brazil tried the same line on Ron, a freshman from Ashland, Virginia. The expected catharsis was not there. Students did not respond well and avoided her after that. They regarded her fearfully as rumors floated around campus. Some of what was said got back to Brazil, heightening a sense of shame that drove him deeper into his isolation. He knew he could never have friends because if anyone got close, the truth would be known. Even West had been confronted the first time she had called his house. Brazil was still perplexed, if not stunned, that this had not seemed to affect the deputy chief's opinion of him.

"Mom, how about I cook us up some eggs?" Brazil paused in the doorway. Light from the television flickered in the dark living room.

"I'm not hungry," she said, staring at the screen.

"What have you eaten? Probably nothing, right? You know how bad that is for you, Mom."

Pointing the remote control, she changed to another channel, where people were laughing and exchanging bad lines.

"How 'bout a grilled cheese?" her son tried again.

"Well, maybe." She changed channels again.

It was hard for her to be still when her son was nearby. It was hard to look at his face and meet his eyes. The nicer he was to her, the more abusive she felt, and she had never figured out why. She would not make it without him. He bought food and kept the house going. Her social security checks and a small pension from the police department supplied her liquids. It didn't take as much to get drunk these days, and she knew what this said about her liver. She wished she would go on and die, and she worked at it every day. Her eyes filled with tears and her throat closed as her son rattled around in the kitchen.

Alcohol had been the enemy the first time she'd ever touched it, when she was sixteen and Micky Latham took her to Lake Norman at night and got her drunk on apricot brandy. She vaguely remembered lying in the grass, watching stars reconfigure and blur as he breathed hard and clumsily worked on her blouse as if buttons had just been invented. He was nineteen and worked in Bud's Garage, and his hands were calloused and felt like claws on breasts that had never been touched before this intoxicated moment.

That was the night sweet Muriel lost her virginity, and it had nothing to do with Micky Latham, and everything to do with the bottle in its ABC store brown paper bag. When she drank, her brain lifted as if it might sing. She was happy, brave, playful, and witty. She was driving her father's Cadillac the afternoon Officer Drew Brazil pulled her over for speeding. Muriel was seventeen and the most beautiful, worldly woman he'd ever met. If he thought he smelled alcohol on her breath that afternoon, he was too mesmerized to put it in perspective. He was rather glorious in his uniform, and the ticket never got written. Instead, they went to Big Daddy's fish camp after he got off duty. They married that Thanksgiving when she had missed her period two months in a row.

Muriel Brazil's son reappeared with grilled cheese on wheat bread, cooked just right and cut diagonally, the way she liked it. He'd put a dollop of ketchup on the side so she could dip, and he brought her water that she had no intention of drinking. He looked so much like his father it was more than she could bear.

"I know how much you hate water, Mom," he said, setting the plate and napkin in her lap. "But you got to drink it, okay? Sure you don't want salad?"

She shook her head and wished she could thank him. She was impatient because he was blocking her view of the TV.

"I'll be in my room," he said.

He dry-fired until his finger bled. He was remarkably steady because years of tennis had strengthened the muscles of his hands and forearms. His grip was crushing. The next morning he woke up excited. The sun was shining, and West had promised to take him to the range again late afternoon to work with him further. It was Monday, and he had the day off. He didn't know what he would do between now and then, or how he would make hours pass. Brazil could not endure free time and usually gave it away to some project.

The grass was heavy with dew when he slipped out of the house at half past seven. Carrying tennis rackets and a hopper of balls, he walked first to the track, where he ran six miles and did push-ups, sit-ups, and crunches, to get his fix of endorphin. By now, the grass was warm and dry, and he lay in it long enough for his blood to stop pounding. He listened to the buzzing of insects in clover and smelled bittersweet green vegetation and wild onions. His gym shorts and tank top were saturated as he trotted downhill to the outdoor tennis courts.

Ladies were playing doubles, and he politely trotted behind them on their court, going to the other end so he could be as far away from anyone as possible. He didn't want to disturb people with the hundreds of balls he intended to kill. Brazil served in deuce court and ad court, on one side, then the other, picking up after himself with the bright yellow hopper. He was slightly annoyed. Tennis was unforgiving if he didn't practice. His usual precision wasn't there, and he knew what this boded. If he didn't start playing again, he was going to lose one of the few things he'd ever been good at. Damn. The ladies on court one noticed a marked deterioration in their own games as they continued to watch with envy the young man on court four hit balls so hard they sounded like baseballs cracking against bats.

Chief Hammer's concentration was in and out, too. She was presiding over an executive staff meeting in her private conference room, in her sizable corner of the third floor. Windows overlooked Davidson and Trade, and she could see the mighty USBank Corporate Center topped by its silly aluminum headdress, which oddly brought to mind a wild man with a bone in his nose, perhaps from some "Little Rascals" episode from years long past. At exactly eight this morning as Hammer was carrying her first cup of coffee to her desk, the CEO of that sixty-story erection had called her.

Solomon Cahoon was Jewish, and the Old Testament factored into his mother's choice of names for her firstborn male child. Her son would be a king who would make wise decisions, such as the one this Friday, when he had informed his police chief that she would hold a press conference to let citizens know that the serial killings in Charlotte were homosexual and of no threat to normal men visiting the Queen City on business. Northside Baptist Church would be holding a prayer vigil for victims' families and the souls of those killed. Police were following very good leads.

"Just a reassurance thing," Cahoon had relayed to the chief over the phone.

Hammer and her six deputy chiefs, along with people from strategic planning and crime analysis, were discussing this latest commandment delivered from on high. Wren Dozier, deputy chief of administration, was especially incensed. He was forty with delicate features and a soft mouth. Unmarried, he lived in a section of Fourth Ward where Tommy Axel and others had condominiums with dusky rose doors. Dozier had known he would never be promoted beyond captain. Then Hammer had come to town, a woman who rewarded people for good work. Dozier would take a bullet for her.

"What a bunch of shit," Dozier said, as he slowly and angrily twirled his coffee mug on the table. "So what about the other side of this, huh?" He met eyes all around. "What about the wives and kids back home? They're supposed to think the last thing Pop did was pay for a homosexual encounter out on some city street somewhere?"

"There's no evidence to support such a thing," West said, and she was unhappy, too. "You can't say something like this." She stared at Hammer.

The chief and Cahoon could agree on nothing, and she knew he was going to have her fired. It was all a matter of time and would not be a first, either. At her level, it was all politics. The city got a new mayor, who brought along his own chief, which was what had happened to her in Atlanta and would have in Chicago had she not left. She really could not afford to get reshuffled again. Each city would get only smaller, until one fine day she ended up right where she'd started, in the economically languishing one-horse town of Little Rock.

"Of course I will not get up in front of reporters and spread such crap," the chief said. "I won't."

"Well, it can't hurt to remind the public that we are following leads and are on the case," said the public information officer.

"What leads?" said West, who headed investigations, and should be privy to such things.

"If we get any, we'll follow them," said Hammer. "That's the point."

"You can't say that, either," worried the PIO. "We have to leave out the *if we get any* part of . . ."

Hammer impatiently cut her off. "Of course, of course. That

goes without saying. I didn't mean literally. Enough of this. Let's move on. Here's what we're going to do. A press release." She regarded the PIO over reading glasses. "I want it on my desk by ten-thirty and out to the press by midafternoon so they can meet their deadlines. And I will see if I can get up with Cahoon, talk him down from this."

This was very much like securing an audience with the Pope. Hammer's secretary and another assistant traded phone calls with Cahoon's people for most of the day. Finally, the meeting was barely arranged for late that afternoon, sometime between four-fifteen and five, depending on when a gap appeared in the CEO's impossible schedule. Hammer had no choice but to show up at the early end of this interval and hope for the best.

At four she left her police department and walked through downtown on a lovely afternoon that, before this moment, she had not noticed. She followed Trade to Tryon to the corporate center, with its eternal torch and sculptures. Inside a huge lobby of polished stone, she walked briskly, her heels clicking over marble as she passed rich wood paneling and famous fresco paintings depicting the Shingon philosophy of chaos, creativity, making, and building. She nodded at one of the guards, who nodded back and tipped his cap. He liked that lady chief and had always thought she walked like she knew how, and she was nice and didn't disrespect anyone, whether they were a real cop or not.

Hammer boarded a crowded elevator and was the last to get off at the top of the crown, which at this dizzying level, really was aluminum pipes. Hammer had visited Cahoon before. Rarely a month went by that he didn't summon her to his suite of mahogany and glass overlooking his city. As was true of Hampton Court Palace, visitors were required to pass through many outer layers and courts to get to the king. Should a crazed gunman decide to carry out his mission, by the time he reached the throne many secretaries and assistants might be dead, but Cahoon, quite likely, would not have heard the noise.

Several outer offices later, Hammer entered the one occupied by the executive secretary, Mrs. Mullis-Mundi, also known as M&M by those who did not like her, which was virtually all. She was candy-coated, but with nuts. She would melt in the mouth and break teeth. Hammer frankly had no use for this perky young thing who had gotten married and kept her name while appropriating that of her husband, Joe Mundi. Mrs. Mullis-Mundi was bulimic, and had breast implants and long dyed blond hair. She wore size four Anne Klein. Her cologne was Escada. She worked out daily in Gold's Gym. She did not wear slacks, and was simply biding time before she sued for sexual harassment.

"Judy, great to see you." The executive secretary stood and offered her hand with the same lilting style that Hammer had observed in devout bowlers. "Let me see how he's doing."

A half hour later, Hammer remained seated on a buttery-soft ivory leather couch. She was reviewing statistics, memos, and attending to the armies marching restlessly inside her briefcase. Mrs. Mullis-Mundi never got off the phone or grew tired of it. She took one earring off, then the other, then rotated the phone again to a hand less weary, as if to emphasize the painful demands of her career. Often she looked at her large scratch-proof Rado watch, and sighed, flipping her hair. She was about to die to smoke one of her skinny menthol cigarettes that had flowers around the filter.

Cahoon was able at last to fit the chief in at precisely thirteen minutes past the hour. As usual his day had been long, with far too much in it, and all insisting that they could speak to no one but him. In truth he had never been in a hurry to let Hammer into his office, regardless of the minor fact that it was he, versus her, who had demanded a meeting. She was ornery and opinionated and had treated him like a bad dog the first time they'd met. As a result he was one without fail and consistently, when dealing with her. One of these days he would send her down the road and bring in a progressive man, the sort who snapped open a briefcase with the *Wall Street Journal* and a Browning Hi-Power inside. Now, that was

Cahoon's idea of a chief, someone who knew the market, would shoot to kill, and showed a little respect to leaders of the community.

Hammer's first thought whenever she was face to face with the ruler of the city was that he had made his fortune on a chicken farm and had attributed his history to someone else by another name. Frank Purdue, she almost believed, was an alias. Holly Farms was a front. Solomon Cahoon had made his millions off plump breasts and thighs. He had gotten rich off fryers and fat roasters and their little thermometers that popped up at precisely the right time when things were heating up. Clearly, Cahoon had dovetailed these experiences and resources into banking. He had been wise enough to realize that his past might pose a credibility problem for one securing a mortgage through USBank, if this person happened to see the CEO smiling on chicken parts at Harris-Teeter. Hammer couldn't blame him for coming up with an alias or two, if this was what he had in fact done.

His desk was burled maple, not old but magnificent, and much more expansive than the ninety-six inches of wood veneer, including a return, that the city furnished her. Cahoon was creaking in an apple green English leather chair with brass studs and the same burled armrests, talking on the phone, looking out spotless glass and beyond aluminum pipes. She sat across from him and was on hold again. It really didn't bother her all that much anymore, for Hammer could transport herself just about anywhere. She could solve problems, make decisions, come up with lists of matters to be investigated, and deliberate what would be good for dinner and who should cook it.

To her, Cahoon always looked naked from the neck up. His hair was a bristly silver fringe he wore like a crown. Cropped short, it stood up straight in different lengths and was shaped like a crescent moon in back. He was perpetually tan and wrinkled from his passion for sailboats, and he was vital and distinguished in a black suit, crisp white shirt, and Fendi silk tie filled with gold and deep red clocks.

"Sol," she politely greeted him, when he eventually hung up the phone.

"Judy, thanks so much for fitting me in," he said in his soft Southern voice. "So what are we going to do about these gay bashings, these queer killin's? These fag-fisher-queens trolling in our city? You understand the false impression all of it is giving to other corporations and companies thinking of relocating here? Not to mention what it does to business in town as usual."

"*Fag-fisher-queens,*" Hammer slowly, thoughtfully repeated. "*Trolling.*"

"Yes, ma'am." He nodded. "You want some Perrier or something?"

She shook her head, and measured her words. "Gay bashings. Queer killings. This came from where?" She was not on his same planet, and that was her choice.

"Oh come on." He leaned forward, propping elbows on his rich desk. "We all know what this is about. Men come to our city. They cut loose, give in to their perversion, think no one will be the wiser. Well, the angel of death for these sickos is swooping in." He nodded deeply. "Truth, justice, and the American way. God putting his foot down."

"Synonymous," she said.

"Huh?" He frowned in confusion.

"All are synonymous?" she said. "Truth. Justice. American way. God putting his foot down."

"You bet, honey." He smiled.

"Sol, don't call me that." She jabbed her finger the same way she did when making points while West was driving her around the city. "Don't. Not ever."

He settled back in his leather chair and laughed, entertained by this lady. What a trip. Thank God she had a husband to set her straight and put her where she belonged. Cahoon was willing to bet that Hammer's man called her honey and she waited for it, apron tied in back, like Heidi, Cahoon's first and only wife. Saturday mornings, Heidi served him breakfast in bed, providing he was in town. She continued this even now, after so many faithful years, although the effect wasn't quite the same. What happened to the female body after it turned thirty? Men were ready and willing until death. They sat tall in the saddle and were unaffected by gravity and this was why it wasn't out of the question for the male to seek out younger females eventually.

"You understand the definition of honey?" Hammer started in on this again. "A food for larvae. To be flattering or obsequious. Cajolery. What you say to get your socks darned and buttons sewn on. Christ, why did I come to this city?" She shook her head, not kidding.

"Atlanta wasn't much better," he reminded her. "Certainly not Chicago, or it wouldn't have been for long."

"True, true."

"What about your press conference?" He moved on to more important matters. "I passed along a very appropriate suggestion. And what?" He shrugged thin shoulders. "Where's my press conference? Was it so much for me to ask? This building is a beacon bringing business to Charlotte-Mecklenburg. We need to disseminate positive information, such as our hundred and five percent clearance rate for all violent crimes last year . . ."

She interrupted him, because she couldn't let this pass. "Sol, this is not financial smoke and mirrors. You cannot manipulate the bottom line on paper and in computers and get everyone to accept it. We're talking tangibles. Rapes, robberies, B&E's, homicides, with real flesh and blood victims. You're asking me to convince citizens that we cleared more cases than we had last year?"

"Old cases were solved, that's why the numbers . . ." he started to repeat what he had been told.

Hammer was shaking her head, and Cahoon's infamous impatience was heating up. This lady was the only one who dared talk to him in this fashion, if he didn't include his wife and children.

"What old cases?" Hammer said. "And going back how far?

You know what this is like? It's like someone asking me how much
I make as chief of police and I say a million dollars because I'm
going back ten years."

"Apples and oranges."

"No, no, Sol." She was shaking her head more vigorously. "No
apples and oranges here. Oh no. This is fertilizer."

"Judy." He pointed a bent finger at her. "What about the con-
ventions that decide not to come here because of this . . . ?"

"Oh for God's sake." She waved him off and stood. "Conven-
tions don't decide anything, people do, and I can't hear any more of
this. Just let me handle things, you mind? That's what I'm paid to
do. And I'm not going to spread a lot of crap. You'll have to get
someone else to do it." She started walking out of his office with its
view. "A hundred and five percent." She raised her hands in exas-
peration. "And I'd watch out for your secretary, by the way."

"What does she have to do with this?" Cahoon was most confused, which was fairly normal after a visit with Hammer.

"I know the type," Hammer warned. "How much does she
want?"

"For what?" He was baffled.

"Trust me. She'll let you know," said Hammer, shaking her
head. "I wouldn't be alone with her or trust her. I'd get rid of her."

Mrs. Mullis-Mundi knew the meeting could not have gone well.
Cahoon had not sent for water, coffee, tea, or cocktails. He had not
summoned her on the intercom and asked her to show the chief
out. Mrs. Mullis-Mundi was conjuring up herself in her Chanel
compact, checking her smile in the mirror, when Hammer suddenly
was there. This was not a woman who bleached her teeth or waxed
her legs. The chief tossed some sort of report in a file folder on the
executive secretary's enameled Chinese desk.

"These are my stats, the real ones," Hammer said as she left.
"See to it he gets them when he's feeling open-minded."

School kids were getting the grand tour through the marble
lobby when the chief's rapidly clicking heels carried her out. She

glanced at her Breitling watch without really noting the time. Tonight was her twenty-sixth anniversary of being married to Seth. They were supposed to have a quiet evening at the Beef & Bottle, the rare steak hang-out that he loved and she tolerated. It was on South Boulevard, and it had been her experience whenever she had dined there that she generally represented her gender alone as she picked at her meat.

She began, as always, with baby frog legs sautéed in wine and garlic, and a Caesar salad. The din grew louder around them in this darkly paneled room, where city fathers and planners had met for decades, on their way to heart attacks. Seth, her husband, loved food better than life and was fully engaged with shrimp cocktail, hearts of lettuce with famous blue cheese dressing, bread, butter, and a porterhouse for two that he typically did not share. Once upon a time, Seth had been an enlightened and handsome assistant to the Little Rock city manager, and he had run into Sergeant Judy Hammer on the capitol grounds.

There had never been any question about who was the engine driving the train in this relationship, and this was part of the attraction. Seth liked her power. She liked his liking it. They were married and began a family that quickly became his responsibility as the wife soared and was called out at night, and they moved. That Hammer was her name and not his made sense for those who knew them and gave the matter a thought. He was soft, with a weak chin that called to mind the watery-eyed knights and bishops of portrait galleries.

"We should pick up some of this cheese spread for the house," Seth said, laying it on thick in candlelight.

"Seth, I worry about what you're doing to yourself," Hammer said, reaching for her pinot noir.

"I guess it's port wine, but it doesn't look like it," he went on. "It might have horseradish in it. Maybe cayenne pepper."

His hobby was studying law and the stock market. His most significant setback in life was that he had inherited money from his family and was not obligated to work, was gentle, and tended to be mild, nonviolent, and tired much of the time. At this stage in life, he was so much like a spineless, spiteful woman that his wife wondered how it was possible she should have ended up in a lesbian relationship with a man. Lord, when Seth slipped into one of his snits, as he was in this very minute, she understood domestic violence and felt there were cases when it was justified.

"Seth, it's our anniversary," she reminded him in a low voice. "You haven't talked to me all evening. You've eaten everything in this goddamn restaurant, and won't look at me. You want to give me a clue as to what's wrong, for once? So I don't have to guess or read your mind or go to a psychic?"

Her stomach was balled up like a threatened opossum. Seth was the best diet she'd ever been on, and could throw her into anorexia quicker than anything. In rare, quiet moments, when Hammer walked alone on a beach or in the mountains, she knew she had not been in love with Seth for most of their marriage. But he was her weight-bearing wall. Were he knocked out, half her world would crash. That was his power over her, and he knew it like any good wife. The children, for example, might take his side. This was not possible, but Judy Hammer feared it.

"I'm not talking because I have nothing to say," Seth reasonably replied.

"Fine." She folded her cloth napkin and dropped it on the table as she began searching for the waitress.

Miles away on Wilkinson Boulevard, past Bob's Pawn Shop, trailer parks, and Coyote Joe's and near the topless Paper Doll Lounge, The Firing Line was conducting a war of its own. Brazil was slaughtering silhouettes screeching down the lane at him. Ejected cartridge cases sailed through the air, clinking to the floor. West's pupil was improving like nothing she'd ever seen. She was proud.

"Tap-tap, you're out!" she rudely yelled, as if he were the village idiot. "Safety on. Dump the magazine, reload, rack it! Ready position, safety off! Tap-tap! Stop!"

This had been going on for more than an hour, and good ole boys were peering out from their booths, wondering what the hell was going on down there. Who was that babe shouting like a drill sergeant at that faggy-looking guy? Bubba, who was begot by a Bubba and probably related to a long line of them, was leaning against a cinder-block wall, an Exxon cap low over his eyes. He was big and bad in fatigues and a camouflage vest, as he watched the target screeching closer and closer to the blond guy.

Bubba was aware of the dense, tight spread, recognizing this guy's skill at head shots. Bubba drooled snuff in a bottle, and glanced back at his own lane to make certain no one thought about touching his Glock 20 ten-millimeter combat-type handgun or his Remington XP-100 with Leupold scope and standard load of fifty-grain Sierra PSP bullets and seventeen grains of IMR 4198 powder. This was a handgun that rested very nicely over sandbags. His Calico model 110 auto pistol, with its hundred-shot magazine and flash suppressor, wasn't half bad, either, nor was the Browning Hi-Power HP-Practical pistol, complete with Pachmayr rubber grips, round-style serrated hammer, and removable front sight.

There was little Bubba liked better than to machine-gun a couple of targets, brass flying like shrapnel, as drug dealers walked behind him, not the least bit interested in messing with the man. Bubba watched the bitch down range unfasten a target from its metal frame. She held it up and looked at her dead-eye, sweet boyfriend.

"Who pissed you off?" she asked Brazil.

Bubba's manly stride carried him their way as more rounds exploded like strings of firecrackers.

"What is this? Some kind of school going on here?" Bubba asked, as if he owned the place.

The woman gave him her attention, and he didn't like what he saw in her eyes. This one didn't know fear. Clearly, she didn't have sense enough to appreciate what she was looking at, and Bubba went over to her lane and helped himself to her Smith & Wesson.

"Pretty big piece for a little gal like you." Bubba grinned in his cruel way, dribbling more snuff in his jar.

"Please put it down," West calmly told him.

Brazil was intrigued and appropriately nervous about where this was going. The big-bellied pig dressed like Ruby Ridge or Oklahoma City looked like he had hurt people in the past and was proud of it. He did not put West's gun down, but was now dropping out the magazine, checking the slide, and ejecting the cartridge from the chamber. It occurred to Brazil that West was disarmed, and he could not help her, because the .380 was out of ammunition, too.

"Put it down. Now." West was most unfriendly. "It's city property, and I am a city police officer."

"How 'bout that?" Bubba was beginning to enjoy himself immensely. "Little woman here's a cop. Well, golly gee."

West knew better than to announce her rank, which would make matters only that much worse. She stepped so close to him, the toes of their shoes were about to touch. Her chest would have pressed against his belly had she not decided against it.

"This is the last time I ask you to put my gun right back where you found it," she said, staring up into his homely, whisky-flushed face.

Bubba fixed his sights on Brazil, deciding this pretty boy might be in for a life lesson. Bubba strode over to West's lane, set down her gun, walked up to Brazil, tried to grab the .380 for inspection. Brazil slugged Bubba and broke his nose. Bubba bled over camouflage and dripped on assault weaponry as he hastily packed his duffel bag. It was Bubba's Last Stand when he cried out from the steps that the lady and her boyfriend had not heard the last from Bubba.

"Sorry," Brazil said right off when he and West were alone again.

"Jesus Christ. You can't just hit people like that." She was mostly embarrassed that she hadn't resolved the conflict herself.

He was loading magazines and realizing he had never struck anybody in his life. He wasn't sure what he felt about it as he lovingly studied West's .380 pistol.

"What does one of these cost?" he asked, with the reverence of the poor.

"You can't afford it," she said.

"What if I sold your story to *Parade* magazine. My editor thinks they'd go for it. I could make some money. Maybe enough . . ."

This was just what West wanted, another story.

"How about I make a deal with you," she said. "No *Parade* magazine. Borrow the Sig until you can afford one of your own. I'll work with you a little more, maybe on an outdoor range. We'll set up some combat situations. The way you piss people off, it's a good idea. Rule of etiquette. Pick up your brass."

Hundreds of shiny cartridge cases were scattered in their area. Brazil got down and began plucking them up, clinking them into a metal can while West gathered her belongings. She had an unpleasant thought and looked at him.

"What about your mother?" she asked.

He kept working, glancing up, a shadow passing behind his eyes. "What about her?"

"I'm just wondering about a gun being in the house."

"I got good at hiding things a long time ago." He loudly clanged brass into the can, making his point.

Bubba was waiting in the parking lot, inconspicuous inside his spotless chrome and black King Cab pickup truck with gun rack, Confederate flag mud flaps, roll bar, KC fog lights, Ollie North bumper sticker, PVC pipes for holding fishing poles on the front grille, and neon lights around the license plate. He held a wadded-up undershirt to his bleeding nose, watching as the lady cop and her asshole boyfriend emerged from the firing range, walking through the gathering dusk. Bubba waited long enough to see her get out keys and head for an impeccable white Ford Explorer in a corner of the unpaved lot. Her personal wheels, Bubba supposed, and this was even better. He climbed down from his cab, a tire jack in a meaty fist, ready for a little payback.

West was expecting him. She was practiced in the modus operandi of Bubbas, for whom revenge was a reflex, like getting up for a beer during commercials. She had already dipped into her tote bag for what looked like a black golf club handle.

"Get in the car," she quietly ordered Brazil.

"No way," he said, standing his ground as Bubba strode toward them, a menacing sneer on his gory face.

Bubba didn't get within six feet of her car before West was walking to meet him. He was surprised, not expecting kick-ass aggression from this little lady cop. He tapped the tire iron against a thick thigh as a warning, then raised it, eyeing the Ford's spotless front windshield.

"Hey!" Weasel, the manager, yelled from the range's entrance. "Bubba, what d'ya think you're doing, man!"

The retractable steel baton snapped out like a whip, suddenly three feet long with a hard knobby tip that West pointed at Bubba. She drew slow circles in the air, like a fencer.

"Put it down and leave," she commanded Bubba in her police tone.

"Fuck you!" Bubba was really losing his temper now because he was losing his nerve. He had seen weapons like hers at gun shows and knew they could be mean.

"Bubba! You quit right now!" screamed Weasel, who ran a clean business.

Brazil noticed that the manager was most upset but did not get one step closer to the trouble. Brazil was casting about, wanting to help. He knew better than to get in her way. If only the .380 was loaded. He could shoot out this goon's tires or something, perhaps cause a diversion. West caused her own. Bubba raised the tire iron again, this time completely dedicated to connecting it with her car, because he had committed himself. It no longer mattered what he felt. He had to do it, especially now that Weasel and a gathering crowd were watching. If Bubba didn't carry out his threat and avenge his injured nose, everyone in the Charlotte-Mecklenburg region would know.

West smacked the bony part of Bubba's wrist with the baton, and he howled in pain as the tire iron clanked to the parking lot. That was the end of it.

"Why didn't you arrest him?" Brazil wanted to know a little later, as they drove past Latta Park in Dilworth, close to where she lived.

"Wasn't worth it," she replied, smoking. "He didn't damage my car or me."

"What if he takes out warrants on us, for assault?" The thought was weirdly appealing to Brazil.

She laughed as if her ride-along hadn't lived much. "Don't think so." She turned into her driveway. "Last thing he wants is the world knowing he got beat up by a woman and a kid."

"I'm not a kid," he said.

Her house was as he remembered it, and the fence was no further along. Brazil asked no questions but followed her through the backyard to her small workshop, where there was a table saw and a vast collection of tools neatly organized on pegboards. West built bird houses, cabinets, even furniture, it appeared to him. He had done enough odd jobs around his house during his life to have a healthy respect for her obvious ability. He found it a strain to even assemble K-Mart bookcases.

"Wow," he said, looking around.

"Wow what?" She shut the door behind them and turned on a radio.

"What made you decide to do all this?"

"Survival," she said, squatting to open a small refrigerator. Bottles rattled as she brought out two long-neck Southpaw Lights.

Brazil did not like beer, in truth, even though he drank it from time to time. It tasted rotten and made him silly and sleepy. He would die before he let her find this out.

"Thanks," he said, screwing off the cap and tossing it in the trash.

"When I was getting started, I couldn't afford to hire people to help me out around here. So I learned on my own." She opened hard cases and got out guns. "Plus, as you know, I grew up on a farm. I learned whatever I could from my dad and the hired hands."

"What about from your mom?"

West was disassembling the pistols as if she could do it in her sleep. "Like what?" She glanced across the table at him.

"You know, domestic stuff. Cooking, cleaning, raising kids."

She smiled, opening a tackle box stocked with gun-cleaning paraphernalia. "Do I cook and clean for myself? You see a wife anywhere?" She handed him a cleaning rod and a stack of patches.

He took a big swig of beer and swallowed it as fast as he could, trying not to taste it, as usual. He was feeling braver and trying not to notice how good she looked in her gray tee shirt and jeans.

"I've done shit like that all my life, and I'm not a wife," he said.

"What do you know?" she asked as she dipped her rod into a small brown bottle of solvent.

"Nothing." He said this as a sulking challenge.

"Don't give me your moods, okay?" West replied, refusing to play games because, frankly, she was too old for them.

Brazil threaded a patch through his rod and dipped it in Hoppes. He loved the smell and had no intention of confessing anything else to her. But the beer had a tongue of its own.

"Let's talk about this wife-shit again," she pushed him.

"What do you want me to say?" Brazil, the man, replied.

"You tell me what it means." She really wanted to know.

"In theory"—he began to clean the barrel of the .380—"I'm not entirely sure. Maybe something to do with roles, a caste system, a pecking order, a hierarchy, the ecosystem."

"The ecosystem?" She frowned, blasting her barrel and other parts with Gunk Off.

"Point is," he explained, "that being a wife has nothing to do with what you do, but with what someone thinks you are. Just like I'm doing something you want me to do right now, but that doesn't make me a slave."

"Don't you have the roles a little reversed here? Who was giving who firearms instruction?" She scrubbed the inside of the barrel with a toothbrush. "You're doing what you want to do. I'm doing what you want me to do. For nothing, for the record. And who's the slave?" She sprayed again and handed him the can.

He reached for his beer. It was his limited experience that the warmer beer got, the worse it got.

"So let's say you grow up and get married someday," she went on. "What are you going to expect of your wife?"

"A partner." He tossed his bottle into the trash. "I don't want a wife. I don't need anybody to take care of me, clean for me, cook for me." He got out two more beers, popped them open, and set one within her reach. "Saying I'm too busy to do all that shit for myself someday? I'll hire a housekeeper. But I'm not going to marry one," he said as if this was the most ridiculous notion society had ever devised.

"Uh huh."

She reached for the barrel of the .380, checking his work. Man talk, she thought. The difference was, this one could put words together better than most. She didn't believe a thing he said.

"It should look like a mirror inside." She slid the barrel in front of him. "Scrub hard. You can't hurt it."

He picked up the barrel, then his beer. "See, people should get married, live together, whatever, and do things just like this," he went on as he dipped a brush in solvent and resumed scrubbing. "There shouldn't be roles. There should be practicalities, people helping out each other like friends. One weak where the other's strong, people using their gifts, cooking together, playing tennis, fishing. Walking on the beach. Staying up late talking. Being unselfish and caring."

"Sounds like you've thought about this a lot," she said. "A good script."

He looked puzzled. "What script?"

She drank. "Heard it all before. Seen that rerun."

So had Bubba's wife, Mrs. Rickman, whose first name had ceased to be important when she had gotten married twenty-six years ago in the Tabernacle Baptist Church. This had been down the road in Mount Mourne where she worked every day at the B&B, known for the best breakfast in town. The B&B's hot dogs and burgers were popular, too, especially with Davidson students, and of course, with other Bubbas on their way for a day of fishing at Lake Norman.

When gun cleaning was completed and Brazil suggested to West that they stop for a bite to eat, neither of them had a way to know that the overweight, tired woman waiting on them was Bubba's wretched wife.

"Hi, Mrs. Rickman," Brazil said to the waitress.

He gave her his bright, irresistible smile and felt sorry for her, as he always did when he came to the B&B. Brazil knew how hard food service was, and it depressed him to think of what it had been like for his mother all those years when she could still get out and go anywhere. Mrs. Rickman was happy to see him. He was always so sweet.

"How's my baby?" she chirped, setting plastic laminated menus in front of them. She eyed West. "Who's your pretty lady friend?"

"Deputy Chief Virginia West with the Charlotte police," Brazil made the mistake of saying.

So it was that Bubba would learn the identities of his attackers.

"My, my." Mrs. Rickman was mighty impressed as she got an eyeful of this important woman sitting in a B&B booth. "A deputy chief. Didn't know they had women that high up. What'll be? The pork barbecue's extra good tonight. I'd get it minced."

"Cheeseburger all the way, fries, Miller in the bottle," West said.

"Extra mayonnaise and ketchup. Can you put a little butter on the bun and throw it on the grill?"

"Sure can, honey." Mrs. Rickman nodded. She didn't write down anything as she beamed at Brazil.

"The usual." He winked at her.

She walked off, her hip killing her worse than yesterday.

"What's the usual?" West wanted to know.

"Tuna on wheat, lettuce, tomato, no mayo. Slaw, limeade. I want to ride patrol with you. In uniform," he said.

"In the first place, I don't ride patrol. In the second place, in case you haven't noticed, I have a real job, nothing important. Just the entire investigative division. Homicide. Burglary. Rape. Arson. Fraud. Auto theft. Check theft," she said. "White collar, computer, organized crime, vice. Juvenile. Cold case squad. Of course, there's a serial killer on the loose, and it's my detectives on the case, getting all the heat."

She lit a cigarette and intercepted her beer before Mrs. Rickman could set it down. "I would prefer not to work twenty-four hours a day, if it's all the same to you. You know how my cat gets? Won't touch me, won't sleep with me? Not to mention, I haven't gone out to a movie, to dinner, in weeks." She drank. "I haven't finished my fence. When was the last time I cleaned my house?"

"Is that a no?" Brazil said.

Chapter Eight

Bubba's Christian name was Joshua Rickman, and he was a forklift operator at Ingersoll-Rand in Cornelius. Perhaps the manufacturer's greatest claim to fame came and went in the early eighties when it manufactured a snow machine that was used in the winter Olympics somewhere. Bubba wasn't clear on the details and didn't care. Air compressors were what one saw on life's highways. They were in demand all over the world. His was an international career. This early Monday morning he was deep in thought as he skillfully deposited crates on a loading dock.

His wife happened to have mentioned the Davidson kid who was dating some big-shot policewoman. Yo. Bubba didn't have to strain himself to add two and two. His nose hurt like shit but no way he was going to a doctor. For what? It was his philosophy that there was nothing to be done about a busted nose or ripped ears, knocked-out teeth and other non-life-threatening head injuries, unless one had some queerbait interest in plastic surgery, which

Bubba clearly did not. His nose was a blimp and always had been, so the setback in this case was pain and pain alone. Every time he blew his nose, blood gushed and tears filled his eyes, all because of that little son of a bitch. Bubba wasn't about to forget.

He had books for life's problems and referred to them as needed. *Make 'Em Pay* and *Get Even 1* and *2* were especially insightful. These were the ultimate revenge technique manuals penned by a master trickster and privately published out of Colorado. Bubba had discovered them at gun shows here and yon. Bombs were an idea. What about a television tube that would explode, or a Ping-Pong ball loaded with potassium chlorate and black powder? Maybe not. Bubba wanted some real damage here but wasn't interested in the FBI Hostage Rescue Team (HRT) fast roping in or staking out his property. He didn't want prison time. Maybe what was called for was the trick where certain scents available at the hunt shop would draw every rodent, neighborhood pet, bug, reptile, and other critter into the yard, that all might ruin it during the night. Bubba slammed the forklift in reverse, thoughts buzzing.

Or he could feed beer-laced urine through a tube inserted under the police lady's front door. He could mail hair to her, anonymously. Eventually, would she move? Hell yes. She'd want to, oh yeah. Or maybe Sea Breeze in the jock strap of that blond kid she was jerking off with, unless both of them were queer and, frankly, Bubba had his opinion. Honestly, there was no way a man could look that good or a woman could be that powerful unless they were suspect. Bubba could see it now. The pretty boy getting what he deserved, from the rear, from a manly man like Bubba, whose favorite movie was *Deliverance*. Bubba would teach the little asshole, oh yes he would. Bubba hated fags so intensely that he was on the lookout for them in every sports bar and truck stop and in all vehicles he passed on life's highways, and in politics and the entertainment industry.

West and Brazil could not know of their personal peril. They were not thinking of themselves this Tuesday night as emergency lights flashed on broken glass and the torn, crumpled remains of a patrol car that had crashed in the affluent residential neighborhood of Myers Park. Raines and other paramedics were using hydraulic tools to get bodies out of a Mercedes 300E that was wrapped around a tree. Everyone was tense and upset as a siren screamed, and police had set up a barricade, blocking off the street. Brazil parked his BMW as close as anyone would let him. He ran toward red and blue lights and rumbling engines.

West arrived, and cops moved sawhorses to let her through. She spotted Brazil taking notes. He was dazed by horror as Raines and other paramedics lifted another bloody dead body out of the Mercedes and zipped it inside a pouch. Rescuers lowered a victim next to three others on pavement stained with spilled oil and blood. West stared at the totaled Charlotte cruiser with its hornet's nest emblem on the doors. She turned her attention to another cruiser not far away, where Officer Michelle Johnson was collapsed in the back-seat, holding a bloodstained handkerchief to her devastated face as she trembled and shook. West swiftly walked that way. She opened the cruiser's back door and climbed in next to the distraught officer.

"It's going to be okay," West said, putting an arm around a young woman who could not comprehend what had just happened to her. "We need to get you to the hospital," West told her.

"No! No!" Johnson screamed, covering her head with her hands, as if her plane were going down. "I didn't see him until he was through the light. Mine was green! I was responding to the ten-thirty-three, but my light was green. I swear. Oh God! No, no. Please. No. Please, please, please."

Brazil was inching closer to the cruiser and heard what Johnson said. He stepped up to the door and stared through the window, watching West comfort a cop who had just smashed into another car and killed all its occupants. For an instant, West looked out. Her eyes met his and held. His pen was poised and filled with quotes he now knew he would never put in any story. He lowered the pen and notepad. Slowly, he walked away, not the same reporter or person he had been.

Brazil returned to the newspaper. He walked in no hurry and was not happy to be here as he headed for his desk. He took his chair, typed in his password, and went into his computer basket. Betty Cutler, the night editor, was an old crow with an underbite. She had been pacing and waiting for Brazil and swooped in on him. She began her annoying habit of sniffing as she spoke. It had occurred to Brazil that she might have a cocaine problem.

"We got to ship this in forty-five minutes," she said to him. "What did the cop say?"

Brazil began typing the lead and looking at his notes. "What cop?" he asked, even though he knew precisely whom she meant.

"The cop who just wiped out an entire family of five, for Chrissake." Cutler sniffed, her lower teeth bared.

"I didn't interview her."

Cutler, the night editor, didn't believe this. She refused to believe it. Her eyes glittered as she gave him a penetrating stare. "What the hell do you mean, you didn't interview her, Brazil!" She lifted her voice that all might hear. "You were at the scene!"

"They had her in a patrol car," he said, flipping pages.

"So you knock on the window," Cutler loudly berated him. "You open her door, do whatever you have to!"

Brazil stopped typing and looked up at a woman who truly depressed him. He didn't care if she knew it. "Maybe that's what you would do," he said.

When the paper thudded on his front porch at six o'clock the next morning, Brazil was already up. He had already run five miles at the track. He had showered and put on his police uniform. He opened the door, snatched the paper off the stoop, and rolled off the rubber band, eager to see his work. His angry steps carried him through the sad living room and into the cramped dingy kitchen where his mother sat at a plastic-covered table, drinking coffee held in trembling hands. She was smoking and momentarily present. Brazil tossed the paper down on the table. The front page, above-the-fold headline screamed POLICE CRASH KILLS FAMILY OF FIVE. There were large color photographs of broken glass, twisted metal, and Officer Michelle Johnson weeping in the cruiser.

"I can't believe it!" Brazil exclaimed. "Look! The damn headline makes it sound like it was the cop's fault when we don't even know who caused the wreck!"

His mother wasn't interested. She got up, moving slowly toward the screen door that led out to the side porch. Her son watched with dread as she swayed and snatched keys from a hook on the wall.

"Where are you going?" he asked.

"The store." She dug inside her big old pocketbook.

"I just went yesterday," he said.

"I need cigarettes." She opened her billfold and scowled.

"I bought you a carton, Mom." Brazil stared at her.

He knew where his mother was really going and felt the same old defeat. He sighed angrily as his mother clutched her pocketbook and counted dollar bills.

"You got a ten-spot?" she asked him.

"I'm not buying your booze," he stated.

She paused at the door, regarding an only child she had never known how to love. "Where are you going?" she said, with a cruel expression that made her face ugly and unfamiliar. "A costume party?"

"A parade," Brazil answered. "I'm directing traffic."

"Parade charade." She sneered. "You're not police, never will be. Why do you want to be going out there to get killed?" She got sad just as quickly as she had turned mean. "So I can end up all alone?" She yanked the door open.

The morning got no better. Brazil drove fifteen minutes through the police department deck, and finally left his BMW in a press space, even though he really wasn't on official press business. The day was lovely, but he took the tunnel from the deck to the first level of police headquarters because he was feeling especially anti-social. Whenever he had encounters with his mother, he got very quiet inside. He wanted to be alone. He did not want to talk to anyone.

At the Property Control window, he checked out a radio and was handed keys for the unmarked vehicle he would be driving in the Charlie Two response area between Tryon and Independence Boulevard for the annual Freedom Parade. It was a modest cele-bration sponsored by local Shriners in their tasseled hats and on their scooters, and Brazil could not have been assigned a worse car. The Ford Crown Victoria was dull, scratched black and had been driven hard for a hundred and sixteen thousand miles. The trans-mission was going to drop out any moment, providing the damn thing started, which it didn't seem inclined to do.

Brazil flipped the key in the ignition again, pumping the accel-erator as the old engine tried to turn over. The battery supplied enough juice to wake up the scanner and radio, but forget about going anywhere, as the car whined and Brazil's frustration soared.

"Shit!" He pounded the steering wheel, accidentally blaring the horn. Cops in the distance turned around, staring.

Chief Hammer was causing her own commotion not too far away inside the Carpe Diem restaurant on South Tryon, across the street from the Knight-Ridder building. Two of her deputy chiefs, West and Jeannie Goode, sat at a quiet corner table, eating lunch and discussing problems. Goode was West's age and jealous of any female who did anything in life, especially if she looked good.

"This is the craziest thing I've ever heard," Goode was saying as she poked at tarragon chicken salad. "He shouldn't be out with us to begin with. Did you get a load of the headline this morning? Im-plying we caused the accident, that Johnson was pursuing the Mer-cedes? Unbelievable. Not to mention, skid marks indicate it wasn't us who ran the red light."

"Andy Brazil didn't write the headline," West said, turning to Hammer, her boss, who was working on cottage cheese and fresh fruit. "All I'm asking is to ride routine patrol with him for maybe a week."

"You want to respond to calls?" Hammer reached for her iced tea.

"Absolutely," West said as Goode looked on with judgment.

Hammer put down her fork and studied West. "Why can't he ride with regular patrol? Or for that matter, we've got fifty other volunteers. He can't ride with them?"

West hesitated, motioning to a waiter for more coffee. She asked for extra mayonnaise and ketchup for her club sandwich and fries, and returned her attention to Hammer as if Goode were not at the table.

"No one wants to ride with him," West said. "Because he's a reporter. You know how the cops feel about the *Observer*. That won't go away overnight. And there's a lot of jealousy." She looked pointedly at Goode.

"Not to mention, he's an arrogant smartass with an entitlement attitude," Goode chimed in.

"Entitlement?" West let the word linger like a vapor trail in the rarified air of Carpe Diem, where high feminine powers met regularly. "So tell me, Jeannie, when was the last time you directed traffic?"

It was an odious job. Citizens did not take traffic cops seriously. Carbon monoxide levels got dangerously high, and the cardinal rule that one must never turn his back to traffic was irrelevant in four-way intersections. How could anyone face four directions simultaneously? Brazil had questioned this since the academy. Of course it made no sense, and added to the mix was a basic disrespect problem. Already, he'd had half a dozen teenagers, women, and businessmen make fun of him or offer gestures that he was not allowed to reciprocate. What was it about America? Citizens were all too aware of law enforcement officers such as himself, who wore no gun and seemed new at the job. They noticed. They commented.

"Hey, Star Trek," a middle-aged woman yelled out her window. "Get a phaser," she said as she gunned onto Enfield Road.

"Shooting blanks, are we, fairy queen?" screamed a dude in an Army-green Jeep with a basher bumper, sports rack, and safari doors.

Brazil directed the Jeep through with a hard stare and set jaw, halfway wishing the shithead would stop and demand a fight. Brazil was getting an itch. He wanted to deck someone and sensed it was only a matter of time before he busted another nose.

Sometimes, Hammer got so sick of her diet. But she remembered turning thirty-nine and getting a partial hysterectomy because her uterus had pretty much quit doing anything useful. She had gained fifteen pounds in three months, moving up from a size four to an eight, and doctors told her this was because she ate too much. Well, bullshit. Hormones were always to blame, and for good reason. They were the weather of female life. Hormones moved over the face of the female planet and decided whether it was balmy or frigid or time for the storm cellar. Hormones made things wet or dried them. They made one want to walk hand-in-hand in balmy moonlight or be alone.

"What does directing traffic have to do with anything?" Goode wanted to know.

"Point is, this guy works harder than most of your cops," West replied to Goode. "And he's just a volunteer. Doesn't have to. Could have a real attitude problem but doesn't."

Hammer wondered if salt would hurt her much. Lord, how nice it would be to taste something and not end up looking like her husband.

"I'm in charge of patrol. That's where he is right now," Goode said, turning over lettuce leaves with her fork to see if anything good was left. Maybe a crouton or a walnut.

Brazil was sweating in his uniform and bright orange traffic vest. His feet were on fire as he blocked off a side street. He was turning cars around left and right, routing them the other way, blowing his whistle, and making crisp traffic motions. Horns were honking, and another driver began yelling rudely out the window for directions. Brazil trotted over to help, and was not appreciated or thanked. This was a terrible job, and he loved it for reasons he did not understand.

"So he relieves at least one sworn officer from traffic duty," West was saying as Hammer chose to ignore both of her deputy chiefs.

Frankly, Hammer could take but so much of the bickering between the brass. It never ended. Hammer glanced at her watch and imagined Cahoon at the top of his crown. The fool. He would turn this city into the prick of America, peopled by yahoos with guns and USAir Gold cards and box seats for the Panthers and Hornets if someone did not stop him.

Cahoon had been stopped three times on his way to lunch on the sixtieth floor in the corporate dining room. Awaiting him amid linen and Limoges were a president, four vice-presidents, a chairman and a vice-chairman, and a top executive with the Dominion Tobacco Company, which over the next two years would be borrowing more than four hundred million dollars from USBank for a cancer research project. Computer printouts had been stacked high by Cahoon's plate. There were fresh flowers on the table, and waiters in tuxedos hovered.

"Good afternoon." The CEO nodded around the table, his eyes lingering on the tobacco executive.

Cahoon didn't like the woman and wasn't sure why, beyond his rabid hatred of smoking, which had begun seven years ago after he had quit. Cahoon had serious misgivings about granting such a huge loan for a project so scientific and secretive that no one could tell him precisely what it was about, beyond the fact that USBank would be instrumental in the development of the world's first truly healthy cigarette. He had reviewed endless charts and diagrams of a long and robust cylinder with a gold crown around the filter. The amazing product was called *USChoice.* It could be smoked by all, would harm none, and contained various minerals, vitamins, and calming agents that would be inhaled and absorbed directly into the bloodstream. Cahoon was reminded of what his bank's contribution would mean to humanity, as he reached for his bubbly water, and felt happy.

The people along Eastway Drive were also happy as they waited for the Freedom Parade. It was always full of hope and bounce, Shriners zigzagging on their scooters, waving at the crowd, reminding all of burn units and good deeds. Brazil was slightly concerned that other cops at other intersections seemed bored and restless. There were no floats. He scanned the horizon and saw nothing but a patrol car in a hurry heading his way. A horn blared and another driver yelled, this time an angry old woman in a Chevrolet. No matter how much Brazil tried to help, she was determined to be unpleasant and unreasonable.

"Ma'am," he politely said, "you have to turn around and take Shamrock Drive."

She flipped him a bird and roared off, as the frantic, irritated cop in the patrol car rolled up on Brazil's intersection.

"The parade and a funeral somehow got routed through here at the same time," the cop hastily explained.

"What?" Brazil asked, baffled. "How . . . ?"

But the patrol car sped off.

"Doesn't matter who he relieves from traffic," Goode was saying as she gave up on food in hopes it would give up on her. "I don't want him. He's a spy, CIA, KGB, whatever you want to call him."

"Now how stupid is that?" West pushed her plate away. "For Chrissake."

Hammer said nothing as she looked around the restaurant to see who else she recognized. The book columnist for the *Observer* and an editorial writer were eating lunch, but not together. Hammer trusted none of them. She had spent no time with Andy Brazil, but thought maybe it wouldn't be a bad idea. He sounded interesting.

When the hearses slowly appeared, they were gleaming black, with headlights burning. Brazil watched their formidable approach as he struggled to keep his side street blocked and continued to direct cars to turn away. The endless funeral procession crept past with precision and dignity, and hundreds of people waiting for Shriners and scooters drank sodas and watched and waved. This wasn't exactly what they had expected when they'd headed out into the morning for a little free excitement, but they were here and would take whatever they could get.

Inside a black Lincoln Continental stretch limousine with white leather interior and a television and VCR, the bereft brother and the widow were dressed for Sunday and staring out tinted glass. They were impressed by all the spectators lining the street to pay last respects. A lot of them had brought snacks, drinks, kids, and small American flags. They were waving and cheering, which was the way it ought to be, a celebration, as one crosses over to the other side, into the loving arms of Jesus.

"I had no idea Tyvola had so many friends," the brother marveled, waving back.

"And all these police came out." The widow shyly waved, too.

Brazil blew his whistle and almost got run over by an old man in a Dodge Dart who didn't seem to understand that a policeman holding out both palms was a hint that the driver might want to stop. The unbroken caravan of stretch limousines, town cars, hearses, all black with lights on, didn't seem to send any direct message to Howie Song in his Dart. By now, Song was halfway out into the intersection with a line of cars bumper to bumper behind him. It was not possible he could back up unless everyone else did.

"Don't you move!" Brazil warned the impatient old man, who had his radio turned up as high as it would go, playing a country western tune.

Brazil set three traffic cones in front of the Dart. They scattered like bowling pins the instant Brazil stepped back to direct other cars to back up. Song in his Dart helped himself to the Boulevard, certain the lumbering funeral cars would let him through so he could get to the hardware store.

That's what you think, thought Chad Tilly, director of the Tilly Family Mortuary, which was famous for its air-conditioned building, plush slumber parlors, and quality caskets. His big ad on page 537 of the Yellow Pages was unfortunately positioned directly next to Fungus and Mold Control. Tilly's secretary was forever telling people who called that although they had similar concerns in the funeral business, they could not help with basement moisture problems or sump pumps, for example.

Tilly had driven in more funeral processions than he could remember. He was a formidable businessman who hadn't gotten his fine suits and rings by being a pushover. He not only didn't let that little piece of law-breaking banged-up blue Dodge shit through, but Tilly got on his two-way radio. He raised his lead car on the air.

"Flip," he said to his number-two man in the company.

"Coming at ya, boss."

"Put the brakes on up there," Tilly told him.

"You sure?"

"Always am," said Tilly.

This stopped the entire line of black cars with lights burning. The Dart could not get across the boulevard now, and Song was momentarily confused. He stopped, too, long enough for a cop to yank open his door and get the crabby old man out of the car.

"Flip." Tilly was back on the air. "Move along." He chuckled.

Hammer was not amused as she applied lipstick after lunch and listened to her two female deputy chiefs bickering like rival siblings.

"I'm in charge of patrol," Goode announced inside the Carpe Diem, as if the restaurant's name applied to her. "And he's not riding with us. God only knows what will end up in the newspaper. You're so hot on him, let him ride with your people."

Hammer got out her compact and glanced at her watch.

"Investigations doesn't have ride-alongs. Ever," West replied. "It's against department policy and always has been."

"And what you're proposing isn't?" Goode demanded.

"Ride-alongs, volunteers, have been riding with patrol for as long as I've been here," West reminded her in a strained voice.

Hammer got out her wallet and studied the bill.

"I'm wondering if there's some personal agenda here," Goode went on.

West knew exactly what the bitch was implying. It had been duly noted around the department that Andy Brazil was rather good to look at, and West had never been famous for dating. The current theory circulating was that she had found a boy toy because she couldn't get a man. Long ago, she had learned to ignore such gossip.

"The bigger issue," Goode was saying, "is that volunteers don't routinely ride with a deputy chief who hasn't made an arrest or written a ticket in fifty years. He's probably not even safe out there with someone like you."

"We've handled some situations a lot better than patrol did," West let her know.

Hammer had heard enough. "Here's what we're going to do," she spoke. "Virginia, I'm going to approve your riding patrol with

him. It's an interesting idea. We might learn something new. I probably should have done the same thing a long time ago."

She put money on the table. West and Goode did the same.
Hammer nailed Goode with a look.

"You'll do everything you can to help," Hammer said to her.

Goode was cold as she got up and turned to West for one last re-
mark. "Hope there's no problem. Remember, your rank is unclassi-
fied."

"As is yours," Hammer said to Goode. "I can fire you without
cause. Just like that." She snapped her fingers and wished Goode
had gone into some other profession. Maybe undertaking.

Chapter Nine

Chad Tilly could have used another undertaker at exactly that moment. He had brilliantly outmaneuvered the Dodge Dart with its kamikaze old man rocking to country western. That round the funeral director had won without effort, but it had also been Tilly's experience that when he was relaxed and not looking, he usually got his butt kicked. Tilly was creeping along again when he decided to light a cigar and fiddle with the radio at the same time.

Tilly did not notice the blond kid in uniform and no gun, suddenly halting the procession as, of all things, a Fourth of July–looking float appeared on the horizon, running the lead limo off the road. This was amazing. Sweet Jesus, this could not be so. Tilly slammed on brakes at the same moment his assistant's inability to completely shut the hearse's tailgate became known. The copper-tinted casket with deep satin lining slammed one way and ricocheted out the other like a lightweight alloy bullet. The casket and its occupant skittered over pavement and kept going, for as luck would have it, the procession was momentarily on a slight hill.

Brazil had not been trained to handle such a situation and was on his radio in a flash as yet a second float glided into view. This was awful. It was his intersection. He would be blamed. His armpits were soaked and his heart was out of control as he tried to contain the disaster of the world. Men in dark suits with lots of rings and gold crowns on their teeth were flying out of stretch limousines and chasing a runaway gaudy electroplated casket down the boulevard. Oh God. No. Brazil blew his whistle and stopped all traffic, including floats. He raced after the casket as it continued its lonely journey. People stared at the cop chasing it. They cheered.

"I'll get it," Brazil called out to men in suits, as he sprinted.

The foot pursuit was brief, order restored, and a dapper man who identified himself as Mr. Tilly formally thanked Brazil for all to hear.

"Is there anything else I can do to help?" replied Brazil, the community-oriented cop.

"Yeah," the funeral home director boomed. "Get them motherfucking floats outa my way."

Floats were pulled over to make room, and none moved an inch for an hour. Not one spectator went home, and others came as word traveled around. This was the best Freedom Day in the history of Charlotte.

Goode, head of patrol, did not share quite the same enthusiasm, since traffic control was her responsibility and a runaway casket was not something she wanted to hear about on the evening news. It was a matter she intended to resolve in person, but not until it was dark out. Then she packed up her slim, soft leather satchel and headed to the parking deck, where the city paid nineteen dollars a month for her reserved parking space. She preferred driving her personal car back and forth to work and got inside her black Miata.

Goode opened her satchel, dug for Obsession, and strategically sprayed. She dry-brushed her teeth. She worked on her hair a bit, and threw the car in reverse, loving the engine throbbing beneath her. She headed out to Myers Park, the wealthiest, oldest neighborhood, where huge mansions with slate roofs gathered their cobblestone skirts around them lest they be splashed by the dirtier elements of the city.

Myers Park Methodist Church was gray stone and rose from the horizon like a castle. Goode had never been to a service here, but the parking lot she knew very well, for she worshiped in it regularly. Brent Webb was on his break after the six o'clock news, his Porsche idling beneath a large magnolia tree in a far corner. He shut down the engine as his other one got going. He got out of his car, looking each way, as if about to cross traffic, and slid inside Goode's Miata.

Rarely did they talk, unless she had a scoop he must know. Their lips locked, sucked, bit, probed, and invaded, as did tongues and hands. They drove each other further than either had ever been, each time more primitive and special, each frenzied by the other's power. Webb had secret fantasies of Goode in uniform, whipping out her handcuffs, and her gun. She liked to watch him on TV, when she was alone at home, savoring his every syllable as he alluded to her and secretly quoted her to the world.

"I assume you know about the casket problem." Goode could barely talk.

"Whose?" asked Webb, who never knew anything unless the information was stolen or leaked.

"Never mind."

They were breathing heavily, the Pointer Sisters jumping on the radio. They made out in the front seat, maneuvering around the stick shift as best they could. Through the front windshield the lit-up city skyline was close, the USBank Corporate Center very much a symbol of Webb's good mood. He unfastened her bra, never sure why he bothered, and he imagined her tie, her police belt, and his excitement grew.

🧚 Officer Jenny Frankel was typically excited, as well, for she was young and still enthusiastic about her job. She looked for trouble, begged, and even prayed for it, so when she noticed two vehicles pulled off in a remote corner of the Myers Park Methodist Church parking lot, she had to check it out. In the first place, choir practice was yesterday and AA didn't meet until Thursday. Plus, there were drug dealers everywhere, threatening to take over. Fuck no, was her position. She would take the city back, return it to decent, hardworking men and women if it was the last thing she did in life.

She pulled into shadows and stopped, now close enough to notice movement in the front seat of a late-model black Miata that looked vaguely familiar, for some reason. Frankel suspected the active silhouettes were two men, based on the hair. She typed plate numbers into her MDT and patiently waited as the two guys kissed, fondled, and sucked. When Deputy Chief Goode's and Brent Webb's Department of Motor Vehicle information returned to the video display, Frankel rapidly left the area. Other than her sergeant, with whom she went out drinking several times a week, Frankel told no one what she had observed this night. The sergeant also told only one person, and this discreetly went on.

🧚 Brazil's day had been long, but he did not want to go home. After working traffic, he had changed his clothes and done his eight hours for the *Observer*. Now it was almost one A.M. The late shift had been slow. For a while he had hung around the press room watching newspapers race toward their final destination of puppy crates and recycling bins. He had stood, mesmerized, unable to see his byline this time because all he had been able to bring in was a local metro story about a pedestrian run over in Mint Hill. The victim was a known drunk and night editor Cutler didn't think the story merited more than three inches.

Brazil got in his BMW and headed back toward Trade Street. This was not a safe thing to do, and no one needed to tell him that. He rumbled past the stadium and the Duke Power transfer station, stopping at a dead end at West Third where the old crumbling building seemed even more haunted and menacing at this hour. Brazil sat and stared, imagining murder, and believing there was a person who had heard the gunshots and spraying of paint. Somewhere, someone knew. Brazil left his engine running, the Sig Sauer between the front seats and within reach.

He began walking around, probing with a flashlight, his eyes nervous, as if he feared he was being watched. Old blood on pavement was black, and an opossum was working on it, eyes white in the flashlight as it spied the intrusion and scuttled off. The woods teemed with restless insects, and fireflies winked. A far-off train rumbled down rusty tracks, and Brazil was chilled, his attention darting around like static. He felt murder in this place. He sensed a sinister energy that bristled and coiled and waited to claim more. These killings were common and cold, and Brazil believed that the monster was known by the people of the night, and fear kept identity hidden.

Brazil did not believe prostitution was right. He did not think that anyone should have to pay for such a thing. He did not believe that anyone should have to sell such a thing. All of it was depressing, and he imagined being a homely middle-aged man and accepting that no woman would want him without his wallet. Brazil imagined a woman worrying about servicing the next client in order to feed her child or herself or avoid another beating from her pimp. A horrid slavery, all of it dreadful and hard to imagine. This moment, Brazil entertained little hope about the human condition when he considered that heartless behavior had evolved not one level higher since the beginning of time. It seemed that what had changed, simply, was the way people got around and communicated, and the size of the weapons they used against each other.

On Highway 277, he saw one of these very sad creations on the shoulder, walking languidly, in tight jeans and no bra, her chest thrust out. The young hooker was pointed and tattooed, in a skimpy white knit shirt. He slowed, meeting bold, mocking eyes that didn't know fear. She was about his age and missing most of her front teeth, and he tried to imagine talking to her, or picking her up. He wondered if the appeal was stolen fire, some sort of mythical thing, an ill-gotten rush that made people feel powerful, her over him, him over her, if only for a dark, degrading moment. He imagined her laughing at her johns and hating them as much as she hated herself and all. He followed the young hooker in his rearview mirror as she stared back at him, with a slight, quizzical smile, waiting for the boy to make up his mind. She could have been pretty once. Brazil sped up as a van cruised close to her and stopped.

The next night, Brazil was out on the street again, and reality seemed different and odd, and at first, he thought it was his imagination. From the moment he left the *Observer* in his BMW, he saw cops everywhere in spotless white patrol cars. They were watching and following him, and he told himself this could not be true, that he was tired and full of fantasy. The evening was slow, with no good reports in the press basket, unless Webb had already stolen them. There were no good calls over the scanner until a fire broke out. Brazil didn't waste time. The blaze was huge and he could see it against the night sky in Adam One, close to where Nations Ford and York Roads met. Brazil's adrenaline flooded him with nervous energy. He was focused on getting to the scene and not getting lost, when suddenly a siren sounded behind him, and he checked his rearview mirror.

"Shit," he said.

Moments later, he was in the passenger's seat of a police cruiser, getting a ticket as the distant fire burned without him.

"My speedometer is broken." Brazil tried that shopworn line.

"Get it fixed." The officer was unfriendly and taking her time.

"Could you please hurry with that, ma'am?" Brazil then politely said. "I've got to get to my story."

"You should have thought about that before you broke the law." She was not nice about it.

A half hour later, Brazil was talking on the two-way radio, and leaving the fire scene, where an abandoned building was still fully involved. Flames danced from the roof, as fire fighters on cranes blasted water through broken windows. News helicopters hovered nearby. Brazil was telling a metro editor what he'd found.

"Unoccupied, an old warehouse. No injuries," he said into the mike.

In the rearview mirror, a patrol car was following him. He couldn't believe it. Another cop was staring right at him.

"Just do a couple graphs," the editor told him over the air.

He would get to it. Right now, Brazil had more important concerns. This was not an imagined threat, and he could afford no more tickets or points on his record. He started driving the way he played tennis, serving up this and that, slicing, sending a ball top-spinning over his opponent's head. Asshole, he thought, as the same car bird-dogged him. Like anybody else, Brazil could and would take but so much.

"That's it," he snapped.

The patrol car was behind him in the right lane. Brazil continued at a steady speed and took a left on Runnymede Lane. The cop stayed on Brazil's bumper, and they slowed to a stop at a red light. Brazil did not look over or acknowledge in any way that he was aware of the problem. He was cool in his saddle-leather seat, preoccupied with adjusting the radio, which had been silent for years. At the last second, he swerved into the left lane, and the officer pulled up beside him, with an icy smile that Brazil returned. The ruse was up. They were squared off. This was war. There was no turning back. Brazil thought fast. Officer Martin, with his .40 caliber pistol, shotgun, and 350 V8, didn't need to think.

The light turned green and Brazil threw his old car into neutral, gunning it like he was going to blast off like the space shuttle. Officer Martin gunned his car, too, only the big horsepower Ford was in drive. It was already through the intersection by the time Brazil had finished his U-turn, flying the other way on Barclay Downs. He caromed off on Morrison and cut a tangled path that ended in a dark alleyway in the heart of Southpark Mall, next to a Dumpster.

His heart was hammering as he turned off headlights and sat, his thoughts frantic and frightened. He was trying to figure out what might happen if the cop found him again. Would the officer arrest Brazil for trying to elude, for resisting arrest? Would the cop show up with other goons and beat the shit out of Brazil in a place like this, remote and dark, with no chance of discovery by a citizen with a video camera? Brazil gasped as a burglar alarm suddenly sounded like a clanging jackhammer, shattering the absolute quiet. At first, he thought it was a siren that was somehow related to his fugitive status, then a back door swung open and slammed against brick. Two young males hurried out, loaded down with electronics they had just stolen from Radio Shack.

"911!" Brazil yelled into the mike connecting him into the newsroom. Disgusted, he yelled at himself this time, "Oh now that was helpful."

"What was that?" the newsroom crackled back.

Brazil squealed off in pursuit, flipping headlights on. The thieves were having a hard time moving fast and holding on to their hard-earned rewards. Smaller boxes dropped first, primarily Walkmans, portable CD players, and computer modems. Brazil could tell that these two would hang on to boom boxes and miniature televisions until the bitter end. He raised the newsroom on the radio, and this time instructed an editor to call 911 and put the phone near the base station so a dispatcher could hear what Brazil was saying.

"Burglary in progress." He was talking like a machine gun,

weaving after his quarry. "Southpark Mall. Two white males running east on Fairview Road. I'm in pursuit. You might want a unit
at the rear of Radio Shack to collect what they've dropped before
someone else does."

The thieves cut through a parking lot, then through another alleyway. Brazil broadcast their every step, on their heels like a bor-
der collie herding sheep. Neither young man could legally buy beer
and both had been smoking dope, stealing, lying, and jailing since
they were old enough for their pants to fall off. Neither was in pre-
miere shape. Shooting hoops and boogeying in front of friends and
on street corners was one thing. But running wide open for blocks
was definitely another. Devon, especially, knew one lung, and possibly both, would rupture any second. Sweat was stinging his eyes.
His legs might buckle, and unless he was having vision distur-
bances, too, the flashing red and blue lights of his childhood were
closing in like UFOs from all corners of the planet.

"Man!" Devon gasped. "Let's drop it! Run!"

"I am running, man!"

As for Ro, whose name was short for something no one could recall, he would be damned before he would relinquish what he had
his arms around. The TV alone would keep him in rocks for a
week, unless he traded it in on a new pistol, this time one with a
holster. The Smith & Wesson stainless steel .357 revolver with its
four-inch barrel jammed in the back of his baggy jeans wasn't
going to stay put much longer. Ro could feel it slipping as sweat
blurred his vision and sirens screamed.

"Shit," Ro complained.

The gun was completely submerged now, and working its way
down. Oh Lord, he hoped he didn't shoot himself in some private
place. He would never live it down. The revolver slid through layers of huge boxer shorts, burrowing down his thigh, his knee, and
finally peeking out at the top of a leather Fila. Ro helped it along by
shaking his leg. This was no easy feat while running with half the

Charlotte Police Department and some crazy-ass white boy in a BMW about to run Ro down. The gun clattered against pavement as the circle of white cars with flashing lights was complete around Devon and Ro. The two bandits simply stopped in their tracks.

"Shit," Ro said again.

In all fairness, Brazil's reward for his valiant contribution to community policing should have been the pleasure of cuffing the suspects and tucking them into the back of a patrol car. But he had no enforcement powers. For that matter, he was on the newspaper's payroll this night, and it was no simple matter to explain why he happened to be parked in a dark alleyway behind a Radio Shack when the burglary occurred. He and Officer Weed went round and round about this as Brazil gave his statement in the front seat of Weed's cruiser.

"Let's try this again," Weed was saying. "You were sitting back there with your headlights off for what reason?"

"I thought I was being followed," Brazil patiently explained one more time.

Weed looked at him, and had no idea what to make of this one except that she knew the reporter was lying. All of them did. Weed was willing to bet the guy had parked back there to sleep on the job, maybe jerk off, smoke a little weed, or all of the above.

"Being followed by who?" Weed had her shiny metal clipboard in her lap, as she worked on her report.

"Some guy in a white Ford," Brazil said. "Wasn't anybody I knew."

It was late by the time Brazil rolled away from the Southpark scene, without a word of thanks from any officer there, he noted. The way he calculated it, he had about an hour to kill before he needed to get back to the newsroom and write up what he'd gotten during his eight-hour shift, which wasn't much, in his mind.

He wasn't far from the area of Myers Park where Michelle Johnson's horrible accident had occurred, and for some reason, he was haunted by that awful night, and by her. He cruised slowly past the mansions of Eastover and fantasized about who lived inside them and what they must feel about the neighbors killed. The Rollins family had lived around the corner from the Mint Museum. When Brazil was in front of their stately white brick house with its copper roof, he stopped. He sat and stared. The only lights on were for the benefit of burglars, because nobody in the family was home, or ever would be. He thought of a mother, a father, and three young children, gone in one violent minute, life lines randomly intersecting in exactly the horribly wrong way, and all was lost.

Brazil had never heard much about rich people dying in car wrecks or shoot-outs. Now and then their private planes went down, and he recalled there had been a serial rapist in Myers Park back in the eighties. Brazil imagined a young male in a hood knocking on doors, his sole intention to rape a woman home alone. Was it resentment that fired such cruelty? An *up yours* to the rich? Brazil tried to put himself in the mindset of such a young violent man as he watched lighted windows flow past.

He realized the rapist had probably done exactly what Brazil was doing this night. He would have browsed, stalked, but most likely on foot. He would have spied and planned, the actual awful act incidental to the fantasy of it. Brazil could not think of much worse than to be sexually violated. He had been scorned by enough rednecks in his brief life to fear rape as a woman might. He would never forget what Chief Briddlewood of Davidson security had told him once. *Don't ever go to jail, boy. You won't stand up straight the whole time you're there.*

The wreck was right about where Selwyn and the various Queens Roads got confused, and Brazil recognized the scene instantly as he approached. What he had not expected was the Nissan pulled off the street. As he got closer, he was shocked to recognize Officer Michelle Johnson inside it, crying in the dark. Brazil parked on the shoulder. He got out and walked toward the officer's personal car, his footsteps sure and directed as if he were in charge of whatever was going on. He stared through the driver's window, transfixed by the sight of Johnson crying, and his heart began to thud. She looked up and saw him and was startled. She grabbed her pistol, then realized it was that reporter. She relaxed but was enraged. She rolled her window down.

"Get the fuck away from me!" she said.

He stared at her and could not move. Johnson cranked the engine.

"Vultures! Fucking vultures!" she screamed.

Brazil was frozen. He was acting so oddly and atypically for a reporter that Johnson was taken aback. She lost interest in leaving. She did not move, as they stared at each other.

"I want to help." Brazil was impassioned.

A streetlight shone on broken glass and black stains on pavement and illuminated the gouged tree the Mercedes had been wrapped around. Fresh tears started. Johnson wiped her face with her hands, her humiliation complete as this reporter continued to watch her. She heaved and moaned, as if overwhelmed by a seizure, and was aware of the pistol that could end all of it.

"When I was ten," the reporter spoke, "my dad was a cop here. About your age when he got killed on duty. Sort of like you feel you've been."

Johnson looked up at him as she wept.

"Eight-twenty-two P.M., March twenty-ninth. A Sunday. They said it was his fault," Brazil went on, his voice trembling. "Was in plain clothes, followed a stolen car out of his district, wasn't supposed to make a traffic stop in Adam Two. The backup never got there. Not in time. He did the best he could, but . . ." His voice caught, and he cleared his throat. "He never had a chance to tell his story."

Brazil stared off into the dark, furious at a street, at a night, that had robbed him of his life, too. He pounded his fist on top of the car.

"My dad wasn't a bad cop!" he cried.

Johnson had gotten strangely quiet and felt empty inside. "I'd rather be him," she said. "I'd rather be dead."

"No." Brazil bent down, at her eye level. "No." He saw her left hand on the steering wheel and the wedding band she wore. He reached in and gripped her arm. "Don't leave anybody behind," he said.

"I turned in my badge today," Johnson told him.

"They made you do that?" he protested. "There's no evidence you . . ."

"No one made me. I did it," she cut him off. "They think I'm a monster!" She broke down more.

Brazil was determined. "We can change that," he said. "Let me help."

She unlocked her car and he got in.

Chapter Ten

Chief Hammer was watering her plants when West walked in the next morning. West carried coffee and another healthy breakfast from Bojangles, this time a sausage-egg biscuit and Bo-Rounds, for a little variety. The chief's phone was going crazy, but Hammer was busy atomizing orchids. She glanced up without a greeting. Hammer was well known for one-two punch announcements in her faint Arkansas accent.

"So." She sprayed. "He gets in a pursuit, resulting in two arrests. Single-handedly cracking a string of Radio Shack burglaries that has plagued the city for eight months."

She examined an exotic white blossom and sprayed again. Hammer was striking in a black silk suit with subtle pinstripes, and a black silk blouse with a high collar and black onyx beads. West loved the way her boss dressed. West was proud to work for a woman who looked so sharp and had good legs, and was decent to people and plants, and could still kick butt with the best of them.

"And he somehow managed to get the truth from Johnson." Hammer nodded at the morning paper on her desk. "Clearing up this notion that she's responsible for those poor people's deaths. Johnson's not going to quit."

Hammer moved over to a calamondin tree near a window and plucked dead leaves from bushy branches that always bore fruit. "I talked to her this morning," she went on. "All this, and Brazil wasn't even riding with us." She stopped what she was doing and looked up at her deputy chief. "You're right. He can't be out by himself. God knows what he'd do if he had a uniform on. I wish I could transfer him to another city about three thousand miles from here."

West smiled as her boss worried about spider mites and quenched a corn plant with a small plastic watering can. "What you wish," West said to her, "is that he worked for you." Paper crackled as she dug into her Bojangles bag.

"You eat too much junk," Hammer told her. "If I ate all the crap you do, I'd be a medicine ball."

"Brazil called me." West finally got around to this as she folded back a greasy wrapper. "You know why he was behind that Radio Shack?"

"No." Hammer started on African violets, glancing curiously at West.

Five minutes later, Hammer was walking with purpose down a long hallway on the first floor. She did not look friendly. Police she passed stared and nodded. She reached a door and opened it. Uniformed officers inside the roll call room were startled to see their well-dressed leader walk in. Deputy Chief Jeannie Goode was in the midst of briefing dozens of the troops about her latest concerns.

"All, I mean *all* inquiries get routed to the duty captain . . ." Goode was saying before the vision of Hammer walking toward her cut the meeting short. Goode knew trouble when she saw it.

"Deputy Chief Goode," Hammer said for all to hear. "Do you know what harassment is?"

The color drained from Goode's face. She thought she might faint, and leaned against the blackboard while cops stared, paralyzed. Goode could not believe the chief was about to dress her down in front of thirty-three lowly David One street cops, two sergeants, and one captain.

"Let's go upstairs to my office," Goode suggested with a weak smile.

Hammer stood in front of her troops and crossed her arms. She was very calm when she replied, "I think everyone could benefit from this. It has been reported to me that officers tailed an *Observer* reporter all over the city."

"Says who?" Goode challenged. "Him? And you believe him?"

"I never said it was a him," Hammer informed her.

The chief paused for a long time and the silence in the room gave Goode chills. Goode thought about the pink Kaopectate tablets in her desk drawer. The third floor seemed very far away.

"One more time." Hammer looked at everyone. "It will cost you."

High heels snapped as she walked out. When she tried to reach Andy Brazil at home, someone else answered the phone. The woman was either drunk or did not have her teeth in, perhaps both. Hammer hung up and tried Panesa.

"Judy, I will not have my reporters intimidated, bullied . . ." Panesa jumped right in.

"Richard, I know," Hammer simply said, staring out at the skyline and discouraged. "Please accept my apology and my promise that something like this will not happen again. I'm also giving Brazil a special commendation for his assisting the police last night."

"When?"

"Immediately."

"And we can put that in the paper," Panesa said.

Hammer had to laugh. She liked this man. "Tell you what," Hammer said. "You put that in the paper, but do me a favor. Leave out the part about why Brazil was hiding in an alleyway."

Panesa had to think about this for a moment. Generally, cops abusing their power, harassing a citizen, was a much better story than something positive, such as a citizen helping or making a difference by doing the right thing, and demonstrating community responsibility and being appreciated for it.

"Now listen," Hammer spoke again. "It happens again, then run it one-A, Richard, okay? I wouldn't blame you. But don't punish the entire police department because of one asshole."

"Which asshole?" Now Panesa was really interested, and maybe pulling Hammer's chain just a little.

"It's been taken care of." Hammer had nothing more to say about it. "What's Brazil's phone number? I'm going to call him."

This impressed Panesa even more. The publisher could see Brazil beyond glass. As usual, Brazil was in early, working on something no one had asked him to do. Panesa scanned a phone sheet and gave Hammer Brazil's extension. Panesa thoroughly enjoyed watching Brazil's stunned expression when he snatched up his phone a moment later and it was the chief of police.

"Judy Hammer." The familiar voice was strong over the line.

"Yes, ma'am." Brazil sat up straighter, knocked over his coffee, shoved back his chair, and grabbed notepads out of the way of a tepid flood.

"Look, I know all about last night." The chief went straight to the point. "I just want you to hear from me that this sort of behavior is absolutely not condoned by the Charlotte Police Department. It is not condoned by me and will not be repeated. Please accept my apology, Andy."

Hearing her say his name made him warm all over. His ears turned red. "Yes, ma'am" was all he seemed capable of uttering, repeatedly.

He used words for a living, and were there any available when he needed them? He was devastated when she hung up. She had to think he was lobotomized, a wimp, a dolt. He could have at least thanked her, for God's sake! Brazil wiped up coffee. He stared blankly into his computer screen. She wouldn't get on the phone if he called her back, he supposed. She would be off on other important things by now. No way she'd waste any more time on him. Brazil was oblivious to the story he was writing about First Union Bank's minimal losses in a fraud case. Tommy Axel, not so far away, typically, did not exist.

Axel had been looking at Brazil all morning and was certain Brazil's feelings were stirring. The guy was blushing even as Axel stared. That definitely was a good sign. Axel could hardly concentrate on his Wynonna Judd review, which was unfortunate for her. What might have been a splashy story about her latest fabulous album was destined for mindless jargon that no doubt would cost her millions in sales. Axel had that power. He sighed, working up the courage to ask Brazil yet one more time to do dinner, a concert, or a club with male strippers. Maybe he could get Brazil drunk, get him to smoke a little dope, jazz him up, and show him what life was about.

Brazil was in despair as he glanced again at the phone. Oh, what the hell. What happened to having guts? He grabbed the receiver, flipped through his Rolodex, and dialed.

"Chief Hammer's office," a man answered.

Brazil cleared his throat. "Andy Brazil with the *Observer*," he said in a remarkably steady voice. "I wonder if I might have a word with her."

"And this is in regard to what?"

Brazil was not about to be scared off the case. It was too late. There was no place to run, really.

"I'm returning her phone call," he bravely said, as if it were perfectly normal for the chief to call him and for him to get back to her.

Captain Horgess was thrown off. What did Hammer do? Dial

this reporter's number herself? Horgess hated it when she did that instead of placing all calls through him. Damn it. He couldn't keep track of that woman. She was out of control. Horgess punched the hold button without bothering to tell Brazil. Two seconds later, Hammer's voice was on the line, shocking Brazil.

"I'm sorry to bother you," he quickly said to her.

"That's quite all right. What can I help you with?" she replied.

"Oh, not a thing. I mean this isn't about a story. I just wanted to thank you for what you did."

Hammer was quiet. Since when did reporters thank her for anything?

Brazil interpreted the silence wrongly. Oh God, now she really thought he was stupid. "Well, I won't take up your time." He was talking faster and faster, thoroughly decompensating. "Uh, I, well. It's just that it was a big thing to do. I thought so. When you didn't have to. Someone in your position, I mean. Most wouldn't."

Hammer smiled, drumming her nails on a stack of paperwork. She needed a manicure. "I'll see you around the department," she told him, and her heart was pricked as she hung up.

She had two sons and they hurt her on a regular basis. This did not prevent her from calling them every Sunday night, or setting up a college trust for the grandbabies, and offering to send plane tickets whenever a visit was possible. Hammer's sons did not have her drive, and she secretly blamed this on the bad genetic wiring of their father, who was all egg white and no yolk, in truth. No bloody wonder it had always required so many tries for Hammer to get pregnant. As it turned out, Seth's sperm count could be done on one hand. Randy and Jude were single, with families. They were still finding themselves in Venice Beach and Greenwich Village. Randy wanted to be an actor. Jude played drums in a band. Both of them were waiters. Hammer adored them. Seth did not, and this was directly related to how seldom they came to town and why their mother ached in private.

The chief was suddenly depressed. She felt as if she might be coming down with something. She buzzed Captain Horgess. "What do I have scheduled for lunch?" she asked.

"Councilman Snider," came the reply.

"Cancel him and get West on the phone," she said. "Tell her to meet me in my office at noon."

Chapter Eleven

The Presto Grill was an acronym for Peppy Rapid Efficient Service Tops Overall and was not in a good part of town. Every cop in the greater Charlotte-Mecklenburg area knew that Hammer and West ate breakfast at the Presto every Friday morning. This was monitored far more closely than the cops supposed either woman knew, for there wasn't an officer interested in survival who would take even the slimmest chance that something bad might happen to the chief or deputy chief on his beat.

The small grill looked as it had in the forties, when it was built. It was on West Trade Street and surrounded by eroded parking lots, just down from the Mount Moriah Primitive Baptist Church. Hammer preferred walking from headquarters when the weather was nice, as it was this day. West never walked when she could ride, but it was not her call.

"Nice suit," Hammer said to West, who had opted to give her uniform a day off and was dressed in a red blouse and a bright blue pants suit. "Why do you never wear skirts?" Hammer asked her.

It was not a criticism, just curiosity. West had a very nice figure and slender legs.

"I hate skirts," West said, breathing hard, for Hammer did not walk at a normal pace. "I think hose and high heels are a male conspiracy. Like binding feet. To cripple us. Slow us down." She breathed.

"Interesting," Hammer considered.

David One Officer Troy Saunders spotted them first and was instantly palsied by indecision as he quickly turned off on Cedar Street, out of sight. Did he alert his buddies out here? He was reliving the nightmare of Hammer's surprise appearance at roll call, and her severe warning about cops following people and harassing, spying, tailing no matter the motive. Wouldn't it be harassment in the chief's eyes if he, Saunders, instigated her and West being spied upon, or tailed, during lunch? Christ. Saunders came to a dead halt in an All Right parking lot, his heart out of control.

He checked his mirrors and scanned parked cars, deliberating. It wasn't worth the risk, he decided. Especially since he had been right there and had heard every word Hammer had said to Goode. The chief sure as hell could check roll call and know for a fact that Saunders had been sitting three chairs away from her. She'd be all over his ass for insubordination, for disobeying a direct order. He was certain that her eyes had burned through him when she'd said, *Next time, it will cost you.* Saunders raised no one on his radio. He parked in the farthest corner of the pay lot and smoked.

By twenty minutes past noon, the regulars had found their favorite stools lining the Formica counter inside the grill. Gin Rummy was the last to sit, the usual banana in his back pocket that he planned to save for later on in the day when he got hungry again while driving his red and white Ole Dixie taxicab.

"You can fix me a hamburger?" Gin Rummy asked Spike at the grill.

"Yeah, we can fix you a hamburger," Spike said, pushing the bacon press.

"Know it's early."

"Man, it's not early." Spike scraped clean an area of the grill, and slapped down a frozen hamburger patty. "When's the last time you looked at a clock, Rummy?"

His friends called him that for short. Rummy smiled, shaking his head sheepishly. He usually came in for breakfast but was running a little late today. Seems like those two white ladies usually came in for breakfast, too. Maybe that was the problem. Everything was confusing. He shook his head again, grinned, and adjusted his banana so he didn't bruise any part of it.

"Why you carry your banana like that?" asked his neighbor, Jefferson Davis, who operated a yellow Caterpillar and still bragged that he had helped build USBank. "Put it in your shirt pocket." He tapped the pocket on Rummy's red-checked shirt. "Then you don't sit on it."

Other men at the counter, and there were eight of them, got into a deep discussion about Rummy's banana and Davis's suggestion. Some were eating beef tips and gravy, others sticking with the fried livermush, collard greens, and cheese grits.

"I put it in my shirt pocket and I see it the whole time I'm driving." Rummy was trying to explain his philosophy. "Then I eat it sooner. See? It never makes it till three or four o'clock."

"Then stick it in the glove box."

"No room in there."

"What about the passenger's seat up front? All your fares ride in back, right?" Spike set down the burger, all the way, thousand island instead of mayo, double American cheese, and fried onions on the side.

"Won't work. Sometimes bags go up front." Rummy neatly cut his lunch in half. "Or I pick up four fares at the bus station, and one of 'em gotta go up there. They see a banana on the seat, think I eat on the job."

"Well, you do, man."

"That's so."

"The truth."

"Tell it, brother."

"Not with no one in with me, I don't." Rummy shook his head, chewing, the banana remaining in his back pocket where it belonged.

Hammer did not recall the Presto being this loud. She eyed the men at the counter, halfway expecting them to get into a fight any minute. Seems one told another to stick something somewhere and others were agreeing. She hadn't been in a good fight in a while, if she didn't count arguments with Seth. Of course, she was no fool. She knew there were at least twenty patrol cars cruising the area, watching every bit of Cobb salad she speared with her fork. It was annoying, but she didn't blame her troops and in fact appreciated their attention and care. She found it touching, even though she knew the motive was their butts and not her well-being, really.

"I probably should have confronted her in private," Hammer was saying.

West wished Hammer had reprimanded Goode in front of the entire police department, all sixteen hundred of them, or at a televised city council meeting.

"You're being too hard on yourself," West diplomatically said, as she finished her Reuben and fries.

"I swear, the food here really is the best," said Hammer. "Look at those hash browns. Everything from scratch."

West watched Spike cooking, flinging, slamming away, as men on their stools continued arguing about where to hide stolen goods, or maybe drugs. The glove box. Under the seat. On their persons. West couldn't believe how brazen criminals were these days. While it was true that she and her chief were both in plain clothes, everyone knew who they were, and West's portable radio was upright on the table, chattering away. Did these dudes care; were they even remotely intimidated by the law?

"Tell you what," one of them railed on, jabbing a finger at the man in the red-checked shirt. "You want to know what to do with it? I'm here to tell you. Eat it. Quick before anybody sees. Then what's anybody gonna say 'bout it? Huh?"

"Can't say nothing."

"Not one thing."

"You got that right."

"Sitting on it ain't the answer, Rummy," Spike spoke his mind. "Besides, it's not like you can't get the same thing here. High quality, imported, good price. Fresh every morning." He folded a ham and cheese omelet. "But oh no. Every stinking day you come in with the same damn thing stuffed in your pocket. Like what? Maybe you think you're impressing the women or something? Make 'em think you're happy to see 'em?"

Everyone laughed, except West, head of investigations for the city. She was going to get some of her guys on this right away and bust this ring wide open, trace it back to Colombia, get the DEA or ATF in on it, if need be.

"Drugs," she mouthed to her boss.

Hammer was preoccupied and still so angry at Goode that Hammer's blood felt hot as it raced around her body. How dare that lamebrain overpromoted bitch jeopardize the reputation of the entire police department and of women everywhere. Hammer could not remember the last time she was this furious. West was enraged, too, Hammer could tell, and found this somewhat soothing. Not many people understood what it was like to have the chief's responsibility and stress, and West had integrity, damn it. She knew how wrong it was to abuse power.

"Can you believe it?" West asked her, angrily crumpling her napkin as she glared at the drug dealer in his red-checked shirt, with a banana in his back pocket. "Can you believe people?"

Hammer shook her head, about to boil over. "No," she said. "I never cease to be amazed. . . ."

Both of them got quiet as the call came over the radio.

"Any unit in the area, six hundred block West Trade. Robbery in progress, armed white male on a bus, robbing passengers . . ."

Hammer and West were on their feet and running out the door to the Greyhound bus terminal next door. David One units were responding, but it seemed not one car was within blocks. This baffled Hammer as she ran with some difficulty in high-heeled Ferragamos. West was slightly behind her. They sped around the station to a lane on the side where a forty-seven-passenger bus filled to capacity was idling, with doors open wide.

"We'll get on pretending to be passengers," West whispered as they slowed their pace.

Hammer nodded, knowing exactly how this would go down. "I'll go first," she said.

This was not quite what West had in mind, but the last thing she intended to do now or ever was imply that Hammer had forgotten how to be a cop. Hammer's black pumps were loud on metal steps as she smiled, climbing aboard, oblivious and on her way somewhere. People were terrorized in their seats as the sinister young white male made his way down the aisle, collecting wallets, cash, jewelry, and dropping them in a plastic trash bag.

"Excuse me," Hammer politely said to anyone listening.

Magic the Man whipped around and fixed on the fine lady in her fine black suit as she spotted his gun. Her smile faded and she froze, as did another lady right behind her. This was getting better. These bitches looked rich.

"Is this the bus for Kannapolis?" the older bitch in black stammered.

"This is the bus for you giving me your money." Magic jabbed the .22 pistol her way.

"Yes sir. I don't want a problem," the lady in black said.

Magic thought she seemed confused, as if she might pass out or pee in her pants. She shakily moved closer to him, as she rooted around in her big black leather pocketbook. Magic might just take that too, for his mama. Maybe those bad black shoes, too. Wonder what size they were? He found out as much as he would ever need to know about those shoes when the bitch suddenly kicked him so hard in the shin with a knife-pointed toe that he bit his tongue. She suddenly had a big pistol out and was poking it against his head as his gun instantly vanished from behind, and then he was facedown in the aisle, and the other bitch was jerking his wrists together and wrapping them tight with a flex cuff.

"Man, oh man. That's too tight," Magic said as his shin throbbed. "I think my leg's broke."

Innocent passengers on the bus stared slack-jawed, in speechless wonder as the two well-dressed ladies led that son-of-a-bitch murderer off into the bright afternoon. Police cars were suddenly roaring up, blue and red lights whirling, and all on the bus knew the ladies somehow had made that happen, too.

"Thank you Jesus," someone thought to say.

"Lord be praised."

"It's a miracle."

"Batman and Robin."

"Hand that bag over here so I can get my gold chain back."

"I want my ring."

"Everybody, remain where you are and don't touch anything," said a cop as he boarded.

Officer Saunders hoped the chief wouldn't notice him as he climbed out of his cruiser.

"Where were you?" she asked him as she briskly walked past. She then commented to West, "Don't you find that a little odd? Usually they're all over the place when we're around."

West didn't understand it, either, but she did have more respect for the chief's skirts and pumps. Not only had they not slowed her up enough to matter, but the shoes, at least, had come in handy. She was proud of her boss as they walked back inside the Presto to pay their bill. The men at the counter were smoking now, still arguing, and oblivious to what had just gone down next door at the

Greyhound station. Not that a bunch of drug dealers cared about innocent people getting robbed, West thought. She threw them another menacing look as her boss drank one last swallow of her unsweetened iced tea and glanced at her watch.

"Well, I guess we'd better be getting back," Hammer suggested.

Andy Brazil had heard about the incident at the bus station when it crackled over his scanner while he was working on a substantial story about the long-term consequences of violence on victims and the relatives left behind. By the time he ran down the escalator, got into his car, and raced to the six hundred block of West Trade, the drama apparently had ended in an arrest.

He was trotting past the Presto Grill when West and Hammer were walking out of it. Startled, Brazil stopped and stared at both of them. In the first place, he didn't understand why two of the most prominent people in the city would eat in such a dive. Nor could he fathom how they could continue with lunch when lives were in danger not fifty yards away, and they had to have known. West was carrying her police radio.

"Andy." Hammer nodded her greeting to him.

West shot him a glance that dared him to ask questions. He noted that both were in handsome business suits and that the chief's black leather handbag included a secret compartment for her pistol. He supposed her badge was somewhere in there, too, and he liked the way her calves knotted as she briskly walked off. He wondered what West's legs looked like as he hurried on to the bus station. Cops were busy taking statements, and this was no small chore. Brazil counted forty-three passengers, not including the driver, who proved to be a pretty great interview.

Antony B. Burgess had been a professional bus driver for twenty-two years and had seen it all. He had been mugged, robbed, hijacked, and stabbed. He'd been shot at the Twilight Motel in Shreveport when he picked up a she who was a him (sh'im) by mistake. He told all this to Brazil and more, because the blond dude was nice as hell, and discerning enough to recognize a raconteur when he met one.

"Had no idea they was cops," Burgess said again, scratching under his cap. "That one never would have entered my mind. They come on board all in black, and red and blue, like Batman and Robin. And next thing Batman's kicked the fool out of the little bastard and's about to blow his fucking brains all over my bus while Robin cuffs 'im. Ho-ly smoke." He shook his head, as if he'd seen a vision. "And that's the po-lice chief. That's what I heard. Can you believe it?"

By five P.M., the story was in the bag and destined for 1-A above the fold. Brazil had already seen the headline in the composing room:

POLICE CHIEF AND DEPUTY FOIL ABDUCTION OF BUS
BATMAN AND ROBIN IN HEELS?

West got a preview a little later when Brazil, in uniform, hopped in her car for another night out on the town. He was full of himself and thought this story was his best yet. He was thrilled over what Hammer and West had pulled off, almost wanted their autographs, or a poster of the two of them to hang in his room.

"Jesus fucking Christ," West exclaimed again as they sped along South Boulevard not going anywhere in particular. "You didn't have to put in the Batman shit."

"Yes I did," Brazil insisted, his mood sinking like the sun as his world got dark and stormy. "It was a quote. It's not like I made it up."

"Fuck." West would be the laughingstock of the entire department tomorrow. "Goddamn son-of-a-bitch." She lit a cigarette, imagining Goode laughing.

"This is an ego thing." Brazil didn't like his work criticized and could take but just so much of it. "You're just pissed because you don't like being a sidekick, Robin instead of Batman, because it reminds you of your real situation. You aren't Batman. She is."

West gave him a look that was heat-seeking, like a missile. He would not survive this night and probably should have remained silent.

"I'm just being honest," he added. "That's all."

"Oh yeah?" She launched another look. "Well, let me tell you *honest* for a minute. I don't give a flying fuck what someone quotes to you, okay? You know what quotes like that are called in the real world? They're called bullshit. They're called perjury, hearsay, impeaching a witness, slander, dis-fucking-respect."

"How do you spell that last one? I guess it's hyphenated?" Brazil was trying not to laugh and pretending to take notes as West gestured with her cigarette and got increasingly ridiculous.

"Point is, just because someone says something, Sherlock, doesn't mean it's gospel, worth repeating, worth printing. Got it?"

He nodded with mock seriousness.

"And I don't wear high heels and don't want anybody thinking I do," she added.

"How come?" he asked.

"How come what?"

"You don't want people thinking it," he said.

"I don't want people thinking about me, period."

"How come you don't ever wear high heels. Or skirts?" He wasn't going to let her duck him.

"Not any of your goddamn business." She tossed the cigarette out her window.

The police radio took charge, broadcasting an address on Wilkinson Boulevard that anyone who knew anything would recognize as the Paper Doll Lounge. The striptease joint had been in Charlotte longer than sex, staffed by women with nothing on but a g-string, and tormenting men with jeans full of dollar bills. This night, derelicts were swigging from quart bottles of beer brilliantly disguised by brown paper bags. Not far away, a damaged young man joyfully rooted around inside a Dumpster.

"She wasn't much older than me," Brazil was telling West about the young hooker he'd noticed the other night. "Most of her front teeth gone, long dirty hair, tattoos. But I bet she was pretty once. I wish I could talk to her and find out what happened to turn her into something like that."

"People repeat their histories, find other people to abuse them," West said, strangely impatient with his interest in a hooker who might have been pretty once.

They got out of the car. West approached a drunk in a Chick-Fil-A cap. He was swaying, clutching his bottle of Colt 45.

"We're having a lot of fun tonight," West said to him.

The man was staggering, but jolly. "Cap'n," he slurred. "You're lookin' mighty fine. Who dat wid ya?"

"You can pour it out or go to jail," West said.

"Yes, ma'am. That's an easy 'cision! No questi'n 'bout it!"

He emptied beer on the parking lot, almost falling headlong into it and splashing Brazil's uniform trousers and impeccable boots. Brazil was a good sport. He jumped back a little late, wondering where the nearest men's room was and certain West would take him there straight away. She scattered the drunks, emptying their lives on pavement while they watched and counted their change in their minds, calculating how quickly they could get back to Ray's Cash & Carry, the Texaco Food Mart, or Snookies'.

Brazil followed West back to their car. They climbed in and fastened their seatbelts. Brazil was embarrassed by the sour smell seeping up from his lower legs. This part of the job he could do without. Drunks disturbed him in a deep way, and he felt anger as he watched the men through his window. They were staggering off and would be drinking something else before West and Brazil were even a mile down the road. That was the way people like that were, addicted, wasted, no good on this earth and hurting everyone.

"How can anybody sink that low?" he muttered, staring out and ready to leave.

"Any of us could," West said. "That's what's scary. One beer at a time. Any one of us."

There had been times in her life when she had found herself on that same road, night after night drinking herself to sleep, not remembering the last thing she thought or read, and sometimes waking up with lights still on. The impaired young man was joyfully ambling over to their car, and West wondered what trick in reality placed some people where she was sitting and consigned others to parking lots and Dumpsters. It wasn't always a choice. It hadn't been for this one, who was known by the police and was a permanent resident of the street.

"His mother tried to abort him and didn't quite pull it off," West quietly told Brazil. "Or that's the story." She hummed open Brazil's window. "He's been out here forever." She leaned across the front seat, and called out, "How goes it?"

He couldn't speak any language that Brazil might recognize. He was gesturing wildly, making strange sounds that shot fear through Brazil. Brazil wished West would drive off quickly and get them out of here before this creature breathed or drooled on him. God, the guy smelled like dirty beer bottles and garbage, and Brazil pulled back from the window, leaning against West's shoulder.

"You stink," West said to him under her breath as she smiled at their visitor.

"It's not me," Brazil said.

"Yes it is." To their visitor, she added, "What you doing out here?"

He gestured, getting more excited as he told the nice police lady everything he'd been up to, while she smiled and clearly enjoyed hearing about it. Her partner needed to lighten up a little.

Boy, as he had always been called, knew when cops were brand new. Boy could tell by how tense they got, by the look on their faces, and this always invited Boy to have a little fun with them. He stared at Brazil and gave him his gummy, gaping grin, as if he were some exotic creature new to the planet. When Boy poked the rookie, the rookie flinched. This excited Boy more than ever, and he got louder, dancing around, poking the rookie again. West laughed, winking at her ride-along.

"Uh oh," she said. "I think he's sweet on you."

She finally rolled up the window, and by now Brazil felt completely soiled. He had beer on his uniform and had been mauled by someone with no teeth who spent his life inside Dumpsters. Brazil thought he might throw up. He was indignant and hurt as West laughed and drove off, lighting a cigarette. Not only had she not prevented his degradation, she had made it happen and was savoring it. He fumed in silence as she headed out on West Boulevard, toward the airport.

She cut over on the Billy Graham Parkway, wondering what it would be like to have a major highway named after her. She wasn't sure she would appreciate cars and trucks rolling over her day and night, leaving ratty recaps and skid marks, while drivers made obscene comments to other drivers and gave them the finger and pulled out guns. There was nothing Christian about a road, the more West thought about it, unless it was used in Biblical analogies, such as the road to hell and what it was paved with. The more she contemplated all this as she drove, the sorrier she felt for the Reverend Billy Graham, who had been born in Charlotte, in a house that against his will had been appropriated by a nearby religious theme park.

Brazil had no idea where they were going, except it was not where the action was, and it was apparent West had no intention of taking him someplace where he could clean up. He was riveted to the scanner, and things were popping in Charlie Two on Central Avenue. So why were they heading in the opposite direction on this parkway? He remembered his mother watching Billy Graham on TV all the time, no matter what else was on or what Brazil might want to see. He wondered how hard it might be to get a quote from the famous evangelist, maybe inquire about the Reverend Graham's views on crime, one of these days.

"Where are we going?" Brazil asked as they turned off on Boyer toward Wilkinson Boulevard again.

This was definitely the sinful strip, but West did not stay on it long. She sped past Greenbriar Industrial Park and turned left on Alleghany Street, heading into Westerly Hills, a nothing neighborhood near Harding High School. Brazil's mood got worse. He suspected West was up to her old tricks, and it not only reminded him that she really did not want to be out here with him but hinted rather strongly that he had no business on police calls and would not be on many, if she had her way about it.

"Any unit in the area of the twenty-five hundred block of Westerly Hills Drive." The scanner shattered West's peace of mind. "Suspicious subjects in the church parking lot."

"Shit," West said, speeding up.

What lousy luck. They were in Westerly Hills on Westerly Hills Drive, The Jesus Christ Is Lord Glorious United Church of the Living God right in front of them. The small white frame church was Pentecostal, and deserted this night, not one car in the parking lot when West turned in. But there definitely were subjects loitering, half a dozen young males with their mother, who was full of herself and feisty in a wheelchair. All stared hatefully at the cop car. Not sure what to make of the situation, West ordered Brazil to stay put, as both their doors opened and both climbed out.

"We got a call of . . ." West started to say to Mama.

"Just passing through," her oldest son, Rudof, volunteered.

Mama gave Rudof a killing look, holding his eyes. "You don't got to answer to no one!" she snapped at him. "You hear me? Not to no one!"

Rudof looked down, his pants about to fall off and red boxer shorts showing. He was tired of being dissed by his mama and hassled by the police. What had he done? Nothing. Just walking home from the E-Z mart because she needed cigarettes, all of them going with her, taking a nice walk and cutting through the church parking lot. What was so wrong with that?

"We didn't do nothing," Rudof folded his arms and said to the cops.

Brazil knew a fight was coming, just like he could smell a storm before the front moved in. His body tensed. He scanned the small, violent crowd standing restlessly in the dark. Mama wheeled closer to West. Mama had something on her mind she'd been wanting to deliver for a long time, and now was as good an opportunity as any. All her children would hear, and these two police didn't look like they would hurt anybody unnecessarily.

"We just got here," Mama said to West. "We were just coming home, walking like anybody else. I'm tired of you people prosecuting us."

"Nobody is . . ." West tried again.

"Oh yes. Oh yes, uh huh, you are." Mama got louder and angrier. "This is a free country! We was white, you think anybody would've called the police?"

"You have a good point," West reasonably replied.

Mama was amazed. Her children were baffled. For a white lady cop to admit such a thing was unheard of and miraculous.

"So you're agreeing that you were called because we're black." Mama wanted to make sure.

"That would be my guess, and it absolutely isn't fair. But I didn't know you were black when the call came over the radio," West went on in the same calm but sure tone. "We didn't respond because we thought you were black, white, Asian, whatever. We responded because it's our job, and we wanted to make sure everything was all right."

Mama tried to be hateful as she wheeled on her way, her brood in her wake. But she was wavering. She felt like she might cry and didn't know why. The police got back in their shiny new car and drove away.

"Rudof, pull up your pants, son," Mama complained. "You gonna trip and break your neck. Same with you, Joshua. I swear." She wheeled ahead in the night, in the direction of their poor apartment.

Brazil and West were quiet as they got back on Wilkinson Boulevard. He was thinking about what she'd said to that family. West had said *we* several times, when most people would have said *I*, as if Brazil wasn't there. It felt really good when she included him, and he was touched by her gentleness with that wounded, hateful family. Brazil wanted to say something to West, to let her know, to somehow show his appreciation. But he was oddly tongue-tied again, just as he had been with Hammer.

West headed back into the city, thinking, and wondering why her ride-along was so quiet. Maybe he was angry with her for avoiding calls, or trying to avoid them, at any rate. She felt bad. How would she like it were the roles reversed? It wasn't very kind, and he had every right to resent her for it. West was totally ashamed of herself. She turned up the scanner, and picked up the mike.

"700," she said.

"700," the dispatcher came back.

"I'm ten-eight."

Brazil couldn't believe it. West had just told the radio that she was in service, meaning she wanted to take calls like everyone else on the street. The two of them would actually be assigned situations. They were available for trouble. This wasn't long in coming. Their first call was to Our Lady of Consolation Catholic Church.

"Check for loud music coming from the club in the shopping center across the street," came the instruction over the air.

The dispatcher's nickname was Radar, and there were reasons for this. First, Radar had started his career with the North Carolina Highway Patrol, where he was famous for clocking cars, abutments, buildings, trucks, signs, pedestrians, low-flying planes, helium balloons, trees, and nailing all for exceeding the speed limit. He simply loved the radar gun. He deeply loved being a Smoky out on life's highways and pulling the unaware outlaws as they hurried to important places or away from them. Radar retired. He bought an RV and began a new career as a dispatcher to pay for it. It was believed by the 911 operators that Radar could sense trouble before it hit. The call at the church, for example, he had a feeling about, a real bad one.

Thus he had assigned it to Deputy Chief West, because it was

Radar's personal conviction that no woman should be in a uniform unless she was naked beneath it and on the cover of those detective magazines he also loved. In addition to an intuition that bordered on the psychic, Radar knew that the complainant in this case, Fat Man's Lounge, was run by a bunch of thugs who held his same beliefs about a woman's place. Colt, the bouncer, whom Radar personally knew, would not respond well when West with all her brass, ass, and big tits rolled up.

West knew none of this as she lit a cigarette and made a U-turn on Statesville Avenue. She nodded at the MDT. "It took me forty minutes to learn how to use this thing," she said to Brazil. "You got ten."

Our Lady of Consolation Catholic Church was having a special night of music, and the parking lot was packed with cars. Listings for Catholic places of worship were brief in the Charlotte Yellow Pages. Choices were far more abundant for churches that were Baptist, Advent Christian, Presbyterian, Apostolic, Assembly of God, Evangelical, Pentecostal, Non-Pentecostal, Gospel, Full Gospel, Foursquare Gospel, to name but a few. These outnumbered the Catholics about twenty-eight to one.

Indeed, Catholic places of worship were sandwiched between the one Buddhist church in the city and the charismatics who spoke in tongues. So it was, that Catholics did not take their church for granted, never knowing when it might be burned by men in disguises or criticized in editorials. The congregation of Our Lady of Consolation was rocking the block this night, its stained glass windows glowing in the dark, Jesus bright and colorful in many poses, and sheep.

"You sure it isn't the bar complaining about the church?" Brazil wondered out loud.

West was finding the situation rather odd, too. How the hell could anyone inside that church hear a thing beyond their own choir, which was belting out some hymn and accompanied by guitars, the organ, drums, and possibly a violin or two. She turned into the shopping center directly across the street and cut through the parking lot. Fat Man's Lounge wasn't doing nearly the business the church was. A couple of shifty-looking dudes were hanging out in front, drinking beer, smoking, and glaring.

Brazil did not hear any noise, not one sound drifting out of the lounge. He suspected someone in the church had complained just to hassle Fat Man's, which clearly was a den of iniquity. Members of Our Lady would, without a doubt, have preferred another establishment across the street from them, something wholesome and family-oriented, like a Shoney's, a Blockbuster Video store, or maybe another sports bar. The dudes out front followed the cop car with hostile eyes as West parked. She and Brazil got out and approached their welcoming committee.

"Where's all the noise?" West asked. "We got a complaint."

"Only noise is that over there," a dude said, jutting his chin at the church. He boldly took a swig of beer, drunk and mean.

"Word's the noise is coming from here." West held her ground.

She started walking toward the lounge, Brazil with her, the dudes moving out of their way. Fat Man's was a depressing, dark den, smoke hanging in the air and music playing, but not too loudly. Men were drinking at wooden tables, watching a woman on stage, in g-string and tassels, as she twirled heavy, sagging breasts. Brazil didn't want to stare too hard, but he was pretty sure that the left one was tattooed with the planet Saturn, bright yellow, with rings orbiting fast. In big circles. These were, without a doubt, the biggest breasts he had ever seen in person.

The stripper, whose stage name was Minx, needed another Valium. She was thirsty, had to have a cigarette, and damn it all, the fucking cops were here. What this time? She started twirling the other way, then did two different directions at once. This usually got the men going, but tonight's stingy crowd was about as excitable as a cemetery. Minx smiled. The boy cop couldn't take his eyes off her.

"Never seen tits before?" she asked him as he went by.

Brazil was indifferent. West shot Minx a cool look, and thought the stripper's fried egg tattoo on her left breast was rather clever, not to mention apropos. Lord, this one even had stretch marks, cellulite, her clients not interested in anything that wasn't in a glass. Colt, the bouncer, was the exception. He was heading at the cops like a freight train on a mission. He was big and scary in a shiny black suit, thick gold chains, and a red leather tie. He looked like he might hurt them, starting with Brazil.

"We got a complaint of loud music," West said to Colt.

"You hear it?" Colt lifted his heavy jaw, veins like ropes in his powerful neck.

He was full of hate toward these white cops, especially the bitch. Who did she think she was anyway, strutting into Fat Man's in her fancy uniform with all its shiny shit meant to hurt hardworking people like him? He glanced at Minx, making sure she wasn't letting up. It seemed not a night went by when he didn't have to smack a little more energy into her, give her pain someplace where it wouldn't show, encouraging her to do her job. She was slinging away. Nobody cared. Nobody tipped. Two of the regulars were getting up, and leaving, the night still young. The cops were to blame.

Colt jerked open the side door leading out into an alleyway. He grabbed Brazil by the front of his uniform shirt with such force, it ripped.

"*Heyyyy!*" Brazil yelled.

Colt lifted the punk off his feet and threw him outside in the trash, where he belonged. Garbage cans clattered against pavement, bottles clanging. It was just a good thing Brazil was dirty, anyway. He got to his feet in time to see West whipping out her handcuffs. Colt had her by her uniform shirt, intending to pitch her, too, as the little shit yelled *"Mayday! Mayday!"* into his police radio.

Chapter Twelve

Colt gagged, and for a blinding shard of insight thought someone had shoved a pool cue into the hollow of his massive neck. It seeped into his fading consciousness that the bitch was drilling her index finger into that soft hollow over his windpipe. He couldn't breathe. His tongue protruded as she drilled and he gagged, gasping for air, eyes bugging as he dropped to his knees, a gun barrel now staring at his nose. Colt's ears were ringing, blood roaring as the bitch screamed like she was going to eat him tartare.

"You move I'll blow your brains out motherfucker!"

Minx gyrated. Patrons drank. Backup cops burst through the front door, far away across the dark, smoky room. West had a knee on Colt's beefy back, and was busy snapping cuffs on his wrists tight behind him. Brazil looked on in awe. Cops hauled Colt and the drunk dudes to jail. Minx saw her chance and walked off her runway, plucking lousy folded dollar bills out of her garter, wrapping up in a sweatshirt, and lighting a cigarette, out of here for good this time.

"Why did I let you get me into this?" West was saying as she unlocked their car. "I don't do this anymore for a reason." She climbed in, yanking the seatbelt across her chest, cranking the engine.

Both of them were excited and trying not to show it. Brazil held together his ruined uniform shirt, which was missing half its buttons. West noted that he had a very well-developed chest to go with those shoulders and arms and legs. She instantly stopped transmitting any and all signals, such as body language or glances or words or heat. Where was all this coming from anyway? Outer space. Not from her. No sir. She opened the glove box and rummaged until she found the tiny stapler she was sure was in there somewhere.

"Hold still," she said to him, as if it were an order.

She leaned close because there was no other way to correct the situation and gathered his shirt together, and began stapling. Brazil's heart picked up. He could smell her hair, his own seeming to stand on end. He did not move. He was terrified even to breathe as her fingers brushed against him. He was convinced she could tell what he was feeling, and if he as much as twitched and inadvertently touched her somewhere, she would never believe it was an accident. She'd think he was just one more prick out there who couldn't keep it in his pants. She'd never see him as a person, as a sensitive human being. He'd be reduced to this thing, this guy-thing. If she leaned half an inch closer to the right, he would die right there, on her front seat.

"When was the last time you had to do something like that?" he managed to ask.

West covered her repair job with his clip-on tie. The more she tried not to connect with his person, the clumsier her fingers got, fumbling, and touching. She nervously tried to put the stapler away, and dropped it.

"I use it for reports." She groped under the seat. "Don't think

I've ever used it on someone's shirt." She slammed shut the glove box on the third try.

"No," Brazil said, clearing his throat again. "I mean, what you did in there. That guy must weigh two hundred and fifty pounds, and you decked him. All by yourself."

West shoved the car in gear. "You could," she said. "All you need is training."

"Maybe you . . . ?"

She held up a hand as if halting traffic. "No! I'm not a goddamn one-person police academy!" She tapped the MDT. "Clear us outa here, partner."

Brazil was tentative as he placed his fingers on the keyboard. He started typing. The system beeped as if it liked him. "God, this is so cool," he said.

"Small minds," West commented.

"Unit 700," Radar, the dispatcher, said. "Missing person at five-fifty-six Midland."

"Shit. Not again." West grabbed the mike and tossed it to her partner. "Let's see what they're teaching volunteers these days."

"700," he said on the air for all to hear. "We're ten-eighteen five-fifty-six Midland."

Missing person reports were so much paperwork it was unbelievable. Such investigations were almost always fruitless, for either the person really wasn't missing, or he was and dead. Radar's preference was that West had gotten her butt kicked at Fat Man's. At least Radar could ensure that she would be filling out forms the rest of her life, and Midland was government-subsidized housing, definitely not a nice place for a female or her reporter ride-along.

Luellen Wittiker lived in a one-bedroom unit. Her number, 556, like all others in Midland Court, was painted in huge numbers over the door. The city had done this free of charge so the cops could find places fast when out at night with searchlights sweeping and K-9 dogs panting. Luellen Wittiker had just moved here from Mint Hill, where she had worked as a checkout clerk in Wal-Mart until she hit her eighth month of pregnancy and got tired of Jerald coming around. How many times did she have to tell him *no*. N-O.

She paced, wringing her hands, her four-year-old daughter, Tangine, watching from the bed, which was close to the front door. Boxes were still stacked against a wall, although there were not many, since the Wittiker family traveled light. Luellen prayed every hour that Jerald would not find out where she had moved. He would show up. Oh yes. She paced some more. Where the hell were the police? They think this was the lay-away plan? Can't do it now, pick it up later?

Oh yes. He would find her. Because of that bad seed child of hers. Wheatie was out there right now, God only knew where, probably trying to find a way to get hold of Jerald, who was not Wheatie's biological father, but his mother's last boyfriend. Wheatie hero-worshiped Jerald, and that was the problem. Tangine watched her mother pacing. Tangine was eating a Popsicle. Jerald was nothing more than a lowlife drugman, who bought and sold the big stuff, and did it, too.

Cain, crack, diesel, smoke, all that shit. He walked around in his big warm-up suit and Filas like he was in the NBA, and had a diamond earring, too, and a 4×4, black with red and yellow detailing. He'd drive up, and Wheatie would start in, walking, badmouthing, cool-talking, just like Jerald. Next thing, Wheatie would start cussing Luellen and even slapping her around, or smoking marijuana. Just like Jerald. She heard feet on the steps and called out to make sure.

"Police," a woman's voice sounded.

Luellen worked a big cinder block back from the door and removed a concrete support steel bar that she had found on a construction site. She had the same set of improvised locks at the back door, too. Even if Jerald or his bad friends could get in, she'd at least hear things scraping and clanging and have time to get out her matte-black nine-millimeter Baretta Model 92FS pistol with its Tritium night sights, wood grips, and fifteen-shot magazine. The gun had come from Jerald as well, and it had been a big mistake giving her this hand-me-down. If he so much as knocked on her door, it would be his last gesture.

"Come on in," Luellen said to the two police officers at the top of concrete steps.

Brazil's eyes adjusted to the glaring illumination of a naked light bulb in a plastic Greek column lamp. A small TV was on, the Braves playing the Dodgers. There was a boom box in a corner, walls bare, the bed unmade and right there in the living room, a little girl sitting on it. She had braids and sad eyes. It was hot as hell in here, and Brazil started sweating. So did West. She had attached an endless form on top of her metal clipboard, and was prepared to do a lot of writing. Luellen began by telling the police lady all about Wheatie, including that he was adopted and jealous as hell of Tangine and the unborn baby, yet unnamed.

"He called you after he missed the bus," West repeated as she wrote.

"Wanted me to come get him, and I told him I had no way," Luellen said. "Last time I was pregnant, he jumped on me and I lost the baby. He was fifteen then. Always been hateful because he's adopted, like I told you. Trouble from day one."

"You got a recent picture of him?" West asked.

"Packed up. Don't know if I can get to it."

Mother described Wheatie as small, bad skin, wearing Adidas, baggy jeans hanging off, teal-green Hornets tee shirt and baseball cap, and a fade haircut. He could be anywhere, but Luellen worried that he was running with bad kids and into drugs. Brazil felt sorry for Tangine, who seemed unimportant in the grand scheme of things as she climbed down from the bed, fascinated by this blond man in his fancy uniform with all its shiny leather. He got out his Mag-Lite and started bouncing the beam around on the floor, playing with her like she was a cat. Tangine didn't know what to make of this and got scared. She was screaming and did not intend to stop by the time the police left. Mother watched Brazil and West feel their way down the steps in the complete dark.

"Way to go," West said to her partner, as Tangine wailed and shrieked.

Brazil missed a step and landed on his ass.

"I'd put a light on if I had one," Luellen said from the doorway.

The next two hours were spent in the records room. West continued to fill out forms, having no idea that there were so many of them these days. It was astonishing, and she was unfamiliar with anyone back here tonight, and all were rude and not inclined to respect West's rank. Were she paranoid, she might have suspected a conspiracy, as if someone had instructed the clerks to give the deputy chief a bad dose, to stick her but good. Mostly, West got their backs as they typed and sipped their Frescas and Diet Cokes. West could have asserted herself but didn't. She entered the missing person information in NCIC herself.

She and Brazil rode around for a while in the Midland area, hoping they might spot the small adopted son with bad skin and Hornets cap. They drove slowly past kids hanging out on corners, and beneath streetlights, hateful eyes following. Wheatie remained at large, and as the evening wore on, Brazil had developed a relationship with him. Brazil imagined Wheatie's wretched life, his loneliness and anger. What chance did anyone like that have? Nothing but bad examples and cops out there like cowboys waiting to lasso and round him up.

Brazil's early years weren't perfect, either, but there was no comparison. He had tennis courts and nice neighbors. Davidson security treated him like family, and he was always welcome to visit their small brick precinct and listen to their stories and gossip and exaggerations. They made him feel special when he came in. The same was true at the laundry with its rooftop of tangled rusting metal from students picking up laundry and tossing the wire hangers up there, where they stayed for years. Doris, Bette, and Sue always had time for Brazil. The same could be said in the snack bar, the M&M soda shop, the bookstore, anywhere he went, really.

Wheatie had never experienced any of this and quite likely never would. At the very moment West was reprimanding a driver for not wearing a seatbelt, Wheatie was jailing with his heroes in the slums off Beatties Ford Road. There were three friends, all years older than Wheatie. His pals had big pants, big shoes, big guns, and big rolls of cash in their pockets. They were high-fiving, laughing, soaring on wings of smoke. Yes sir, the night had been good, and for one sweet minute, that hollow, hurtful spot in Wheatie's heart was full and feeling fine.

"Give me a gun, I'll go work for you," he said to Slim.

"Little piece like you?" Slim laughed. "Uh uh." He shook his head. "I give you a job, you get spanked and I end up with nothing."

"Bullshit," Wheatie said in his biggest, boasting tone. "Nobody fuck with me."

"Yeah, you bad," said Tote.

"Yeah, you bad," Fright imitated Tote, while popping Wheatie on the head.

"Man, I gotta go get me some food," said Slim, who could eat tires after getting high. "How 'bout we hit Hardee's."

He meant this literally. Slim and company were under the influence and armed, and robbing Hardee's was as good an idea as any they had come up with this night. All of them piled into his red Geo Tracker. They headed out with the radio so loud the bass could be felt five cars away. Wheatie plotted as they drove, thinking about Jerald and how proud he would be of Wheatie right now. Jerald would be impressed with Wheatie's buddies. Wheatie wished Slim, Tote, and Fright could meet Jerald. Shit, wouldn't they step back and give Wheatie a little more respect? Fuck yeah, they would. He watched telephone poles and cars go by, his heart picking up speed. He knew what he had to do.

"Give me a gun, I'll do it," he said loud enough to be heard over heavy metal.

Slim was driving and laughed again, eyeing him in the rearview mirror. "You will? You ever hit anything before?"

"I hit my mother."

They all laughed.

"He *hit* his mother! Woooo-weeee! Bad ass!"

They were choking, guffawing, weaving in and out of traffic. Fright slipped out his high-gloss stainless steel Ruger .357 Black-hawk revolver with its six-and-a-half-inch barrel and walnut grips and adjustable sights. It was loaded with six Hydra-Shoks. He handed his piece to Wheatie, who acted as if he knew all there was to know about guns and owned plenty of them. They pulled up to Hardee's. The friends landed glazed eyes on Wheatie.

"All right, motherfucker," Slim said to him. "You go in and get a twelve-piece dinner, all white meat." He snapped out a twenty-dollar bill. "You pay and wait. Don't do nothing 'til you got the food, you know? Then you tuck it under your arm, pull out the gun, clean out the registers, and run like hell."

Wheatie nodded, heart drilling out of his chest.

"We ain't gonna be sitting right here." Fright made that point, jerking his head at the Payless gas station next door. "Back there by the Dumpster. You take long, motherfucker, we leave your ass."

Wheatie understood. "Get the fuck outa my face," he said, tough and invincible as he tucked the revolver in the front of his pants and pulled his tee shirt over it.

What Wheatie did not understand was that this particular Hardee's had been robbed before, and Slim, Fright, and Tote were aware of it. They were laughing and lighting up another joint even as he walked in and they drove off. Wheatie's little butt was going to get locked up tonight. He'd learn about jailing honestly, his pants falling off because they took his belt, then dropping the rest of the way when some motherfucker got the urge for his sweet lit-tle ass.

"Twelve piece, white meat." Wheatie's voice didn't sound quite so tough now that he was at the counter. He was shaking all over and terrified that the fat black lady in a hair net knew all about his plan.

"What sides you want?" she asked.

Shit. Slim didn't tell him that part. Oh shit. He got it wrong and they'd kill him. His furtive, hard eyes cast about, not seeing the Tracker anywhere.

"Baked beans. Slaw. Biscuits." He did the best he could.

She rang it up, and took his twenty. He left the change on the counter, fearful that tucking it in his pocket might draw attention to the gun. When the big bag of chicken and side orders were gripped under a frail arm, Wheatie drew the gun, not real smoothly, but he got it out and pointed it at the fat lady's startled face.

"Give me all your money, motherfucker!" he commanded in his cruelest voice as the gun shook in his small hands.

Wyona managed this Hardee's and was working the counter because two of her people were out sick tonight. She'd been robbed three times in her life and this little piece of motherfucking white meat wasn't going to make it four. She put her hands on her hips, glaring at him.

"What you gonna do, cock-a-doodle-doo? Shoot me?" she sang.

Wheatie had not anticipated this. He clicked back the hammer, hands shaking harder. He wet his lips, eyes jumping. It was decision time. No way he could let this fat chicken lady dis him. Shit man. He walked out of here without the money and that was the end of his career. He wasn't even sure he'd gotten the sides right. Oh shit, he was in trouble. He closed his eyes and pulled the trigger. The explosion was incredible and the revolver jumped in his hands. The bullet smashed through *large fries $1.99* on the lit-up sign over Wyona's head. She grabbed the big .357 magnum away from him, and he ran like hell.

Wyona was a firm believer in community intervention. She chased Wheatie out the door. She thundered after him through the parking lot, across the way to the Payless, and behind it where a red Tracker was parked, filled with teenagers smoking weed. They locked the doors. Wheatie tugged a handle to no avail, yelling, as the huge woman grabbed the back of his pants, yanking them down to his leather Adidas. He fell to the pavement in a tangle of red denim as she pointed the revolver through glass, at the driver's head.

Slim knew a determined look when he saw it. This bitch was going to shoot him if he so much as blinked. He slowly lifted his hands from the steering wheel and held them up.

"Don't shoot," he begged. "Oh please don't shoot."

"Get on your car phone and call 911 right now," Wyona screamed.

He did.

"Tell them where you are and what you done and that if they don't get here in exactly two minutes, I'm blowing your mother-fucking head off!" she screamed, her foot firmly planted on Wheatie, who was supine and shaking on the pavement, facedown, hands covering his head.

"We just robbed Hardee's and are behind the Payless on Central Avenue!" Slim yelled into the phone. "Please get here quick!"

Selma, the 911 operator who got the call, wasn't certain what this was about. But she gave it a priority one because her instinct prodded her in a tragedy-about-to-occur direction. Radar, mean-while, had not finished with West this night. He passed the emer-gency along to her.

"Goddamn it," West said as she drove past Piedmont Open Middle School. She was trying to avoid other problems and did not wish to hear her unit number one more time, ever.

Brazil couldn't grab the mike fast enough. "700," he said.

"Unknown trouble, four thousand block of Central Avenue," Radar said with a smile.

West floored it, flying down Tenth Street, cutting over to the one thousand block of Central, flying past the Veterans Park and Saigon Square. Other units backed her up, for by now it had occurred to every cop on the street that their deputy chief was handling a lot of dangerous calls unassisted by anyone. When she rolled into the Payless, six cars with lights flashing were behind her. This was uncommon, but West didn't question it and was grateful. She and Brazil got out. Wyona lowered the gun, now that help was here.

"They tried to rob me," she said to Brazil.

"Who did?" West asked.

"The piece of white shit under my foot," she said to Brazil.

West noted the fade haircut, the bad skin, the Hornets cap and shirt. The boy's pants were knotted around his basketball shoes, and he had on yellow boxer shorts. Next to him was a big bag of chicken and side orders.

"He come in, ordered twelve piece all white meat, then pulled out this thing." Wyona handed the gun to Brazil because he was the man and Wyona had never dealt with women police and wasn't about to start now. "I chased him out here to where these sons of bitches are." She gestured furiously at Slim, Fright, and Tote as they cowered inside the Tracker.

West took the gun from Brazil. She looked back at the six other officers standing nearby and observing.

"Let's lock 'em up," she said to the troops. To Wyona, she added, "Thanks."

The boys were rounded up and cuffed. Now that they were official felons again and not about to be killed, their bravery returned. They stared hatefully at the police and spat. In the car West gave Brazil a pointed look. He typed on the MDT, clearing them from the scene.

"Why do they hate us so much?" he said.

"People tend to treat others the way they've been treated," she answered. "Take cops. A lot of them are the same way."

They rode in silence for a while, passing other poor landscapes, the aspiring sparkling city around them.

"What about you?" Brazil asked. "How come you don't hate?"

"I had a good childhood."

This made him angry. "Well, I didn't, and I don't hate everyone," he said. "So don't ask me to feel sorry for them."

"What can I tell you?" She got out a cigarette. "It goes back to Eden, the Civil War, the Cold War, Bosnia. The six days it took God to make all this."

"You got to quit smoking," he said, and he remembered her fingers touching him as she fixed his shirt.

Chapter Thirteen

Brazil had a lot to think about. He wrote his stories fast and shipped them out within seconds of various deadlines for various editions. He was strangely unsettled and not remotely tired. He did not want to go home and had fallen into a funk the instant West had let him out at his car in the parking deck. He left the newsroom at quarter past midnight and took the escalator down to the second floor.

The press room was going full tilt, yellow Ferag conveyors flying by seventy thousand papers per hour. Brazil opened the door, his ears overwhelmed by the roar inside. People wearing hearing protectors and ink-stained aprons nodded at him, yet to understand his odd peregrinations through their violent, dirty world. He walked in and stared at miles of speeding newsprint, at folding machines rat-a-tat-a-tatting, and belt ribbon conveyors streaking papers through the counting machines. The hardworking people in this seldom-thought-of place had never known a reporter to care a hoot about how his clever words and big-shot bylines ended up in the hands of citizens every day.

Brazil was inexplicably drawn to the power of these huge, frightening machines. He was awed to see his front page racing by in a blur, thousands and thousands of times. It was humbling and hard to believe that so many people out there were interested in how he saw the world and what he had to say. The big headline of the night was, of course, Batman and Robin saving the hijacked bus. But there was a pretty decent piece on WHY A BOY RAN AWAY, on the metro section front page, and a few paragraphs on the altercation at Fat Man's Lounge.

In truth, Brazil could have written stories forever about all he saw while riding with West. He wandered up a spiral metal staircase to the mail room and thought of her calling him *partner.* He replayed her voice over and over. He liked the way she sounded, deep but resonate and womanly. It made him think of old wood and smoke, of fieldstone patched with moss, and of lady's slippers in old forests scattered with sun.

Brazil did not want to go home. He wandered out to his car, in a mood to roam and think. He felt blue and did not know the source of it. Life was good. His job couldn't be better. The cops didn't seem to despise him quite as intensely or as universally. He contemplated the possibility that his problem was physical, because he wasn't working out as much as usual and wasn't producing enough endorphin or pushing himself to the point of exhaustion. He cruised down West Trade, looking at the people of the night trolling, offering their bodies for cash. Sh'ims followed him with sick, glowing eyes, and the young hooker was out again, at the corner of Cedar.

She walked seductively along the sidewalk and stared brazenly at him as he slowly drove past. She had on tight cut-off jeans that barely covered firm buttocks, her tee shirt cut off, too, just below her chest. Typically, she wasn't wearing a bra, and her flesh moved as she walked and stared at the blond boy in his black BMW with its loud, rumbling engine. She wondered what he had beneath his hood, and smiled. All those Myers Park boys in their expensive cars, sneaking out here to taste the fruit.

Brazil roared ahead, daring a yellow light to be red. He turned off on Pine and entered Fourth Ward, the lovely restored area where important people like Chief Hammer lived, within walking distance of the heart of the city she was sworn to serve. Brazil had been here many times, mostly to look at huge Victorian homes painted fun colors like violet and robin's egg blue, and at graceful manors with elaborate dentil work trimming slate roofs. There were walls and big azaleas, and trees that could clarify history, for they had been here since horses, shading genteel streets traveled by the rich and well known.

He parked on that special corner on Pine where the white house and its gracious wraparound porch were lit up, as if expecting him. Hammer had liriope grass, periwinkles, pansies, yucca, ligustrum hedges, and pachysandra. Wind chimes stirred in the dark, sending friendly tones of truth, like a tuning fork, welcoming him, her protégé. Brazil would not trespass, would not even think of it. But there were numerous tiny public parks in Fourth Ward, sitting areas with fountains and a bench or two. One such cozy spot was tucked next door to Hammer's house, and Brazil had known about this secret garden for a while. Now and then he sat in the dark there, when he could not sleep or did not want to go home. There was no harm done or imagined.

It wasn't as if he were on her property. He wasn't a stalker or a voyeur. All he wanted, really, was to sit where no one could see him. The most he invaded was the window of her living room, where he saw nothing, for the draperies were always drawn, unless a shadow passed by, someone who belonged in that house and could walk wherever he pleased. Brazil sat on a stone bench that was cold and hard beneath his dirty uniform trousers. He stared, and the sadness he felt was beyond any word he knew. He imagined Hammer inside her fine house, with her fine family and her fine husband. She was in a fine suit, probably talking on a portable phone, busy and important. Brazil wondered what it would be like to be loved by a woman like that.

Seth knew exactly what it was like, and as he finished loading his ice cream bowl into the dishwasher, he entertained violent thoughts. He had been lacing his late-night Chunky Monkey with butterscotch and hot fudge when Chief Wife came in with her bottle of Evian. So what did she do? Nag, nag, nag. About his weight, his coronary arteries, his propensity for diabetes, his laziness, his dental problems. He went into the living room, flipped on "Seinfeld," tried to block her out, and wondered what had ever attracted him to Judy Hammer.

She was a powerful woman in uniform the first time they met. He would never forget the way she stood out in dark blue. What a figure she cut. He had never told her his fantasies about being overpowered by her, cuffed, pinned, held, yoked, and hauled away in the paddy wagon of erotic captivity. After all these years, she did not know. None of it had happened. Judy Hammer had never restrained him physically.

She had never made love to him while she was in uniform, not even now, when she had enough brass and gold braid to impress the Pentagon. When she went to police memorial services and banquets and showed up in dress blues, Seth turned fainthearted. He was overcome, helpless and frustrated. In the end, after all these years and disappointments, she was still splendid. If only she didn't make him feel so worthless and ugly. If only she hadn't driven him to this, forced him into it, caused it, and willed abject ruination upon his life. It was her fault that he was fat and a failure.

The chief, his wife, honestly was not privy to any of her husband's ambitions or lustful imaginings or the complete set of his resentments. She would not have been flattered, amused, or held responsible, for Chief Hammer was not aroused by dominance or prey to control or quick to assume that others might be smitten and excited by her position in life. It would never occur to her that

Seth was eating ice cream with butterscotch, hot fudge sauce, and maraschino cherries at this unhealthy hour because he really wished to be shackled to the bedposts or to be searched inappropriately and for a long time. He wanted her to arrest him for animal desire and throw away the key. He wanted her to languish and doubt herself and all she had done. What did not interest him in the least was to be sentenced to the solitary confinement their marriage had become.

Chief Hammer was not in uniform or even on the portable phone. She was in a long, thick terry cloth robe, and suffering from insomnia, and this was not unusual. She rarely slept much because her mind kept its own hours, the hell with her body. She was sitting in the living room, "The Tonight Show" droning on as she read the *Wall Street Journal*, various memos, another long letter from her ancient mother, and a few salient pages from Marianne Williamson's *A Return to Love*. Hammer did her best to block out Seth making noise in the kitchen.

His failure in his passage through the world felt like hers. No matter what she told herself or the therapists she left in Atlanta and Chicago, profound personal failure was what she felt every hour of every day. She had done something very wrong, otherwise Seth would not be committing suicide with a fork, a spoon, or chocolate sauce. When she looked back, she realized that the woman who had married him was another entity. She, Chief Hammer, was a reincarnation of that earlier lost manifestation. She did not need a man. She did not need Seth. Everyone knew it, including him.

It was a simple fact that the best cops, Marines, Airmen, National Guards, fire fighters, and military people in general who were women did not need men personally. Hammer had commanded many such independents. She would pick them without question, as long as they weren't so much like the men they did not need that they had completely adopted bad male habits, such as getting into fights rather than not, or being clingy and demanding and domineering. What Hammer had concluded after all these years was that she had an overweight, neurotic, nonworking wife who did nothing but bitch. Judy Hammer was ready for change.

Thus it was that she made a tactical error this very early morning, in her long clean robe. She decided to go out on her wraparound porch and sit on the swing, sipping chardonnay, alone with her thoughts, for a spell.

Brazil was mesmerized when she emerged, a vision, a god glowing in lamplight, all in white and shimmering. His heart rolled forward at such a pitch that he could not catch up with it. He sat very still on the cold cement bench, terrified she would see him. He watched every small thing she did, the way she pushed forward and let go, the bend of her wrist as she lifted the tapered glass, her head leaning back against the swing. He saw the slope of her neck as she rocked with eyes shut.

What did she think? Was she a person just like him, with those darker shades, those lonely, cold corners of existence that no one knew? She swung slowly and alone. His chest ached. He was drawn to this woman and had no clear idea why. It must be hero worship. If he had a chance to touch her, he really wouldn't know what to do. But he did want to, as he stared in the night at her. She was pretty, even at her age. Not delicate but fascinating, powerful, compelling, like a collector's car, an older BMW in mint condition, with chrome instead of plastic. She had character and substance, and Brazil was certain that her husband was quite the contender, a Fortune 500 man, a lawyer, a surgeon, someone capable of holding an interesting conversation with his wife during their brief, busy interfaces with each other.

Chief Hammer pushed the swing again and sipped her wine. She would never be completely devoid of street sense, no matter her station in life. She goddamn knew when she was being watched. Abruptly, she stood, feet firmly planted on her porch. She searched the night, detecting the vague silhouette of someone sitting in that annoying little park right slam next to her house. How many times had she told the neighborhood association that she didn't want a public area adjacent to her domicile? Did anyone listen? To Brazil's horror, she walked down porch steps and stood amidst pachysandra, staring right at him.

"Who's there?" she demanded.

Brazil could not speak. Not a fire or a *Mayday* could have pried a word loose from his useless tongue.

"Who's sitting there?" she went on, irritable and tired. "It's almost two o'clock in the morning. Normal people are home by now. So either you're not normal, or you're interested in my house."

Brazil wondered what would happen if he ran as fast as he could. When he was a little boy, he believed that if he sprinted full speed, he would disappear, become invisible, or turn to butter like Little Black Sambo. It wasn't so. Brazil was a sculpture on his bench, watching Chief Judy Hammer step closer. A part of him wanted her to know he was there, so he could get it over with, confess his intensity, have her blow him off, laugh, dismiss him from her police department, and be done with him, as he deserved.

"I'm going to ask one more time," she warned.

It occurred to him that she might have a gun on her person, perhaps in a pocket. Jesus Christ, how could any of this happen? He had meant no harm driving here after work. All he'd wanted was to sit, think, and contemplate his raison d'être and how he felt about it.

"Don't shoot," he said, slowly bringing himself to his feet and holding his hands up in surrender.

Hammer knew for a fact she had a wacko in her midst. *Don't shoot?* What the hell was this? Clearly, this was someone who knew who she was. Why else would the person assume she might be armed and wouldn't hesitate to shoot? Hammer had always nurtured the unspoken fear that in the end, she would be taken out by a loonytune with a mission. Assassinated. Go ahead and try, was her motto. She followed the brick walk through more pachysandra as Brazil's panic level crested. He cast his eyes toward his car on the street, realizing that by the time he raced to it, got in, and drove off, she would have his plate number. He decided to relax and feign innocence. He sat back down as she, in her white robe, floated closer.

"Why are you here?" she asked, hovering mere feet from him now.

"I didn't mean to be disturbing anyone," he apologized.

Hammer hesitated, not getting quite what she had expected. "It's almost two o'clock in the morning," she repeated.

"Actually, it's a little later than that," Brazil said, chin in hand, face shadowed. "Love this place, don't you? So peaceful, great for thinking, meditating, getting into your spiritual space."

Hammer was entertaining second thoughts about this one. She sat down on the bench, next to him.

"Who are you?" she asked, and the indirect light was an artist lovingly painting her face as she studied him.

"Nobody special," Brazil said.

Oh yes he was. She thought of her own horrible life, of the husband in there, where she lived. This one on the bench next to her understood. He appreciated her for who and what she was. He respected her power and wanted her as a woman at the same time. He was deeply interested in her thoughts, her ideas, her memories of childhood. Brazil traced her neck deep down into her plush white terry cloth robe, slowing down, taking his time. He kissed her, tentatively until he was sure she was kissing him back, then he worked on her lower lip until their tongues became acquainted and were friends.

When he woke up inside his locked bedroom, he wasn't finished yet and in agony. It was awful. Please Lord, why couldn't it be true? But it decidedly was not. It was a fact that he had sat in the tiny park staring at Hammer's house and she had come out to drift on her swing. It was not a fact that any of the rest of it had occurred, except in fractured dreams. She did not know that he was there in the dark, hearing her North Carolina flag snap in the wind, over her porch. She did not care. He had never touched his lips to hers, he had never caressed soft skin and never would. He was terribly ashamed. He was frustrated and confused. She was probably thirty years older than Brazil. This was sick. Something must be terribly wrong with him.

He had played the messages on his answering machine when he had come home at quarter of three in the morning. There had been four, all of them hang-ups. This had only worsened his mood. He could not help but think that the pervert was after him because he, too, was some sort of deviant. There had to be a reason a sick person would be drawn to him. Brazil was angry as he yanked on running clothes at dawn. He grabbed a tennis racquet, the hopper of balls, and trotted out the door.

The morning was wet with dew, the sun already making its potent presence known. Magnolias were dense and heavy with waxy white blossoms that smelled like lemon as he passed beneath them. He cut through the Davidson campus, sprinting along the small road winding behind Jackson Court, heading to the track. He ran six fast miles, and furiously served tennis balls. He worked out with weights in the gym, sprinted several laps, and did push-ups and sit-ups until his body's natural opiates kicked in.

Hammer was preoccupied with her ruined morning. This was what she got for altering her routine and having lunch with West, who clearly could not keep out of trouble. Hammer had worn her uniform this day, which in itself was exceedingly unusual. She had not found it necessary to argue court dates with the district attorney in fifteen years and wanted no problem here. She believed in the power of personal confrontations and determined that the D.A. was about to have one. By nine A.M. Hammer was inside the big granite Criminal Court Building, waiting in the reception area of the city's top prosecutor.

Nancy Gorelick had been reelected so many times she ran unopposed, and most of the population would not have bothered to go to the polls were there not other officials to vote for or against. She and Hammer were not personal friends. The D.A. certainly knew very well who the chief was and in fact had read about Hammer's heroics in the morning paper. Batman and Robin. Oh please. Gorelick was a ruthless Republican who believed in hanging first and sorting out later. She was tired of people who thought special excuses should be made for them, and there was no doubt in her mind about the reason for Hammer's impromptu visit.

Gorelick made Hammer wait long enough. By the time the D.A. buzzed her secretary to say that the chief could be shown in, Hammer was pacing the reception area, looking at her watch and getting more irritated by the second. The secretary opened a dark wooden door and Hammer strode past her.

"Good morning, Nancy," the chief said.

"Thank you." The D.A. nodded with a smile, hands folded on top of her neat desk. "What can I do for you, Judy?"

"You know about the incident at the Greyhound bus station yesterday."

"The whole world knows," said Gorelick.

Hammer pulled a chair around to the side of the desk, refusing to sit directly across from Gorelick with a big block of wood between them. There was little more valuable than office psychology, and Hammer was a master at it. Right now, the D.A.'s setup was blatantly overpowering and unwelcoming. Gorelick was leaning forward with hands on the blotter, assuming a posture of superiority and dominance. She was visibly bothered that Hammer had rearranged the order and was now facing the D.A., with nothing between them but crossed legs.

"The Johnny Martino case," Gorelick said.

"Yes," Hammer said. "Also known as Magic the Man."

"Thirty-three class D felony charges of robbery with a dangerous weapon," Gorelick went on. "He'll plea bargain. We'll sock him with maybe ten, get him to agree to consolidate sentencing under five counts. Since he's a prior record level two, he's going to be out of circulation for so long he'll turn into a skeleton."

"When do you anticipate setting the court date, Nancy?" Hammer wasn't impressed and, frankly, believed not a word. This guy would get the minimum. They all did.

"I've already set it." The D.A. picked up her big black date book and flipped pages. "Set for superior court, July twenty-second."

Hammer wanted to kill her. "I'm on vacation that entire week. In Paris. It's been set for a year. I'm taking my sons and their families, and I've already bought the tickets, Nancy. That's why I came by this morning. Both of us are busy professionals with crushing schedules and responsibilities. You know perfectly well, Nancy, that police chiefs normally do not make arrests and end up in court. When was the last time that you heard of such a thing? I'm asking you to work with me on this."

Gorelick didn't care who anybody was, especially not this chief of police with her personal wealth and fame. All in Gorelick's courtroom had jobs waiting for them, busy schedules, and demands on their time, except the defendants, of course, who generally had nothing in their Day Timers but empty spaces to fill with trouble. Gorelick had never been especially fond of Judy Hammer. The chief was arrogant, competitive, power drunk, noncollaborative, and vain. She spent considerable money on designer suits and pearls and accessories, and, in a word, did not suffer from the same problems, such as body fat, adult acne, estrogen volatilities, and rejection, as others.

"I was not elected to work with you or anyone," Gorelick stated. "It is my job to set trial dates that please the court, and that is what I have done. Vacation plans are not the business of the court, and you will have to make whatever adjustments are necessary. As will everyone else involved."

Hammer noted that Gorelick was overbuffed as usual. She had a penchant for short skirts, bright colors, and open necklines that were an invitation whenever she bent over to look at documents, dockets, or cases. She wore too much makeup, especially mascara. There were rumors about her many affairs, but Hammer had chosen to view these as unfounded until this moment. This was the woman the cops called the D.A. *Whorelick.* She was lower than dirt and a slut. Office psychology dictated that Hammer should get up from her chair.

She did, and leaned against the desk, helping herself to her opponent's domain, breathing all the air she wished, picking up a crystal paperweight of USBank and fiddling with it. Hammer was very comfortable and in charge. She spoke rationally, softly, and sincerely.

"The press, of course, has been calling me about yesterday's incident," Hammer confessed, and her fooling with the paperweight was clearly bothering Gorelick. "National press. The *Washington Post, Time, Newsweek, CBS This Morning,* Jay Leno, *New York Times,* Don Imus, Howard Stern." She began to pace, tapping the USBank in her palm, as if it were a slapjack. "They'll want to cover the trial, I'm sure. It's a big story, I guess." She paced and tapped. "I suppose when you stop to think about it, when has something like this ever happened? That reminds me." She laughed. "Some studio and a couple producers from Hollywood called, too. Can you imagine?"

Gorelick wasn't feeling well. "It is an unusual situation," she had to agree.

"An amazing example of community policing, Nancy. People doing the right thing." Hammer paced and gestured with the little crystal building wearing a crown. "Your treating a chief and deputy chief just like anyone else, making no special considerations." She nodded. "I think all those reporters are going to like that. Don't you?"

Gorelick would be ruined, would look like the dickhead she was. Someone would run against her next fall. She'd have to go work in a law firm as a lowly junior attorney to a bunch of overbearing partners who wouldn't want her to join their exclusive ranks.

"I'm going to tell them all about it." Hammer smiled at her. "Right now. I guess the best thing would be a press conference."

The court date was moved ahead a week and landed on a day

convenient for all, except Johnny Martino, a.k.a. Magic the Man, who was sitting in his jail cell, dejected in a blaze orange jumpsuit with DEPT OF CORR stenciled in on the back. Everybody in the Corr wore one, and now and then, when he gave much thought to the matter, he wondered what the hell the *Corr* was. As in Marine Corps, Peace Corps, *C&O RailRoad* maybe? His old man worked for Amtrak, cleaning up cars after all those passengers got off.

No way young Martino was ever doing shitwork like that. No fucking way. He couldn't believe how bad his leg hurt from where that bitch kicked him. The guns people carried these days, women especially. Both of them pointing *forty-fucking-caliber semiautomatics* at his head. Now where the hell did that come from? Fucking Mars? These ladies beam down, or something? He was still stunned and had sat up on his narrow bunk this morning thinking yesterday on the bus didn't happen.

Then he focused on the steel toilet bowl that he had not bothered to flush last night. His shin was throbbing so bad and had a lump on it the size of an orange, the skin broken in the middle, like a navel, where that pointy metal toe had connected. Now that he explored the situation a little further, he should have been suspicious of two rich ladies like that getting on the Greyhound. No way people like them take the bus. Some of the guys were talking and laughing up and down the cells, going on and on about him getting his ass kicked by some old woman with a big pocketbook, everybody making fun of Martino. He got out a cigarette and thought about suing. He thought about getting another tattoo, might as well while he was here.

Brazil's day was not going especially well, either. He and Packer were editing another self-initiated, rather large piece Brazil was doing on mothers alone in a world without men. Brazil continued to come across typos, spaces, blank lines that he knew he had not caused. Someone had been breaking into his computer basket and going through his files. He was explaining this to his metro editor, Packer, as they rolled through paragraphs, inspecting the violation.

"See," Brazil was hotly saying, and he was in uniform, ready for yet another night on the street. "It's weird. The last couple days I keep finding stuff like this."

"You sure you're not doing it? You do tend to go through your stories a lot," Packer said.

What the editor had observed about Brazil's remarkable productivity had now reached the level of *not humanly possible*. This kid dressed like a cop frightened Packer. Packer didn't even much want to sit next to Brazil anymore. Brazil wasn't normal. He was getting commendations from the police and averaging three bylines every morning, even on days when he supposedly was off. Not to mention, his work was unbelievably good for someone so inexperienced who had never been to journalism school. Packer suspected that Brazil would win a Pulitzer by the time he was thirty, possibly sooner. For that reason, Packer intended to remain Brazil's editor, even if the job was exhausting, intense, and unnerving, and caused Packer to hate life more with each passing day.

This morning was a typical example. The alarm had buzzed at six, and Packer did not want to get up. But he did. Mildred, his wife, was her cheery self, cooking oatmeal in the kitchen, while Dufus, her purebred Boston Terrier puppy, skittered around sideways and wall-eyed and looking for something else to chew, or pee or poop on. Packer was tucking in his shirt all the way around as he entered this domestic scene, trying to wake up, and wondering if his wife was losing what marbles she had left.

"Mildred," he said. "It's summer. Oatmeal is not a good hot-weather food."

"Of course it is." She happily stirred. "Good for your high blood pressure."

Dufus jumped and fussed at Packer, dancing around his feet, trying to climb him, grabbing cuffs in snaggly teeth. Packer never touched his wife's puppy if he could help it and had refused any input into its development beyond naming it, over objections from Mildred, who had made it a condition of their marriage that she would never be without one of these ugly little dogs from her childhood. Dufus did not see very well. From his perspective, Packer was a very big and unfriendly tree, a utility pole, some other edifice, maybe a fence. Whenever Packer came within scent, Dufus was airborne and in grass and squatting and relieving other basic functions that meant nothing to Dufus. He untied both of Packer's shoelaces.

Packer made his way across the newsroom as if he saw no color in the world, only gray. He was tucking in his shirt, heading to the men's room, feeling like he had to go and knowing nothing would happen again and reminded that next Wednesday at two P.M., he had an appointment with his urologist.

Brazil was running down the escalator, deciding to take matters into his own hands. He pushed through several sets of doors, finally entering the rarified air-conditioned space where Brenda Bond ruled the world from an ergonomically correct green fabric chair with rollers. Her feet were on an adjustable footrest, her valuable hands poised over a contoured keyboard designed to prevent carpal tunnel syndrome.

Bond was surrounded by IBM and Hewlett Packard mainframes, multiplexors, modems, cabinets containing huge tape reels, decoders, and a satellite feed from the Associated Press. It was her cockpit, and he had come. She could not believe that Brazil was standing before her, had sought her out, and wanted to be with her and no one but her this very second in time and space. Her face got hot as she looked him up and down. God almighty, was he built, and he knew it, and was already showing his contempt for her.

"I think someone's getting into my basket and going through my files," Brazil announced.

"Impossible," Bond, the genius, arrogantly told him. "Unless you've given out your password."

"I want it changed," he demanded.

She was studying his uniform trousers and the way they fit him, particularly in the area of his zipper, appropriating and full of her superiority. Brazil made a big point of looking where she was looking, as if there must be something on his pants.

"What? I spill something?" he said, walking off.

It was not that his trousers were too tight, nor were they provocative in any way. Brazil never wore anything for the purpose of drawing attention to himself or impressing others. For one thing, shopping had never been an option. The entirety of his wardrobe could be accommodated by two dresser drawers and about twenty coat hangers. Mostly, he had uniforms, and tennis clothes supplied by the tennis team and by Wilson, which had put him on a free list when he was in high school and consistently ranked in the top five juniors in the state. Brazil's uniform trousers were, in truth, baggy if anything. Yet people like Brenda Bond still stared. So did Axel.

When Brazil was in midnight blue and black leather, he had no idea what effect it had on others. If he had paused to analyze the matter, he might have discovered that uniforms were about power, and power was an aphrodisiac. Axel knew this for a fact. He got up and trotted out of the newsroom, in pursuit. Brazil was notorious for his sprints down the escalator and into the parking deck. Axel worked out in the Powerhouse Gym every early morning and was rather spectacularly sculpted.

Axel drank Met-Rx twice a day and was very much admired when he was gleaming with sweat and in a tank top and a weight belt, pumping, veins standing out, in his skimpy shorts. Other fit people stopped what they were doing just to watch. He had been stalked several times by residents of his apartment complex. In truth, Tommy Axel could have anybody and probably had at any given time. But he was not into aerobic exercise because it was not a spectator sport. He got winded easily.

"Shoot," Axel said when he burst through glass doors leading into the parking deck, as Brazil was driving his old BMW out of it.

Publisher Panesa had a black-tie dinner this night and was going home unusually early. The publisher was starting his silver Volvo, with its unrivaled safety record and two airbags, and was witness to Axel's shameless behavior.

"Christ," Panesa muttered, shaking his head as he pulled out of his reserved space in the center of the best wall, no more than twenty steps from the front glass doors. He rolled down a window, stopping Axel cold.

"Come here," Panesa told him.

Axel gave his boss a crooked, sexy Matt Dillon smile and strolled over. Who could resist? "What's going on?" Axel said, moving in a way that showed muscle to its best advantage.

"Axel, leave him alone," Panesa said.

"Excuse me?" Axel touched his chest in pure hurt innocence.

"You know exactly what I mean." Panesa roared off, fastening his shoulder harness, locking doors, checking mirrors, and snapping up the mike of his private frequency two-way radio to let the housekeeper know he was en route.

The longer Panesa had worked in the newspaper business, the more paranoid he had become. Like Brazil, Panesa had started out as a police reporter, and by the time he was twenty-three, knew every filthy, nasty, cruel, and painful thing people did to one another. He had done stories on murdered children, on hit and runs, and husbands in black gloves and knit caps stabbing estranged wives and friends before cutting their throats and flying to Chicago. Panesa had interviewed women who lovingly seasoned home cooking with arsenic, and he had covered car wrecks, plane crashes, train derailments, skydiving gone bad, scuba diving gone worse, bungee jumping by drunks who forgot the cord, and fires and drownings. Not to mention other horrors that did not end in death. His marriage, for example.

Panesa frantically ran through downtown traffic like a Green Bay Packer, cutting in and out, the hell with you, honk all you want, get out of my way. He was going to be late again. It never failed. His date tonight was Judy Hammer, who apparently was married to a slob. Hammer avoided taking her husband out in public when she could, and Panesa did not blame her, if the rumor was true. Tonight was USBank's Public Service Awards banquet, and both Panesa and Hammer were being honored, as was District Attorney Gorelick, who had been in the news a lot lately, scorching the N.C. General Assembly for not coughing up enough money to hire seventeen more assistant D.A.s, when it was clear that what the Charlotte-Mecklenburg region really needed was another medical examiner or two. The banquet was held at the Carillon, with its wonderful paintings and mobiles. Panesa was driving.

Hammer's personal car was a Mercedes, but not new and with only one airbag, on the driver's side. Panesa would not ride in anything that did not have a passenger's side airbag, and this had been made clear up front. Hammer, too, was rushing home early from the office. Seth was working in the garden, weeding and fertilizing. He had made cookies, and Hammer smelled the baked butter and sugar. She noted the telltale traces of flour on the counter. Seth waved a handful of wild onions at her as she peered out the kitchen window at him. He was civil enough.

She was in a hurry as she headed to her bedroom. God, the image staring back at her in the mirror was frightening. She washed her face, squirted nonalcohol styling gel into her hands and riffled through her hair. She started all over again with makeup. Black-tie affairs were always a problem. Men owned one tux and wore it to everything, or they rented. What were women supposed to do? She hadn't given any thought to what she might put on until she was walking into a house that smelled like a bakery. She pulled out a black satin skirt, a gold and black beaded short-waisted jacket, and a black silk blouse with spaghetti straps.

The truth was, Hammer had gained four pounds since she had worn this ensemble last at a Jaycee's fundraiser in Pineville about a year ago, if memory served her well. She managed to button her skirt but was not happy about it. Her bosom was more out front than usual, and she did not like drawing attention to what she normally kept to herself. She irritably yanked her beaded jacket around her, muttering, wondering if dry-cleaning might have shrunk anything and the fault, therefore, not hers. Changing earrings to simple diamond posts with screw-backs was always troublesome when she was rushed and out of sorts.

"Darn," she said, closing the drain just in time before a gold back sailed down the sink.

Panesa did not need a personal shopper, had no weight concerns, and could wear whatever he wished whenever he wished. He was an officer in the Knight-Ridder newspaper chain, and preferred black-label Giorgio Armani that he did not get in Charlotte. Hornets fans had priorities other than draping themselves in two-thousand-dollar foreign suits, it seemed, and shopping remained a difficulty in the Queen City. Panesa was as it turned out dazzling in a tuxedo with satin lapels and trousers with stripes. His was black silk, and he wore a matte-finished gold watch and black lizard shoes.

"So tell me," Panesa said when Hammer climbed into the Volvo. "What's your secret?"

"What secret?" Hammer had no idea what this was about as she fastened her shoulder harness.

"You look stunning."

"Of course I don't," Hammer said.

Panesa backed out of the driveway, checking his mirrors, noticing the fat man working on geraniums. The fat man was watching them leave, and Panesa pretended not to notice as he adjusted the air conditioning.

"Do you shop around here?" Panesa asked.

"Lord, I need to." Hammer sighed, for when did she have time?

"Let me guess. Montaldo's."

"Never," Hammer told him. "Have you noticed how they treat you in places like that? They want to sell me something because I can afford it and then treat me like an inferior. If I'm so inferior, I ask myself, then why are they the ones selling hose and lingerie?"

"That is absolutely the truth," said Panesa, who had never shopped in a store that did not have clothes for men. "Same thing in some restaurants I won't go to anymore."

"Morton's," Hammer supposed, although she had never eaten there.

"Not if you're on their V.I.P. list. They give you a little card, and you can always get a table and good service." Panesa switched lanes.

"Police officials have to be careful of things like that," Hammer reminded the publisher, whose paper would have been the first to print a story about Hammer's V.I.P. status or any other special favors possibly resulting in one establishment getting more police protection than another.

"Truth is, I don't eat much red meat anymore," Panesa added.

They were passing the Traveler's Hotel, upstairs from the Presto Grill, which Hammer and West had made rather famous of late. Panesa smiled as he drove, reminded of Brazil's Batman and Robin story. The hotel was a horrific dive, Hammer thought as she looked out her window. Appropriately, it was across Trade Street from the city's unemployment office and next door to the Dirty Laundry Cleaner & Laundry. No eating or drinking was allowed in the lobby of the Traveler's. They'd had an axe murder there several years earlier. Or was that the Uptown Motel? Hammer couldn't remember.

"How do you stay in shape?" Panesa continued the small talk.

"I walk whenever I can. I don't eat fat," Hammer replied, digging in her purse for lipstick.

"That's not fair. I know women who walk on the treadmill an hour every day, and their legs don't look like yours," Panesa observed. "I want to know precisely what the difference is."

"Seth eats everything in my house." Hammer was out with it. "He eats so much, I lose my appetite on a regular basis. You know what it does to you to walk in at eight o'clock, after a hellish day, and see your husband parked in front of the TV, watching 'Ellen,' eating his third bowl of Hormel chili with beef and beans?"

Then the rumors were true, and Panesa suddenly felt sorry for Hammer. The publisher of *The Charlotte Observer* went home to no one but a housekeeper who prepared chicken breasts and spinach salads. How awful for Hammer. Panesa looked over at his peer in satin and beads. Panesa took the risk of reaching out and patting Hammer's hand.

"That sounds absolutely awful," the publisher sympathized.

"I actually need to lose a few pounds," Hammer confessed. "But I tend to put it on around my middle, not my legs."

Panesa searched for parking around the Carillon, where Morton's of Chicago steak house was doing quite a business without them. "Watch your door there. Sorry," Panesa said. "I'm a little close to the meter. I don't guess I need to put anything in it?"

"Not after six," said Hammer, who knew.

She thought how nice it would be to have a friend like Panesa. Panesa thought how nice it would be to go sailing with Hammer, or jet skiing, or do lunch or Christmas shopping together, or just talk in front of the fire. Getting drunk was also a thought when normally it was a big problem for the publisher of a nationally acclaimed newspaper or the chief of a formidable police department. Hammer had overdone it with Seth now and then, but it was pointless. He ate. She passed out. Panesa had gotten drunk alone, which was worse, especially if he had forgotten to let the dog back in.

Being drunk was a rarified form of beaming-out-of-here, and it was all about timing. It was not something that Hammer ever discussed with anyone. Panesa did not, either. Neither of them had a therapist at this time. This was why it was rather much a miracle that the two of them, after three glasses of wine, got on the subject while someone from USBank was pontificating about economic incentives and development and company relocations and the nonexistent crime rate in Charlotte. Panesa and Hammer hardly touched the salmon with dill sauce. They switched to Wild Turkey. Neither of them fully recalled receiving their awards, but all who witnessed it thought Hammer and Panesa were animated, witty, gracious, and articulate.

On the way home, Panesa got the daring idea of tucking his car near Latta Park in Dilworth and playing tunes and talking, with headlights out. Hammer was not in the mood to go home. Panesa knew that going home was soon followed by getting up in the morning and going to work. His career was not as interesting as it used to be, but he had yet to admit this even to himself. His children were busy with involved lives. Panesa was dating a lawyer who liked watching tapes of Court TV and talking about what she would have done differently. Panesa wanted out.

"I guess we should go," Hammer volunteered, about an hour into their sitting inside the dark Volvo and talking.

"You're right," said Panesa, who had a trophy in the backseat and an emptiness in his heart. "Judy, I have to say something."

"Please," said Hammer.

"Do you have a friend or two you just have fun with?"

"No."

"I don't either," Panesa confessed. "Don't you think that's rather incredible?"

Hammer took a moment to analyze. "No," she decided. "I never had a friend or two. Not in grammar school, when I was better than everyone in kickball. Not in high school, when I was good in math and the president of the student body. Not in college. Not in the police academy, now that I think about it."

"I was good in English," Panesa thought back. "And dodgeball, I guess. A president of the Bible Club one year, but don't hold that against me. Another year on the varsity basketball team but horrible, fouled out the one game I played in when we were forty points behind."

"What are you getting at, Richard?" asked Hammer, whose nature it was to walk fast and rush to the point.

Panesa was silent for a moment. "I think people like us need friends," he decided.

West needed friends, too, but she would never admit this to Brazil, who was determined to solve every crime in the city that night. West was smoking. Brazil was eating a Snickers bar when the scanner let them know that any unit in the area of Dundeen and Redbud might want to look for a dead body in a field. Flashlights cut across darkness, the sound of feet moving through weeds and grass as Brazil and West searched the dark. He was obsessed and managed to get ahead of West, his flashlight sweeping. She grabbed him by the back of his shirt, yanking him behind her, like a bad puppy.

"You mind if I go first?" West asked him.

Panesa stopped in Fourth Ward, in front of Hammer's house, at twenty minutes past one A.M. "Well, congratulations on your award," Panesa said again.

"And to you," Hammer said, gripping the door handle.

"Okay, Judy. Let's do this again one of these days."

"Absolutely. Award or not." Hammer could see the TV flickering through curtains. Seth was up and probably eating a Tombstone pizza.

"I really appreciate your allowing Brazil to be out with your folks. It's been good for us," Panesa said.

"For us, too."

"So be it. Anything innovative, I'm all for it," said Panesa. "Doesn't happen often."

"Rare as hen's teeth," Hammer agreed.

"Isn't that the truth."

"Absolutely."

Panesa controlled his impulse to touch her. "I need to go," he said.

"It's late," she completely agreed.

Hammer finally lifted the door handle, letting herself out. Panesa drove off in the direction of his empty house and felt blue. Hammer walked into her space, where Seth lived and ate, and was lonely.

West and Brazil were working hard and unmindful of the time. They had just pulled up to the federally subsidized housing project of Earle Village and entered apartment 121, where there were suspicious signs of money. A computer was on the coffee table, along with a lot of cash, a calculator, and a pager. An elderly woman was composed on the couch, her raging old drunk boyfriend dancing in front of her, his finger parried at her. Police were in the room, assessing the problem.

"She pulled a .22 revolver on me!" the boyfriend was saying.

"Ma'am," West said. "Do you have a gun?"

"He was threatening me," the woman told Brazil.

Her name was Rosa Tinsley, and she was neither drunk nor excited. In fact, she didn't get this much attention except once a week, when the police came. She was having a fine time. Billy could just hop around, threaten away like he always did when he went to the nip joint and lost money in poker.

"Come in here doing all his drug deals," Rosa went on to Brazil. "Gets drunk and says he's gonna cut my throat."

"Are there drugs here?" West asked.

Rosa nodded at Brazil and gestured toward the back of the house. "The shoe box in my closet," she announced.

Chapter Fourteen

There were many shoe boxes in Rosa's closet, and West and Brazil went through all of them. They found no drugs, the boyfriend was evicted, and Rosa was rewarded with instant gratification. West and Brazil headed back to their car. Brazil felt they had accomplished a good thing. That rotten, stinking, besotted old man was out of there. The poor woman would have some peace. She was safe.

"I guess we got rid of them," Brazil commented with pride.

"She was just scaring him, like she does once a week," West replied. "They'll be back together by the time we drive off."

She started the engine, watching the old boyfriend in her rearview mirror. He was standing on the sidewalk, carrying his things, staring at the dark blue Crown Victoria, waiting for it to disappear.

"One of these days he'll probably kill her," West added.

She hated domestic cases. Those and dog bite reports were the most unpredictable and dangerous to the police. Citizens called the cops, and then resented the intervention. It was all very irrational. But perhaps the worst feature of people like Rosa and their boyfriends was the codependency, the inability to do without the other, no matter how many times partners brandished knives and guns, slapped, stole, and threatened. West had a difficult time dealing with people who wallowed in dysfunction and went from one abusive relationship to the next, never gaining insight and hurting life. It was her opinion that Brazil should not live with his mother.

"Why don't you get an apartment and be on your own for once?" West said to him.

"Can't afford it." Brazil typed on the MDT.

"Sure you can."

"No, I can't." He typed some more. "A one-bedroom apartment in a decent neighborhood is about five hundred a month."

"So?" West looked over at him. "And your car is paid for, right? You owe any money to Davidson?"

It wasn't any of her business.

"You could afford it," West preached on. "What you got is a sick relationship. You don't get away from her, you'll grow old together."

"Oh really?" Brazil looked up at West, not appreciating her remarks in the least. "You know all about it, do you?"

"I'm afraid so," West said. "In case you haven't figured it out yet, Andy, you aren't the first person in the world to have a codependent, enabling relationship with a parent or spouse. Your mother's crippling, self-destructive disease is her choice. And it serves one important function. It controls her son. She doesn't want you to leave, and guess what? So far you haven't."

This was also Hammer's problem, although she had yet to face it fully. Seth, too, was a cripple. When his powerful, handsome wife breezed in with her trophy in the early morning hours, he was surfing hundreds of cable channels made possible by his eighteen-inch satellite dish on the back porch. Seth liked country western music and was looking for just the right band. It was not true that he was eating a Tombstone pizza. That had been earlier, when it had gotten to be midnight and his wife still was not home. Now he was working on popcorn drenched with real butter he had melted in the microwave.

Seth Bridges had never been much to look at. Physical beauty was not what had attracted Judy Hammer to him long ago in Little Rock. She had loved his intelligence and gentle patience. They had started out as friends, the way everyone would were the world filled with good sense. The problem lay in Seth's capacity. He grew as his wife did for the first ten years. Then he maxed out, and simply could stretch no further as a spiritual, enlightened, big-thinking entity. There was no other way to broaden himself unless he did so in the flesh. Eating, frankly, was what he now did best.

Hammer locked the front door and reset the burglar alarm, making sure the motion sensors were on stay. The house smelled like a movie theater, and she detected a hint of pepperoni beneath a buttery layer of chilled air. Her husband was stretched out on the couch, crunching, fingers shiny with grease as he stuffed popcorn inside a mouth that never completely rested. She walked through the living room without comment as stations changed as fast as Seth could point and shoot. In her bedroom, she angrily set the trophy on the floor in a closet with others she never remembered.

She was overwhelmed with fury and slammed the door, tore her clothes off, and threw them in a chair. She put on her favorite nightshirt and grabbed her pistol out of her pocketbook and walked back out into the living room. She'd had it. No more. Enough. Every mortal had limits. Seth froze mid-shovel when his wife marched in, armed.

"Why drag it out?" she said, towering over him in blue and white striped cotton. "Why not just kill yourself and get it over with? Go ahead."

She racked the pistol and offered it to him, butt first. Seth

stared at it. He had never seen her like this, and he propped himself up on his elbows.

"What happened tonight?" he asked. "You and Panesa get into
a fight or something?"

"Quite the opposite. If you want to end it, go ahead."

"You're crazy," he said.

"That's right, well on my way to it, thanks to you." His wife
lowered the gun and put the safety on. "Seth, tomorrow you go for
help. A psychiatrist and your primary care physician. You
straighten yourself out. Starting this minute. You're a pig. A slob. A
bore. You're committing slow suicide and I do not intend to watch
a minute longer." She snatched the bowl of popcorn out of his oily
hands. "You don't get it fixed, I'm out of here. Period."

Brazil and West also were suffering aftershocks from their con-
frontation in her unmarked car. They had continued arguing about
his living situation, by now both of them in a lather as they drove
through another rough area of the city. Brazil was glaring at her
and not particularly cognizant of the area or its bad people who
were thinking violent thoughts about the cop car cruising past.
Brazil wondered what possessed him to want to spend so much of
his valuable time with this rude, insensitive, inappropriate deputy
chief who was old and backward and, in truth, a jerk.

It seemed that fighting was a cloud layer over the Queen City,
and Panesa's pleasant mood had deteriorated as well when his
lawyer friend called at the precise moment Hammer was locking
her bedroom door and West was telling Brazil to grow up and
Bubba was on the prowl in his King Cab. The lawyer had been
thinking about Panesa, whom she had observed on the late news, in
his stunning tuxedo, receiving a trophy. The lawyer was thinking
about Panesa and his silver hair and wanted to drop by and maybe

stay over. Panesa made it clear that this was not possible and never would be again, as Bubba parked in dark shadows near Latta Park.

Bubba was in camouflage, a black cap pulled low. When he stealthily reached West's house, he was pleased that she wasn't home. Bubba could only suppose that she was being screwed by her sissy boyfriend, and Bubba smiled as he imagined her getting screwed again by Bubba, as he sneaked closer to the front of the brick house. His intention wasn't felonious but would ruin the bitch's mood when she couldn't open her front or back doors because someone had filled the locks with Super Glue. This idea had come from yet another of his anarchist manuals and might well have worked like a charm had circumstances not conspired against him as he unfolded his Buck knife and cut off the tip from the tube of glue.

A car was coming, and Bubba wisely supposed it might be the cop returning home. It was too late to run, and he dove into the hedge. The Cavalier wagon passed, carrying Ned Toms to The Fish Market, where he was about to start his shift, unpacking seafood from boxes of ice. He noticed what he supposed was a big dog moving around in bushes in front of a house where he often saw an unmarked cop car parked, then his Cavalier was gone like a breeze.

Bubba emerged from the hedge, his fingers glued together and left hand completely fastened to the right inner thigh of his fatigues. He rapidly hobbled away, looking remarkably like a hunchback. He could not unlock his truck or drive without freeing one hand, and this required his removing his pants, which he was in the process of doing when Officer Wood happened by on routine patrol, checking the park for perverts. Bubba was arrested for indecent exposure.

West and Brazil heard the call over the scanner but were not even close and were busy discussing Brazil's life.

"What the hell do you know about my mother or why I choose to take care of her?" Brazil was saying.

"I know a lot. Social services, juvenile court, are overwhelmed by cases just like yours," West said.

"I've never been a social service case. Or in juvenile court."

"Yet," she reminded him.

"Mind your own business for once."

"Get a life," she said. "Declare your independence. Go out on a date."

"Oh, so now I don't date, either," he snapped.

She laughed. "When? While you're brushing your teeth? You're out every night working and then show up in the newsroom by nine, after you've run your ass off around the track and hit a million tennis balls. You tell me when you date, Andy? Huh?"

Fortunately, Radar the dispatcher hailed them exactly at this moment. Apparently there was an assault on Monroe Road.

"Unit 700 responding," Brazil irritably said into the mike.

"They call you Night Voice," West told him.

"Who's they?" he wanted to know.

"Cops. They know when you get on the radio that you're not me."

"Because my voice is deeper? Or maybe because I use proper grammar?" he said.

West was making her way through more menacing-looking government-subsidized housing. She was constantly checking her mirrors. "Where the hell are my backups?" she said.

Brazil had his eye on something else, and excitedly pointed. "White van, EWR-117," he said. "From the APB earlier."

The van was moving slowly around a corner, and West sped up. She flipped on lights and siren, and twenty minutes later, cops hauled someone else to jail as West and Brazil drove on.

Radar wasn't finished with them yet. A call came in for a car broken into at Trade and Tryon, and he assigned this to unit 700 as well, while other cops rode around with nothing much to do.

"Subject a black male, no shirt, green shorts. May be armed," Radar's voice came over the scanner.

At the scene, West and Brazil discovered a Chevrolet Caprice with a smashed windshield. The upset owner, Ben Martin, was a law-abiding citizen. He'd had his fill of crime and violence and did not deserve to have his brand-new Caprice mauled like this. For what? His wife's coupon book that looked like a wallet in the backseat? Some shithead hooligan destroyed Martin's hard-earned ride to get fifty cents off Starkist albacore tuna, or Uncle Ben's, or Maxwell House?

"Last night, same thing happened to my neighbor over there," Martin was explaining to the cops. "And the Baileys over there got hit the night before that."

What had gone wrong in the world? Martin remembered being a boy in Rock Hill, South Carolina, where they did not lock their doors and a burglar alarm was when you walked in on the sucker cleaning you out and he was surprised. So you beat the fool out of him, and that was the end of it. Now there was nothing but randomness, and strangers brutalizing a new Caprice for manufacturers' coupons camouflaged by a red fabric wallet fastened with Velcro.

Brazil happened to notice a black male in green shorts running a block away, headed toward the dark, ancient Settlers Cemetery. "That's him!" Brazil shouted.

"Get on the radio!" West ordered.

She took off. It was instinct and had nothing to do with reality, which revealed her as a middle-aged, out of shape, Bojangles-addicted smoker. She was at least a hundred feet behind the subject and already heaving. She was sweating and clumsy, her body and heavy Sam Browne belt simply not designed for this. The bastard had no shirt on, his muscles rippling beneath gleaming ebony skin. He was a damn lynx. How the hell was she supposed to catch something like this? No way. Subjects didn't used to be this fit. They didn't used to drink Met-Rx and have fitness clubs in every jail.

Even as she was thinking these thoughts, Brazil passed her, flying like an Olympic athlete. He was gaining on Green Shorts, closing in as they entered the cemetery. Brazil zeroed in on the muscular V-shaped back. This dude had maybe five percent body fat, was shiny with sweat, running his scrawny butt off and believing he would get away with stealing that coupon book. Brazil shoved him as hard as he could from the rear and sent him sprawling to the grass, coupons fluttering. Brazil jumped on top of Green Shorts and dug a knee in the common thief's spine. Brazil pressed his Mag-Lite, like a gun, against Green Shorts's skull.

"Move I'll blow your brains out motherfucker!" Brazil screamed.

He looked up, proud of himself. West had finally gotten around to showing up, heaving and sweating. She would have a heart attack, of this she was certain.

"I stole that line from you," Brazil told her.

She managed to detach handcuffs from the back of her belt, having no clear recollection of when she might have used them last. Was it when she was a sergeant and got in a foot pursuit with a sh'im in Fourth Ward, way back when, or in Fat Man's? She felt lightheaded, blood pounding her neck and ears. West traced her deterioration back to her thirty-fifth year when, coincidentally, Niles had deposited himself on her back stoop one Saturday night. Abyssinians were exotic and quite expensive. They were also difficult and eccentric, possibly explaining why Niles had been available for adoption. Even West had moments when she wanted to boot him out the car door on one of life's highways. Why the scrawny, cross-eyed kitten with memories of the pyramids had picked West remained unknown.

The stress brought on by Niles's addition to the family precipitated a self-destructiveness in West that had nothing to do with her growing isolation as she continued to get promoted in a man's world. Her increased smoking, consumption of fat and beer, and her refusal to exercise were completely unrelated to her breaking up with Jimmy Dinkins, who was allergic to Niles, and frankly hated the cat to the point of pulling his gun on Niles one night when Dinkins and West were arguing and Niles decided to insert himself by pouncing on Dinkins from the top of the refrigerator.

West was still sweating, her breathing labored, as she led their prisoner back to the car. She thought she might throw up.

"You got to quit smoking," Brazil said to her.

West stuffed the subject into the back of the car, and Brazil climbed in the front.

"You got any idea how much fat's in Bojangles, and all that other shit you eat?" Brazil went on.

Their prisoner was silent, his eyes bright with hate in the rearview mirror. His name was Nate Laney. He was fourteen. He would kill these white cops. All he needed was a chance. Laney was bad and had been since birth, according to his biological mother, who also had always been bad, according to her own mother. This bad seed could be traced back to a prison in England, where the original bad seed had been shipped out to this country around the same time the troops in the Queen City had been chasing Cornwallis down the road.

"I bet you never exercise." Brazil did not know when to quit.

West gave him a look as she wiped her flushed face with a tissue. Brazil had just sprinted a hundred yards and wasn't even breathing. She felt old and crabby, and sick and tired of this kid and his naive, self-righteous opinions. Life was entirely more complicated than he thought, and he would begin to see it for himself after he'd been out here a year or two with nothing but fried chicken places on every corner. Bojangles, Church's, Popeye's, Chic N Grill, Chick-Fil-A, Price's Chicken Coop. Plus, cops didn't make much money, certainly not in their early years, so even off-duty options for dining were limited to the pizza, burgers, and bar food that were plentiful in Charlotte, where citizens loved their Hornets and Panthers and NASCAR race-car drivers.

"When was the last time you played tennis?" Brazil asked as their prisoner plotted in the backseat.

"I don't remember," she said.

"Why don't we go out and hit some."

"You need your head examined," she said.

"Oh come on. You used to be good. I bet you used to be in shape, too," he said.

The massive concrete jail was in the heart of downtown. It had been built at the same time as the big new police department, in this city that enjoyed a crime clearance rate that exceeded the actual number of cases, according to some. There were many levels of security to go through at the jail, starting with lockers where police were to deposit their guns on the way in. At a desk, deputies checked all who entered, and Brazil looked around, taking in yet another new, scary place. A Pakistani woman in dark clothing and a veil was being processed for shoplifting. Drunks, thieves, and the usual drug dealers were being herded by cops, while the sheriff's department supervised.

In the Central Warrant Repository, West searched her prisoner, emptying his pockets of Chap Stick, one dollar and thirteen cents, and a pack of Kools. She shuffled through his paperwork. He was happy now, laughing, full of himself, checking to see who was watching Nate the Man.

"You able to read?" West asked him.

"My bond on there?" Her prisoner was jailing, wearing three pairs of boxer shorts, two pairs of shorts, the outer ones green, falling off, no belt, looking around and unable to stand still.

"'Fraid not," West said.

Inside blue metal solitary holding cells, another young boy beyond redemption stared out with forlorn, killing eyes. Brazil stared back at him. Brazil looked at the Holding Area, where a cage was packed with men waiting to be transported to the jail on Spector Drive until the Department of Corrections transferred them to Camp Green or Central Prison. The men were quiet, peering out, gripping bars like animals in the zoo, nothing else to do in their jail house orange.

"I ain't been in here in a while," West's prisoner let her know.

"How long's a while?" West completed an inventory of Nate the Man's belongings.

Nate Laney shrugged, moving around, looking. "'Bout two months," he said.

Chapter Fifteen

West and Brazil ended their ride with breakfast at the Presto Grill. He was wide-eyed and ready for adventure. She was worn out, a new day just begun. She went home long enough to notice a tube of Super Glue in her shrubbery. Nearby was an open Buck knife. She barely remembered hearing something on the scanner about a subject exposing himself in Latta Park. It seemed glue was involved. West bagged possible evidence, getting an odd feeling about why it might have landed in her yard. She fed Niles. At nine A.M., West accompanied Hammer through the atrium of City Hall.

"What the hell are you doing with a summons book in your car?" Hammer was saying, walking fast.

This had gone too far. Her deputy chief had been out all night in foot pursuits. She had been locking people up.

"Just because I'm a deputy chief doesn't mean I can't enforce the law," West said, trying to keep up, nodding at people they passed in the corridor.

"I can't believe you're writing tickets. Morning, John. Ben. Locking people up. Hi, Frank." She greeted other city councilmen. "You're going to end up in court again. As if I can spare you. Your summons book gets turned in to me today."

West laughed. This was one of the funniest things she'd heard in a while. "I will not!" she said. "What did you tell me to do? Huh? Whose idea was it for me to go back out on the street?" Her sleep deficit was making her giddy.

Hammer threw her hands up in despair as they walked into a room where a special city council meeting had been called by the mayor. It was packed with citizens, reporters, and television crews. People instantly were on their feet, in an uproar, when the two women police officials walked in.

"Chief!"

"Chief Hammer, what are we going to do about crime in the east end?"

"Police don't understand the black community!"

"We want our neighborhoods back!"

"We build a new jail but don't teach our children how to stay out of it!"

"Business downtown has dropped twenty percent since these se- rial killing–car jackings started!" another citizen shouted.

"What are we doing about them? My wife's scared to death."

Hammer was up front now, taking the microphone. Councilmen sat around a polished horseshoe-shaped table, polished brass nameplates marking their place in the city's government. All eyes were on the first police chief in Charlotte's history to make people feel important, no matter where they lived or who they were. Judy Hammer was the only mother some folks had ever known, in a way, and her deputy was pretty cool, too, out there with the rest of them, trying to see for herself what the problems were.

"We will take our neighborhoods back by preventing the next crime." Hammer spoke in her strong voice. "Police can't do it with- out your help. No more looking the other way and walking past." She, the evangelist, pointed at all. "No more thinking that what happens to your neighbor is your neighbor's problem. We are one body." She looked around. "What happens to you, happens to me."

No one moved. Eyes never left her as she stood before all and spoke a truth that power brokers from the past had not wanted the people to hear. The people had to take their streets, their neighborhoods, their cities, their states, their countries, their world, back. Each person had to start looking out his window, do his own bit of policing in his own part of life, and get irate when something happened to his neighbor. Yes sir. Rise up. Be a Minuteman, a Christian soldier.

"Onward," Hammer told them. "Police yourself and you won't need us."

The room was frenzied. That night, West was ironically reminded of the overwhelming response as she and Brazil sped past the stadium rising eerily, hugely, against the night, filled with crazed, cheering fans celebrating Randy Travis. West's Crown Victoria was directed and in a hurry as it passed the convention center where a huge video display proclaimed WELCOME TO THE QUEEN CITY. In the distance, cop cars went fast, lights strobing blue and red, protesting another terrible violation. Brazil, too, could not help but think of the timing, after all Hammer had said this morning. He was angry as they drove.

West knew fear she would not show. How could this happen again? What about the task force she had handpicked, the Phantom Force, as it had been dubbed, out day and night to catch the Black Widow Killer? She could not help but think of the press conference and its excerpts on radio and television. West was tempted to wonder if this might be more than coincidental, as if someone was making a mockery of Charlotte and its police and its people.

The killing had occurred off Trade Street, behind a crumbling brick building where the stadium and the Duke Power transfer station were in close view. West and Brazil approached the disorienting strobing of emergency lights, heading toward an area cordoned off by yellow crime-scene tape. Beyond were railroad tracks and a late-model white Maxima, its driver's door open, interior light on, and bell dinging. West flipped open her portable phone and tried her boss's number again. For the past ten minutes, the phone had been busy because Hammer had one son on call waiting and the other on the line. When Hammer hung up, her phone immediately rang with more bad news.

Four minutes later, she drove out of her Fourth Ward neighborhood in a hurry as West folded the phone and handed it to Brazil. He returned it to the leather case on his belt, where there was plenty of room since volunteers packed light. Brazil was pleased to attach anything to his belt that was *road legal*, a Charlottean term, the etymology of which could be traced back to NASCAR gods and the rockets they drove, not one of which, in fact, was permitted on life's highways unless it was chained to a trailer. Brazil envied what most cops complained about. Backaches, inconvenience, and being encumbered did not enter his mind.

Of course, he carried a radio with channels for all response areas, the antenna stubby and prone to probe very short officers' armpits. Brazil also wore a pager no one ever called, a Mini Mag-Lite with two thousand two hundred candlepower in its black leather holster, and West's cellular phone, because he was not allowed to carry the *Observer*'s cellular phone when he was in uniform. Brazil had no gun or pepper spray. His ultra duty belt was without expandable baton, nightstick ring, double magazine holders, handcuffs, or double cuff case. Brazil lacked a long flashlight case or Pro-3 duty holster or clip holder, and had not a single molded belt keeper or for that matter a silent keyholder with Velcro wraparound flap.

West had all this and more. She was fully loaded, and Niles could hear her coming from the far reaches of the city. Minute by minute, the seven-pound Abyssinian waited for the sound, listening for the beloved clanking and creaking and heavy landings. His disappointment was becoming chronic and broaching unforgivable as he sat in his window over the sink, watching and waiting and increasingly fixated by the USBank Corporate Center (USBCC) dominating the sky. Niles in his earlier lives had been intimate with the greatest erections in all of civilization, the pyramids, the magnificent tombs of pharaohs.

In the fantasies of Niles, USBCC was the giant King Usbeecee, with his silver crown, and it was simply a matter of time before his majesty shook loose of his moorings. He would turn right and left, looking at his feeble neighbors. Niles imagined the king stepping slowly, heavily, feeling his way, shaking earth, for the first time. He aroused Niles's fearful reverence because the king had no smile, and when his eyes caught the sun and turned gold, they were overpowering, as was the mighty monarch's sheer weight. King Usbeecee could step on *The Charlotte Observer*, the entire police department, all of the LEC and city hall. He could crush the entire force of armed officers and their chief and deputy chiefs, the mayor, the newspaper's publisher, reducing all to precast dust.

Hammer got out of her car and wasted no time striding through her detectives and uniformed police. She ducked under the tape with its bright yellow warning that always made her ache and full of fear, no matter where she saw it. Hammer was not in the form she would have liked, having even more on her mind than usual. Since her ultimatum to Seth, her quality of life had radically disintegrated. He had not gotten up this morning and was mumbling about Dr. Kevorkian, living wills, and the Hemlock Society. Seth had pontificated about the silliness of assuming that suicide was selfish, for every adult had the right to be absent.

"Oh for God's sake," his wife had said. "Get up and go for a walk."

"No. You can't make me. I don't have to be in this life if I don't want to be."

This had prompted her to remove all firearms from their usual spots. Hammer had collected many over the years and had strategically tucked them in various places around the house. Still at large when West had called was Hammer's old faithful Smith &

Wesson stainless steel five-shot .38 special with Pachmeyer grips. Hammer was fairly certain it was supposed to be in the drawer of her vanity in her bathroom. She was almost positive this was where it had been last time she had rounded up weapons and locked them in the safe before the grandbabies came to town.

Hammer had many concerns. She was depressed and coping the best she could as anxieties from her press conference, which had involved national media, continued to pluck at her. Politics were what she hated most. They honestly were the bane of her existence. *A hundred and five percent clearance rate.* She wished Cahoon could be here in this god-awful place. This was what he needed to see. The Cahoons of the world would lose it, wouldn't be able to handle it, would pale and flee. This gory dead businessman was not about appearances or economic development or the tourist industry. This overgrown, creepy thicket flickering with fireflies near railroad tracks, this Thrifty rental car, open and dinging, was about reality.

Hammer spoke to no one as she approached tragedy, and blue and red lights lit up her hard, distressed face. She joined West and Brazil near the Maxima as Dr. Odom arranged another black pouch around another body. The medical examiner's gloved hands were bloody and sweat dripped in his eyes as his heart beat slow and with force. He had dealt with the savagery of sexual homicide most of his life, but nothing like this. Dr. Odom was a compassionate man, but he was tough. He had learned long ago to keep himself in check and not relate too closely. It was sad but true that it was easier for him to be clinical when the victims were women or obvious gays not getting along or, in some cases, foreigners. It had been comfortable for him to categorize.

Dr. Odom was feeling increasingly shaky about his homosexual serial killing theory. This victim happened to be fifty-four-year-old state senator Ken Butler from Raleigh. The last thing Dr. Odom intended to imply, in any form or fashion, was that the much-beloved black leader was something less than mainstream. Dr. Odom also knew, from his vast experience, that homosexual politicians didn't cruise downtown streets looking for boys. They went to public parks and men's rooms, where they could always swear they were neither exposing themselves nor offering an invitation. They were urinating.

Dr. Odom zipped the pouch over blood and naked flesh, covering the blaze orange hourglass. He looked up at Hammer and shook his head as he stood. His back was killing him. Brazil was staring into the Maxima, hands in his pockets to make sure he didn't inadvertently touch anything and leave his prints. That would be the end of his career. He might even become a suspect. After all, didn't he coincidentally happen to be in the area every time one of these bodies turned up? He nervously glanced around him, wondering if this might remotely occur to anyone. Dr. Odom was busy giving Hammer and West his opinions.

"This is a fucking nightmare," the medical examiner was saying. "Jesus Christ."

He ripped off his gloves and wasn't quite sure what to do with them. He cast about, looking for a receptacle for biological hazards. Catching the eye of Denny Raines, he gave the paramedic a nod and the big, handsome guy came through with his stretcher and crew. Raines winked at West, drinking in the sexy sight of her in uniform. She was pretty unbelievable, and Hammer was hot, too. Brazil's eyes fixed on Raines. Brazil got a strange feeling as he watched the overbuilt ambulance attendant eyeing West and Hammer. Brazil wasn't sure what the problem was, but he was suddenly anxious and a little sick to his stomach. He wanted to get in Raines's face, beg him to start something so Brazil could finish it, or at least order Raines to leave the scene.

"Well, it's all yours now," Dr. Odom went on to Hammer as stretcher legs clacked. "I'm not releasing a damn thing to the media. Never do. Any statement will have to come from you."

"We're not releasing his identity tonight." Hammer was adamant. "Not until he's been positively identified."

There was no doubt in her mind. His driver's license was on the floor of the Maxima, on the passenger's side. Hammer recognized the senator's imposing stature, the gray hair and goatee and heavy face. He hadn't survived long enough to have tissue response to his horrendous injuries, no swelling or bruising. Butler did not look so different from when Hammer had seen him last, at a cocktail party in Myers Park. She was terribly upset and determined that it would not show. She approached Brazil. He was prowling around the car, taking notes.

"Andy," she said, touching his arm. "I'm sure I don't need to tell you how sensitive this is."

He got still, looking at her as if she were the reason people went to church every Sunday. She was God. Hammer was distracted as her gaze wandered inside the car, to the black leather briefcase stamped with the gold initials K.O.B. It was in back, open, as were an overnight bag and a suit bag, everything dumped out. She made a silent inventory of keys, a calculator, USAir peanuts and tickets, a portable phone, pens, paper, address book, Tic Tacs, lubricated Trojan condoms, shoes, socks, and Jockey shorts, all scattered by hard, heartless hands.

"Are we sure it's the senator?" Brazil managed to ask.

Hammer gave him her upset eyes again. "Not sure enough for you to release that yet."

"Okay," he said. "As long as you don't give it out to someone else first."

"Never. You do the right thing, so will I." She said the usual. "Call me tomorrow at five P.M. I'll give you a statement."

She walked off. His eyes followed her as she left the crime scene and ducked under tape, walking briskly through the strobing blue and red night. Television crews, radio reporters, and mobs of reporters darted at her like barracuda. She waved them off and got into her chief's car. Brazil prowled some more, disturbed in a way he did not understand as he got closer to where the senator had been killed. Raines and other paramedics were carrying the body to the ambulance, and the Ace twenty-four-hour towing and recovery truck was rolling in to haul the Maxima to the police department.

The ambulance beeped as it backed up, carrying the dead senator to the morgue while cameras caught it all. Brent Webb watched Brazil with jealous eyes. It wasn't fair Brazil got such special treatment and could wander around the crime scene with a flashlight as if he belonged there. Brazil's privileged position, his golden touch, would end soon enough, Webb knew. The television reporter smoothed his perfect hair and lubricated his lips with lip balm. He looked sincerely into the camera and told the world the latest tragic news as a Norfolk-Southern train loudly lumbered past.

Chapter Sixteen

Brazil's flashlight swept gravel and weeds at the edge of rusty railroad tracks as the last train car loudly rumbled through the dark, hot night. Coagulating blood glistened bright red in the strong beam, illuminating a dingy washcloth and bloody quarters, pennies, and dimes that must have come out of pockets when the murdered senator's pants were pulled down. Blood and gore clung to kudzu, and there were fragments of skull and brain. Brazil took a deep breath, looking down dark tracks, the skyline huge and bright.

Seth had images of his own blood and gore and savored the imagined reaction of Chief Wife when she walked into his room and found him on top of his bed, where he sat up now drinking beer, the .38 revolver in his lap. He could not take his eyes off the gun, which was loaded with one Remington +P cartridge. Intermittently, Seth

had been spinning the cylinder for hours as he watched "Friends,"
"Mary Tyler Moore," and other reruns, and tested his luck. It
wasn't good. So far, out of perhaps a hundred dry runs, he had
committed suicide successfully but twice. How could that be possible? Didn't this go against the law of averages? He figured the cartridge should have lined up fatally at least twenty times, since it
was a five-shot revolver, and five divided into one hundred was
twenty.

He had never been good in math. Seth had never been good in
anything, he decided. Everyone would be better off without him,
including his wimpy sons and his emasculating wife. She'd benefit
the most, walking in, finding him slumped over, shot in the head
through a pillow, blood everywhere, finished, end of story. No
longer a problem. No more taking fatso Seth places and being
ashamed, while younger men still looked at her with interested
eyes. Seth would show her. Take that. Let his final chapter haunt
her the rest of her big-shot days.

He would never go through with it, Hammer was quite sure of
this. Certainly, when she had slid open her vanity drawer and
found the .38 missing, it had occurred to the top police officer in
Charlotte that her depressed, self-destructive spouse might have a
clue as to the gun's whereabouts. And for what? Self-protection.
Hardly. Seth rarely remembered to set the burglar alarm. He did
not like to shoot and had never carried a gun, not even in Little
Rock when he was a member of the NRA because most people
were. Hammer deduced and worried as she drove.

The fool. Wouldn't this be his last and greatest revenge? Suicide
was a mean and skulking act, unless one was dying anyway and desired an earlier flight out of pain and suffering. The vast majority
of people killed themselves for payback purposes. Some of the nastiest notes Hammer had ever read were the last comments of just
such people. She had not much sympathy because there wasn't a
soul she knew who didn't bump over bad stretches of life's high-

ways now and again, struggle over long, lonely miles where it entered the mind that maybe one should run off the road, be done with it. Hammer was not exempt. She was well aware of her own spells of destructive eating, drinking, not exercising, laziness. They happened, and she picked herself up and went on. She always chose a better lane and got healthy again. She would not die, because she was responsible, and people needed her.

She walked into her house, not knowing what she would find. Locking the door, she reset the alarm. The TV was loud in Seth's bedroom across from the kitchen. For a moment, his wife hesitated, tempted to walk back and check, but she couldn't. Suddenly, she was afraid. She headed to her own part of the house, her heart filled with dread as she freshened up in the bathroom. It was late, but she didn't change into her nightshirt yet or pour herself a Dewar's. If he had done it, there would be people all over her property within minutes. There was no point in getting out of her clothes or smelling like booze. Judy Hammer began to cry.

Brazil was thinking about the deal he had made with Hammer as he flew through his story. Still in uniform, he sat before his computer, fingers dancing as he typed and flipped through his notepad. He included incredible detail about this night's Black Widow killing. With photographic total recall, he showed what was inside the car, describing bloody money, and what the police and medical examiner had done, and how violent death felt and smelled and looked. His piece was graphic and moving, but it did not include the victim's identity. Brazil kept his word.

This was very stressful. The journalist in him screamed that he had to print the truth, whether or not it was known for a fact. Brazil was honorable. He could not betray the police. He assuaged himself with the reality that Chief Hammer would never screw him, and he knew that West wouldn't. Brazil would get his quote tomorrow at five P.M., and no one, especially Webb, would catch on until they read it in the *Observer* the following morning.

Webb had just come on the air for the eleven o'clock news when Hammer walked into her husband's bedroom. Her heart slowed a little when she saw no blood. Nothing, in the least, stood out. Seth was on his side, head deep in the pillow. Webb's voice was unusually solemn, the killing the lead story.

". . . the shocking revelation in this night's tragedy is that the victim is believed to be Senator Ken Butler . . ."

Hammer turned to stone, riveted to the TV. Seth sat straight up in bed, startled.

"My God," Seth exclaimed. "We just had drinks with him last month."

"Shhhhhhhhh," Hammer silenced her self-destructive husband.

". . . once again, the peculiar symbol of an hourglass was spray-painted on the body. Butler was believed to have been shot at close range with a high-velocity hollowpoint ammunition known as Silvertips . . ."

Hammer snatched up the portable phone from the table by Seth's bed, where there were three Miller Lite cans and a glass of what looked like bourbon.

"Where's my .38?" she said to him as she dialed.

"Got no idea." He could feel the revolver between his legs, which was not an ideal place for it. But it had rearranged itself when he had fallen asleep.

". . . sources say his briefcase, tote bag, and suit bag were riffled through inside the rental Maxima. Butler had picked up the Thrifty rental car at five-fifteen this afternoon. His money was gone, except for bloody change found under his body. Blood money, as the Black Widow claims number five . . ." Webb's voice lowered, resonating tragic irony.

Brazil was getting his fix of press room sound and fury and therefore was not at his desk to receiver Hammer's call. He watched thousands of newspapers speeding on a conveyor belt. His front page headline was an inch high and blurred, but he could still read it from where he stood.

BLOODY MONEY—BLACK WIDOW CLAIMS NUMBER FIVE

He couldn't quite make out his byline, but he knew it was there. Workers dozed in chairs, waiting for technical problems. Brazil watched one-ton newsprint reels eerily floating up from underground, carried slowly along tracks past barrels of liquid alum and vats of yellow, red, blue, and black ink. Metal clanked as dollies carried newsprint that reminded him of giant rolls of toilet paper. He wandered to the mail room, staring at palates of bundled papers, listening to the loud click-clicking of the Muller Martini machine feeding inserts into papers as a belt carried them into the counting machine. His enthusiasm had left him, for some reason. He felt listless. He was restless, nocturnal again, and still sort of off-line in a way he did not understand.

It was a sweet-sick feeling. His heart was heavy and ached, and when he thought of that beefcake paramedic winking at West and looking at Hammer with lust in his eyes, Brazil felt a tightness and a rage. He felt fright. He experienced the same weak, chilly sensation he associated with barely escaping a car accident or almost losing a tennis match. Was it possible either woman might like Raines, that meatloaf of a paramedic who had to have a meager mental bank account to spend so much time working out? Of late, Brazil recently had caught the rumors about Hammer's pitiful marriage to a fat guy who was unemployed. A dynamic woman like her would have needs and urges. How did Brazil know that she might not go for it and decide to meet Raines somewhere?

It was important for Brazil's peace of mind and spiritual development that he know Hammer had, in fact, driven straight home. He could not trust her unless he knew, with certainty, that she would not betray him and the world by stooping so low as to sneak around with Denny Raines. Brazil drove quickly through Fourth

Ward. He was stunned to see an ambulance parked in front of Hammer's house and her dark blue police car gleaming in the driveway. Brazil's heart was boxing his ribs as he parked some distance away, staring in horror and disbelief. How in God's name could she be so blatant?

A madness invaded Brazil's otherwise sound mind. He got out of his BMW and strode toward the house of the woman he worshiped but no longer respected or would ever speak to or think of or wonder about again. He would air his righteous thoughts, but there would be no violence unless Raines started it. If so, Brazil would sock him to Oz, ace him, smash him. He tried not to think about Raines's size, or that the paramedic did not appear to be scared of much. Brazil was having second thoughts when Hammer's front door opened.

Raines and another paramedic wheeled out a stretcher bearing a fat older man. Chief Hammer followed and seemed in shock, and Brazil was stunned and baffled in the middle of Pine Street. Hammer was distraught as practiced hands loaded her husband into the ambulance.

"You sure you don't want me to ride with you?" Hammer asked the fat man.

"I'm sure." The fat man was in pain and sluggish, perhaps from whatever was dripping into him intravenously.

"Well, have it your way," Hammer told him.

"I don't want her coming," the fat man instructed Raines.

"Not to worry." Hammer sounded hurt as she walked back to the house.

She stood in the doorway, watching the ambulance drive off. Squinting, she noticed Brazil on her dark street, staring. She recognized him, and it all came back to her. Oh Christ. As if she didn't have problems enough.

"I tried to get you earlier. Give me a chance to explain," she called out to him.

Now he was completely baffled. "Excuse me?" He stepped closer.

"Come here." Hammer wearily motioned to him.

He sat on her porch swing. She turned out the light and sat on the steps, certain this young man must think she was the biggest, most dishonest bureaucrat he had ever encountered. Hammer knew this might be the night her controversial community policing project would go to hell along with everything else.

"Andy," she began, "you've got to believe that I said nothing to anyone. I swear I kept my promise to you."

"What?" He was getting a very bad feeling. "What promise?"

She realized he did not know. "Oh God," she mumbled. "You didn't hear the news tonight?"

"No, ma'am. What news?" He was getting excited, his voice rising.

Hammer told him about Channel 3 and Webb's scoop.

"That's impossible!" Brazil exclaimed. "Those are my details! How could he know the stuff about the bloody money, the washcloth, any of it! He wasn't there!"

"Andy, please lower your voice."

Lights were blinking on. Dogs were barking. Hammer stood.

"It's not fair. I play by the rules." Brazil felt as if his life were over. "I cooperate with you, help as much as I can. And get crucified for it." He got up, too, the swing moving, slowly swaying, and empty.

"You can't stop doing what's right just because others do things that are wrong." She spoke quietly and from experience as she opened the door that would lead her back inside her fine home. "We've done some pretty wonderful things, Andy. I hope you won't let this ruin it."

Her face was kind but sad as she looked at him. He felt the ache in his heart, and his stomach was doing something strange, too. He was sweating and chilled as he stared at her, unable to imagine what it must have been like for her children to be raised by such a person.

"Are you all right?" Hammer thought he was acting oddly.

"I don't know what my problem is." He wiped his face with his hands. "I think I've been trying to get sick or something. It's none of my business, but is your husband all right?"

"A flesh wound," she replied, weary and depressed again as moths fluttered past, into her house, where soon they would die from pesticide.

Misfires rarely occurred with double-action revolvers. But when Hammer had demanded that Seth return the .38 to her, he had gotten angry and mean. He'd had enough of being bossed around by this woman, who next would begin searching him and his bedroom. There was no way out. Unfortunately, she'd walked in before he'd had a chance to stash the gun in a place she couldn't find it. Worse, Seth had been sleeping in a drunken position that had resulted in tingling and numbness in his right hand. When he had decided to send this same hand down to his crotch to fish out the revolver, it had not been a wise move. It was also Seth's bad luck that the one time he did not want the cartridge lined up with the firing pin was precisely then.

"His left buttock," Hammer was explaining to Brazil, who was inside the house with her now, because she could not leave her front door open all night.

Brazil looked around at vibrant oriental rugs on polished hardwood floors, at fine oil paintings and handsome furniture in warm fabrics and rich leathers. He was standing in the foyer of Chief Hammer's splendid restored home, and no one else was around. It was just the two of them, and he began sweating profusely again. If she noticed, she did not let on.

"They'll X-ray, of course," she was saying, "to make certain the bullet isn't lodged close to anything important."

There was a dark side of +P hollowpoints, Hammer thought. The objective of their design was for the lead projectile to expand and rip through tissue like a Roto-Rooter. Rarely did the bullets exit, and there was no telling how much lead was scattered through Seth's formidable lower region. Brazil was listening to all this, wondering if the chief would ever get around to calling the police.

"Chief Hammer," Brazil finally felt compelled to speak. "I don't guess you've called this in?"

"Oh dear." It hadn't even occurred to her. "You're absolutely right. I guess a report has to be taken." She began pacing as the reality hit. "Oh no, oh no. That's all I need! So now I get to hear about this on TV, the radio. In your paper. This is awful. Do you realize how many people will enjoy this?" She envisioned Cahoon sitting in his crown, laughing as he read about it.

POLICE CHIEF'S HUSBAND SHOOTS SELF
RUSSIAN ROULETTE SUSPECTED

No one would be fooled, not for a minute. A depressed, unemployed, obese husband in bed with his wife's .38 loaded with only one cartridge? Every cop who worked for Hammer would know that her husband had been flirting with suicide. All would know that there were serious problems in her house. Some would even suspect that she had shot her husband and knew exactly how to get away with it. Maybe it wasn't his left buttock she had been aiming at, either. Maybe he had turned around just in the nick of time. Hammer went into the kitchen and reached for the phone.

There was simply no way she was dialing 911 and having the call broadcast to every cop, paramedic, reporter, and person who owned a scanner in the region. She got the duty captain on the line. It happened to be Horgess. He was fiercely loyal to his boss, but not especially quick-thinking or known for shrewd judgment.

"Horgess," she said. "I need an officer over to my house ASAP to take a report. There's been an accident."

"Oh no!" Horgess was upset. If anything ever happened to his chief, he'd answer directly to Goode. "Are you all right?"

She paced. "My husband's at Carolinas Medical. I'm afraid he had an accident with a handgun. He should be fine."

Horgess immediately grabbed his upright portable radio. He ten-fived David One unit 538, a rookie too scared to do anything other than what she was told. This decision would have been good had Horgess not failed to overlook the reason Hammer had called him, the duty captain, directly.

"Need you over there *now* to take an accidental shooting report," Horgess excitedly said into his radio.

"Ten-four," Unit 538 came back. "Any injuries?"

"Ten-four. Subject en route to Carolinas Medical."

Every officer on duty, and some who weren't, and anyone else with a scanner, heard every word of the broadcast. Most assumed Chief Hammer had been accidentally shot, meaning Jeannie Goode this very instant was the acting chief. Nothing could have sent the force into more of a panic. Hammer had a base radio station in her kitchen and it was on.

"Horgess, you idiot!" she exclaimed in disbelief to no one in particular, inside her kitchen.

She stopped pacing. It struck her that Andy Brazil was still standing in the doorway. She was not entirely sure why he was here and suddenly doubted the wisdom of a handsome young reporter dressed like a cop being in the house with her, in the wake of a domestic shooting. Hammer also knew that her entire evening shift was heading toward her address, flying to investigate the fate of their leader.

Goode never kept her radio on at home or in her car, but a source had tipped her off, and she was already putting on her uniform, preparing to take over the Charlotte Police Department, as Unit 538 sped through Fourth Ward. Unit 538 was terrified. She worried she might have to stop to vomit. She turned on Pine Street, and was stunned to find five other police cars already in front of Hammer's house, lights strobing. In Unit 538's rearview mirror, more cars came, miles of them, speeding through the night to help their fallen chief. Unit 538 parked, shakily gathered her metal clipboard, wondering if she could just leave and deciding probably not.

Hammer went out on the porch to reassure her people. "Everything is under control," she spoke to them.

"Then you're not injured," said a sergeant whose name she did not recall.

"My husband is injured. We don't think it's serious," she said.

"So everything's okay."

"Man, what a scare."

"We're so relieved, Chief Hammer."

"See you in the morning." Hammer dismissed them with a wave.

That was all they needed to hear. Each officer secretly keyed his mike, broadcasting several clicks over the air, signaling comrades everywhere that all was ten-four. Only Unit 538 had unfinished business, and she followed Hammer into the rich, old house. They sat in the living room.

"Before you even start," Hammer said, "I'm going to tell you how this is going to be done."

"Yes, ma'am."

"There will be no implication that the right thing was not done here, that exceptions were made because the subject involved happens to be married to me."

"Yes, ma'am."

"This is routine and will be worked according to the book."

"Yes, ma'am."

"My husband should be charged with reckless endangerment and discharging a firearm in the city limits," Hammer went on.

"Yes, ma'am."

Unit 538's handwriting was unsteady as she began filling out the accidental shooting report. This was amazing. Hammer must not like her husband much. Hammer was nailing him with the maximum charge, locking him up and throwing away the key. It just proved Unit 538's theory that women like Hammer got where they were by being aggressive hardasses. They were men poured into the wrong form at the factory. Hammer recited all the necessary information. She answered Unit 538's banal questions and got the cop out as fast as possible.

Brazil remained seated at the kitchen table in Chief Hammer's house, wondering if anyone might have recognized his distinctive

BMW parked out front. If the cops ran his tag, what would they think? Who was he here to see? He remembered with a sinking feeling that the condominiums Axel and friends lived in were just around the corner. Cops with their suspicious minds might think Brazil had parked a street away, trying to fool everybody. If word got back to Axel, he'd believe Brazil was stalking him, had a thing for him.

"Andy, let's wind this up." Hammer walked in. "I suppose it's too late to get this in the paper for tomorrow."

"Yes, chief. The city edition deadline was hours ago," Brazil replied, glancing at his watch, and startled that she would want a word of this in the paper.

"I'm going to need you to help me and have to trust that you will, even after what happened with Channel Three," she said.

There was no one Brazil would rather assist.

Hammer looked at the clock on the wall, in despair. It was almost three A.M. She had to get to the hospital, whether Seth liked it or not, and she needed to be up in three hours. Hammer's body did not appreciate all-nighters anymore, but she would make it. She always did. Her plan was the best she could devise under circumstances which were truly extreme and upsetting. She knew tomorrow's news would bristle with Seth's bizarre shooting and what it might imply. She could not preempt the television and radio stations, but at least could straighten out the facts the following day with a true, detailed account by Brazil.

Brazil was silent and stunned as he sat in the passenger's seat of Hammer's impeccable Crown Victoria. He took notes while she talked. She told him all about her early life and why she had gone into law enforcement. She talked about Seth, about what a support he had been as she was fighting her way through the ranks of what was truly a male militia. Hammer was exhausted and vulnerable, her personal life in shambles, and she had not been to a therapist in two years. Brazil had caught her at a remarkable time, and he was moved and honored by her trust. He would not let her down.

"It's a perfect example of the world not allowing powerful people to have problems," Hammer was explaining as she drove along Queens Road West, beneath a canopy of great oak trees. "But the fact is, all people have problems. We have tempestuous and tragic phases in relationships we don't have time enough to tend to, and we get discouraged and feel we have failed."

Brazil thought she was the most wonderful person he had ever met. "How long have you been married?" he asked.

"Twenty-six years."

She had known the night before her wedding that she was making a mistake. She and Seth had united out of need, not want. She had been afraid to go it alone, and Seth had seemed so strong and capable back then.

As he lay on his stomach in the E.R., after X-rays and scrubbing and being rolled all over the place, Seth wondered how this could have happened. His wife had once admired him, valued his opinion, and laughed at his witty stories. They were never much in bed. She had far more energy and staying power, and no matter how he might have wanted to please, he simply could not carry her same tune, didn't have as many pages, usually was snoring by the time she'd returned from the bathroom, ready for the next act.

"Ouch!" he yelled.

"Sir, you're going to have to hold still," the stern nurse said for the hundredth time.

"Why can't you knock me out or something!" Tears welled in his eyes as he clenched his fists.

"Mr. Hammer, you're very fortunate." It was the triage surgeon's voice now, rattling X-rays that sounded like saw blades. She was a pretty little thing with long red hair. Seth was humiliated that her only perspective on him was his corpulent fanny that had never seen the sun.

Chapter Seventeen

The Carolinas Medical Center was famous for its triage, and patients were med-flighted in from all over the region. This early morning, helicopters were quiet silhouettes on red helipads centered by big H's on rooftops, and shuttle buses moved slowly from parking lots to different areas of the massive concrete complex. The medical center's fleet of ambulances was teal and white, the colors of the Hornets and much of what filled Charlotte with pride.

The entire hospital staff knew that a V.I.P. had arrived. There would be no waiting, no bleeding in chairs, no threatening, no shortcuts or neglect. Seth Hammer, as he had been erroneously registered and referred to most of his marriage, had been taken straight into the E.R. He had been rolled in and out of many rooms. He wasn't certain he understood the pretty surgeon's vernacular, but it seemed, according to her, that although the bullet's destruction of tissue had been significant, at least no major arteries or veins had been hit. However, because he was a V.I.P., no chances could be taken. It was explained that medical personnel would do arteriography and shoot him full of dye and see what they found. Then they would give him a barium enema.

Hammer parked in a police slot outside the emergency room at not quite four A.M. Brazil had filled twenty pages in his notepad and knew more about her than any reporter who had ever lived. She fetched her large pocketbook with its secret compartment and took a deep breath as she got out. Brazil was struggling with his next question but had to ask. It was for her own good, too.

"Chief Hammer." He hesitated. "Do you suppose I could get a photographer here to maybe get something of you on your way out of the hospital, later?"

She waved him off as she walked. "I don't care."

The more she thought about it, the more she realized it didn't matter what he wrote. Her life was over. In the course of one short day, all was lost. A senator had been murdered, the fifth in a series of brutal slayings committed by someone the police were no closer to catching. USBank, which owned the city, was at odds with her. Now her husband had shot himself in the ass while playing Russian roulette. The jokes would be endless. What did this suggest about where he assumed his most vital organ was, after all? Hammer would lose her job. What the hell. She may as well offer her two cents' worth on her way out the door. Brazil had just gotten off a pay phone and was walking fast to keep up with her.

"We'll also be running the Black Widow story, if there's a positive I.D.," he nervously reminded her.

She didn't care.

"I'm wondering," Brazil pushed his luck, "if you'd have a problem with my slipping in a few details or two that might trick the killer."

"What?" Hammer glanced blankly at him.

"You know, if I messed with him a little. Well, Deputy Chief West didn't think it was a good idea, either," he conceded.

The enlightened chief caught on to what he was suggesting and was interested. "As long as you don't release sensitive case details."

She fixed on the triage nurse in her console and headed there. No introduction was necessary.

"He's on the way to the O.R. right now," the nurse said to the police chief. "Do you want to wait?"

"Yes," Hammer decided.

"We have a private room the chaplain uses, if you'd like a little quiet," the nurse said to this woman who was one of her heroes.

"I'll just sit where everybody else does," Hammer said. "Someone might need that room."

The nurse certainly hoped not. Nobody had died in the last twenty-four hours, and this had better not change on her shift. Nurses always got the raw end of that deal. Doctors suddenly vanished. They were off to their next bit of drama, leaving the nurses to take out tubes, tie on toe tags, wheel the body to the morgue, and deal with bereft relatives who never believed it and were going to sue. Hammer found two chairs in a corner of the reception area. There were maybe twenty distressed people waiting, most accompanied by someone trying to comfort them, most arguing, others moaning and bleeding into towels or cradling broken limbs and holding ice on burns. Almost all were weeping or limping to the restroom, and drinking water from paper cups and fighting another wave of nausea.

Hammer looked around, pained by what she saw. This was why she had chosen her profession, or why it had chosen her. The world was falling apart, and she wanted to help. She focused on a young man who reminded her of Randy, her son. The young man was alone, five chairs away. He was burning up with fever, sweating and shivering and having a difficult time breathing. Hammer looked at his earrings, his chiseled face and wasted body, and she knew what was wrong with him. His eyes were shut as he licked cracked lips. It seemed everyone was sitting as far from him as possible, especially those leaking body fluids. Hammer got up. Brazil never took his eyes off her.

The triage nurse smiled at Hammer's approach. "What can I do for you?" the nurse said.

"Who's the young man over there?" Hammer pointed.

"He's got some sort of respiratory infection." The nurse became clinical. "I'm not allowed to release names."

"I can get his name from him myself," Hammer told her. "I want a large glass of water with a lot of ice, and a blanket. And when might your folks get around to seeing him? He looks like he could pass out any minute and if he does, I'm going to know about it."

Some seconds later, Hammer was returning to the waiting area with water and a soft folded blanket. She sat next to the young man and wrapped him up. He opened his eyes as she held something to his lips. It was icy cold and wet and felt wonderful. Warmth began to spread over him, and his shivering calmed as his feverish eyes focused on an angel. Harrel Woods had died, and he was relieved as he drank the water of life.

"What's your name?" the angel's voice sounded from far away.

Woods wanted to smile, but his lips bled when he tried.

"Do you have a driver's license with you?" the angel wanted to know.

It blearily occurred to him that even Heaven required a picture I.D. these days. He weakly zipped open his black leather butt pack and handed the license to the angel. Hammer wrote down the information, in the event he might need a shelter somewhere if he ever got out of here, which wasn't likely. Two nurses were making their way to him with purpose, and Harrel Woods was admitted to the ward for AIDS patients. Hammer returned to her chair, wondering if she might find coffee somewhere. She digressed more about helping people. She told Brazil that when she was growing up, it was all she had wanted to do in life.

"Unfortunately, policing seems to be part of the problem these days," she said. "How often do we really help?"

"You just did," Brazil said.

She nodded. "And that's not policing, Andy. That's humanity. And we've got to bring humanity back into what we do or there's no hope. This is not about politics or power or merely rounding up offenders. Policing always has been and always must be about all of us getting along and helping each other. We're one body."

Seth's body was in dire straits in the O.R. His arteriogram was fine and he hadn't leaked any barium from his bowels, but because he was a V.I.P., no chance would be taken. They had draped and prepped him, and he was facedown again, and nurses had pierced his tender flesh repeatedly with excruciatingly painful injections and a Foley catheter. They had rolled in a tank of nitrogen and connected it to a tube. They began subjecting him to what they called a Simpulse irrigation, which was nothing more than a power wash with saline and antibiotics. They were blasting him with three thousand cc's, suctioning, debriding, as he complained.

"Put me under!" he begged.

There was too much risk.

"Anything!" he whined.

They compromised and gave him an amnesiac they called Midazolam, which did not relieve pain but caused it to be forgotten, it seemed. Although the bullet was located on the X ray, they would never locate it in so much fat, not without dicing Seth as if he were destined for a chef salad, the surgeon knew. Her name was Dr. White. She was a thirty-year-old graduate of Harvard and Johns Hopkins, and had done her residency at the Cleveland Clinic. Dr. White would not have been as concerned about leaving the bullet were it the typical semi-jacketed, round-nosed variety.

But hollowpoints opened like a flower on impact. The deformed missile in the chief's husband had cut a swath, exactly as planned by Remington, and might continue to do damage after the fact. Without question, it put him at considerable risk for infection. Dr. White made an incision so the wound could drain, and it was packed and dressed. The sun was rising by the time Dr. White met Chief Hammer in recovery, where Seth was groggy, lying on his side, tethered by IV lines, a curtain drawn to give him the privacy afforded V.I.P.s, as set by the medical center's unwritten policy.

"He should be fine," Dr. White was saying to Hammer.

"Thank God," Hammer said with relief.

"I want to keep him overnight in isolation and continue the IV antibiotics. If he spikes a fever during the first twenty-four hours, we'll keep him longer."

"And that could happen." Hammer's fears returned.

Dr. White could not believe she was standing here and the police chief was looking to her for answers. Dr. White had read every article written about this incredible woman. Hammer was what Dr. White wanted to be when Dr. White was older and powerful. Caring, strong, good-looking, kick-ass in pearls. Nobody pushed Hammer around. It wasn't possible that Hammer put up with the same shit Dr. White did, from the old boy surgeons. Most were graduates of Duke, Davidson, Princeton, and UVA, and wore their school bow ties to the symphony and cocktail parties. They didn't think twice when one of their own took a day off to boat on Lake Norman or play golf. But should Dr. White need a few hours to go to her gynecologist, to visit her sick mother, or give in to the flu, it was another example of why women didn't belong in medicine.

"Of course, we're not expecting any problem," Dr. White was reassuring Hammer. "But there is extensive tissue damage." She paused, searching for a diplomatic way to explain. "Ordinarily, a bullet of that power and velocity would have exited when fired at such close range. But in this case, there was too much mass for the bullet to pass through."

The only image that came to Hammer's mind was tests the firearms examiners conducted by shooting into massive shimmering blocks of ballistic jelly, manufactured by Knox. Brazil was still taking notes. Nobody cared. He was such a respectful, helpful presence he could have continued following Hammer for years and it would not have been a problem. It was entirely possible she would not have been fully cognizant of it. If her imminent termination were not an inevitability, she might have assigned him to her office as an assistant.

Hammer spent little time with her husband. He was checked

out on morphine and would have nothing to say to her were this not the case. She held his hand for a moment, spoke quiet words of encouragement, felt terrible about all of it, and was so angry with him she could have shot him herself. She and Brazil headed out of the hospital as the region headed to work. He hung back to allow the *Observer* photographer to get dramatic shots of her walking out the E.R. entrance, head down, grimly following the sidewalk as a Medvac helicopter landed on a nearby roof. Another ambulance roared in, and paramedics rushed to get another patient out as Hammer made her way past.

That photograph of her by the ambulance, a helicopter landing in the background, her eyes cast down and face bravely tragic, was sensational. The next morning it was staring out from racks, boxes, and stacks of papers throughout the greater Charlotte-Mecklenburg area. Brazil's story was the most stunning profile of courage Packer had ever seen. The entire metro desk was in awe. How the hell did he get all this? Hammer wasn't known for di-vulging anything personal about herself or her family, and sud-denly, in a time when discretion was most vital, she revealed all to this rookie reporter?

The mayor, city manager, city council, and Cahoon were not likewise impressed. They were interviewed by several television and radio reporters and were openly critical of Hammer, who con-tinued to draw far too much attention to the serial murders and other social problems in the Queen City. It was feared that several companies and a restaurant chain were reconsidering their choice of Charlotte as a new location. Businessmen were canceling meet-ings. It was rumored that sites for a computer chip manufacturing plant and a Disney theme park were being scouted in Virginia.

Charlotte's mayor, city manager, and several city councilmen promised that there would be a full police investigation into the ac-cidental shooting. Cahoon, in a brief statement, agreed this was fair. The men smelled blood and were crazed by it. Panesa did not often get directly involved in choosing sides, but he rolled up his sleeves on this one and penned an impassioned editorial on the Opinion page that ran Sunday morning.

It was called HORNET'S NEST, and in it, Panesa went into great detail about the city's ills as seen through the eyes of an un-flagging, humane woman, their beloved chief, who was embattled by her own demons and yet "has never let us down or burdened us with her private pain," Panesa wrote. "Now is the time to support Chief Hammer, to show her respect and caring, and prove that we, too, can stand up and make the right choices." Panesa went on to allude to Brazil's story of Hammer in the E.R. bringing a blanket and water to a young man dying of AIDS. "That, citizens of Char-lotte, is not only community policing but Christianity," Panesa wrote. "Let Mayor Search, city council, or Solomon Cahoon throw the first stone."

This went on for days, things stirred up, hostility rising from Cahoon's crown and swarming through the mayor's window. Tele-phone lines angrily buzzed as the city fathers plotted on secure phones, devising a way to run Hammer out of town.

"It's got to be the public that decides," the mayor said to the city manager. "The citizens have got to want it."

"No other way," Cahoon agreed in a conference call from his mighty desk, as he viewed his kingdom between aluminum pipes. "It's entirely up to the citizens."

The last thing Cahoon wanted was pissed-off people changing banks. If enough of them did and went on to First Union, CCB, BB&T, First Citizens Bank, or Wachovia, it could catch up with Ca-hoon and hurt him. It could become an epidemic, infecting the big, healthy investors like a computer virus, Ebola, salmonella, hemor-raghic fever.

"The problem, damn it, is Panesa," opined the mayor.

Cahoon felt a fresh wave of outrage. He would not soon recover from the publisher's Sunday editorial with its comment about throwing stones. Panesa had to go, too. Cahoon's brain raced through his formidable network, contemplating allies in the

Knight-Ridder chain. This would have to come from on high, at the level of chairman or president. Cahoon knew them all, but the media was a goddamn centipede. The minute he gave it a prod, it curled up tight and took care of its own.

"The only person who can control Panesa is you," the mayor said to Cahoon. "I've tried. He won't listen to me. It's like trying to talk sense to Hammer. Forget it."

Both the publisher and the police chief were unreasonable. They had agendas and had to be stopped. Andy Brazil was becoming a problem, as well. Cahoon had been around the block enough times to know exactly where he would attack.

"Talk to the boy," Cahoon said to the mayor. "He's probably been trying to get quotes from you anyway, right?"

"They all do."

"So let him come see you, Chuck. Pull him over to our side, where he belongs," Cahoon said with a smile as he gazed out at the hazy summer sky.

Brazil had turned his attention to the Black Widow killings, which he was certain would not stop. He had become obsessed with them, determined that somehow he would uncover that one detail, that important insight or clue that might lead police to the psychopath responsible. He had gotten FBI profiler Bird on the phone, and had written a chillingly accurate but manipulative story. Last night, Brazil had returned to the train tracks on West Trade Street to explore the razed brick building, his flashlight shining on crime-scene tape stirred by the wind. He had stood still, looking around that forsaken, frightening scene, trying to read the emotion of it. He tried to imagine how the senator had stumbled upon the place.

It was possible the senator had plans to meet someone, back in the dark overgrowth where no one would see. Brazil wondered if the autopsy had revealed drugs. Did the senator have a secret vice that had cost him his life? Brazil had cruised South College Street, looking out at the hookers, still not sure which were men or vice cops. The young one he had seen many times before, and it was obvious that she now recognized him in his BMW as she languidly strolled and boldly stared.

Brazil was tired this morning. He could barely finish four miles at the track and didn't bother with tennis. He hadn't seen much of his mother, and she punished him by not speaking on those rare occasions when she was awake and up. She left him notes of chores she needed done and was more slovenly than usual. She coughed and sighed, doing all she could to make him miserable and stung with guilt. Brazil continued to think of West's lecture to him about dysfunctional relationships. He heard her words constantly in his head. They pounded with each step he ran, and blinked in the night as he tried to sleep.

He had not seen or talked to West in days and wondered how she was and why she never called to go shooting or to ride or just to say hi. He felt out of sorts, moody and introverted, and had given up trying to figure out what had gotten into him. He did not understand why Hammer hadn't contacted him to say thanks for his profile. Maybe something in it had pissed her off. Maybe he had gotten a fact wrong. He had really put his heart into that story and had worked himself almost sick. Panesa seemed to be ignoring him also, now that Brazil was making a list. Brazil told himself that if he were as important as any one of these powerful people, he would be more sensitive. He would try to think of the little person's feelings and make that person's day by picking up the phone or sending a note or maybe even flowers.

The only flowers West had in her life this moment were the ones Niles had shredded all over the dining-room table. This was after he had scattered litter in the bathroom while his owner was in the shower, her wet bare feet about to step on grit and unpleasant things coated in it. West's mood was volatile, anyway. She was incensed over the storm of controversy surrounding her beloved boss, and fearful of where it all might end. The day Goode became acting chief was the day West moved back to the farm. West knew all about Brazil following Hammer into very private rooms that not even West had entered.

It was all so typical, she thought as she cussed Niles, rinsed her feet, and cleaned up the bathroom floor. Brazil used West to gain a foothold with the chief. Brazil had acted like a friend, then the moment he got a chance to ingratiate himself with a higher power, West didn't hear a word from him ever again. Wasn't that the way things went? The son of a bitch. He hadn't called to go shooting, to ride, or even to make sure she was still alive. West discovered what was left of the blood lilies from her garden as Niles darted under the couch.

The resurrection lilies Hammer carried into Seth's hospital room at ten A.M. were magenta and appropriately named. Hammer set them on a table and pulled a chair close. The bed was raised, allowing her husband to eat, read, visit, and watch TV on his side. His eyes were dull with the strep infection that had invaded from unknown colonies. Fluids and antibiotics ready for combat marched nonstop through narrow tubes and into needles taped to each arm. Hammer was getting frightened. Seth had been in the hospital three nights now.

"How are you feeling, honey?" she asked, rubbing his shoulder.

"Shitty," he said, eyes wandering back to Leeza on TV.

He had seen, heard, and read the news. Seth knew the terrible thing he had done to himself. Most of all, he knew what he had done to her and his family. Honestly, he had never meant any of it. When he was in his right mind, he'd rather die than hurt anyone. He loved his wife and could not live without her. If he ruined her career in this city, then what? She could go anywhere, and it would be ever so much easier for her to leave him behind, as she had already threatened, if she had to move anyway.

"How are things with you?" Seth mumbled as Leeza argued with a gender-reassigned plumber who had cleavage.

"Don't you worry about me," Hammer firmly said, patting him again. "All that matters right now is that you get better. Think positively, honey. The mind affects everything. No negativity."

This was like telling the dark side of the moon to lighten up a bit. Seth stared at her. He couldn't remember the last time she'd called him *honey*. Maybe never.

"I don't know what to say," he told her.

She knew precisely what he meant. He was poisoned by remorse and guilt and shame. He had set out to ruin her life and the lives of his children and was getting good at it. He ought to feel like shit, if the truth was told.

"You don't have to say anything," Hammer gently reassured him. "What's done is done. Now we move on. When you leave here, we're going to get you some help. That's all that matters now."

He shut his eyes and tears swam behind the lids. He saw a young man in baggy white trousers and bow tie and snappy hat, grinning and happy on a sunny morning as he skipped down the granite steps of the Arkansas state capitol. Seth had been charming and sure of himself once. He had known how to have fun and party with the rest of them and tell funny tales. Psychiatrists had tried Prozac, Zoloft, Nortriptylene, and lithium. Seth had been on diets. He had stopped drinking once. He had been hypnotized and had gone to three meetings of Overeaters Anonymous. Then he had quit all of it.

"There's no hope," he sobbed to his wife. "Nothing left but to die."

"Don't you dare say that," she said, her voice wavering. "You hear me, Seth? Don't you dare say that!"

"Why isn't my love enough for you!" he cried.

"What love?" She stood, anger peeking around her curtain of self-control. "Your idea of love is waiting for me to make you happy while you do nothing for yourself. I am not your caretaker. I am not your zookeeper. I am not your innkeeper. I am not your keeper, period." She was pacing furiously in his small private room. "I am supposed to be your partner, Seth, your friend, your lover. But you know what? If this were tennis, I'd be playing goddamn singles in a goddamn doubles match on both sides of the net while you sat in the shade hogging all the balls and keeping your own private score!"

Brazil had spent the better part of the morning wondering if he should call West to see if she wanted to play some tennis. That would be innocent enough, wouldn't it? The last thing he wanted was to give her the satisfaction of thinking he cared a hoot that he hadn't heard from her in three and a half days. He parked at the All Right lot on West Trade near Presto's and went inside the grill for coffee, starved, but saving himself for something healthy. Later, he'd drop by the Just Fresh, the *eat well feels good* fast food restaurant in the atrium of First Union. That and Wendy's grilled chicken filet sandwiches with no cheese or mayonnaise were about all he lived on these days, and he was losing weight. He secretly wondered if he were getting anorexic.

He sat at the counter, stirring black S&D coffee, waiting for Spike to stop cracking eggs with one hand over a bowl. Brazil wanted to chat. The Michelob Dry clock on the wall over Spike's head read ten-forty-five. There was so much to do and Brazil had to get it done by four P.M., when his beat for the newspaper formally began. As much as Packer loved Brazil's scoops, the regular news of burglaries, robberies, rapes, suicides, fistfights in sports bars, white-collar bank crimes, drug busts, domestic problems, dog bites, and other human interest stories needed to be covered. Most of those reports Webb stole long before anyone else could see them. In fact, the situation was so acute that the rest of the media now referred to the Charlotte Police Department's press basket as *The Webb Site.*

West, having recalled Brazil's early complaint about this, had finally done her bit by calling Channel 3 and complaining to the general manager. This had solved nothing. Nor was Goode receptive when West had brought it up to her, not realizing that Goode, in fact, regularly logged into The Webb Site. These days she and Brent Webb parked all over the city in her Miata. This was not due to a problem with their going to her apartment, where she lived alone. The risk of exposure was a huge turn-on to the couple. It was not unusual for them to park within blocks of his house, where his wife waited dinner for him and picked up his dirty clothes and sorted his socks.

Chapter Eighteen

The task force West had assembled to investigate drug deals going down at the Presto Grill also had much dirt to find, sort through, and hopefully match with other crime trends in the city. Mungo was an undercover detective, and he was eating grilled chicken tips and gravy in the grill while Brazil, whom Mungo did not know, sipped black coffee. Mungo had gotten his street name for obvious reasons. He was a mountain in jeans and Panthers tee shirt, his wallet chained to his belt, long bushy hair tied back, and a bandanna around a sloping forehead. He wore an earring. Mungo was smoking, one eye squinting as he watched the blond guy quiz Spike at the grill.

"No, man." Spike was flipping a burger and chopping hash browns. "See, none's from around here, know what I mean?" He spoke with a heavy Portuguese accent.

"Where they come from doesn't matter," Brazil said. "It's what happens once they get here. Look, the source of the bad shit going down is right where we are." He was talking the language, drumming his index finger on the counter. "Local. I'm sure of it. What do you think?"

Spike wasn't going to explore this further, and Mungo's radar was locked in. That blond pretty-boy looked familiar. It seemed Mungo had seen him somewhere and that made him only more convinced that he was going to develop Blondie as a suspect. But first things first. Mungo needed to sit here a little longer, see what else was going down, and he hadn't finished his breakfast.

"I need more toast," he said to Spike as Blondie left. "Who's he?" Mungo jerked his head in the direction of the shutting front door.

Spike shrugged, having learned long ago not to answer questions, and Mungo was a cop. Everybody knew it. Spike started filling a toothpick holder while Brazil made his next stop. Adjoining the Presto was the Traveler's Hotel, where one could get a room for as little as fifty dollars per week, depending on how well one negotiated with Bink Lydle at the desk. Brazil asked his questions to Lydle and got the same information he'd been handed next door.

Lydle was not especially hospitable, his arms folded across his narrow chest as he sat behind the scarred reception desk with its bell and one-line telephone. He informed this white boy that Lydle knew nothing about these businessmen being whacked around here and couldn't imagine that the "source of this bad shit going down" was local. Lydle, personally, had never seen anyone who made him suspicious, certainly not in his hotel, which was a city landmark, and *the* place to go back in the days of the Old Southern Train Station.

Brazil walked several blocks to Fifth Street and found Jazzbone's Pool Hall. Brazil decided that somebody was going to talk to him, even if he had to take a risk. At this early hour, Jazzbone's wasn't doing much business, just a few guys sitting around drinking Colt 45, smoking, telling favorite stories about binges and women and winning at numbers. Pool tables with shabby green felt were deserted, balls in their triangles, waiting for tonight when the place would be crowded and dangerous until the boozy early morning. If anyone knew what was going on in the neighborhood, Jazzbone was the man.

"I'm looking for Jazzbone," Brazil said to the drinking buddies.

One of them pointed to the bar, where Jazzbone, in plain view, was opening a case of Schlitz and aware of the golden-hair dude dressed like college.

"Yeah!" Jazzbone called out. "What you need."

Brazil walked across cigarette-burned, whisky-smelling carpet. A cockroach scuttled across his path, and salt and cigarette ashes were scattered over every table Brazil passed. The closer he got to Jazzbone, the more he noticed details. Jazzbone wore gold rings, fashioned of diamond clusters and coins, on every finger. The gold crowns on his front teeth had heart and clover cutouts. He wore a semiautomatic pistol on his right hip. Jazzbone was neatly replacing bottles of beer in the cooler.

"All we got cold right now is Pabst Blue Ribbon," Jazzbone said.

Last night had been busy and had wiped Jazzbone out. He had a feeling this boy wanted something other than beer, but he wasn't undercover, like Mungo. Jazzbone could smell police and the Feds the minute they hit the block. He couldn't remember the last time he was fooled. Jazzbone only got spanked by the other dudes out there, people coming into his establishment looking just like him, guns and all.

"I'm with *The Charlotte Observer*," said Brazil, who knew when it was better to be a volunteer cop and when not. "I'd like your help, sir."

"Oh, yeah?" Jazzbone stopped putting away beer, and had always known he'd make a good story. "What kind of help? This for the paper?"

"Yes, sir."

Polite, too, giving the man respect. Jazzbone scrutinized him, and started chewing on a stirrer, cocking one eyebrow. "So, what you want to know?" Jazzbone went around to the other side of the bar and pulled out a stool.

"Well, you know about these killings around here," Brazil said.

Jazzbone was momentarily confused. "Huh," he said. "You might want to specify."

"The out-of-towners. The Black Widow." Brazil lowered his voice, almost to a whisper.

"Oh, yeah. Them," Jazzbone said, and didn't care who heard. "Same person doing all of 'em."

"It can't be helping your business worth a damn." Brazil got tough, acting like he was wearing a gun, too. "Some creep out there ruining it for everyone."

"Now that's so, brother. Tell me about it. I run a clean business here. Don't want trouble or cause none either." He lit a Salem. "It's others who do. Why I wear this." He patted his pistol.

Brazil stared enviously at it. "Shit, man," he said. "What the hell you packing?"

One thing was true, Jazzbone was proud of his piece. He had got it off a drug dealer playing pool, some dude from New York who didn't know that Jazzbone owned a pool hall for a reason. In Jazzbone's mind, when he was good at something, whether it was a woman, a car, or playing pool, he may as well own it, and he was definitely one hell of a pool player. He slipped the pistol out of its holster so Brazil could look without getting too close.

"Colt Double Eagle .45 with a five-inch barrel," Jazzbone let him know.

Brazil had seen it before in *Guns Illustrated.* Stainless steel matte finish, adjustable sights with high-profile three-dot system, wide steel trigger, and combat-style hammer. Jazzbone's pistol went for about seven hundred dollars new, and he could tell the kid was impressed and dying to touch it, but Jazzbone didn't know him well enough for that.

"You think it's the same one whacking all these white men from out of town?" Brazil repeated.

"I didn't say they was white," Jazzbone corrected him. "The last one, the senator dude, wasn't. But yeah, same motherfucker's doing 'em."

"Got any idea who?" Brazil did his best to keep the excitement out of his voice.

Jazzbone knew exactly who and didn't want trouble like this in his neighborhood any more than those rich men wanted it in their rental cars. Not to mention, Jazzbone was a big supporter of free enterprise and collected change from more than pool sharking and beverages. He had an interest in a few girls out there. They earned a few extra dollars and kept him company. The Black Widow was hurting business bad. These days, Jazzbone had a feeling men came to town after watching CNN and reading the paper, and they rented adult movies, stayed in. Jazzbone didn't blame them.

"There's this one punkin head I seen out there running girls," Jazzbone told Brazil, who was taking notes. "I'd be looking at him."

"What's a punkin head?"

Jazzbone flashed his gold grin at this naive reporter boy.

"A *do*." Jazzbone pointed to his own head. "Orange like a punkin, rows of braids close to his head. One mean motherfucker."

"You know his name?" Brazil wrote.

"Don't want to," Jazzbone said.

West, in charge of investigations for the city, had never heard of a punkin head in connection with the Black Widow killings. When Brazil called her from a pay phone, because he did not trust a cellular phone for such sensitive information, he was manic, as if he had just been in a shoot-out. She wrote down what he said, but not a word of it sparked hope. Her Phantom Force had been undercover out on the streets for weeks. Brazil had spent fifteen minutes at Jazzbone's and had cracked the case? She didn't think so. Nor was she feeling the least bit friendly toward Brazil's two-timing, user-friendly ass.

"How's the chief?" he asked her.

"Why don't you tell me," she said.

"What?"

"Look, I don't have time to chitchat," she rudely added.

Brazil was on a sidewalk in front of the Federal Courthouse, hateful people looking at him. He didn't care.

"What did I do?" he fired back. "Tell me when's the last time I've heard from you? I haven't noticed you picking up the phone, asking me to do anything or even to see how I am."

This had not occurred to West. She never called Raines. For that matter, she did not call guys and never had and never would, with the occasional exception of Brazil. Now why the hell was that, and why had she suddenly gotten weird about dialing his number?

"I figured you'd get in touch with me when you had something on your mind," she replied. "It's been hectic. Niles is driving me crazy. I may turn him over to the juvenile courts. I don't know why I haven't gotten around to calling you, okay? But a lot of good it's going to do for you to punish me for it."

"You want to play tennis?" he quickly asked.

West still had a wooden Billie Jean King racquet, clamped tight in a press. Neither were manufactured anymore. She had an ancient box of Tretorn balls that never went dead but broke like eggs. Her last pair of tennis shoes were low-cut plain white canvas Converse, also no longer made. She had no idea where anything was and owned no tennis clothes, and didn't especially enjoy watching the sport on TV but preferred baseball at this stage in her personal evolution. There were many reasons she gave the answer she did.

"Forget it," she said.

She hung up the phone and went straight to Hammer's office. Horgess was not his usual informative, friendly self. West felt sorry for him. No matter how many times Hammer had told him to let it go, he never would. He had picked up the radio instead of the phone. Horgess, the sycophantic duty captain, had made sure all the world knew about the embarrassing shooting at the chief's house. That's all anybody talked and speculated about. The expected jokes were ones West would never want her boss to hear. Horgess was pale and depressed. He barely nodded at West.

"She in?" West asked.

"I guess," he said, dejected.

West knocked and walked in at the same time. Hammer was on the phone, tapping a pen on a stack of pink telephone messages. She looked amazingly put together and in charge in a tobacco-brown suit and yellow and white striped blouse. West was surprised and rather pleased to note that her boss was wearing slacks and flats again. West pulled up a chair, waiting for Hammer to slip off the headset.

"Don't mean to interrupt," West said.

"Quite all right, quite all right," Hammer told her.

She gave West her complete attention, hands quietly folded on top of the neatly organized desk of someone who had far too much to do but refused to be overwhelmed by it. Hammer had never been caught up and never would be. She didn't even want to get to all of it. The older she got, the more she marveled over matters she once had considered important. These days, her perspective had shifted massively, like a glacier forming new continents to consider and cracking old worlds.

"We've not really had a chance to talk," West proceeded delicately. "How are you holding up?"

Hammer gave her a slight smile, sadness in her eyes before she could run it off. "The best I can, Virginia. Thank you for asking."

"The editorials, cartoons, and everything in the paper have been really terrific," West went on. "And Brazil's story was great." She hesitated at this point, the subject of Andy Brazil still disturbing, although she didn't understand it, entirely.

Hammer understood it perfectly. "Listen, Virginia," she said with another smile, this one kind and slightly amused. "He's pretty sensational, I have to admit. But you have nothing to worry about where I'm concerned."

"Excuse me?" West frowned.

Brazil was out in bright sunshine, walking along the sidewalk in an area of the city where he should not have been without armed guards. This was a very special juncture known as Five Points, where the major veins of State, Trade, and Fifth Streets, and Beatties Ford and Rozzelles Ferry Roads branched out from the major artery of Interstate 77, carrying all traveling on them into the heart of the Queen City. This included the thousands of businessmen coming from Charlotte-Douglas International Airport and those bad dudes waiting, including the serial killer, Punkin Head.

Punkin Head was believed to be a sh'im by those who had laid eyes on the pimp, which were few. It held its own council, as a rule, in an '84 Ford cargo van, dark blue, 351 V8, which it was especially fond of because the van had windows only in front. Whatever business Punkin Head chose to run out of the back remained private, as it should have, and this included sleeping. This fine morning Punkin Head was parked in its usual spot on Fifth Street, in the Preferred Parking lot where the attendant knew to leave well enough alone and was now and then rewarded with services Punkin Head's business could provide.

Punkin Head was reading the paper and eating its third take-out bacon and egg sandwich with hot sauce and butter, brought by the attendant. Punkin Head saw the white boy walking around, snooping, a notepad in hand. Word on the street was the dude's name was Blondie, and Punkin Head knew exactly who Blondie was trying to snitch on, and Punkin Head wasn't appreciative. It watched, thinking, as it finished its breakfast and popped open a Michelob Dry, taking another look at the front page story in this morning's *Observer*.

Some South American reporter named Brazil was getting far too personal about Punkin Head, and it was not pleased. In the first place, it was incensed that when the masses thought about Punkin Head, they envisioned a spider, and that all believed the orange symbol Punkin Head painted on each body was an hourglass. Punkin Head painted what it did because it liked orange. It also intended to whack and rob eight businessmen and no more, before it moved on. To linger longer in the same area would be pressing its luck, and the figure eight was simply a reminder, a note to itself, that soon it would be time for Punkin Head and Poison to head out in the van, maybe up to the D.C. area.

In an article this morning, the reporter named Brazil had quoted an FBI profiler as saying that the Black Widow was a failure in interpersonal relationships, had never married or held a job long, was inadequate sexually and in every other way, and suffered from a sexual identity crisis, according to Special Agent Bird. Punkin Head, who of course was not referred to by name, but simply as "the killer," had read and viewed considerable violent pornography throughout its life, had come from a dysfunctional home, and had never finished college, if it had ever gone at all. It owned a vehicle, probably old and American, and still lived with its father, which it hated, or had for much of its adult life. Punkin Head was slovenly, possibly fat, and a substance abuser.

S.A. Bird, the article went on to say, predicted that Punkin Head would soon begin to decompensate. Punkin Head would make mistakes, overstep itself, become disorganized, and lose control. All psychopaths eventually did. Punkin Head threw the newspaper into the back of the van in disgust. Someone was snitching, leaking personal details about Punkin Head to the press, and it glared out at Blondie pausing at the Cadillac Grill, where the sh'im's sandwiches had been carefully prepared. Blondie decided to go inside.

The clientele at the Cadillac Grill wasn't happy to see Blondie walk in. They knew he was a reporter and wanted nothing to do with him or his questions. What did he think? They were crazy? They're suppose to risk getting Punkin Head pissed off, turn it meaner than usual and end up with Silvertips in their heads? That sh'im was the nastiest, most hateful of all time, and the truth was that the business community of Five Points wanted it to move on or get whacked. But as was often true in fascist regimes, no one had the guts or the time to rise up against Punkin Head. Energy and lucid thought were low among soldiers who stayed up late drinking Night Train, smoking dope, and shooting pool.

The head cook at the Cadillac was Remus Wheelon, a heavyset

Irishman with tattoos. He had heard all about Blondie and didn't want the snitch in his establishment. Remus was well aware that he had just fixed Punkin Head three deluxe Rise and Shine sandwiches, and the cold-blooded killing piece of shit was probably sitting out there in its van, watching and waiting for Remus to so much as serve Blondie a cup of coffee. Remus waited on the counter. He took his time scraping the grill. He made more coffee, fried another batch of baloney, and read the *Observer*.

Brazil had helped himself to a booth and picked up a greasy plastic-laminated menu, handwritten, prices reasonable. He was aware of people staring at him in a manner that was about as unfriendly as he had ever seen. He smiled back, as if this were Aunt Sarah's Pancake House, giving them an attitude that made all think twice. Brazil refused to be deterred from his mission. His pager went off for all to hear, and he grabbed it as if it had bitten him. He recognized the number and was surprised. Brazil looked around, deciding that the venue probably wasn't the best for whipping out his reporter's portable phone and calling the mayor's office.

He was getting up to leave and changed his mind when the door opened, the bell over it ringing. The young hooker walked in, and Brazil's pulse picked up. He wasn't sure why he was so fascinated, but he couldn't take his eyes off her and felt compassion that was equaled by fear. She wore jeans cut off high, sandals with tire tread soles, and a Grateful Dead tee shirt with sleeves torn off. Her naked breasts moved in rhythm as she walked. She took the next booth over, facing him, eyes bold on his as she flipped dirty blond hair out of the way.

Remus brought her coffee before she could even pick up the menu. She studied plastic-covered writing with difficulty, the words tangling like fishing line on the shore of Lake Algae, as the rich folks in Davidson called the pond at Griffith and Main Streets, where her daddy had taken her fishing a few times. This was before she got older and Mom was working in housekeeping at the Best Western. Daddy was a truck driver for Southeastern and kept erratic hours. Mom wasn't always home when her husband rolled in from a long trip.

In the mind of Cravon Jones, his three daughters belonged to him, and how he chose to express affection was his business and his right. There was no question he was partial to Addie, who was named after his wife's mother, whom he hated. Addie was blond and pretty from the day she was born, a special child who loved to cuddle with her daddy and with whom her mother did not bond or get along. Mrs. Jones was tired of coming home to a drunk, disgusting, stinking man, who slapped her around, shoved, and on one occasion broke her nose and jaw. The daughters, understandably, were drawn to him out of fear.

Addie reached her eleventh year, and Daddy crawled in bed with her one night. He smelled like sour sweat and booze as he pressed his hard thing against her and then drove it in while blood-soaked sheets and her silent tears flowed. Addie's sisters were in the same room and heard all of it. No one spoke of the event or acknowledged that it was real, and Mrs. Jones remained selectively ignorant. But she knew damn well, and Addie could tell by her mother's eyes, increased drinking, and growing indifference toward Addie. This went on until Addie turned fourteen and ran away one night while Mrs. Jones was working and Daddy was on the road somewhere. Addie got as far as Winston-Salem, where she met the first man who ever took care of her.

There had been many since, giving her cain and crack, cigarettes, fried chicken, whatever she wanted. She was twenty-three when she stumbled off the Greyhound in Charlotte some months back. Addie didn't remember it much, seemed like last she recalled she was in Atlanta getting high with some rich dude who drove a Lexus and paid an extra twenty dollars to urinate in her face. She could take anything as long as she wasn't present, and the only turnstile to that painless place was drugs. Sea, her last and final man, beat her with a coat hanger because she had cramps and couldn't make any money one night. She ran off for the countless time in her life, headed to Charlotte because she knew where it was and it was all she could afford after grabbing some old lady's purse.

Addie Jones, who had not been called by her Christian name in too many highs to remember, had an Atlanta Braves duffel bag she'd stolen from one of her tricks. In it she had a few things, and both hands had been gripping hard as she had walked along West Trade, nearing the Presto Grill, across from the All Right parking lot where Punkin Head was waiting in its van, fishing. Most of its best catches had come off buses, all those fuck-ups washing ashore like biological hazards, their stories the same. Punkin Head knew this for a fact, having crawled off one of those buses itself some time back.

Fifteen minutes later, Addie had been inside that dark blue van, and Punkin Head knew it had a find this time. Not only did it want this girl for itself, but the johns out there were going to fall hard for her perky body and sultry eyes and swollen mouth. Punkin Head christened its new creature Poison, and the two of them began their unfriendly takeover. Other pimps were flip at first. Then the killings began, and cops were everywhere. There were stories of bad hollowpoints and something painted orange and something else about a spider. All got scared.

"What'll be?" Remus asked Poison as she smoked a cigarette and stared out at the street.

"Some bacon," she said in an accent that no longer sounded white or even American.

It had been Remus's observation throughout his career that hookers took on the accents and mannerisms of their owners. Black hookers sounded white and white hookers sounded black, white gigolos walked with an NBA spring, black gigolos strutted like John Wayne. By now Remus was used to it. He just did his cooking and ran his joint, live and let be. He didn't want trouble, and Poison troubled him like an ice pick too close to his eye. She had a mocking smile, as if she knew the joke was on him. Remus sensed that a cold-blooded killing, including his own, would amuse her.

Brazil sat in his booth for quite some time, watching the clientele thin. He was tapping his menu, his table bare since no one seemed inclined to wait on him. He watched the young hooker finish breakfast. She dropped money on the table and got up. Brazil's eyes followed as she left. He was dying to talk to her, but scared. The bell on the door got quiet in her mysterious wake, and he got up, too. Brazil forgot he had never ordered, and left a tip. He emerged from the grill, notepad out, looking up and down the sidewalk, walking around the block, scanning the parking lot across Fifth Street, not seeing her anywhere. Disappointed, he continued wandering.

A black van with dark tinted glass drove slowly past, but Brazil gave it not a second thought as his mind tried to unlock something he was certain he knew the combination to but could not yet access.

Mungo stared out the van's windshield at Blondie, realizing that this case was getting only bigger. Mungo watched the slow, languid way the guy moved, stopping every now and then to search traffic and stare. Mungo's excitement mounted when Blondie approached Shena, one of the oldest sluts in the area.

She was perched on the front wooden steps of a dilapidated wooden house, sipping Coke, trying to get over the night before and readying herself for the one coming up. Blondie walked up like they knew each other. He started talking to her. She shrugged, gestured, then got pissed and waved him off like he was a pigeon in her way. Uh huh, Mungo thought. This boy-bait was becoming a territorial problem out here, moving in on the other hookers' lemonade stands. Blondie was probably luring men, maybe some women, selling them dope, committing crimes against nature and getting rich from it.

Mungo was convinced that if he dug further he would find out that Blondie was way up there on the drug-dealing chain, probably directly connected to New York. There could be a connection to the Black Widow killings. Mungo got out the video camera and captured what was possibly the best-looking, most clean-cut male prostitute he'd ever seen, except in the movies. Mungo quickly drove back to headquarters.

West had been up all night. She had done her best to make Niles shut up his yowling and kneading. She had thrown him off the bed until her shoulder got tired. She had talked in an adult fashion with him, trying to make him understand her fatigue and need of sleep. She had yelled, threatened, and locked him out of her room. He had been well rested and happily snoozing on his favorite windowsill when West hurried out the door this morning, late for work. She had no patience left. When Mungo walked into the conference room in the midst of her meeting with the Phantom Force, she was not welcoming.

"We're having a meeting," she said to Mungo.

"And I got something you're going to want to hear about." He proudly held up the videotape. "Definitely a player, maybe even more, maybe even our killer or at least involved." Mungo was breathless and looked like a biker.

Hammer had been on the phone ever since West had seen her last, and West got on the radio and told her boss to give her a call.

"I don't want you to get your hopes up," West told her. "But it sounds pretty promising."

"Describe him," Hammer said.

"White male, five-foot-seven, one-thirty pounds, blond, tight black jeans, tight polo-type shirt, Nikes. Strolling the area of Fifth and Trade, looking at cars, talking to hookers. Apparently he was in the Presto talking about the quality of drugs in the area and local sources, words to that effect. Also," West went on, "and this bothers me considerably, chief, you're aware of Poison, a.k.a. Addie Jones?"

"Right." Hammer had no idea.

"They were in the Cadillac Grill together for quite a long time. She left, and he went out right after her. At that point they split, seemingly off to do whatever they were up to."

"Where's this videotape?" Hammer wanted to know.

"I've got it."

"You looked at it yet?"

"We use these handheld JVC Grax 900 camcorders for covert operations. Mungo has gone to get the VHS adapter and should have it for me in a minute."

"Bring it by," Hammer said to her. "Let's take a look."

Chapter Nineteen

In the mayor's office, Brazil was impatiently perched on a couch, making a note of his surroundings and watching the secretary, Ruth Lafone, answer another call. She felt a little sorry for Andy Brazil, well aware that he was being set up as others before him. Her phone rang again. Ruth answered and smiled. She was pleasant and respectful to the man elected by an overwhelming majority to serve the people of the city. She hung up as she rose from her chair, and looked at Brazil.

"The mayor will see you now," she said.

Brazil was slightly bewildered. He had no idea how many times he had tried to get comments, interviews, and opinions from Mayor Search. Now the mayor was calling Brazil, finally following up on a request? Which request? Brazil wished he had dressed a little better this day, something besides black jeans that were too small. He had stopped in the men's room, at least, and had tucked in his faded red Head shirt, which also was a bit too small. Since Brazil had lost a few pounds, his normal clothes were falling off as if he were jailing, so he had dipped into another drawer of jeans and shirts he'd had since high school.

"If you don't mind my asking," he said to the secretary as he got off the couch, "is there some purpose to this interview other than my requests to talk to the mayor that go back to the beginning of my career?"

"I'm afraid he can't always get to everything right away," she apologized as she had learned to so well over the years.

Brazil looked at her for a moment, hesitating, detecting something in the way she averted her gaze from him. "Okay," he said. "Thanks a lot."

"You're so welcome." She led him to the slaughter because she needed her job.

Mayor Search was a distinguished, neat man in a European-cut summer weight gray suit. He wore a white shirt, his tie charcoal and blue paisley with matching suspenders. He did not get up from his huge block of walnut, the skyline of the city filling many windows. USBank Corporate Center was cut off about belt level, directly behind him, and the mayor could not see the crown unless he got on the floor and strained to look up.

"Thank you for finding the time to see me," Brazil said as he sat in a chair across from Search.

"Understand you've got a rather interesting situation here in our city," Search said.

"Yes, sir. And I appreciate it."

This wasn't the typical smartass reporter Search dealt with morning, noon, and night. The kid was Billy Budd, Billy Graham, wide-eyed innocence, polite, respectful, and committed. Search knew the extreme danger of sincere people like this. They died for causes, would do anything for Jesus, served a higher calling, were no respecter of persons, believed in burning bushes, and were not led into sin by Potiphar's wife. This wasn't going to be as easy as Search had supposed.

"Now let me tell you something, son," Search began in his

earnest, overbearing way to this lad who was lucky to get the mayor's time. "No one loves our police department more than I do. But you do realize, I hope, there are two sides to every story?"

"Usually more sides than that, sir, it's been my experience," said Brazil.

Hammer was in her outer office, having a word with Horgess, while she waited for West and a videotape that she prayed might reveal what Mungo seemed to think it did. Maybe her luck would turn for the better for once.

"Fred, enough," Hammer said, standing at the corner of his desk, hands in the pockets of her tobacco brown pants.

"It's just I feel so bad, Chief Hammer. Can't believe I did something like that. Here you trusted me and I'm supposed to make your life better, be a faithful retainer. And look what I did when things got a little stressful," Horgess said in his same sad, hate-me tone.

This was sounding all too much like Seth, and the last thing Hammer needed at present was an office husband as pitiful as the one in room 333 at Carolinas Medical Center.

"Fred, what do we say about mistakes? As part of our vision statement?" she quizzed him.

"I know." He could not look at her.

"First, we allow a mistake if you were trying to do the right thing when you made it, and second, if you tell someone that you made the mistake. And third, if you are willing to talk about your mistake to others so they won't do the same thing."

"I haven't done two and three," he said.

"No, you haven't," Hammer had to agree as West walked in. "Two isn't necessary because in this instance, everybody already knows. No later than seventeen hundred hours, I want a commentary by you for the *Informer*, telling everyone about your mistake. On my desk." She looked at him over the top of her glasses.

Mayor Search did not know the first thing about a community policing vision statement or any other vision statement that did not slaughter people for making mistakes, especially of the egregious nature that caused Hammer such embarrassment. This was not about to happen to him because the mayor knew how to handle people, including the media.

"It absolutely is untrue that the city is unsafe," he stated to Brazil, and the office seemed to have gotten airless and hot and maybe smaller.

"But five businessmen from out of town have been murdered in the last few weeks," Brazil said. "I don't know how you can . . ."

"Random. Isolated. Incidents." Sweat rolled down his sides. Search felt his face getting red.

"Downtown hotels and restaurants claim business has dropped more than twenty percent." Brazil wasn't trying to argue. He just wanted to get to the bottom of this.

"And people like you are only going to make that worse." Search mopped his forehead, wishing Cahoon had never passed this goddamn assignment along to him.

"All I want is to tell the truth, Mayor Search," Billy Budd, Billy Graham, said. "Hiding it won't help resolve this terrible situation."

The mayor resorted to sarcasm, laughing at this simple boy's simple logic. He felt that bitter juice seep through his veins, the bile rising as his face reddened dangerously, his rage a solar flare on the surface of his reason. Mayor Search lost control.

"I can't believe it." He laughed derisively at this reporter who was nothing in life. "*You're* giving *me* a lecture. Look. I'm not going to sit here and tell you business isn't suffering. *I* wouldn't drive downtown at night right now." He laughed harder, unstoppable, and drunk with his power.

By six P.M., at happy hour, West and Raines were on their way to being drunk at Jack Straw's A Tavern of Taste, next to La-dee-da's and Two Sisters, on East Seventh Street. West had changed out of her uniform and was casual in jeans, a loose denim shirt, and sandals. She was drinking Sierra Nevada Stout, the beer of the month, and still in a state of disbelief over the videotape she had watched with Hammer.

"Do you have any idea how this makes me and my investigative division look?" she said for the fourth time. "Christ. Please tell me this is a nightmare. Please, please. I'm going to wake up, right?"

Raines was drinking Field Stone chardonnay, the wine of the month. In gym shorts, Nikes with no socks, and a tank top, he was turning all heads except for the one across the table from him. What was it with her? All she ever talked about was work and that twit from the paper she rode around with. And Niles, oh yes, let's not forget that fucking, God-save-the-queen, cat. How many times had that cat ruined a building moment? Niles seemed to know exactly when to cause a distraction. A jump on Raines's back or head, a bite of a sock-covered toe. How about the time Niles sat on the remote control until the volume of Kenny G sounded like an air raid?

"It's not your fault," Raines said again, working on the spinach dip.

West ate another pickle fried in beer batter as Jump Little Children began setting up all their equipment and instruments. This small place with blue plastic tablecloths and funky art in screaming colors by someone named Tryke was going to rock tonight, jam, trot out primitive ids and libidos. Raines hoped he could make West stay at least until the second set. Actually, Raines thought what had happened to her all in a day's work was hilarious. It was all he could do to look tender and concerned.

He imagined Mungo-Jumbo swinging into the Presto to chow down. He spots a dude with a banana in his pocket who's the head of the Geezer Grill Cartel. A task force is formed, ending with a videotape of Blondie, the King of Vice and top suspect in the Black Widow serial murders, as he cruises Five Points in his tight black jeans and reporter's notepad. What wouldn't Raines have paid to see a videotape of Hammer sitting in her important conference room watching this shit! Christ! He fought a smile again and was losing. His face was aching and his stomach hurt.

"What's wrong with you?" West gave him a look. "There's nothing fucking funny about this."

"There certainly isn't," he said weakly as he dissolved into laughter, doubled over in his chair, howling as tears streamed down his face.

This went on as Jump Little Children set up amplifiers, and checked Fender electric guitars, Pearl drums with Zildjian medium crash cymbals, and Yamaha keyboards. They gave each other sly looks, flipping long hair out of the way, earrings glinting in the dim light. This guy was fried. Man, look at him go. Cool. The girlfriend wasn't digging it, either. Him taking a trip she's not on. Kind of weird he's drinking chardon-fucking-nay.

West was so angry she wanted to flip over the table, cowboy style. She wanted to jump on top of Raines, flex-cuff his ankles and feet, and just leave his sorry ass in the middle of Jack Straw's on a hot Thursday night. She halfway believed the only person Mungo was undercover for was Goode. Maybe Goode had gotten to him and promised him favors if he would set up West and destroy her credibility, her good relationship with Hammer. Oh God. When they had been sitting at that polished table and the video had flickered on, at first West was certain some mistake had been made. Brazil, big as life, was walking along to the sound of traffic, making notes, for Chrissake! How many serial killers or drug kingpins walk around in the middle of the day making notes?

As for Brazil's physical description, Mungo-the-Woolly-Mammoth had missed that by about forty pounds and six inches, although West had to admit she'd never seen Brazil in clothes that tight. She didn't know what to make of it. Those black jeans were so tight she could see the muscles in the back of his thighs flex as he walked, the red polo shirt fitting like paint, muscles lean and well defined, and he had veins. Maybe he was trying to blend out there. That would make sense.

"Tell me what she did," Raines choked, wiping his eyes.

West motioned to the waitress for another round. "I don't want to talk about it."

"Oh come on, Virginia. Tell me, tell me. You got to." He straightened up a bit. "Tell me what Hammer did when she saw the tape."

"No," West said.

Hammer hadn't done much, in truth. She'd sat in her usual spot at the head of the table, staring without comment at the twenty-four-inch Mitsubishi. She'd watched the entire tape, all forty-two minutes of it, every bit of Brazil's long promenade and indistinct conversations with the city's unsavory downtown folks. West and Hammer had watched Brazil point, shrug, jot, scan, and squat to tie shoelaces twice, before finally returning to the All Right to re-trieve his BMW. After a pregnant silence, Chief Hammer had taken off her glasses and voiced her opinion.

"What was this?" she had said to her deputy in charge of inves-tigations.

"I don't know what to tell you," West had said, feeling dark hate for Mungo.

"And this all began the day we had lunch at the Presto and you saw a man with a banana in his pocket." Hammer had wanted to make sure she was clear on the facts of the case.

"I really don't think it's fair to link the two."

Hammer had gotten up, but West knew not to move.

"Of course it's fair," Hammer had said, hands in her pockets again. "Don't get me wrong, I'm not blaming you, Virginia." She'd begun pacing. "How could Mungo not recognize Andy Brazil? He's out there morning, noon, and night, either for the *Observer* or us."

"Mungo is deep cover," West had explained. "He generally

avoids any place police or the press might be. I don't think he reads much, either."

Hammer had nodded. She could understand this, actually, and she was raw. Hammer was not ready or willing to react violently to the embarrassments and honest mistakes of others, whether it was Horgess, Mungo, or even West, who really had made no error, except perhaps in her choice of Mungo to do anything in life.

"Do you want me to destroy it?" West had asked as Hammer popped the tape out of the VCR. "I mean, I'd prefer not to. Some of that footage includes known prostitutes. Sugar, Double Fries, Butterfinger, Shooter, Lickety Split, Lemon Drop, Poison."

"All of them were in there?" Hammer was perplexed as she had opened the conference room door.

"They blend in. You have to know where to look."

"We'll hang on to it," Hammer had decided.

Raines was laughing so hard, West was furious with herself for telling him the rest of the story. He had his head on the table, hands covering his face. She wiped her forehead with a napkin, perspiring and flushed, as if she were in the tropics. The band would be cranking up soon, and Jack Straw's was getting crowded. She noticed Tommy Axel walk in, recognizing him from his picture in the paper. He had another guy with him, both dressed a lot like Raines, showing off. Why was it most of the gay guys were so good-looking? West didn't think it was fair. Not only were they guys in a guy's world, with all the benefits, but their DNA had somehow managed to appropriate the good stuff women had, too, like gracefulness and beauty.

Of course, gay guys got some of the bad stuff, too. Sneakiness, game playing, compulsive grooming, vanity, and shopping. Maybe it had nothing to do with gender, after all, West considered. Maybe there was no such thing as gender. Maybe biological people were just vehicles, like cars. She'd heard that overseas the steering wheels were on one side, while here they were on the other. Different genders? Maybe not. Maybe just different cars, the behavior of all determined by the spirit in the driver's seat.

"I've had enough," West hissed at Raines.

She drained her Sierra Nevada and started on another one. She might just tie one on tonight. Raines was driving.

"I'm sorry. I'm sorry." He took another deep breath and was spent. "You look like you don't feel too good," he said with one of his concerned expressions. "It is a little hot in here."

West mopped her face again, her clothes getting damp but not in the way Raines might have hoped. She was feeling the heaviness in her lower nature, the goddess of fertility reminding West with more volatility every month that time was running out. West's gynecologist had warned her gravely and repeatedly that troubles would begin about her age. She, Dr. Alice Bourgeois, spoke of punishment when there were no children and none on the way. *Never underestimate biology,* Dr. Bourgeois always said.

West and Raines placed an order for cheeseburgers, fries, and another round of drinks. She wiped her face again and was getting cold. She wasn't sure she could eat anything else, not another fried pickle. She watched the band setting up, her attention wandering to people at other tables. She was quiet for a long time, overhearing a couple not so far away speaking a foreign language, maybe German. West was getting maudlin.

"You seem preoccupied," said Raines the intuitive.

"Remember when those German tourists got whacked in Miami? What it did to the tourist industry?" she said.

Raines, as a man, took this personally. He had seen the bodies in the Black Widow slayings, or at least several of them. It was unthinkable to have a gun shoved against your head, your brains blown out. There was no telling what indignities those guys had been subjected to before the fact, and how did anyone really know that their pants hadn't been pulled down first, that maybe they hadn't been raped and then spray-painted? If the killer had been wearing a condom, who was going to know? West had said just the right thing to put Raines in a mood. Now he was totally pissed, too.

"So this is about the tourist industry," he said, leaning across the table and gesturing. "Forget guys being jerked out of their cars, brains blown all over, balls spray-painted with graffiti!"

West wiped her face again and dug Advil out of her butt pack. "It's not graffiti. It's a symbol."

Raines crossed his legs, feeling endangered. The waitress set down their dinner. He grabbed the ketchup bottle as he folded a french fry between his lips.

"It makes me sick," he said.

"It should make everybody sick." West could not look at food.

"Who do you think's doing it?" He dipped a bouquet of french fries into a red puddle.

"Maybe a sh'im." She was soaked in cold sweat. Her hair was wet around her face and neck, as if she'd just been in a foot pursuit.

"Huh?" Raines glanced up at her, biting into his dripping burger.

"She-him. Woman one night, man the next, depending on the mood," she said.

"Oh. Like you." He reached for the dish of mayonnaise.

"Goddamn it." West shoved her plate away. "I must be about to start."

The first twangs on electric guitars shattered the din, and sticks beat-beat and beat-beat-beat. Cymbals crashed and crashed as Axel snaked his foot around Jon's ankle and thought about Brazil for the millionth time this day.

Packer was thinking about Brazil, too, as the editor carried Dufus out the back door like a small, squirming football, headed for the same Japanese maple. Dufus had to go in the same place, get used to it, and be able to find his smells. It didn't matter that the tree was in the hinterlands and that it had started to rain. Packer dropped his wife's wall-eyed dog in the same bald spot next to the same gnarled root. Packer was out of breath, watching Dufus curtsey to the Queen.

"Why don't you lift your leg like a man," Packer muttered as bulging eyes watched him, speckled pink nose twitching. "Sissy," Packer said.

The worn-out editor's pager had vibrated earlier this evening while he was mowing the grass on his vacation day. It had been Panesa calling to tell him that the mayor had admitted that even he wouldn't drive downtown at night right now! Jesus living God, this was unbelievable. Surely the paper was well on its way to winning a Pulitzer for a series that made a difference in society, one that changed history. Why the hell did this wait to happen when Packer was out of the newsroom? He'd been there thirty-two years. The moment he decided to put life in perspective, ward off that heart attack perched outside the window of his existence, Andy Brazil showed up.

Now it was run-through-the-yard time to get Dufus's bowels wound up that they might unleash what, in Packer's mind, should have been a humiliation to any creature, except maybe a small domestic cat. Dufus would not chase Packer or come, and this was not new. The editor sat on the back porch steps while his wife's dog chewed mulch until it was time to drop his niggling gifts. Packer sighed and got up. He walked back into the air-conditioned house, Dufus on his heels.

"There's my good little boy," Mildred cooed as the dog hopped and licked until she picked him up and rocked him in loving arms.

"Don't mention it," Packer said, falling into his recliner chair, flicking on television.

He was still sitting there hours later, eating chicken nuggets, and dipping them in Roger's barbecue sauce. He loudly dug into a big bag of chips, swiping them in sauce, too. After several Coronas with lime, he had forgotten about the window and the heart attack perched beyond it. Mildred was watching *Home for the Holidays* again, because she thought it was their life. Go figure. In the first place Packer did not play the organ and she did not wear a wig or smoke, and they did not live in a small town. Their daughter had never gotten fired, at least not from an art gallery. That was one place she had never worked, probably because she was color blind.

Nor was their son gay that Packer knew of or cared to know of and any intimations to the contrary by his wife went into the Bermuda Triangle of their marital news hole. The editor didn't listen and the story didn't run. The End.

Packer pointed the remote control with authority. The volume went up, the ubiquitous Webb staring at the camera in a way that Packer knew meant trouble.

"Shit," Packer said, hitting a lever on his chair, cranking himself up.

"In a rare, if not shocking, moment of candor today," Webb said with his sincere expression, "Mayor Charles Search said that because of the Black Widow serial killings, hotel and restaurant business has dropped more than twenty percent, and he himself would not feel safe driving downtown at night. Mayor Search implored Charlotte's citizens to help police catch a killer who has ruthlessly murdered five . . ."

Packer was already dialing the phone, bag of potato chips falling out of his lap, scattering over the rug.

". . . an individual the FBI has profiled as a sexual psychopath, a serial killer who will not stop . . ." Webb went on.

"Are you listening to this?" Packer exclaimed when Panesa picked up his phone.

"I'm taping it," he said in a homicidal tone Packer rarely heard. "This has got to stop."

Chapter Twenty

Brazil never watched television because his mother monopolized the one at home, and he did not frequent Charlotte's many sports bars, where there were big screens in every corner. He knew nothing about what had been on the eleven o'clock news this Thursday night, and no one paged him or bothered to find him. All was peaceful as he ran on the Davidson track in complete darkness, close to midnight, no sound but the rhythm of his breathing and falling feet. As pleased as he was about his amazing nonstop journalistic home runs, he could not say that he was happy.

Other people were getting a lot of the same stuff. Webb was, for example, and no matter how informative or compassionate the story, the bottom line was the scoop. Brazil, of late, was scooping no one, if the truth be told. It just seemed he was because what he wrote routinely ended up on the front page and changed public opinion and seemed to rattle a lot of cages. Brazil would have been satisfied to spend the rest of his days writing pieces that did just this and nothing else. Prizes didn't matter much, really. But he was realistic. If he didn't beat everybody to the quote, the revelation, or the crime scene, one of these days he might not get paid anymore to write.

At which point he could become a cop, he supposed, and this turned his mind to West again, sailing him off firm ground into a dark, tangled, painful thicket that hurt and frustrated him the more he tried to fight his way out of it. He ran harder, bending around goal posts, passing empty bleachers filled with the memories of games, mostly lost, during fall nights when he had usually been studying or walking the frosty campus beneath stars he tried to describe as no one ever had. He would tuck his chin into his hooded sweatshirt, heading to the library or a hidden corner of the student lounge, to work on a term paper or poetry, not wanting couples he passed to notice him.

Even if West hadn't wanted to play tennis, there was no need for her to have been rude about it unless she hated him. *Forget it.* Her voice saying those heartless words followed him as he ran harder, lungs beinning to burn, catching fire around the edges as his legs reached farther and sweat left a trail of scattered spots. He tried to outrun the voice and the person who owned it, anger flinging him through the night and past the fifty yard line. Legs wobbled as he slowed. Brazil fell into cool, damp grass. He lay on his back, panting, heart thundering, and he had a premonition that he was going to die.

Virginia West felt like it. She lay in bed, lights out, a hot water bottle held close as contractions prepared her for birth for no good cause. Ever since she was fourteen, she'd gone into labor once a month, some episodes worse than others. On occasion, the pain was debilitating enough to send her home from school, a date, or work, lying about what was wrong as she gulped Midol. After a sullen Raines, the paramedic, had dropped her off, she'd taken four Motrin, a little too late. Hadn't Dr. Bourgeois told her to take two hundred milligrams of ibuprofen four times a day *three days before* trouble started so it could be prevented, *and don't cut yourself or get a nosebleed, Virginia?* West, as usual, had gotten too busy to bother with anything so mundane, so trivial, as her health. Niles recognized the cyclical emergency and responded, curling around his owner's neck and head, keeping her warm. He was pleased she wasn't going anywhere and he didn't have to share their bed.

Chief Judy Hammer was having morbid premonitions and was bedside, too, in the Surgical Intensive Care Unit (SICU) of Carolinas Medical Center, where Seth's condition was serious and on the wrong side of getting better. Hammer was in shock, dressed in gown, mask, and gloves, sitting by his bed. High dose penicillin, clindamycin, and immunic globulin dripped into her husband's veins in an effort to counter necrotizing fasciitis (NF). It was a rare infection associated with systemic infection and a fulminant course, according to Hammer's personal observations and the notes she had been taking every time the infectious disease doctor spoke.

This was all somehow related to everyday group A beta-hemolytic streptococci and *Staphylococcus aureus*, which Hammer could not comprehend beyond figuring out that the microscopic bastards were eating her husband alive. Meanwhile, Seth's oxygen content in his bloodstream had dropped below normal, and the medical center was in a panic. Personnel had made Seth, the V.I.P., a top priority, and specialists were in and out. Hammer could not keep them straight. She could not think as she stared at her husband's slack, feverish face and smelled his death through the mask she wore.

During the Civil War, surgeons would have diagnosed her husband's condition as simple gangrene. No fancy Latin term changed the reality of flesh turning black and green at a wound site, with limbs and eventually the person rotting alive. The only treatment for NF was antibiotics, surgery, and amputation. About a third of the three to five hundred people who got the disease in the

U.S. annually died, or approximately thirty percent, according to what Hammer had found through searches on America Online.

Nothing she had discovered about the disease had consoled or given hope. The deadly bacteria burst upon the scene in recent years when it killed eleven people in Great Britain. KILLER BUG ATE MY FACE, screamed the *Daily Star*. DEADLY FLESH EATING BACTERIA, other tabloids proclaimed. It had killed Jim Henson of the Muppets, Hammer had discovered on the Internet, and was believed to be a virulent form of a strep that had caused scarlet fever in the 1800s. In some cases, NF spread too rapidly for antibiotics to work, and it was feared that Seth would be the latest statistic. His V.I.P. status had ensured aggressive treatment since admission, so the problem lay not in the hospital, but in his general condition.

Seth had poor nutrition. He was clinically depressed. He had a history of heavy drinking and arteriosclerotic vascular disease. He had received a trauma resulting in an open wound and a foreign body that could not be removed. Seth, according to Dr. Cabel, was immunosuppressed and was losing approximately a pound of flesh per hour. This did not include layers lost by surgeons fileting to the next level of healthy, bleeding tissue, which soon after turned black and green, despite all efforts and prayers. Hammer was motionless in her chair, reliving every word she'd ever spoken to her husband, every deed that had been angry or unkind. None of his flaws would come to her now.

This was all her fault. It had been her .38 special, her Remington hollowpoint +P cartridge. It had been her order that he root under the sheets for that gun and hand it over to her *this minute.* It had been Hammer giving him the ultimatum about his weight, and she halfway believed that what he suffered from now was no coincidence but a functional illness. Seth was melting before her eyes, an inch smaller every hour, slabs lighter after every surgery. This was not the weight-loss plan she would have wished for him. He was punishing her for all those years he had lived in her shadow, the wind beneath her wings, her inspiration and biggest fan.

"Chief Hammer?"

She realized someone was speaking, and her eyes focused on Dr. Cabel in surgical greens, cap, mask, gloves, and shoe covers. He was no older than Jude. God help me, Hammer thought with a deep, quiet breath as, once again, she got out of her chair.

"If you'll give me a minute with him," Dr. Cabel said to her.

Hammer went out into the antiseptic, bright corridor. She watched nurses, doctors, family members, and friends alight on different rooms where more suffering lay tethered to narrow hydraulic beds and machines monitored the life force as it struggled on. She stood, in a daze, until Dr. Cabel returned, slipping Seth's chart in the envelope on the back of the door.

"How is he?" Hammer asked the same question, pulling her mask down around her neck.

Dr. Cabel left his mask on. He took no chances and didn't even shower at home anymore without lathering from head to toe with antibacterial soap. He shut Seth's door, eyes troubled. Hammer was shrewd and not interested in further euphemisms, convolutions, and evasions. If this young infectious disease doctor thought he could hide the truth from her, she was about to add to his education.

"We're going to take him back into surgery," Seth's doctor said. "Which is fairly typical at this point."

"And which point is this point, exactly?" Hammer wanted to know.

"Day two of progressive streptococcal gangrene and necrotizing fasciitis," he replied. "The necrosis is visibly beyond the margins of the original debridement."

While Dr. Cabel respected Chief Hammer, he did not want to deal with her. He cast about for a nurse. Shit. All were busy elsewhere.

"I need to get started," he said.

"Not so fast," Hammer let him know. "Exactly what are you going to do in surgery?"

"We'll know better when we go in."

"How about hazarding a guess." She might slap him.

"Generally, at this stage, the wound is debrided again down to bleeding, healthy tissue. We'll probably irrigate with saline and pack the wound with Nu-Gauze. We'll continue with hyperbaric oxygen therapy twice a day, and I recommend total parenteral nutrition."

"Multivitamins then," she said.

"Well, yes." He was mildly surprised by her ability to connect the dots.

Hammer had been buying vitamins for years and failed to see anything special about the suggestion. Dr. Cabel started to walk off. She snatched him back by his greens.

"Let's cut to the chase," she said. "Seth has had strep throat a dozen times in his life. Why has it turned into this now? Aside from his lousy immune system."

"It's not exactly the same thing as the strep that causes a sore throat."

"Clearly."

This lady was not going to let him go. Dr. Cabel felt sorry for Seth in a different way, now. Living with this woman would wear out anybody. Imagine asking her to fetch coffee or take your word for it? When all else failed, Dr. Cabel switched to the language that only his super race understood.

"It's quite possible strep has acquired new genetic information, picked up genes. This can happen through infection by a bacteriophage," Dr. Cabel informed her.

"What's a bacteriophage?" She wouldn't give up.

"Uh, a virus that can incorporate its DNA into a bacterial host," he said. "The hypothesis is, that some M1 strain of group A strep in approximately forty percent of recent invasive infections seems to have acquired genetic material from a phage. This is according to WHO."

"*Who?*" Hammer frowned.

"Exactly." He looked at his watch long enough to give her a broad hint.

"Who the hell is *who?*" She would get an answer.

"World Health Organization. They have a strep reference laboratory. The long and short of it, this may all be connected to a gene that encodes a toxin called superantigen which is widely believed to be connected to toxic-shock syndrome."

"My husband has the same thing you get from a tampon?" Hammer raised her voice.

"A distant cousin."

"And since when do you amputate for that?" she demanded as passersby glanced curiously at the two people in greens arguing in the spotless, well-lit corridor.

"No, no." He had to get away from this woman, so he, the English major, threw Shakespeare at her. "Ma'am, with what your husband's got, surgery remains the most effective treatment. 'Be bloody, bold and resolute,'" he quoted. *"King Lear."*

"Macbeth," Hammer, who loved the theater, said as Dr. Cabel hurried off.

She lingered long enough to see her husband wheeled back to the O.R., then Hammer went home. By nine o'clock she had collapsed in bed, too exhausted and distressed to remain in a conscious state effectively. She and her deputy chief, in their respective homes, one with a pet, one without, slept fitfully the rest of the night.

Brazil tossed and yanked sheets this way and that, over his feet, under them, back over them again, on his side, on his belly. Finally, he lay on his back, staring up into the dark, listening to the TV murmur through the wall as his mother lay passed out on the couch again.

He kept thinking about what West had said. He should move out, find an apartment. Yet whenever he followed this scary, exciting path a few steps further, he always ran slam into the same scarecrow that sent him fleeing the other way. What was he supposed to do about his mother? What would happen to her if he left her alone? He supposed he could still bring by groceries, stop in to check on her, fix things, and run errands. Brazil worried as he thrashed in bed, listening to the eerie strains of what must have been some three A.M. half-a-star horror flick. He thought about West and felt depressed again.

Brazil decided that he did not like West in the least. She was not the kind, enlightened woman that Hammer was. One day, Brazil would find someone like Hammer. They would enjoy and respect each other, and play tennis, run, work out with weights, cook, fix the cars, go to the beach, read good fiction and poetry, and do everything together, except when they needed space. What did West know about any of this? She built fences. She cut her own grass with a rider mower because she was too lazy to use a push one, and her yard was barely half an acre. She had disgusting eating habits. She smoked. Brazil turned over again, hanging his arms off either side of the mattress, miserable.

At five, he gave up and went back to the track to run again. He clipped off eight more miles and could have gone farther, but he got bored and wanted to get downtown. It was strange. He'd gone from exhaustion to hyperactivity in a matter of days. Brazil could remember no other time in his life when his chemistry had swung him around like this. One minute he was dragging, the next he was high and excited with no explanation. He contemplated the possibility that his hormones were going through a phase, which he expected would be normal for one his age. It was true that if the male did not give in to his drives between the ages of sixteen and twenty, biology would punish him.

His primary care physician had told him exactly that. Dr. Rush, whose family practice was in Cornelius, had warned Brazil about this very phenomenon when Brazil had a team checkup his freshman year at Davidson. Dr. Rush, recognizing that Brazil had no father and needed guidance, said many young men made tragic mistakes because their bodies were in a procreation mode. This, said Dr. Rush, was nothing more than a throwback to colonial times when sixteen was more than half of the male's life expectancy, assuming Indians or neighbors didn't get him first. When viewed in this fashion, sexual urges, albeit primitive, made perfect sense, and Brazil was to do his best not to act on them.

Brazil would be twenty-three next May, and the urges had not lessened with time. He had been faithful to Dr. Rush, who, according to local gossip, was not faithful to his wife and never had been. Brazil thought about sexuality as he ran a few sprints before trotting home. It seemed to him that love and sex were connected but maybe shouldn't be. Love made him sweet and thoughtful. Love prompted him to notice flowers and want to pick them. Love crafted his finest poetry, while sex throbbed in powerful, earthy pentameters he would never show to anyone or submit for publication.

He hurried home and took a longer than usual shower. At five past eight, he was moving through the cafeteria line in the Knight-Ridder building. He was in jeans, pager on his belt, people staring curiously at the boy wonder reporter who played police and always seemed alone. Brazil selected Raisin Bran and blueberries as the intercom piped in WBT's wildly popular and irreverent *Don't Go Into Morning* show with Dave and Dave.

"In a fast-breaking story last night," Dave was saying in his deep radio voice, "it was revealed that even our city's mayor won't go downtown at night right now."

"Question is, why would he anyway?" quipped Dave.

"Same thing Senator Butler should have asked."

"Just checking on his constituents, Dave. Trying to be of service."

"And the eensy weensy spider crawled up his water spout . . ."

"Whoa, Dave. This is getting out of control."

"Hey, we're supposed to be able to say anything on this show. That's in the contract." Dave was his usual witty self, better than Howard Stern, really.

"Seriously. Mayor Search is asking everybody to help catch the Black Widow killer," Dave said. "And next up is Madonna, Amy Grant, and Rod Stewart . . ."

Brazil had stopped in the middle of the line, frozen as the radio played on and people made their way around him. Packer was walking in, heading straight toward him. Brazil's world was Humpty Dumpty off the wall, cracks happening everywhere at once. He paid for his breakfast and turned around to face his ruination.

"What's going on?" he said before his grim editor could tell him.

"Upstairs now," Packer said. "We got a problem."

Brazil did not run up the escalator. He did not speak to Packer, who had nothing more to say. Packer wanted no part of this. He wasn't going to insert his foot in his mouth. The great Richard Panesa could fix this one. That's why Knight-Ridder paid him those big bucks. Brazil had been marched to the principal's office only twice during his early school years. In neither case had he really done anything wrong. The first time he had poked his finger into the hamster cage and had gotten bitten. The second time of trouble occurred when he inserted his finger into the hole at the top of his clipboard and had gotten stuck.

Mr. Kenny used wire cutters to free young Brazil, who had been humiliated and heartbroken. The blue Formica clipboard with its map of the United States was destroyed. Mr. Kenny threw it into the trash while Brazil stood bravely by, refusing to cry and knowing his mother could not afford to buy him another one. Brazil had meekly asked if he could stay after school for a week, dusting erasers on back steps to earn enough to buy something new to hold notebook paper and write on. That had been okay with all.

Brazil wondered what he could offer to Panesa to make up for whatever he had done to cause such a problem. When he walked into the publisher's intimidating glass office, Panesa was sitting behind his mahogany desk, in his fine Italian suit and leather chair. Panesa didn't get up or acknowledge Brazil directly but continued reading a printout of the editorial for the Sunday paper, which slammed Mayor Search for his glib, albeit true, comment about his reluctance to travel downtown these nights.

"You might want to shut the door," Panesa quietly said to his young reporter.

Brazil did and took a seat across from his boss.

"Andy," he said, "do you watch television?"

His confusion grew. "I rarely have time . . ."

"Then you may not know that you are being scooped right and left."

The dragon inside Brazil woke up. "Meaning?"

Panesa saw fire in his eyes. Good. The only way this sensitive, brilliant young talent was going to last in this criminal world was if he were a fighter, like Panesa was. Panesa wasn't going to give him a breath of comfort. Andy Brazil, welcome to Hell School, the publisher thought as he picked up a remote control from his mighty desk.

"Meaning"—Panesa hit a button and a screen unrolled from the ceiling—"that the last four or five major stories you've done have been aired on television the night before they ran in the paper, usually on the eleven o'clock news." He pressed another button, and the overhead projector turned on. "Then the radio stations pick them up first thing in the morning. Before most people get a chance to read what we've plastered on the front page of our paper."

Brazil shot up from his chair, horrified and homicidal.

"That can't be! No one's even around when I'm out there!" he exclaimed, fists balled by his sides.

Panesa pointed the remote control, pressed another button, and instantly Webb's face was huge in the room.

". . . in a Channel Three exclusive interview said she returns to the scene of the crash late at night and sits in her car and weeps. Johnson, who turned in her badge this morning, said she wishes she had been killed, too . . ."

Panesa looked at Brazil. Brazil was speechless, his fury toward Webb coalescing into hatred for all. Moments passed before the young police reporter could gather his wits.

"Was this after my story?" Brazil asked, though he knew better.

"Before," Panesa replied, watching him carefully, and assessing. "The night before it ran. Like every other one that's followed. Then this bit with the mayor. Well, that clinched it. We know that was a slip on Search's part and not something Webb could know unless he's got the mayor's office bugged."

"This can't be!" Brazil boiled over. "It's not my fault!"

"This is not about fault." Panesa was stern with him. "Get to the bottom of it. Now. We're really being hurt."

Panesa watched Brazil storm out. The publisher had a meeting, but sat at his desk, going through memos dictating to his secretary while he observed Brazil through glass. Brazil was angrily opening desk drawers, digging in the box under it, throwing notepads and other personal effects into his briefcase. He ran out of the newsroom as if he did not plan on coming back. Panesa picked up the phone.

"Get Virginia West on the line," the publisher said.

Tommy Axel was staring after Brazil's wake, wondering what the hell was going on and at the same time suspicious. He knew about Webb and had heard about the leaks and didn't blame Brazil for being out of his mind. Axel couldn't imagine the same thing happening to him, someone stealing brilliant thoughts and analyses from his music columns. God. Poor guy.

Brenda Bond also was alert to the uproar as she worked on a computer that had gone down three days in a row because the idiot garden columnist had a knack for striking combinations of keys that somehow locked him out or translated his files into pi signs. Bond had a strange sensation as she went into System Manager. She found it hard to concentrate.

West was standing behind her desk, struggling to pack up her briefcase and snap the lid back on her coffee and wrap up the biscuit she didn't have time to eat. She looked worried and frantic as Panesa talked to her on the phone.

"You have any idea where he went?" West inquired.

"Home, maybe?" Panesa said over the line. "He lives with his mother."

West looked hopelessly at the clock. She was supposed to be in Hammer's office in ninety seconds, and there was no such thing as putting the chief on hold or being late or not showing up or forgetting. West shut her briefcase and slid her radio into the case on her belt. She was at a loss.

"I'll do what I can," she promised Panesa. "Unfortunately, I've got court this morning. My guess is he's just blowing off steam. As soon as he cools down, he'll be back. Andy's not a quitter."

"I hope you're right."

"If he hasn't shown up by the time I get back, I'll start looking," West said.

"Good idea."

West hoped that Johnny Martino would plead guilty. Hammer didn't. She was in a mood to cause trouble. Dr. Cabel had done her a favor, really. He had ignited a few sparks of anger, and the brighter they got, the more the mist of depression and malaise burned off. She was walking the fastest West had ever seen her, a zip-up briefcase under an arm, sunglasses on. Hammer and West made their way through the sweltering piedmont morning to the Criminal Court Building, constructed of granite in 1987 and therefore older than most buildings in Charlotte. Hammer and West waited in line with everyone else at the X-ray machine.

"Quit worrying." West tried to reassure her boss as they inched foward behind some of the city's finer citizens. "He'll plead." She glanced at her watch.

"I'm not worried," said Hammer.

West was. There were a hundred cases on the docket today. In truth, this was a bigger problem than whether Martino pled guilty versus taking his chances before a jury of his peers. Deputy Octavius Able eyed the two women getting closer in line and was suddenly alert and interested in his job. West had not passed through his X-ray machine since it resided in the old courthouse. Never had Able so much as laid eyes on Hammer in person. He had never had complete control over her. West was in uniform and walked around the door frame that was beeping every other second as pagers, change, keys, good luck charms, and pocketknives went into a cup. Hammer walked around, too, assuming the privilege of her position.

"Excuse me, ma'am!" Deputy Able said for all to hear. "Ma'am! Please step through."

"She's the chief of police," West quietly told him, and she knew damn well it went without saying.

"Need some identification," the powerful deputy said to Hammer.

A long line of restless feet stopped, all eyes on the well-dressed lady with the familiar face. Who was that? They'd seen her somewhere. Maybe she was on TV, the news, a talk show? Oh heck. Then Tinsley Owens, six deep in line, here for reckless driving, got it. This lady in pearls was the wife of someone famous, maybe Billy Graham. Hammer was nonplussed as she dug through her pocketbook, and this made Deputy Able's assertion of self not quite as rewarding. She smiled at him, holding up her badge.

"Thanks for checking." She could have knocked him over when she said that. "In case anybody had any doubts about the security of our courthouse." She leaned close to read his nameplate. "O.T. Able," she repeated, committing it to memory.

Now the deputy was dead. She was going to complain.

"Just doing my job," he weakly said as the line got longer, winding around the world, the entire human race witnessing his destruction.

"You most certainly were," Hammer agreed. "And I'm going to make sure the sheriff knows how much he should appreciate you."

The deputy realized the chief meant every word of it, and Able was suddenly taller and slimmer. His khaki uniform fit perfectly. He was handsome and not nearly as old as he had been when he was at the BP pumping gas this morning and a carload of juveniles yelled, calling him *Deputy Dawg, Hawaii Five-O, Tuna Breath,* and other racial slurs. Deputy Octavius Able was ashamed of himself for throwing his weight around with this woman chief. He never used to be that way and did not know what had happened to him over the years.

Chapter Twenty-one

Hammer and West signed in at the Court Liaison Office and punched time cards. On the second floor, they followed a long corridor crowded with people looking for a pay phone or the bathroom. Some were sleeping on maple benches, or reading the *Observer* to see if their cases might be mentioned. When West opened the door to 2107, her anxiety increased. The courtroom was packed with defendants waiting for punishment, and with cops whose fault it was. Hammer led the way to the very front, sitting on the side for lawyers and police. Assistant District Attorney Melvin Pond spotted the two powerful women instantly and got excited. He had been waiting for them. This was his chance.

Fourth Circuit Judge Tyler Bovine of the Twenty-fifth Prosecutorial District had been waiting, too, as had the media from far and near. *Batman and Robin*, she, Judge Bovine, thought with intense pleasure as she departed from her chambers. She'd see about that when she reigned on high in the long black robe that covered her massive body of law. West felt increasingly troubled for a number of reasons. She was worried about Brazil and afraid she'd never get out of here to check on him. Tyler Bovine, as was true of the rest of the judicial herd, was a traveling judge. She resided on the other side of the Catawba River and despised Charlotte and all that was good about it, including its citizens. The judge was confident that it was only a matter of time before Charlotte annexed her hometown of Gastonia, and all else Cornwallis had failed to seize.

"All rise for the judge."

All got around to it, and Judge Bovine smiled to herself as she entered the courtroom and spotted Hammer and West. The judge knew that the press had been tipped not to waste their time hanging around here this day. Batman and Robin would be back on Monday. Oh yes they would. The judge sat and put on her glasses, looking important and godlike. A.D.A. Pond stared at the docket as if he had never seen one before this morning. He knew he had a battle on his hands but was determined he would prevail.

"The court calls the case of the State of North Carolina versus Johnny Martino," he said with confidence he did not feel.

"I'm not ready to hear that now." Judge Bovine sounded bored.

West nudged Hammer, who was thinking about Seth and not sure what she would do if he died. It did not matter how much they fought or drove each other crazy or proved irrefutably that men and women could not be soulmates or friends. Hammer had a tragic look on her face, and A.D.A. Pond took it as a slight to his knighthood and professional future. He had failed this wonderful, heroic woman whose husband was shot and in the hospital. Chief Hammer did not need to be sitting here with all these cretins. Judge Bovine saw the look on Hammer's face, too, and also misinterpreted, and was further aroused. Hammer had not supported Bovine in the last election. Bovine would see how big and important Hammer was now.

"When I call out your name, please stand. Maury Anthony," announced A.D.A. Pond.

Pond scanned despondent faces. He searched people slumped

back, pissed off, and sleeping. Maury Anthony and his public defender rose near the rear. They came forward and stood before the A.D.A.'s table.

"Mr. Anthony, how do you plead to possession with the intent to sell cocaine?" the A.D.A. asked.

"Guilty," Mr. Anthony spoke.

Judge Bovine stared out at the defendant who was no different than all others. "Mr. Anthony. You realize that by pleading guilty you have no right to appeal," she stated rather than asked.

Mr. Anthony looked at his public defender, who nodded. Mr. Anthony returned his attention to the judge. "Yes, sir," he said.

Laughter was scattered among those awake and alert. Mr. Anthony realized his egregious error and grinned sheepishly. "I'm sorry, ma'am. My eyes ain't what they once was."

More laughter.

Judge Bovine's big flat face turned to concrete. "What says the state," she ordered as she sipped from a two-liter bottle of Evian.

A.D.A. Pond looked over his notes. He glanced at Hammer and West, hoping they were attentive and impressed. This was his opportunity to be eloquent, no matter what a dog of a case it was.

"Your Honor," the A.D.A. began as he always did, "on the night of July twenty-second, at approximately eleven-thirty, Mr. Anthony was drinking and socializing in an establishment on Fourth Street near Graham . . ."

"The court requires the exact address," Judge Bovine interrupted.

"Well, Your Honor, the problem is, there's not one."

"There has to be one," said the judge.

"This is an area where a building was razed in nineteen-ninety-five, Your Honor. The defendant and his associates were back in weeds . . ."

"What was the address of the building that was razed?"

"I don't know," said the A.D.A., after a pause.

Mr. Anthony smiled. His public defender looked smug. West

was getting a headache. Hammer had drifted further off. The judge drank from her bottle of water.

"You will provide that for the court," the judge said, screwing on the cap.

"Yes, Your Honor. Only, where this transaction occurred isn't precisely at the old address, but rather farther back, approximately eighty feet, and then another fifty feet, I'd say, at a sixty-degree angle, northeast, from the Independence Welfare building that was there, that was razed, in a thicket where Mr. Anthony had set up a hobo camp of sorts for the purposes of buying and selling and smoking crack cocaine and eating crabs with associates on that night. Of July twenty-second."

A.D.A. Pond had the attention, however briefly, of Hammer, and West, plus Johnny Martino's mother and the conscious courtroom, in addition to two bailiffs and a probation officer. All stared at him with a mixture of curiosity and lack of comprehension.

"The court requires an address," the judge repeated.

She took another gulp of water and felt contempt for her psychiatrist and for manic-depressive people everywhere. Not only did lithium necessitate drinking a tub of water daily but it caused frequent urination, which by Judge Bovine's definition was double jeopardy. Her bladder and kidneys were a drip coffee maker that she could feel and measure as she drove back and forth from Gaston County and sat on the bench and went to the movies and flew on crowded airplanes or walked on the track and found the fieldhouse locked.

Because she was a superior court judge, she could adjourn every fifteen, twenty, or thirty minutes, or until after lunch if her need was great and she so chose. She could wheel in a damn Porta-John, do whatever she liked, *ipso facto*. But what she would never do, not once during this life and on this planet, was to interrupt a case after it was started, because above all else, the judge was a well-bred lady who had grown up in an antebellum house and gone to Queens College. Judge Bovine was tough but never rude. She did not tolerate fools or classless people, and no one could accuse her of anything less than impeccable manners. There was nothing more important than manners, really.

A.D.A. Pond hesitated. Hammer had faded away again. West could not get comfortable. The bench seat was wood, and it pressed her police belt and the small of her back. She was perspiring and waiting for her pager to vibrate. Brazil was decompensating. It was something West sensed, yet she wasn't certain why or what to do about it.

"Mr. Pond," the judge said, "please continue."

"Thank you, Your Honor. On this particular night of July twenty-second, Mr. Anthony did sell crack cocaine to an undercover Charlotte police officer."

"Is this officer in the courtroom?" The judge squinted at the sea of wretches below her.

Mungo stood. West turned around, dismayed when she saw who had caused such creaking and shuffling and whispering. *Oh God, not again.* West's sense of foreboding darkened. Hammer remembered Seth bringing her breakfast in bed and dropping keys on the tray. The new Triumph Spitfire was green with burl wood, and she had been a sergeant with free time, and he was the rich son of a rich land developer. Back then, they went on long drives and had picnics. She would come home from work, and music filled the house. When did Seth stop listening to Beethoven, Mozart, Mahler, and Bach, and start turning on the TV? When did Seth decide he wanted to die?

"The subject, Mr. Anthony," Mungo was saying, "was sitting on a blanket in the thicket Mr. Pond has just described. He was with two other subjects, drinking Magnum Forty-four and Colt Forty-five. Between them they had a dozen steamed crabs in a brown paper bag."

"A dozen?" Judge Bovine queried. "You counted them, Detective Mungo?"

"Most were gone, Your Honor. I was told there had been a dozen originally. When I looked there were three left, I believe."

"Go on, go on." What patience the judge had for this drivel from the dregs of humanity was inversely proportional to her filling bladder as she took another slug of water and thought of what she would eat for lunch.

"The subject, Mr. Anthony, offered to sell me a rock of cocaine in a vial, for fifteen dollars," Mungo continued.

"Bullshit," was Mr. Anthony's comment. "I offered you a fucking crab, man."

"Mr. Anthony, if you aren't quiet, I will hold you in contempt of court," Judge Bovine warned.

"It was a crab. Only time I used the word *crack* was when I told him to *crack* it himself."

Mungo said, "Your Honor, I asked the subject what was in the bag, and he distinctly replied, 'crack.'"

"Did not." Mr. Anthony was about to approach the bench, his public defender restraining him by a sleeve that still had the label sewed on it.

"Did too," Mungo said.

"Did not!"

"Too."

"Uh uh."

"Order!" the judge declared. "Mr. Anthony, one more outburst and . . ."

"Let me tell my side for once!" Mr. Anthony went on.

"That is what you have a lawyer for," the judge said severely, and she was beginning to feel the pressure of water and a loss of composure.

"Oh yeah? This piece of shit?" Mr. Anthony glowered at his free-lunch defense.

The courtroom was awake and interested, more so than A.D.A. Pond had ever witnessed before this morning. Something was going to happen and no one was about to miss it, people nudging each other and making silent bets. Jake on the third row, defendant's side, was putting his money on Mr. Anthony ending up with his butt in jail. Shontay two rows over was betting on the undercover detective who reminded her of a haystack wearing a wrinkled pin-striped suit. Cops always won, no matter how wrong they might be, it was her belief, based on hearsay. Quik, way in the back, didn't give a fuck as he practiced flicking his thumb out like a switchblade. As soon as he could, the asshole responsible for Quik's *show cause warrant* was gonna pay. Ratting on him like that. Man.

"Detective Mungo." Judge Bovine had had enough. "What probable cause did you have to search Mr. Anthony's brown paper bag?"

"Your Honor, it's like I said." Mungo was unmoved. "I asked him what was in the bag. He told me."

"He told you crabs and suggested you crack these crabs yourself," said the judge, who really had to go now.

"Gee. I don't know. I thought he said crack." Mungo tried to be fair.

This sort of thing happened to Mungo more times than not. He'd always found it easier to hear whatever he wanted, and when one was as big as him, one could. The case was dismissed, and before the judge could adjourn to her chambers, the agitated A.D.A. called the next, and the next, and the next, and the judge did not interrupt, because it was one thing she would not do. Citizens arrested for burglaries, car thefts, rape, murder, and more drug dealers and those who patronized them stood with their public defenders. A.D.A. Pond was mindful of the judge's constricted body language and miserable demeanor. Pond was accustomed to the judge's frequent visits to her chambers and knew that capitalizing on her disability was his only hope.

Each time Her Honor started to rise from her bench, A.D.A. Pond was off and running on the next case. As fast as he could, he announced Johnny Martino once again, in hopes Pond would break the judge, wear her down, and subject her to the water treatment until she could take no more. Her Honor would hear the state of North Carolina versus Johnny Martino so Hammer and West could return to life's highways and the hospital. A.D.A. Pond prayed

Hammer would think kindly of him when he ran for D.A. in three years.

"Johnny Martino," A.D.A. Pond said as fast as he could, again, moments later.

"I'm not ready to hear that case yet." The judge could barely talk.

"Alex Brown," the A.D.A. blurted out.

"Yeah." Mr. Brown stood, as did his counsel.

"How do you plead to malicious wounding?"

"He started it," Mr. Brown stated for the record. "What I'm supposed to do, huh? In Church's getting a quart of chicken livers and he decides he wants the same thing, only he's going to get mine and not pay."

Hammer had tuned back in long enough to make an assessment of her surroundings and those in it. This was much more disheartening than she had imagined. No wonder her beat officers and investigators got so discouraged, so jaded and cynical. There had been a time when she'd had no sympathy or use for people like this. They were lazy, no-account, self-destructive, self-absorbed wastrels who added nothing to society and took from everyone around them. She thought of Seth, of his money, privilege, and opportunity. She thought of the love she and others had given him. Chief Hammer thought of many people she knew who were no better than anybody in this courtroom, really.

West wanted to kill Judge Bovine. It was outrageous making a chief and deputy chief sit through all this. West's attention wandered back to Brazil about every other minute. She wondered if he had returned to the newspaper, and her ominous foreshadowing got denser and more chilling. If she didn't get out of this courtroom soon, she might cause a scene. Her boss, oddly, had returned to the present and seemed fascinated by everything around her, as if Hammer could sit here all day and think those private thoughts that had made her who and what she was.

"Johnny Martino," A.D.A. Pond struck again.

"I'm not going to hear that case now," the judge snapped as she carefully got to her feet.

That would be the end of it for at least half an hour, West thought with fury. So she and Hammer would get to sit in the hall-way and wait. Oh great. This would have been exactly right had Johnny Martino's mother permitted it. Like West, Mrs. Martino had been pushed too far. Mrs. Martino knew exactly what was going on. She knew that those two ladies in front were Batman and Robin, and that the judge had to pee. Mrs. Martino rose before Her Honor could climb down from her throne.

"Now hold on one minute," Mrs. Martino loudly said as she made her way over people and up to the bench, in her nice dress and loafers. "I been sitting here this whole time seeing exactly what's going on."

"Ma'am . . . !" the judge protested, by now standing and in cri-sis, as a reporter for New Country WTDR radio slipped into the back of the courtroom.

"Don't you ma'am me!" Mrs. Martino wagged her finger. "The boy who robbed all those innocent folks is my son. So I got a right to say whatever the hell I want. And I also know who these women are." She gave them a deep nod. "Risking themselves to help all those poor folk when that rotten-ass boy of mine climbed on that bus with the gun he got from some drug dealer out there. Well, I tell you what."

West, Hammer, A.D.A. Pond, and the courtroom listened to Mrs. Martino with keen interest. The judge deemed it best to reseat herself and hold tight. Mrs. Martino had been waiting all her life for her day in court, and she began to pace like an experienced trial lawyer. Radio reporter Tim Nicks was writing down everything, his blood singing and playing drums in his ears. This was too good to be true.

"Let me tell you something, judge," Mrs. Martino went on. "I know a game when I see one. And every time you could let those poor busy ladies out of here, you pass on it, say move on, no way, not now, ummm ummm." She shook her head, striding, swinging arms wide. "Now why you want to be doing that to people who help, to people trying to make a difference out there? It's a disgrace, that's *exactly* what it is."

"Ma'am, please be seated . . ." Her Honor tried again.

Johnny Martino was in Mecklenburg orange and flip-flops when he was brought in from the jail. He raised his right hand and swore to tell the truth one more time in his life. Hammer was sitting up straight, filled with shining admiration for Mrs. Martino, who had no intention of being silenced and in fact now that her son had appeared, was only getting started. West was fascinated by how Judge Cow was going to get herself out of an udder disaster, ha! West stifled laughter, suddenly on the verge of hysteria and another hot flash. A.D.A. Pond smiled, and Reporter Nicks wrote furiously in his notepad.

"You want me to sit down, judge?" Mrs. Martino walked up closer to the bench and put her hands on her sturdy hips. "Then I tell you what. You do the right thing. You hear Johnny's case this minute, listen to his guilty lying stealing ass. Then let these fine crusading ladies be on their way out there saving more lives, helping more folks who can't help themselves, delivering us from evil."

"Ma'am, I am hearing the case," Judge Bovine tried to explain. "That's what we're doing . . ."

But Mrs. Martino had her mind made up about the way things were. She turned around and gave Johnny the eye.

"Tell me now." She swept her arms over the courtroom, touching all. "Anybody here who insists on stepping ahead of these Christian ladies?" She looked around, taking in the silence, not finding a raised hand to count. "Speak now," she called out. "All right then! Do we want to set these ladies free?"

The courtroom cheered and roared, people doing high-fives for Batman and Robin, who could do nothing but watch, enchanted.

"Johnny Martino, how do you plead to ten counts of robbery with a dangerous weapon?" the A.D.A. called out.

Judge Bovine's teeth were clamped and a sleeve of her robe flapped empty and useless as she held in her objections, her legs crossed.

"Guilty," Johnny Martino mumbled.

"What says the state," the judge whispered, in pain.

"Mr. Martino boarded a Greyhound bus on July eleventh at one-eleven P.M.," A.D.A. Pond summarized. "He robbed ten passengers at gunpoint before being apprehended and retrained by Chief Judy Hammer and Deputy Chief Virginia West . . ."

"Yo Batman," someone yelled.

"Robin!"

The cheering began again. Judge Bovine could endure no more. She might have called the sheriff for intervention, but she had more pressing concerns. She had been polite, well mannered, well bred, and had lost control of her courtroom. This was a first. Someone had to pay. It might as well be the son of a bitch who caused all this when he climbed on that damn bus.

"The state agrees to consolidate sentencing under ten counts," the judge announced rapidly and with no attempt at drama. "Defendant is a prior record level two and will receive in each of the ten counts a sentence of seventy months minimum or ninety-three months maximum for a total of seven hundred months minimum and nine hundred and thirty months maximum. The court is recessed until one." She gathered her robe in one hand and fled as Mr. Martino checked the judge's math.

Reporter Nicks fled back to South McDowell Street, where *Today's Hot New Country and Your All Time Favorites* could be heard on 96.9. It was rare his station got breaking news, scoops, tips, or leaks, as if to imply that a country music audience didn't vote or care about crime or want crack dealers in jail. The point was, no city official or Deep Throat had ever bothered to think of Nicks when something went down. This was his day, and he was out of his '67 Chevelle with such urgency that he had to run back twice to get his notepad and lock the doors.

Chapter Twenty-two

The sensational courtroom drama of the caped cru-saders sitting on the front row while the joker of the judge dissed them, bristled over the airwaves. It was bounced from radio tower to radio tower throughout the Carolinas. Don Imus picked it up, embellishing as only he could, and Paul Harvey told the rest of the story. Hammer was back and forth to SICU and aware of little else, and West drove Charlotte's streets, looking for Brazil, who had not been seen since Thursday. It was Saturday morning now.

Packer was out with the dog again when West called. He got on the phone, irritable and perplexed. He had heard nothing from Brazil, either. In Davidson, Mrs. Brazil snored on the living-room couch, sleeping through Billy Graham's televised service, as usual. The phone rang and rang, an overflowing ashtray and bottle of vodka on the coffee table. West was driving past the Knight-Ridder building, hanging up her portable phone in frustration.

"Goddamn it!" she blurted. "Andy! Don't do this!"

Mrs. Brazil barely opened her eyes. She managed to sit up an inch, thinking she heard something. A choir in blue with gold stoles praised God. Maybe that was the noise. She reached for her glass, and it shook violently as she finished what she had started the night before. Mrs. Brazil fell back into old sour couch cushions, the magic potion heating blood, carrying her away to that place nowhere special. She drank again, realizing she was low on fuel with nothing nearby but the Quick Mart. She could get beer or wine, she supposed. Where was Andy? Had he been in and out while she was resting?

Night came, and West stayed home and did not want to be with anyone. Her chest was tight and she could not sit long in any one spot or concentrate. Raines called several times, and when she heard his voice on the machine, she did not pick up. Brazil had vanished, it seemed. West could focus on little else. This was crazy. She knew he wouldn't do anything stupid. But she was revisited by the horrors she had worked in her career.

She had seen the drug overdoses, the gunshot suicides not discovered until hunters returned to the woods. She conjured up images of cars covered by the clandestine waters of lakes and rivers until spring thaws or hard rains dislodged those who had chosen not to live.

Even Hammer, with all her problems and preoccupations, had contacted West several times, voicing concern about their young at-large volunteer. Hammer's weekend, so far, had been spent at SICU, and she had sent for her sons as their father settled deeper into the valley of shadows. Seth's eyes stared dully at his wife when she entered his room. He did not speak.

He did not think complete thoughts, but rather in shards of memories and feelings unexpressed that might have formed a meaningful composite had he been able to articulate them. But he was weak and sedated and intubated. During rare lucid flickers during days he could not measure, when he might have given Hammer enough to interpret his intentions, the pain pinned him to the bed. It always won. He would stare through tears at the only woman he had ever loved. Seth was so tired. He was so sorry. He'd had time to think about it.

I'm sorry, Judy. I couldn't help any of it ever since you've known me. Read my mind, Judy. I can't tell you. I'm so worn out. They keep cutting on me and I don't know what's left. I punished you because I couldn't reward you. I have figured that out too late. I wanted you to take care of me. Now look. Whose fault is it, after all? Not yours. I wish you would hold my hand.

Hammer sat in the same chair and watched her husband of twenty-six years. His hands were tethered to his sides so he would not pull out the tube in his trachea. He was on his side, his color deceivingly good and not due to anything he was doing for himself but to oxygen, and she found this ironically typical. Seth had been drawn to her because of her strength and independence, then had hated her for the way she was. She wanted to take his hand, but he was so fragile and inflexible and trussed up by tubes and straps and dressings.

Hammer leaned close and rested her hand on his forearm as his dull eyes blinked and stared and looked sleepy and watery. She was certain that at a subconscious level he knew she was here. Beyond that, it was improbable much registered. Scalpels and bacteria had ravaged his buttocks and now were fileting and rotting his abdomen and thighs. The stench was awful, but Hammer did not really notice it anymore.

"Seth," she said in her quiet, commanding voice. "I know you may not hear me, but on the off chance you can, I want to tell you things. Your sons are on their way here. They should arrive sometime late this afternoon and will come straight to the hospital. They are fine. I am hanging in there. All of us are sad and sick with worry about you."

He blinked, staring. Seth did not move as he breathed oxygen and monitors registered his blood pressure and pulse.

"I have always cared about you," she went on. "I have always loved you in my own way. But I realized long ago that you were attracted to me so you could change me. And I was drawn to you because I thought you'd stay the same. Rather silly, now that I look at it." She paused, a flutter around her heart as his eyes stared back at her. "There are things I could have done better and differently. I must forgive you, and I must forgive myself. You must forgive me and you must forgive yourself."

He didn't disagree with this and wished he could somehow indicate what he thought and felt. His body was like something unplugged, broken, out of batteries. He flipped switches in his brain and nothing happened. All this because he drank too much in bed while playing with a gun to punish her.

"We go on from here," Chief Judy Hammer said, blinking back tears. "Okay, Seth? We put this behind us and learn from it. We move ahead." It was hard to talk. "Why we got married isn't so important anymore. We are friends, companions. We don't exist to procreate or perpetuate endless sexual fantasies for each other. We're here to help each other grow old and not feel alone. Friends." Her hand gripped his arm.

Tears spilled from Seth's eyes. It was the only sign he gave, and his wife dissolved. Hammer cried for half an hour as his vital signs weakened. Group A strep oozed toxins around his soul and did not give a damn about all those antibiotics and immunoglobulin and vitamins being pumped into its plump host. To his disease, he was a rump roast. He was carrion on life's highway.

Randy and Jude entered their father's SICU room at quarter of six and did not see him conscious. It was not likely Seth knew they were by his bed, but knowing they were coming had been enough.

West cruised past the Cadillac Grill, Jazzbone's, and finally headed to Davidson, deciding that Brazil might be hiding out in his own house and not answering the phone. She pulled into the eroded driveway and was crushed that only the ugly Cadillac was home.

West got out of her police car. Weeds grew between cracks in the brick walk she followed to the front door. She rang the bell several times and knocked. Finally, she rapped hard and in frustration with her baton.

"Police!" she said loudly. "Open up!"

This went on for a while until the door opened and Mrs. Brazil blearily peered out. She steadied herself by holding on to the door frame.

"Where's Andy?" West asked.

"Haven't seen him." Mrs. Brazil pressed her forehead with a hand, squinting, as if the world was bad for her health. "At work, I guess," she muttered.

"No, he's not and hasn't been since Thursday," West said. "You're sure he hasn't called or anything?"

"I've been sleeping."

"What about the answering machine? Have you checked?" West asked.

"He keeps his room locked." Mrs. Brazil wanted to return to her couch. "Can't get in there."

West, who did not have her tool belt with her, could still get into most things. She took the knob off his door and was inside Brazil's room within minutes. Mrs. Brazil returned to the living room and settled her swollen, poisoned self on the couch. She did not want to go inside her son's room. He didn't want her there anyway, which was why she had been locked out for years, ever since he had accused her of taking money from the wallet he tucked under his socks. He had accused her of rummaging through his school papers. He had blamed her for knocking over his eighteen-and-under singles state championship tennis trophy, badly denting it and breaking off the little man.

The red light was flashing on the answering machine beside Brazil's neatly made twin bed with its simple green spread. West hit the play button, looking around at shelves of brass and silver trophies, at scholastic and creative awards that Brazil had never bothered to frame but had thumbtacked to walls. A pair of leather Nike tennis shoes, worn out from toe-dragging, was abandoned under a chair, one upright, one on its side, and the sight of them pained West. For a moment, she felt distressed and upset. She imagined the way he looked at her with blue eyes that went on forever. She remembered his voice on the radio and the quirky way he tested coffee with his tongue, which she had repeatedly told him wasn't a smart way to determine whether something was too hot. The first three calls on his machine were hang-ups.

"Yo," began the fourth one. "It's Axel. Got tickets for Bruce Hornsby . . ."

West hit a button.

"Andy? It's Packer. Call me."

She hit the button again and heard her own voice looking for him. She skipped ahead, landing on two more hang-ups. West opened the closet door and her fear intensified when she found nothing inside. She, the cop, went into drawers and found them empty, as well. He had left his books and computer behind, and this only deepened her confusion and concern. These were what he loved the most. He would not abandon them unless he had embarked upon a self-destructive exodus, a fatalistic flight. West looked under the bed and lifted the mattress, exploring every inch of Brazil's private space. She did not find the pistol he had borrowed from her.

West drove around the city much of the night, mopping her face, popping Motrin, and turning the air conditioner on and off as she vacillated between hot and cold. On South College, she slowly passed street people staring hard at each, as if she expected Brazil to have suddenly turned into one of them. She recognized Poison, the young hooker from Mungo's videotape, undulating along the sidewalk, smoking a cigarette and enjoying being watched. Poison followed the dark blue cop car with haunted, glassy eyes, and West looked back. West thought of Brazil, of his sad curiosity about bad people and what had happened to make them that way.

They make choices. West said that all the time, and it was true. But she envied Brazil's freshness, his innocent clarity of vision.

In truth, he saw life with a wisdom equal to her own, but his was born of vulnerability and not of the experience that sometimes crowded West's compassion and cloaked her feelings in many hard layers. Her condition had been coming on for a long time and most likely was irreversible. West accepted that when one is exposed to the worst elements of life, there comes a point of no return. She had been beaten and shot, and she had killed. She had crossed a line. She was a missionary, and the tender, warm contours of life were for others.

On Tryon Street, she was stopped at a traffic light near Jake's, another favorite spot for breakfast. Thelma could do anything with fried steak and biscuits, and the coffee was good. West stared ahead, several blocks away, just past First Union Bank with its giant painted hornet bursting out of one side of the building. She recognized the dark car's boxy shape and conical taillights glowing red. She wasn't close enough to see the tag yet and was going to do something about that.

The light turned green and West gunned the Ford's powerful engine until she was on the old BMW's bumper. Her heart thrilled as she recognized the plate number. She honked her horn and motioned, and Brazil kept going. West followed, honking again and longer, but clearly he had no intention of acknowledging her as she followed his shiny chrome bumper through downtown. Brazil knew she was there and didn't give a damn as he threw back another gulp from the tallboy Budweiser he was holding between his legs. He broke the law right in front of Deputy Chief West and knew she saw it, and he didn't give a shit.

"Goddamn son of a bitch," West exclaimed as she flipped on flashing lights.

Brazil sped up. West couldn't believe what was happening. How could he do anything this stupid?

"Oh for fuck's sake!" She hit the siren.

Brazil had been in pursuits, but he had never been the lead car. Usually, he was back there sitting in the front seat with West. He drank another swallow of the beer he had bought at the 76 truck stop just off the Sunset East exit. He needed another one, and decided he might as well hit I-77 off Trade Street and cruise on back for a refill. He tossed his empty in the backseat, where several others clinked and rolled on the floor. His broken speedometer faithfully maintained its belief that the BMW was going thirty-two miles per hour.

In fact, he was going sixty-three when he turned onto the interstate. West doggedly pursued as her alarm and anger grew. Should she call for other cars, Brazil was ruined, his volunteer days ended, his real troubles only begun. Nor was there a guarantee that more cops would effect a stop. Brazil might decompensate further. He might feel desperate, and West knew how that might end. She had seen those final chapters before, all over the road, crumpled metal sharp like razors, glass, oil, blood, and black body bags on their way to the morgue.

His speed climbed to ninety miles per hour and he maintained it, with her steadily behind him, lights and siren going full tilt. It penetrated his fog that she had not gotten on the radio for help. He would have heard it on his scanner and backup cars surely would have shown up by now. He didn't know if this made him feel better or worse. Maybe she didn't take him seriously. Nobody took him seriously, and nobody ever would again, because of Webb, because of the unfairness, the heartlessness of life and all in it.

Brazil shot onto the exit of Sunset Road East and began to slow. It was finished. In truth, he needed gas. This chase had its limits anyway. He might as well stop. Depression settled heavier, crushing him into his seat as he parked at the outer limits of the tarmac, far away from eighteen-wheelers and their bright-painted shiny cabs with all their chrome. He cut the engine and leaned back, shutting his eyes, as punishment approached. West wouldn't cut him any slack. She, in her uniform and gun, was above all else a cop, and a hard, unkind one at that. It mattered not that they were partners and went shooting together and talked about things.

"Andy." She loudly rapped a knuckle on his window. "Get out," she commanded this common lawbreaker.

He felt tired as he climbed out of a car that his father, Drew, had loved. Brazil took off his father's jacket and tossed it in the backseat. It was almost eighty degrees out, gnats and moths swarming in sodium vapor lights. Brazil was soaked with sweat. He tucked the keys in a pocket of the tight jeans that Mungo believed pointed to Brazil's criminal leanings. West shone her flashlight through the back window, illuminating aluminum tallboy beer cans on the mat in back. She counted eleven.

"Did you drink all these tonight?" she demanded to know as he shut his door.

"No."

"How many have you had tonight?"

"I didn't count." His eyes were hard and defiant on hers.

"Do you always elude police lights and sirens?" she said, furious. "Or is tonight special for some reason?"

He opened the back door of his BMW, and angrily grabbed out a tee shirt. He had no comment as he peeled off his wet polo shirt, and yanked on the dry one. West had never seen him half naked.

"I ought to lock you up," she said with not quite as much authority.

"Go ahead," he said.

Randy and Jude Hammer had flown into the Charlotte-Douglas International Airport within forty-five minutes of each other, and their mother had met them downstairs in baggage. The three were somber and distracted as Hammer returned to Carolinas Medical Center without delay. She was so happy to see her boys, and old memories were reopened and exposed to air and light. Randy and Jude had been born with their mother's handsome bones and straight white teeth. They had been blessed with her piercing eyes and frightening intelligence.

From Seth, they had received their four-cylinder engines that moved them slowly along with little direction or passing power or drive. Randy and Jude were happy enough simply to exist and go nowhere in a hurry. They drew gratification and joy from their dreams and regular customers in whatever restaurant employed them from one year to the next. They were happy with the understanding women who loved them anyway. Randy was proud of his bit parts in movies no one saw. Jude was thrilled to be in any jazz bar he and the guys got gigs in, and he played the drums with passion, whether the audience was ten people or eighty.

Oddly, it had never been their rocket-charged mother who could not live with the sons' something less than stellar accomplishments in life. It was Seth who was disgusted and ashamed. Their father had proved so totally lacking in understanding and patience that the sons had moved far away. Of course, Hammer understood the psychological dynamics. Seth's hatred for his sons was his hatred for himself. It didn't take great acumen to deduce that much. But knowing the reason had changed nothing. It had required tragedy, a grave illness, to reunite this family.

"Mom, you holding up?" Jude was in back of Hammer's personal car. He was rubbing her shoulders as she drove.

"I'm trying."

She swallowed hard as Randy looked at her with concern from the front passenger's seat.

"Well, I don't want to see him," said Randy, cradling flowers he had bought for his father, in the airport.

"That's understandable," Hammer said, switching lanes, eyes in the mirrors. It had begun to rain. "How are my babies?"

"Great," Jude said. "Benji's learning to play sax."

"I can't wait to hear it. What about Owen?"

"Not quite old enough for instruments, but she's my boogie baby. Every time she hears music, she dances with Spring," Jude went on, referring to the child's mother. "God, Mom, you'll die when you see it. It's hilarious!"

Spring was the artist Jude had lived with in Greenwich Village for eight years. Neither of Hammer's sons was married. Each had two children, and Hammer adored every fine golden hair on their small lovely heads. It was her bleeding, buried fear that they were growing up in distant cities with only infrequent contact with their rather legendary grandmother. Hammer did not want to be someone they might someday talk about but had never known.

"Smith and Fen wanted to come," said Randy, taking his mother's hand. "It's gonna be all right, Mom." He felt another stab of hate for his father.

West didn't know what to do with her prisoner of the evening. Brazil was slumped down in the seat, arms crossed, his posture defiant and decidedly without remorse. He refused to look at her now but stared out the windshield at bugs and bats swirling beneath lights. He watched truckers in pointed cowboy boots and jeans strolling out to their mighty steeds and leaning against cabs, propping a foot on the running board, hands cupped around a cigarette, as they lit up like the Marlboro Man.

"You got your cigarettes?" Brazil asked West.

She looked at him as if he had lost his mind. "Forget it."

"I want one."

"Yeah, right. You've never smoked in your life and I'm not going to be the reason you start," she said, and she wanted one, too.

"You couldn't possibly know whether I've ever smoked a cigarette or pot or anything else," he said in the strange tone of intoxication. "Ha! You think you know so much. You don't know shit. Cops. And their dark, narrow alleyways for minds."

"Really? I thought you were a cop. Or have you quit that, too?"

He stared miserably out his side window.

West felt sorry for him, mad as she was. She wished she knew what was wrong, exactly.

"What the hell's gotten into you?" She tried another tactic, poking Brazil, this time not playfully.

He did not respond.

"Trying to ruin your life? What if some other cop spotted you first?" She was no-nonsense. "Got any idea how much trouble you'd be in?"

"I don't care," he said, and his voice caught.

"Yes, you do, goddamn it! Look at me!"

Brazil stared out, his eyes swimming as he dully watched bleary images of people in and out of the truck stop, men and women whose lives were different from his and who would not understand what it was like to be him. They would look at all that he was and despise him for being privileged and spoiled, because they could not comprehend his reality.

Bubba felt precisely this, and just so happened to be parking his King Cab at the pumps. He spotted the BMW first, then the cop car with the enemy in it. Bubba could not believe his good fortune. He went in for Pabst Blue Ribbon and Red Man and picked up the latest *Playboy*.

Brazil was struggling to control himself, and West could be hard but so long. She cared about him in a way that fit no easy definition, and this was partly why he unsettled and confused her so much. She enjoyed him as a talented, precocious recruit, someone she could mentor and get a kick out of watching as he learned. She did not have a brother and would have liked one exactly like him, someone young, smart, sensitive, and kind. He was a friend, although she did not give him much of a chance. He was a pretty incredible-looking guy and didn't seem to notice.

"Andy," she quietly said, "please tell me what happened."

"Somehow he got in my computer basket, my files. Everything over the news channels before the paper came out. Scooped." His voice trembled, and he did not want West to see him like this.

West was stunned. "He?" she asked. "Who's he?"

"Webb." He could barely bring himself to say that name. "Same piece of shit screwing your deputy chief!"

"What?" Now West was truly lost.

"Goode," he said. "Everybody knows."

"I didn't." West wondered how she could have missed intelligence like that.

Brazil's heart was broken forever. West wasn't quite sure what to do as she mopped her face again.

Bubba stealthily made his way back to his truck, his thick face with its misshapen nose averted and shadowed by a baseball cap. Climbing up into his cab with his purchases, he sat watching the cop car out his windshield. For a while, he flipped through his magazine, pausing at the really big stories. There were many of them, and he tried not to think about his wife or make comparisons as he calculated the best method of attack.

He had packed light tonight, just a Colt .380 caliber seven-shot pistol in an ankle holster, which would not have been his first choice had he known he might have a standoff with the cops. It was a good thing he had a backup between the seats, a Quality Parts Shorty E-2 Carbine, .223 caliber with thirty-shot magazine, adjustable sights, chrome-lined barrel finished in manganese phosphate that didn't shine at night. For all practical purposes, this was an M-16 and with it, Bubba could riddle West's car Bonnie and Clyde style. He turned a page and massaged more big ideas as he enjoyed the dark.

West had never really been called upon to comfort a member of the male gender. Rarely was such a thing needed or requested, and having no precedent to follow, she used common sense. Brazil was hiding his face in his hands. She felt terribly sorry for him. What an unfortunate state of affairs.

"It's not that bad, really," she kept saying. "Okay?" She patted his shoulder. "We'll find a way out of this. Okay?"

She patted him again, and when this did not make a dent, she finally broke down. "Come here," she said.

West put an arm around him and pulled him close. Suddenly, he

was in her lap, his arms clamped around her as he held her like a
child, which he was not. West's hot flashes seemed worse as she
thought fast and hormones spiked. He nuzzled her, holding tight,
and her insides woke up, startling her. Brazil was suffering from a
similar response and moved up her body, to her neck, until he
found her mouth. For moments, at least, they were completely out
of control and out of orbit. Their traumatized brains went into
shock, allowing other instincts to have their way, for Mother Nature
worked in this fashion to trick couples into procreating.

West and Brazil had not gotten to the point of worrying about
what sort of birth control was best suited to their anatomies, needs,
tastes, belief systems, personal choices, fantasies, secret pleasures,
or faith in consumer reports. This way of communicating with each
other was new, so they took the time to linger in places they had always wondered about. Then reality asserted itself with alacrity, and
West suddenly sat up and looked out the windows of her police car,
remembering she was on duty with a man in her lap.

"Andy," she said.

He was busy.

"Andy," she tried again. "Andy, get up. You're on my . . . gun."

She tried to move him, with no energy or enthusiasm, not wanting him to go anywhere ever again. Hell was here and she was finished.

"Sit up," she said, wiping her face again. Her life was ruined.
"This is incest, pedophilia," she muttered, taking a deep breath as
he went on with what he was doing.

"You're right, you're right," he mumbled with absolutely no
conviction as he explored the wonders of her existence in a way that
was unknown and overwhelming to her.

It was difficult to predict exactly where this might have gone
had Bubba not intervened. There was a Holiday Inn Express not
too far away on I-77, and it had an indoor pool, forty-two-channel
cable TV, and free local calls and newspaper, and complimentary
continental breakfasts. Possibly, West and Brazil would have made
their way to one of those rooms before morning and gotten into

even more trouble at a bargain price. They possibly would have slept together, and that was where West always drew the line. Sex was one thing, but she did not sleep with someone she was not in love with, meaning she slept with no living soul except Niles.

Again, such contemplations are moot when there is a sharp rap on the window and one peers into the barrel of a carbine rifle reminiscent of Bosnia, or perhaps Miami. West did not have her glasses on, but the redneck with his assault rifle outside her police car looked familiar in a fuzzy sort of way.

"Sit up very slowly," she said to Brazil.

"What for?" He wasn't ready yet.

"Trust me," she told him.

It was just as well that condensation had formed on the glass. Bubba could not see exactly what was going on inside the dark blue Ford Crown Victoria, but he had a pretty good idea. This heightened his excitement, making him more certain that he was going to waste these two after doing something really, really bad to them first. If there were two things Bubba could not endure in life, they were queers making out, and straights making out. When he saw queers flirting, touching, Bubba wanted to beat the shit out of them and leave them dying in a ditch. When he saw what he thought he was looking at right now inside this police car, he felt pretty much the same impulse. People with money, importance, or a good sex life, and especially all three, made Bubba insane with righteous outrage. It was his calling, he was sure, to smite them in the name of America.

West was not as frightened by the rifle with thirty rounds as most people would have been, and her brain was powering up. It seemed this was the creep from The Firing Line who had gotten arrested for exposing himself in Latta Park. She had a pretty good idea why she had found Super Glue in her shrubs, and she wished like hell that Brazil hadn't busted the guy's nose. All the same, West was ready for violence. When anyone pointed a gun at her, there was a true cause and effect that rapidly clicked into gear. Unhooking the mike, she placed it next to her hip. She keyed it with her right hand, locking out all radio traffic in her response area. Dispatchers, cops, reporters, and criminals with scanners could hear nothing but her. She rolled down her window a few inches.

"Please don't shoot," she said loudly.

Bubba was surprised and pleased by her rapid submission. "Unlock the doors," he ordered.

"Okay, okay," West continued in the same loud, tense voice. "I'm going to unlock the doors real slowly. Please don't shoot. Please. We can work this out, all right? And if you start shooting here, everyone at the Seventy-six truck stop will hear, so what good will it do?"

Bubba had already thought about this, and she was right. "The two of you are getting in my truck," he said. "We're taking a ride."

"Why?" West kept on. "What do you want from us? We have no problem with you."

"Oh yeah?" He gripped the carbine tighter, loving the way the bitch in uniform was groveling before him, the great Bubba. "How about at the range the other night when Queerbait there hit me?"

"You started it," Brazil said to him and all listening to channel two.

"We can work this out," West said again. "Look. Let's just get right back on Sunset, maybe meet somewhere where we can talk about this? All these trucks coming in here, they're looking. You don't want witnesses, and this isn't a good place to be settling a dispute."

Bubba thought they had already gone over this point. What he planned to do was shoot them out near the lake, weigh their bodies down with cinder blocks, and dump them where no one would find them until mud turtles had eaten important features. He heard that happened. Crabs were bad on dead bodies, too, as were household pets, especially cats, if locked up with dead owners and not fed and eventually having no choice.

As Bubba deliberated, eight Charlotte patrol cars with flashing lights were speeding along I-77, now within minutes of the truck stop. Shotguns were out and ready. The police helicopter was lifting from the helipad on top of the LEC, sniper shooters poised. The SWAT team had been deployed. The FBI had been called and agents were on standby in the event hostage or terrorist negotiators or the Child Abduction Serial Killer Unit or the Hostage Rescue Team might be what it took to save the day.

"Get out of the car," said Bubba.

In his mind, he was not in plaid shorts, white tube socks, Hush Puppies, and a Fruit of the Loom white tee shirt that had never been washed with bleach. In his mind, he was in military fatigues, with black grease under his eyes, hair a buzz cut, sweaty muscles bunching as he gripped his weapon and prepared to score two more points for his country and the guys at the hunt club. He was Bubba. He knew the perfect sliver of undeveloped lake property where he could do his duty, having his way with the woman first. *Take that,* he would think as he drove home his point. *Now who's got the power, bitch?*

Police cars turned onto Sunset East. They traveled single file, lights going, in a neat flashing line. Inside the truck stop, several truckers, who believed they had been stagecoach drivers in an earlier life, had lost interest in microwave nachos, cheeseburgers, and beer. They were looking out plate glass, watching what was going on at the edge of the parking lot as pulsing blue and red lights showed through trees.

"No way that's a rifle," Betsy was saying as she chewed on a Slim Jim.

"Oh yeah it is too," said Al.

"Then we should go on out and help."

"Help which one?" asked Tex.

All contemplated this long enough for police cars to get closer and the sound of chopper blades to be barely discernible.

"Looks to me like Bubba started it," decided Pete.

"Then we should go get him."

"You hear about the guns he's got?"

"Bubba ain't gonna shoot us."

The argument was moot. Bubba could feel dark armies closing around him and he got desperate.

"*Git out now or I'm going to let loose!*" he screamed, racking a cartridge into a chamber that already had one.

"Don't shoot." West held up her hands, noting the double feed that had just jammed his gun. "I'm opening the door, okay?"

"NOW!" Bubba pointed and yelled.

West positioned herself before the door as best she could and planted a foot on it. She raised the handle and kicked with all her strength as eight police cars roared in, sirens ripping the violent night. Bubba was slammed in his midsection and flew back, landing on his back, the rifle skittering across tarmac. West was out and on him before her feet hit the ground. She did not wait for her backups. She didn't care a shit about the big, burly drivers boiling out of the truck stop to help. Brazil leapt out, too, and together they threw Bubba on his fat belly and cuffed him, desperate to beat him half to death, but resisting.

"*You goddamn son-of-a-bitch piece of chicken-eating shit!*" Brazil bellowed.

"*Move and your head's all over with!*" exclaimed West, her pistol pressed hard against the small of Bubba's thick neck.

The force hauled Bubba away, with no assistance from the truckers, who returned their attention to snacks for the road and cigarettes. West and Brazil sat in silence for a moment inside her car.

"You always get me into trouble," she said, backing up.

"Hey!" he protested. "Where are you going?"

"I'm taking you home."

"I don't live at home anymore."

"Since when?" She tried not to show her surprised pleasure.

"Day before yesterday. I got an apartment at Charlotte Woods, on Woodlawn."

"Then I'll take you there," she told him.

"My car's here," he reminded her.

"And you've been drinking all night," she said, buckling her shoulder harness. "We'll come back and get your car when you're sober."

"I am sober," he said.

"Compared to what?" She drove. "You won't remember any of this tomorrow."

He would remember every second of it for the rest of his tormented life. He yawned and rubbed his temples. "Yeah, you're probably right," he agreed, deciding it had meant nothing to her. It also meant nothing to him.

"Of course I'm right." She smiled easily.

She could tell he was indifferent. He was one more typical asshole-user guy. What was she anyway but a middle-aged, out-of-shape woman who'd never been to a city bigger or more exciting than the one she had worked in since she had graduated from college? He was just trying her on for size, taking his first test drive in an old, out-of-style car that he could afford to make mistakes in. She felt like slamming on the brakes and making him walk. When she pulled into the tidy apartment complex parking lot and waited for him to get out, she offered not a word of friendship or meaning.

Brazil stood outside her car, holding the door open, staring in at her. "So, what time tomorrow?"

"Ten," she said, shortly.

He slammed the door, walking away fast, hurt and upset. Women were all the same. They were warm and wonderful one minute and turned-on and all over him the next, which was followed by moody and distant and didn't mean what happened.

Brazil didn't understand how he and West could have had such a special moment at the truck stop and now it was as if they weren't even on a first-name basis. She had used him, that's what. It was empty and cheap to her, and he was certain this was her modus operandi. She was older, powerful, and experienced, not to mention good-looking with a body that caused him serious pain. West could toy with anyone she wanted.

So could Blair Mauney III, his wife feared. Polly Mauney could not help but worry about what her husband might engage in when he traveled to Charlotte tomorrow, on USAir flight number 392, nonstop from Asheville, where the Mauneys lived in a lovely Tudor-style home in Biltmore Forest. Blair Mauney III was from old money and had just come in from the club after a hard tennis match, a shower, a massage, and drinks with his pals. Mauney had come from many generations of banking, beginning with his grandfather, Blair Mauney, who had been a founding father of the American Trust Company.

Blair Mauney III's father, Blair Mauney, Jr., had been a vice president when American Commercial merged with First National of Raleigh. A statewide banking system was off and running, soon followed by more mergers and the eventual formation of North Carolina National Bank. This went on and, with the S&L crisis of the late 1980s, banks that had not been bought up were offered at fire sale prices. NCNB became the fourth-largest bank in the country and was renamed USBank. Blair Mauney III knew the minutia about his well-respected bank's remarkable history. He knew what the chairman, the president, the vice chairman and chief financial officer, and CEO got paid.

He was a senior vice president for USBank in the Carolinas and routinely was required to travel to Charlotte. This he rather much enjoyed, for it was good to get away from wife and teenaged children whenever one could, and only his colleagues in their lofty offices understood his pressures. Only comrades understood the fear lurking in every banker's heart that one day Cahoon, who tolerated nothing, would inform hard workers like Mauney that they were out of favor with the crown. Mauney dropped his tennis bag in his recently remodeled kitchen and opened the door of the refrigerator, ready for another Amstel Light.

"Honey?" he called out, popping off the cap.

"Yes, dear." She briskly walked in. "How was tennis?"

"We won."

"Good for you!" She beamed.

"Withers must have double-faulted twenty times." He swallowed. "Foot-faulted like hell, too, but we didn't call those. What'd you guys eat?" He barely looked at Polly Mauney, his wife of twenty-two years.

"Spaghetti Bolognese, salad, seven grain bread." She went through his tennis bag, fishing out cold sweat-soaked, smelly shorts, shirt, socks, and jock strap, as she always had and would.

"Got any pasta left?"

"Plenty. I'd be delighted to fix you a plate, dear."

"Maybe later." He fell into stretches. "I'm really getting tight. You don't think it's arthritis, do you?"

"Of course not. Would you like me to rub you down, sweetheart?" she said.

While he was drifting during his massage, she would bring up what her plastic surgeon had said when she had inquired about a laser treatment to get rid of fine lines on her face and a copper laser treatment to eliminate the brown spot on her chin. Polly Mauney had been filled with terror when her plastic surgeon had made it clear that no light source could substitute for a scalpel. That was how bad she had gotten.

"Mrs. Mauney," her plastic surgeon had told her. "I don't think you're going to be happy with the results. The lines most troublesome are too deep."

He traced them on her face so gently. She relaxed, held hostage by tenderness. Mrs. Mauney was addicted to going to the doctor. She liked being touched, looked at, analyzed, scrutinized, and checked on after surgery or changes in her medication.

"Well," Mrs. Mauney had told her plastic surgeon, "if that's what you recommend. And I suppose I am to assume you are referring to a face lift."

"Yes. And the eyes." He held up a mirror to show her.

The tissue above and below her eyes was beginning to droop and puff. This was irreversible. No amount of cold water splashes, cucumbers, or cutting down on alcohol or salt would make a significant difference, she was informed.

"What about my breasts?" she then had inquired.

Her plastic surgeon stepped back to look. "What does your husband think?" he asked her.

"I think he'd like them bigger."

Her doctor laughed. Why didn't she state the obvious? Unless a man was a pedophile or gay, he liked them bigger. His gay female patients felt the same way. They were just better sports about it, or pretended to be, if the one they loved didn't have much to offer.

"We can't do all of this at once," the plastic surgeon warned Mrs. Mauney. "Implants and a face lift are two very different surgeries, and we'd need to space them apart, giving you plenty of time to heal."

"How far apart?" she worried.

Chapter Twenty-three

It did not occur to West until she was home and locking herself in for the night that she would have to set her alarm clock. Perhaps one of her few luxuries in life was not getting up on Sunday morning until her body felt like it, or Niles did. Then she took her time making coffee and reading the paper as she thought about her parents heading off to Dover Baptist Church, not far from the Chevon or from Pauline's Beauty Shop, where her mother got her hair fixed every Saturday at ten in the morning. West always called her parents on Sunday, usually when they were sitting down to dinner and wishing her place wasn't empty.

"Great," she muttered to herself, grabbing a beer as Niles sat on the windowsill over the sink. "So now I've got to get up at eight-thirty. Can you believe that?"

She tried to figure out what Niles was staring at. From this section of Dilworth, West would have no reminders of the city she protected were it not for the top thirty stories of USBank rising brightly above West's unfinished fence. Niles had gotten really peculiar lately, it struck West. He sat in the same spot every night, staring out, as if he were ET missing home.

"What are you looking at?" West ran her fingernails down Niles's silky, ruddy spine, something that always made him purr.

He did not respond. He stared as if in a trance.

"Niles?" West was getting a bit worried. "What is it, baby? You not feeling well? Got a hairball? Mad at me again? That's probably it, isn't it?" She sighed, taking a swallow of beer. "I sure wish you'd try to be more understanding, Niles. I work hard, do everything I can to provide you a secure, nice home. You know I love you, don't you? But you gotta try and cut me a little slack. I'm out there all the live-long day." West pointed out the window. "And what? You're here. This is your world, meaning your perspective isn't as big as mine, okay? So you get pissed because I'm not here, too. This isn't fair. I want you to give some serious thought to this. Got it?"

The words of the owner were chatter, the buzzing of insects, the drone of sounds drifting out of the radio on the table by the bed. Niles wasn't listening as he stared out at the forlorn King Usbeecee staring back at him. Niles had been called. There was disaster looming in the land of the Usbeeceeans, and only Niles could help, because only Niles would listen. All others looked up to the mighty King and mocked him in their minds and among themselves, thinking the benevolent monarch could not hear. They, the people, had wanted His Majesty to come. They had wanted his child-care centers and frescos, his career opportunities, and his wealth. Then they had turned jealous of his omniscience, of his all-powerful and praiseworthy presence. Those here and from distant ports were lustful and plotting a takeover that only Niles could stop.

"Anyway," West was saying, popping open another beer as her weird-ass cat continued staring out at the night, "I'm chasing him south on Seventy-seven at about ninety miles an hour? Can you believe it? He should be in jail right now, you ask me."

She took another swallow of Miller Genuine Draft, wondering if she should eat something. For the first time since she'd had the flu several years ago, West was not hungry. She felt light and foreign inside, and awake. She thought back on how much caffeine she'd had this day, wondering if that might be the problem. It wasn't. Hormones, she decided, even though she knew that the beast was no longer raging and in fact had been quiet most of the day, on its way back to its cave until the moon was in position again.

King Usbeecee was a potentate of few words, and Niles had to watch carefully to hear what the King was saying. Sunrise and sunset were the King's most chatty times, when windows flashed white and gold in a firestorm of pontifications. At night, Niles mainly studied the red light winking on top of the crown, a beacon saying to him, repeatedly, *wink-wink-wink.* After a barely perceptible pause, three more winks, and so on. This had gone on for weeks, and Niles knew that the code was directing him to a three-syllable enemy, whose armies this very minute were marching closer to the Queen City that the King ruled.

"Well, since you're so friendly," West said in a snippy tone to her cat, "I'm going to do laundry."

Startled, Niles stretched and stared at her, his eyes crossed as a similar firestorm flared inside his head. What was it the King had said? What, what, what? Earlier this evening, when Niles had been watching the King send him signals with the sun, hadn't the King flashed an agitated pattern, light going round and round the building, back and forth, back and forth, very similar to how the owner's big white box worked when she did *laundry?* A coincidence? Niles thought not. He jumped off the sill, then the counter, and followed his owner into the utility room. The fur stood up on his back when she dipped into pants pockets, pulling out *money* before wadding clothes and dunking them into the machine's basket. Other flashes of insight exploded in Niles's brain. He frantically rubbed against his owner's legs and nipped her, sharpening his claws on her thigh, trying to tell her.

"Goddamn it!" West shook the cat off. "What the hell has gotten into you?"

Brazil lay back in the sleeping bag on the floor of his new one-bedroom unfurnished apartment. He had a headache and couldn't seem to get enough water. He'd been drinking beer for two days, and this frightened him. His mother had probably started exactly the same way, and here he was following her path. He knew enough from all the interest in genetics these days to deduce that he might have inherited his mother's proclivity for self-destruction. Brazil was deeply depressed by this realization. He was ashamed of his behavior and knew for a fact that West had only humored a drunk kid, and the performance would never be repeated.

He lay still, hands beneath the back of his head, staring up at the ceiling, lights out, music on. Beyond his window he could see the top of the USBank Corporate Center almost touching the slivered moon, a red light blinking at the top of the crown. Brazil stared, zoning out again, an unsettling realization coming over him. Tomorrow would be two weeks since the last Black Widow slaying.

"Christ." He sat up, sweating and breathing hard.

He kicked off sheets and stood. He began pacing, with nothing on but gym shorts. He drank more water and stood in his bare kitchen, staring out at USBank, thinking, worrying. Out there somewhere was another businessman about to become a victim! If only there were some way to prevent it. Where was the killer now? What was the bastard thinking as he loaded his gun and thought his evil thoughts, waiting on the web of Five Points for the next rental car to innocently creep into the city?

Niles was following West all over the house. She was certain the cat had gone haywire and knew this was a danger with Siamese, Abyssinians, and all overbred, cross-eyed creatures that had been around for thousands of years. Niles wound through her moving legs, almost tripping her twice, and she had no choice but to boot him across the room.

Niles cried out, but persisted. Then he got angry. One more boot, he thought, and you've had it. West gave him the side of her foot, sending him under the bed, scoring another point.

Niles watched from his dark space between the box spring and hardwood floor, his tail twitching. Niles waited until his owner had taken off shoes and socks, then he shot out and bit the soft spot at the back of her heel, right behind the ankle bone. He knew this hurt because he'd tested it before. His owner chased him around the house for ten minutes, and he ran with sincerity because he recognized true homicidal rage when he saw it. Niles returned to the bed and stayed under it until his owner got tired and wanted to sleep. Sneaking out, Niles returned to the kitchen. He curled up on the sill, where his kind and loving King kept watch over him during dark, lonely nights.

Morning came and brought rain. The unfriendly alarm clock buzzed loudly and stung West awake. She groaned, lying in bed, refusing to get up as heavy drops of water drummed the roof. This was perfect sleeping weather. Why should she get up? Memories of Brazil and his stranded BMW, of Niles and his outrageous behavior last night, depressed and excited her at the same time. This made no sense. She pulled the covers up around her chin and images came, disturbing ones somehow relating to whatever she had dreamt. When she was absolutely still, she could almost feel Brazil's hands and mouth all over her. She was horrified and stayed in bed for quite some time.

Niles, having free rein of the house for a bit, had crept into the laundry room. He was interested in the big white box with wet clothes in it. On top were several folded bills and some change. He jumped up, having yet another idea of how to pass along King Usbeecee's message to Niles's owner. Of course, Niles knew with joy that his owner could do something about the King's endangerment. She could act on it, roar in wearing her important suit with all its leather and metal and dangerous toys. That's what this was all about, Niles was convinced. The King had spoken to him and wanted him to pass along the information to his owner. She in turn would alert other fierce leaders. The troops would be called, the King and all Usbeeceeans saved.

Niles spent a difficult five minutes flipping open the cover on top of the washing machine. He dipped in a paw and pulled out a small, wet article of clothing. He grabbed a folded five-dollar bill in his mouth and jumped back down, excited, knowing his owner would be so pleased. She wasn't. His owner did not seem the least bit thrilled to see Niles, and sat up in a rage when her face was draped with a pair of wet panties that had been dragged across the house. She stared at the panties and the five-dollar bill on her chest, and a chill settled over her.

"Wait a minute," she said to Niles, who was fleeing. "Come back. Really."

Niles stopped and looked at her, thinking, his tail twitching. He didn't trust her.

"Okay. Truce," West promised. "Something's up. This isn't just your acting kooky, is it? Come here and tell me."

Niles knew her tone was honest, and maybe even a little contrite. He walked across the bedroom, and hopped three feet up to the bed, like it was nothing. He sat staring at her as she began to pet him.

"You brought me a pair of panties and money," she said. "Mean something?"

His tail twitched, but not enthusiastically.

"Has to do with panties?"

His tail went still.

"Underwear?"

No response.

"Sex?"

He didn't budge.

"Shit," she muttered. "What else? Well, let me retrace this thing, work it like a crime scene. You went to the washing machine, opened the lid, fished this out, it's wet, and not been in the dryer yet. So what exactly did you intend to fetch and then bring to me? Clothes?"

Niles was getting bored.

"Of course not," West reprimanded herself. Niles could get clothes from anywhere, the chair, the floor. He had gone to a lot of trouble for one pair of panties. "You went into the laundry," she said.

Niles twitched.

"Ah, getting warm. Laundry? Is that it?"

Niles went crazy, twitching and nuzzling her hand. West next started on the five-dollar bill. It took only two tries to affirm that *money* was the operative word.

"Laundry money," West muttered, mystified.

Niles could help her no further and believed he had carried out his assignment. He jumped off the bed and returned to the kitchen, where water washed out the King's morning greeting to his faithful subject. Niles was disappointed, and West was late. She dashed out the door, then dashed back in, having forgotten the most important item, the little box she disconnected from her own telephone. She sped along East Boulevard to South Boulevard and turned off on Woodlawn. Brazil was wearing a windbreaker with a hood and waiting in the parking lot, because he did not want her to see his small place with nothing in it.

"Hi," he said, getting in.

"Sorry I'm late." She could not look at him. "My cat's lost his mind."

This was certainly starting off well, Brazil dismally realized. He was thinking about her, and she was thinking about her cat.

"What's wrong with him?" Brazil asked.

West pulled out of the parking lot as rain sprinkled. Her tires swished over wet streets. Brazil was acting as if nothing had happened. It just went to corroborate her belief that all males were the same. She supposed that his foray through her private possessions was no different than flipping through a magazine full of naked women. A thrill. A passing turn-on like a vibrating motorcycle seat or the right person sitting in your lap when the car was packed with too many passengers.

"He's just crazy, that's all," West said. "Stares out the window all the time. Drags things out of my washing machine. Bites me. Makes weird yowling noises."

"This is new and different behavior?" asked Brazil, the psychologist.

"Oh yeah."

"What kind of yowling sounds?" Brazil went on.

"He goes *yowl-yowl-yowl.* Then he's quiet and does the same thing again. Always three syllables."

"Sounds to me like Niles is trying to give you information and you're not listening. Quite possibly he's pointing out something right under your nose, but either you're caught up in other preoccupations, or you don't want to hear it." Brazil enjoyed making this point.

"Since when are you a cat shrink?" West glanced at him, experiencing that same giddy sensation again, a wiggling in her bowels, as if tadpoles had hatched somewhere down there.

Brazil shrugged. "It's all about human nature, animal nature, whatever you want to call it. If we take the time to try and look at reality from someone else's perspective, try a little compassion, it can make a difference."

"Gag," West said as she flew right by the Sunset East exit.

"You just passed the truck stop. And what do you mean, *gag?*"

"You sure got your lines down pat, don't you, boy?" She laughed in a not-so-nice way.

"I'm not a boy, in case you haven't noticed," he said, and he realized for the first time, to his shock, that Virginia West was scared.

"I'm a legal adult, and I don't deliver lines. You must have met a lot of bad people in life."

This honestly amused her. She started laughing as rain fell harder. She turned on wipers and her radio while Brazil watched her, a smile playing on his lips, although he was clueless as to what he had said to amuse her so.

"Met a lot of bad people." She sputtered, almost helpless. "What do I do for a living, for Christ's sake? Work in a bakery, serve ice cream cones, arrange flowers?" More peals of laughter.

"I didn't mean just what you do for a living," Brazil said. "The bad people you meet in policing aren't the ones who really hurt you. It's people off the job. You know, friends and family."

"Yeah. You're right." She sobered up fast. "I do know. And guess what?" She shot him a glance. "You don't. You don't know the first thing about me and all the shits I've come across when least expecting it."

"Which is why you're not married or close to anyone," he said.

"Which is why we're changing the subject. And you're one to talk, by the way." She turned the radio up loud as rain beat the top of her personal car.

Hammer was watching the rain out the window of her husband's room in SICU, while Randy and Jude sat stiffly in chairs by the bed, staring at monitors, watching every fluctuation in pulse and oxygen intake. The stench got worse every hour, and Seth's moments of consciousness were like weightless airborne seeds that seemed neither to go anywhere nor to land. He drifted and his family could not tell whether he had any awareness of their presence and devotion. For his sons, this was especially bitter. This was more of the same. Their father did not acknowledge them.

Rain streaked glass and turned the world gray and watery as Hammer stood in the same position she had maintained for most of the morning. Arms crossed, she leaned her forehead against the window, sometimes thinking, sometimes not, and praying. Her divine communications were not entirely for her husband. Hammer was more worried about herself, in truth. She knew she had reached a crossroads and something new was meant for her, something more demanding that she might never do with Seth weighing her down, as he had all these years. Her children were gone. She would be alone soon. She needed no specialist to tell her this as she watched the continuing ravenous ingestion of her husband's body.

Whatever you want, I'll do, she told the Almighty. *I don't care what. Why does it matter, really, anyway? Certainly, I'm not much of a wife. I would be the first to confess that I haven't been much in that department. Probably not been much of a mother, either. So I'd like to make it up to everyone out there, okay? Just tell me what.*

The Almighty, who actually spent more time with Hammer and was more related to her than she knew, was pleased to hear her say this, for the Almighty had a rather big plan in store for this special recruit. Not now, but later, when it was time. Hammer would see. It was going to prove rather astonishing, if the Almighty didn't say so Its-Almighty-self. As this exchange went on, Randy and Jude fixed their eyes on their mother for the first time that day, it seemed. They saw her head against the glass, and how still she had gotten for one who generally never stopped pacing. Overwhelmed with the profound love and respect they felt for her, they both got up at once. They came up from behind and arms went around her.

"It's okay, Mom," Randy sweetly said.

"We're here," promised Jude. "I wish I could've grown up into some big-shot lawyer or doctor or banker or something, so you'd know you were going to be taken care of."

"Me too," Randy sadly agreed. "But if you're not too ashamed of us, we'll at least be your best friends, okay?"

Hammer dissolved into tears. The three of them hugged as Seth's heart slowed because it could not go on, or perhaps because some part of Seth Bridges knew it was okay for him to leave just now. He coded at eleven minutes past eleven, and the cart and team could bring him back no more.

Chapter Twenty-four

West had missed the Sunset East exit deliberately. Retrieving Brazil's BMW was not what she intended to take care of first. It was quarter past eleven, and most of the world sat in church and wished the minister would hurry up and end the sermon. West was deep inside her preoccupations. She felt a terrible heaviness that she could not explain and wanted to cry, which she blamed on the time of month, which, of course, had passed.

"You all right?" Brazil felt her mood.

"I don't know," she said, depressed.

"You seem really down," he said.

"It's weird." She checked her speed, glancing around for sneaky state troopers. "It just hit me all of a sudden, this really bad feeling, as if something is horribly wrong."

"That happens to me sometimes, too," Brazil confessed. "It's like you pick up on something from somewhere, you know what I mean?"

She knew exactly what he meant, but not why she should know it. West had never considered herself the most intuitive person in the world.

"I used to get that way about my mom a lot," he went on. "I would know before I walked in the house that she was not in good shape."

"What about now?"

West was curious about all this and not certain she knew what was happening to her. She used to be very pragmatic and in control. Now she was picking up extraterrestrial signals and discussing them with a twenty-two-year-old reporter she had just made out with in a police car.

"My mother's never in good shape now." Brazil's voice got hard. "I don't want to sense much about her anymore."

"Well, let me tell you a word or two, Andy Brazil," said West, who did know about a few things in life. "I don't care if you've moved out of her house, you can't erase her from the blackboard of your existence, you know?" West got out a cigarette. "You've got to deal with her, and if you don't, you're going to be messed up the rest of your life."

"Oh good. She messed up all my life so far, and now she's going to mess up the rest of it." He stared out his window.

"The only person who has the power to mess up your life is you. And guess what?" West blew out smoke. "You've done a damn good job with your life so far, if you ask me."

He was silent, thinking about Webb, the memory of what had happened washing over him like icy water.

"Why, exactly, are we going to my house?" Brazil finally got around to asking that.

"You get too many hang-ups," West replied. "You want to tell me how come?"

"Some pervert," Brazil muttered.

"Who?" West didn't like to hear this.

"How the hell do I know?" The subject bored and annoyed him. "Some gay guy?"

"A woman, I think," said Brazil. "I don't know if she's gay."

"When did they begin?" West was getting angry.

"Don't know." His heart constricted as they pulled into the driveway of his mother's home and parked behind the old Cadillac. "About the time I started at the paper," he quietly said.

West looked at him, touched by the sadness in his eyes as he looked out at a dump he called home and tried not to think of the terrible truths it held.

"Andy," West said, "what does your mother think right now? Does she know you've moved out?"

"I left a note," he answered. "She wasn't awake when I was packing."

By now West had ascertained that *awake* was a code word for reasonably sober. "Have you talked to her since?"

He opened his door. West gathered the Caller I.D. system from the backseat and followed him inside the house. They found Mrs. Brazil in the kitchen, shakily spreading peanut butter on Ritz crackers. She had heard them drive up, and this had given her time to mobilize her defenses. Mrs. Brazil did not speak to either one of them.

"Hello," West said.

"How ya doing, Mom?" Brazil tried to hug her, but his mother wanted none of it and waved him off with the knife.

Brazil noticed that the knob had been removed from his bedroom door, and he looked at West and smiled a little. "I forgot about you and your tools," he said.

"I'm sorry. I should have put it back on." She looked around as if there might be a screwdriver somewhere.

"Don't worry about it."

They walked inside his bedroom. She took off her raincoat, hesitating, looking around as if she had never been here before. She was disturbed by his presence in this intimate corner of his life, where he had been a boy, had turned into a man and dreamed. Another hot flash was coming on, her face turning red as she plugged the Caller I.D. system into his phone.

"Obviously, this won't help when you get your new phone number at your apartment," she explained. "But what's more important is who's been calling this number." She straightened up, her work complete. "Does anybody besides your mother and me know you've moved?"

"No," he replied, his eyes on her.

There had never been a woman in his room before, excluding his mother. Brazil glanced about, hoping there was nothing here that might embarrass him or reveal something to her that he did not want her to know. She was looking around, too, neither of them in a hurry to leave.

"You've got a lot of trophies," she remarked.

Brazil shrugged, moving closer to crowded shelves he paid no mind to anymore. He pointed out especially significant awards and explained what they were. He gave her a few highlights of dramatic matches, and for a while they sat on his bed as he reminisced about days from his youth that he had lived with no audience, really, but strangers. He told her about his father, and she gave him her own vague recollection of Drew Brazil.

"I only knew who he was, that was about it," she said. "Back then I was pretty green, too, just a beat cop hoping to make sergeant. I remember all the women thought he was good-looking." She smiled. "There was a lot of talk about that, and that he seemed nice."

"He was nice," Brazil told her. "I guess in some ways he was old-fashioned, but that was the time he lived in." He picked at his fingernails, his head bent. "He was crazy about my mother. But she's always been spoiled. She grew up that way. I've always thought the biggest reason she couldn't deal with his death is she lost the person who doted on her the most and took care of her."

"You don't think she loved him?" West was curious, and she was very aware of how close they were sitting on his bed. She was glad the door was partially open, the knob off.

"My mother doesn't know how to love anybody, including herself."

Brazil was watching her. She could feel his eyes like heat. Thunder and lightning played war outside the window as rain came down hard. She looked at him, too, and wondered if life would ruin his sweetness as he got older. She felt sure it would, and got up from the bed.

"What you've got to do is call the phone company first thing in the morning," she advised him. "Tell them you want Caller I.D. This little box won't do you a bit of good until they give you that service, okay?"

He watched her, saying nothing at first. Then it occurred to him, "Is it expensive?"

"You can manage it. Who's been hitting on you at work?" she wanted to know as she moved closer to the door.

"Axel, a couple women back in composing." He shrugged. "I don't know, don't notice." He shrugged again.

"Anybody able to get into your computer basket?" she said as more thunder cracked.

"I don't see how."

West looked at his PC.

"I'm going to move that to my apartment. I didn't have room in my car the other day," he volunteered.

"Maybe you could write your next story on it," she said.

Brazil continued to watch her. He lay back on the bed, hands behind his head. "Wouldn't do any good," he said. "Still has to go into the newspaper computer one way or another."

"What if you changed your password?" she asked, slipping her hands in her pockets and leaning against the wall.

"We already did."

Lightning flashed, rain and wind ripping through trees.

"We?" West said.

Brenda Bond was sitting at her keyboard in her room of mainframes, working on Sunday because what else did she have to do? There was little life held for her. She wore prescription glasses in expensive black Modo frames, because Tommy Axel looked good in his. She imitated him in other ways as well, since the music critic looked like Matt Dillon and was clearly cool. Systems Analyst Bond was going through miles of printouts and was not pleased by whatever she was finding.

The general architecture of the newspaper's computerized mail system simply had to be reconfigured. What she wanted was plain and not so much to ask, and she was tired of trying to convince Panesa through presentations that the publisher obviously never even bothered to look at. Bond's basic argument was this: When a user sent a mail message for the UA to relay to the local MTA, the MTA then routed the message to the next MTA, which then routed it to the next MTA, and the next, until the message reached the final MTA on the destination system. With a Magic Marker, Brenda Bond had vividly depicted this in Figure 5.1, with colorful dashed lines and arrows showing possible communication paths between MTAs and UAs.

Bond's ruminations crystallized and she stopped what she was doing. She was startled and confused as Deputy Chief Virginia West, in uniform, suddenly walked in at quarter past three. West could see that Bond was a cowardly little worm, middle-aged, and exactly fitting the profile of people who set fires, sent bombs by mail, tampered with products like painkillers and eyedrops, and harassed others with hate notes and anonymous ugly calls over the telephone. West pulled up a chair and turned it backward, straddling it, arms resting on the back of it, like a guy.

"You know it's interesting," West thoughtfully began. "Most people assume if they use a cellular phone, the calls can't be traced. What they don't realize is calls come back to a tower. These towers cover sectors that are only a mile square."

Bond was beginning to tremble, the bluff working.

"A certain young male reporter has been getting obscene phone calls," West went on, "and guess what?" She paused pointedly. "They come back to the same sector you live in, Ms. Bond."

"I, I, I . . ." Bond stammered, visions of jail dancing through her head.

"But it's breaking into his computer basket that bothers me." West's voice got harder, police leather creaking as she shifted in the chair. "Now that's a crime. Leaking his stories to Channel Three. Imagine! It would be like someone stealing your programs and selling them to the competition."

"No!" Bond blurted. "No! I never sold anything!"

"So you *gave* stories to Webb."

"No!" Bond panicked. "I never talked to him. I was just helping the police."

For an instant, West was quiet. She wasn't expecting this.

"What police?" she asked.

"Deputy Chief Goode told me to." Bond confessed all, out of fright. "She said it was part of an undercover departmental operation."

The chair scraped as West got up. It was when she called Hammer's home that she learned the terrible news about Seth and felt sick.

"Oh my God," West said to Jude, who had answered the phone. "I had no idea. I don't want to bother her. Is there anything at all I can do . . . ?"

Hammer took the phone away from her caretaking son. "Jude, it's all right," she said to him, patting his shoulder. "Virginia?" she said.

Goode was watching a videotape of *True Lies* and relaxing on the couch with her gas fire lit and the air conditioning on high, waiting for Webb to call. He had promised to sneak by before the six o'clock news, and she was getting anxious. If he didn't show up within minutes, there wouldn't be time to do or say a thing. When the phone rang, she snatched it up as if all in life depended on whomever it was. Goode was not expecting Chief Hammer. Goode was not expecting Hammer to somberly tell her that Seth had died and she, the boss, would see Goode in Goode's office at four-thirty sharp. Goode jumped off the couch, energized and euphoric. This could mean but one thing. Hammer was taking a long leave to get her pathetic affairs in order and she was naming Goode acting chief.

Hammer had quite another scenario in mind for Deputy Chief Jeannie Goode. Although those around Hammer did not entirely understand how she could think of work at a time like this, in fact, nothing could have been more therapeutic. Her mind cleared. She woke up, anger a blue flame burning through her veins. She felt she could vaporize someone just by looking at him as she dressed in gray polished cotton slacks and blazer, a gray silk blouse, and pearls. She worked on her hair and sprayed a light mist of Hermès on her wrists.

Chief Judy Hammer went out to her midnight-blue police car and flicked on wipers to slough out leaves knocked down by rain. She backed out of her drive and turned onto Pine Street as sun broke through moiling clouds. A lump formed in her throat and she swallowed hard. Tears burned her eyes, and she blinked and took a deep breath, as she saw her street and the world around it for the first time without him. Nothing looked different, but it was. Oh, it was. She took deep breaths as she drove, and her heart felt bruised while her blood roared for righteous revenge. Goode could not have picked a worse time to pull such a stunt and get caught, of this Hammer was certain.

Goode was filled with confidence and self-importance, and she didn't see any point in putting on her uniform or a suit that might have suggested respect and consideration for her troubled leader. Instead, Goode drove back downtown, dressed in the short khaki skirt and tee shirt she had been in all day, waiting for Webb, who was busy working in the yard, his wife keeping a close eye on him these days. Goode parked her Miata in her assigned spot and was more arrogant than usual to all she met as she took the elevator to the third floor, where her fine office was just around the corner from the suite that soon would be hers.

She shut her door and began her usual routine of dialing Webb's number and hanging up if someone other than the handsome news reporter answered. Goode enjoyed a feature on her police line that scrambled signals and rendered Caller I.D. useless. She was hanging up on Webb's wife when Goode's door suddenly flew open. Chief Hammer walked in, about to live up to her name. Goode's first reaction was how sharp her boss looked in gray. Goode's second and final reaction was that Hammer did not seem to be in mourning as she strode to the desk and snatched up Goode's brass nameplate.

"You're fired," Hammer said in a voice not to be questioned. "I want your badge and gun. Your desk gets cleared out now. Let me help you start."

Hammer threw the nameplate into the trash. She turned without another glance and walked out. Hammer was fury traveling down the corridors of her department, yet she was forthcoming in nods and salutations to troops she passed. Word was already out on the radio about her husband, and members of the Charlotte Police Department were overwhelmed with sorrow and newfound respect for their leader. Throughout it all, she was here, damn it, and she wasn't going to let them down. When a sergeant saw Goode sneaking out to her car with her office crammed in bags and boxes, there was rejoicing throughout Adam, Baker, Charlie, and David response areas, and investigations and support. Cops high-fived and low-tenned in the parking deck and the roll call room. The duty captain lit a rum crook cigar in his nonsmoking office.

Brazil got the good word by pager as he was out in the parking lot changing the oil in his car. He went inside and dialed West's home number.

"Bond won't be bothering you anymore." West tried to be cool, but she was intensely proud of herself. "Goode won't be getting your stories from the little shit and leaking them to Webb."

Brazil was shocked and ecstatic. "No way!"

"Oh yeah. It's done. Hammer's fired Goode and Bond is in a state of paralysis."

"Bond was making those calls?" To Brazil, this seemed incongruous.

"Yup."

He was oddly disappointed that it wasn't someone more dynamic and attractive thinking such thoughts about him.

West sensed this and told him, "You aren't looking at this the right way."

"Looking at what?" He played dumb.

"Andy, I see this kind of thing all the time, doesn't matter whether it's a man or woman doing it, except that women aren't likely to expose themselves to you, so at least you can be grateful for that," she explained. "This sort of thing is not about sex or being attracted to someone in the normal sense of things. It's all about control and power, about degrading. A form of violence, really."

"I know that," he said.

He still wished his verbal assailant had been someone halfway pretty, and he couldn't help but wonder what it was about him that prompted people like the creep at the car wash, and now Brenda Bond, to select him. Why? Did he send out signals that made them think they could take advantage of him? He bet that no one dared do such a thing to West or Hammer.

"Gotta go," West said, leaving Brazil disappointed and irritable.

He got back to changing his oil, in a hurry to finish now. He had an idea.

West had one, too. She called Raines, and this definitely was unexpected and abnormal. West never called him or anyone, except

Brazil, as all around her knew and accepted as fact. Raines had the night off and was looking forward to watching a just-released sports bloopers video he had acquired over the weekend. West was thinking about pizza. They decided they probably could collaborate on this quite nicely, and he headed over to her house in his rebuilt, fully loaded, black on black '73 Corvette Stingray, with headers, tinted glass top, and window sticker. West usually could hear him coming.

Brazil thought he should come up with a way of showing his appreciation to West for resolving his life's crisis. He also imagined the two of them celebrating, and why not? This was a big day for both of them. She had rid him of Bond and Webb, and she and the entire police department were free of Goode. Brazil sped to the nearest Hop-In and picked up the nicest bottle of wine he could find in the glass cooler, a Dry Creek Vineyard 1992 Fume Blanc, for nine dollars and forty-nine cents.

She would be surprised and pleased, and maybe he could pet Niles for a while. Maybe Brazil could spend a little more time inside West's house and learn something more about her. Maybe she would invite him to watch TV with her, or listen to music, the two of them sipping wine in her living room, talking and telling stories about their early years and dreams.

Brazil drove toward Dilworth, overflowing with happiness that his problems had cleared up and he had a friend like her. He thought about his mother, wondering how she was doing, and was pleased that she didn't seem to get him down so much anymore. He didn't seem to feel that her choices were because of what he did or did not do for her.

Lights were out, the TV on in West's living room. She and Raines were on the couch, eating a Pizza Hut triple decker. Raines was perched on the edge of his cushion, drinking a Coors Light, and crazed over his new videotape. Without a doubt it was the best yet, and he wished West would let him watch it undistracted. She was all over him, kissing, nibbling, running her fingers through his thick, curly black hair. She was getting on his nerves, really, and acting out of character, in general.

"What the hell's gotten into you?" he absently said.

He tried to look around her as he twirled her hair with the creative enthusiasm of Niles kneading the rug.

"Yes! Yes! What a dunk! Rip that backboard down! Oh shit! Ahhhh! Look at that! Christ! *Right into the pole.* Oh, man." Raines sat back down.

The next five minutes was ice hockey. The goalie got a stick between his legs. A puck ricocheted off two face masks and hit a referee in the mouth. Raines was going wild. There was nothing he liked better than sports and injuries, especially if the two went together. With each tragedy, he imagined rushing in with his medical kit and stretcher, Raines to the rescue. West was unbuttoning her blouse. She threw herself on top of him, devouring his mouth, and desperate. Raines put down his pizza.

"Hormones again?" He had never seen her this frustrated.

"I don't know." She worked on more buttons and hooks.

They seriously made out on the couch while Niles remained in his sanctuary above the sink. He was not a fan of Tire Man, as Niles called Raines after noticing some radial ad in the newspaper lining his litter box. Tire Man was offensively loud and never warm and appreciative of Niles. Several times, Tire Man had launched Niles off the couch, and this would have been one of those times should Niles have tested his luck, which he did not.

He looked adoringly at his distant, sad King. *I'll help you. Fear not. My owner knows about laundry money. She is very powerful and will protect you and all Usbeeceeans.* Niles twitched an ear, detecting another engine sound, this one a pleasant, deep purring that he recognized. It was Piano Man, the nice one who played his fingers over Niles's spine and ribs and right behind his ears until Niles fell over from sheer pleasure, rattling windowpanes. Niles got up and stretched, excited that Piano Man seemed to be slowing behind the house, where he had parked in the past, on the few times he had stopped by for one reason or another.

West and Raines were not in a good space when the doorbell rang. By now, Raines was completely focused on what he was doing and was within minutes, at most, of victory. It was quite inconvenient and inconsiderate for someone to dare and drop by unannounced. Raines experienced an intense wave of homicidal rage as he withdrew to his end of the couch, sweating and out of breath.

"Goddamn son of a bitch," he furiously blurted.

"I'll get it," West said.

She got up, pulling, zipping, and buttoning, as she walked and combed her fingers through her hair. She was a mess, and as the bell rang again, she hoped it wasn't Mrs. Grabman from two doors down. Mrs. Grabman was a nice enough old woman, but she tended to drop by every weekend West was home, usually offering vegetables from her garden as an excuse to meddle and complain about someone suspicious in the neighborhood. West already had a long row of ripening tomatoes on the counter, and two drawers full of okra, green beans, squash, and zucchini in the refrigerator.

Safety-conscious West, who had never gotten around to installing a burglar alarm, yelled through the door, "Who is it?"

"It's me," Brazil said.

From the bottom of the steps, where he waited with wine, he was excited and clueless. He assumed the old black Corvette on the street belonged to a neighborhood kid. It had never occurred to him that Denny Raines might drive anything besides an ambulance. West opened the door, and Brazil lit up at the sight of her. He offered her the bottle of wine in its brown paper bag.

"I thought we should at least drink a toast . . ." he started to say.

West awkwardly took the wine from him, acutely conscious of his reaction to her tousled hair, to the red marks on her neck and her blouse buttoned crooked. Brazil's smile faded as his eyes wandered around her crime scene. Raines appeared behind his woman and looked down the steps at Brazil.

"Hey, what'cha know, sport?" Raines grinned at him. "Like your stories . . ."

Brazil ran back to his car as if someone were chasing him.

"Andy!" West yelled after him. "Andy!"

She hurried down the steps as his BMW roared off into the setting sun. Raines followed her back into her living room as she buttoned her blouse properly and nervously smoothed her hair. She set the wine on a table, where she did not have to look at it, and be reminded of who had brought it.

"What the hell's his problem?" Raines wanted to know.

"Temperamental writer," she muttered.

Raines wasn't interested. He and West had several downs yet to go, and he tackled her from behind, grabbing, fondling, and working his tongue into her ear. The play was incomplete as she broke free, leaving him yards behind and taking the ball with her.

"I'm tired," she snapped.

Raines rolled his eyes. He'd had enough of her poor sportsmanship and penalty flags.

"Fine," he told her as he ejected his bloopers tape from the VCR. "Let me just ask you one thing, Virginia." He furiously strutted to the door, pausing long enough to fix smoldering eyes on hers. "When you're eating and the phone rings, what happens after you hang up? Do you go back to your meal, or do you forget that, too? Do you just *quit* because you had a tiny interruption?"

"Depends on what I'm eating," West told him.

Brazil's dinner was late and spent at Shark Finn's, on Old Pineville Road, at Bourbon Street. After roaring away from West's house, he had driven around, getting angrier by the moment. It had not been one of his wiser moves, perhaps, to stop by Tommy Axel's Fourth Ward condominium with its blush rose front door. Brazil noticed a number of men noticing him during his approach from the parking lot. Brazil wasn't especially friendly to them, or even to Axel.

What Axel considered a first date and Brazil considered revenge began in Shark Finn's Jaws Raw Bar, where a mounted sailfish caught in a net protested with an open mouth and startled glass eyes. Wooden tables were uncovered, the plank floor unvarnished. There were faces carved on coconuts, and curled starfish and stained glass. Brazil nursed a Red Stripe beer and wondered if he might be going insane as he considered the senseless and impulsive behavior that had landed him here in this place at this moment.

Axel was burning holes in him, living a fantasy, and fearful the vision would vanish if he looked away for even a second. Brazil was certain that other people slipping down raw oysters and getting drunk had figured out Axel's intentions and were miscalculating Brazil's. This was unfortunate since most of the men drove pickup trucks and believed it was their higher calling to get women pregnant, own guns, and kill queers.

"You come here a lot?" Brazil swirled beer in its dark brown bottle.

"Whenever. You hungry?" Axel grinned, displaying his very nice white teeth.

"Sort of," Brazil said.

They got up and moved into the crab shack, which was no different than the raw bar, except there were captain's chairs at the tables and the ceiling fans were working so hard they looked like they might take off. Jimmy Buffett was playing over intercoms. A candle and Tabasco sauce were on their table, which rocked, requiring Brazil to fix it with several packets of Sweet & Low. Axel started by ordering a Shark Attack with lots of Myers's rum, and he convinced Brazil to try a Rum Runner, which had enough liquor in it to turn the lights out in half of Brazil's brain.

As if Brazil were not in enough trouble already, Axel ordered a tin bucket filled with iced-down bottles of Rolling Rock beer. This was going to work just fine, the music critic was sure of it. Brazil was a puppy and could be trained. Axel was stunned to suspect that the guy might never have been drunk in his life. Incredible. What did he grow up in, a monastery, the Mormon church? Brazil was wearing another pair of slightly too small jeans left over from high school days, and a tennis team tee shirt. Axel tried not to think about what it might be like to get those clothes off.

"Everything here's good," Axel said without looking at the menu as he leaned into candlelight. "Conch fritters, crab cakes, Po-Boy sandwiches. I like the baskets and usually get fried scallops."

"Okay," Brazil said to both Axels sitting across from him. "I think you're trying to get me drunk."

"No way," Axel said, signaling for the waitress. "You've hardly had a thing."

"I don't usually. And I ran eight miles this morning," Brazil pointed out.

"Man," Axel said. "You're sheltered. Looks like I'm gonna have to educate you a little, pull you along."

"I don't think so." Brazil wanted to go home and hide in bed. Alone. "I don't feel too good, Tommy."

Axel was insistent that food would prove the cure, and what he said was true to a point. Brazil felt better after he threw up in the men's room. He switched to iced tea, waiting for his internal weather to clear.

"I need to go," he said to an increasingly sullen Axel.

"Not yet," Axel said, as if the decision was his to make.

"Oh yes. I'm out of here." Brazil was politely insistent.

"We haven't had a chance to talk," Axel told him.

"About what?"

"You know."

"Do I have to guess?" Brazil was getting annoyed, his mind still in Dilworth, really.

"You know," Axel said again, his eyes intense.

"I just want to be friends," Brazil let him know.

"That's all I want." Axel couldn't have agreed more. "I want us to get to know each other real well so we can be great friends."

Brazil knew a line when he heard one. "You want to be better friends than I want to be. And you want to start right now. No matter what you claim, I know how it works, Tommy. What you're saying is insincere. If I told you this minute that I'd go home with you, you'd go for it *like that.*" He snapped his fingers.

"What's so wrong about it?" Axel liked the idea quite a lot and wondered if it were remotely possible.

"See. A contradiction. That's not called being friends. That's called being laid," Brazil enlightened him. "I'm not a piece of meat, nor do I care to be a one-night stand."

"Who said anything about one night? I'm a long-term kind of guy," Axel assured him.

Brazil could not help but notice the two guys with bulging muscles and tattoos, in greasy coveralls, drinking long-neck Budweisers, glaring at them as they eavesdropped. This didn't bode well, and Axel was so obsessed he wasn't picking up on the stubby fingers drumming the table and toothpicks agitating in mean mouths, and eyes cutting as plans were being made for the dark parking lot when the fags returned to their vehicle.

"My feelings for you are very deep, Andy," Axel went on. "Frankly, I'm in love with you." He slumped back in his chair, and dramatically threw his hands up in despair. "There. I've said it. Hate me if you want. Shun me."

"Puke," said Rizzo, whose visible tattoo was of a big-breasted naked woman named Tiny.

"I gotta get some air," agreed his buddy, Buzz Shifflet.

"Tommy, I think we should be smart and get out of here as fast as we can," Brazil suggested quietly and with authority. "I made a mistake and I apologize, okay? I shouldn't have come over and we shouldn't be here. I was in a mood and took it out on you. Now we're going to make tracks or die."

"So you do hate me." Axel was into his crushed, you-have-deeply-wounded-me routine.

"Then you stay here." Brazil stood. "I'm pulling your car up to the front porch, and you're going to jump in. Got it?" He thought of West again, and anger returned.

Brazil was looking around, as if expecting a gunfight any moment and ready for one, but aware of his limitations. There were rednecks everywhere, all drinking beer, eating fried fish with tartar and cocktail sauces and ketchup. They were staring at Axel and Brazil. Axel saw the wisdom in Brazil getting the car by himself.

"I'll pay the bill while you do that," Axel said. "Dinner's my treat."

Brazil was completely cognizant of the fact that the two big boys in coveralls were this very second out in the poorly lit parking lot, waiting for the two queers. Brazil wasn't especially concerned by their erroneous impression of him and the choices he made in life, but he was not interested in having the shit beat out of him. He thought fast and tracked down the hostess in the raw bar, where she was parked at a table, smoking and writing tomorrow's specials on a chalkboard.

"Ma'am," he said to her. "I wonder if you could help me with a serious problem."

She looked skeptically at him, her demeanor changing some-what. Guys said similar words to her every night after they'd been through buckets of beer. The problem was always the same thing, and so easy to remedy if she didn't mind slipping off behind the restaurant for maybe ten minutes and dropping her jeans.

"What." She continued writing, ignoring the jerk.

"I need a pin," he said.

"A what?" she looked up at him. "You mean something to write with?"

"No, ma'am. I mean a pin, a needle, and something to sterilize it with," he told her.

"What for?" She frowned, opening her fat vinyl pocketbook.

"A splinter."

"Oh!" Now that she understood. "Don'cha hate it when that happens? This place is full of 'em, too. Here you go, sugar."

She fished out a small sewing kit in a clear plastic box that she'd gotten from the last hotel some rich guy took her to, and she slid out a needle. She handed him a bottle of nail polish remover. He dipped the needle in acetone and bravely retreated to the porch. Sure enough, the two thugs were prowling near cars, waiting. They lurched in his direction when they spotted him, and he quickly stabbed his left index finger with the needle. He stabbed his right index finger and thumb. Brazil squeezed out as much blood as he could, and smeared it on his face, which he then held in his hands as if he were reeling.

"Oh God," he moaned, staggering down steps. "Jesus." He fell against the porch railing, groaning, holding his disgusting, gory face.

"Shit." Rizzo had gotten to him and was completely taken aback. "What the fuck happened to you?"

"My cousin in there," Brazil weakly said.

"You talking about that fag you was sitting with?" asked Shifflet.

Brazil nodded. "Yeah, man. He's fucking got AIDS and he threw up blood on me! You believe that! Oh God."

He staggered down another step. Shifflet and Rizzo moved out of the way.

"It went in my eyes and mouth! You know what that means! Where's a hospital around here, man? I got to get to the hospital! Could you drive me, please?"

Brazil staggered and almost stumbled into them. Shifflet and Rizzo ran. They leapt into their Nissan Hard Body XE with its four-foot-lift oversized tires that spun rocks.

Chapter Twenty-five

The next night, Monday, Blair Mauney III was also enjoying an agreeable meal in the Queen City. The banker was dining at Morton's of Chicago, where he typically went when business called him to headquarters. He was a regular at the high-end steak house with stained-glass windows, next to the Carillon and across from First Presbyterian Church, which also had stained glass, only older and more spectacular, especially after dark when Mauney felt lonely and in the mood to prowl.

Mauney needed no explanation from the pretty young waitress with her cart of raw meat and live lobster waving bound claws. He always ordered the New York strip, medium rare, a baked potato, butter only, and the chopped red onion and tomato salad with Morton's famous blue cheese dressing. This he downed with plenty of Jack Black on the rocks. Tomorrow he would have breakfast with Cahoon and the chairman of corporate risk policy and the chairman of the credit corp, in addition to the chairman of USBank South, plus a couple of presidents. It was routine. They'd sit around a fancy table in Cahoon's fancy Mount Olympus office. There was no crisis or even good news that Mauney knew of, only more of the same, and his resentment peaked.

The bank had been started by his forebears in 1874. It was Mauney who should be ensconced within the crown and have his black and white portrait regularly printed in the *Wall Street Journal.* Mauney loathed Cahoon, and whenever possible, Mauney dropped poison pellets about his boss, spreading malicious gossip hinting at eccentricities, poor judgment, idiocy, and malignant motives for the good in the world Cahoon had done. Mauney requested a doggie bag, as he always did, because he never knew when he might get hungry later in his room at the luxurious Park Hotel, near Southpark Mall.

He paid the seventy-three-dollar-and-seventy-cent bill, leaving two percent less than his usual fifteen-percent tip, which he figured to the penny on a wafer-thin calculator he kept in his wallet. The waitress had been slow bringing his fourth drink, and being busy was no excuse. He returned to the sidewalk out front, on West Trade Street, and the valets scurried, as they always did. Mauney climbed into his rental black Lincoln Continental and decided he really was not in the mood to return to his hotel just yet.

He briefly thought of his wife and her endless surgeries and other medical hobbies, as he cataloged them. What he spent on her in a year was a shock, and not one stitch of it had improved her, really. She was a manikin who cooked and made the rounds at cocktail parties. Buried somewhere deep in Mauney's corporate mind were memories of Polly at Sweetbriar, when a carload of Mauney's pals showed up for a dance one Saturday night in May. She was precious in a blue dress and wanted nothing to do with him.

The spell was cast. He had to have her that moment. Still, Polly was busy, hard to find, and cared not. He started calling twice a day. He showed up on campus, hopelessly smitten. Of course, she knew exactly what she was doing. Polly had been mentored thoroughly at home, at boarding school, and now at this fine women's college. She knew how men were if a girl acknowledged their attentions. Polly knew how to play hard to get. Polly knew that Mauney had a pedigree and portfolio that she had been promised since childhood, because it was her destiny and her entitlement. They were married fourteen months after their first meeting, or exactly two weeks after Polly graduated cum laude with a degree in English which, according to her proud new husband, would make her unusually skilled in penning invitations and thank-you notes.

Mauney could not pinpoint precisely when his wife's many physical complications began. It seemed she was playing tennis, still peppy and enjoying the good fortune he made possible for her, until after their second child was born. Women. Mauney would never figure them out. He found Fifth Street and began cruising, as he often did when deep in thought. He began getting excited as he looked out at the night life and thought about his trip tomorrow afternoon. His wife thought he would be in Charlotte for three days. Cahoon and company believed Mauney was returning to Asheville after breakfast. All were wrong.

While family traveled from the distant airports of Los Angeles and New York, the bereft chief and her sons went through closets and dresser drawers, carrying out the painful task of dividing and disposing of Seth's clothing and other personal effects. Hammer could not look at her late husband's bed, where the nightmare had begun as he got drunk and fantasized about what he could do to really hurt her this time. *Well, you did it, Seth. You figured it out,* Hammer thought. She folded extra-extra-large shirts, shorts, underwear, socks, and placed them in paper bags for the Salvation Army.

They made no decision about Seth's valuables, such as his four different Rolex watches, the wedding band that had not fit him in more than ten years, the collection of gold railroad watches that had belonged to his grandfather, his Jaguar, not to mention his stocks and his cash. Hammer cared nothing about any of it and frankly expected him to zing her one last time in his will. She had never been materialistic and wasn't about to begin now.

"I don't know the details about any of his affairs," she said to her sons, who cared nothing about them, either.

"That figures," said Jude as he removed another suit from a hanger and began folding it. "You would think he might have discussed his will with you, Mom."

"Part of it is my fault." She closed a drawer, wondering how she could have endured this activity alone. "I never asked."

"You shouldn't have to ask," Jude resentfully said. "Part of the whole point of living with someone is you share important things with each other, you know? Like in your case, so you could maybe plan for your future in the event something happened to him? Which was a good possibility with his rotten health."

"I've planned for my own future." Hammer looked around the room, knowing that every molecule within it would have to go. "I don't do so badly on my own."

Randy was younger and angrier. As far as he was concerned, his father had been selfish and neurotic because he was spoiled and made no effort to think about others beyond what function they might have served in his wasteful, rapacious existence. Randy, especially, seethed over the way his mother had been treated. She deserved someone who admired and loved her for all her goodness and courage. He went over and wrapped his arms around her as she folded a Key West shirt she remembered Seth buying on one of their few vacations.

"Don't." She gently pushed her son away, tears filling her eyes.

"Why don't you come stay with us in L.A. for a while?" he gently said, holding on to her anyway.

She shook her head, returning to the business at hand, determined to get every reminder of Seth out of this house as fast as she could, that she might get on with life.

"The best thing for me is to work," she said. "And there are problems I need to resolve."

"There are always problems, Mom," Jude said. "We'd love it if you came to New York."

"You know anything about this Phi Beta Kappa key on a

chain?" Randy held it up. "It was inside the Bible in the back of this drawer."

Hammer looked at the necklace as if she had been struck. The key was hers, from Boston University, where she had enjoyed four very stimulating years and graduated near the top of her class with a double major in criminal justice and history, for she believed that the two were inexorably linked. Hammer had grown up with no special privileges or promise that she would amount to much, since she was a girl amid four brothers in a household with little money and a mother who did not approve of a daughter thinking the dangerous thoughts hers did. Judy Hammer's Phi Beta Kappa key had been a triumph, and she had given it to Seth when they had gotten engaged. He wore it for a long time, until he began to get fat and hateful.

"He told me he lost it," Hammer quietly said as the telephone rang.

West felt terrible about bothering her chief again. West apologized on the cellular phone inside her police car as she sped downtown. Other units and an ambulance roared to the heart of Five Points, where another man from out of town had been brutally slain.

"Oh Lord," Hammer breathed, shutting her eyes. "Where?"

"I can pick you up," West said over the line.

"No, no," Hammer said. "Just tell me where."

"Cedar Street past the stadium," West said as she shot through a yellow light. "The abandoned buildings around there. Near the welding supply company. You'll see us."

Hammer grabbed her keys from the table by the door. She headed out, not bothering to change out of her gray suit and pearls. Brazil had been driving around in a funk when he'd heard the call on the scanner. He got there fast and now was standing beyond crime-scene tape, restless in jeans and tee shirt, frustrated because no one would let him in. Cops were treating him as if he were a reporter no different than others out foraging, and he didn't understand it.

Didn't they remember him in uniform, out with them night after night and in foot pursuits and fights?

West rolled up seconds before Hammer did, and the two women made their way to the overgrown area where a black Lincoln Continental was haphazardly parked far off Cedar and First Streets, near a Dumpster. The welding company was a looming Gothic silhouette with dark windows. Police lights strobed, and in the far distance a siren wailed as misfortune struck in another part of the city. A Norfolk Southern train loudly lumbered past on nearby tracks, the engineer staring out at disaster.

Typically, the car was rented and the driver's door was open, the interior bell dinging, and headlights burning. Police were searching the area, flashguns going off and video cameras rolling. Brazil spotted West and Hammer coming through, reporters moiling around them and getting nothing but invisible walls. Brazil stared at West until she saw him, but she gave him no acknowledgment. She did not seem inclined to include him. It was as if they had never met and her indifference ran through him like a bayonet. Hammer did not seem aware of him, either. Brazil stared after them, convinced of a betrayal. The two women were busy and overwrought.

"We're sure," Hammer was saying to West.

"Yes. It's like the others," West grimly said as their strides carried them beyond tape and deeper inside the scene. "No question in my mind. M.O. identical."

Hammer took a deep breath, her face pained and outraged as she looked at the car, then at the activity in a thicket where Dr. Odom was on his knees, working. From where Hammer stood, she could see the medical examiner's bloody gloves glistening in lights set up around the perimeter. She looked up as the Channel 3 news helicopter thudded overhead, hovering, its camera securing footage for the eleven o'clock news. Broken glass clinked under feet as the two women moved closer, and Dr. Odom palpated the victim's destroyed head. The man had on a dark blue Ralph Lauren suit, a white shirt missing its cufflinks, and a Countess Mara tie. He had graying curly hair and a tan face that might have been attractive, but now it was hard to tell. Hammer saw no jewelry but guessed that whatever this man had owned wasn't cheap. She knew money when she saw it.

"Do we have an I.D.?" Hammer asked Dr. Odom.

"Blair Mauney the third, forty-five years old, from Asheville," he replied, photographing the hateful blaze orange hourglass spray-painted over the victim's genitals. Dr. Odom looked up at Hammer for a moment. "How many more?" he asked in a hard tone, as if blaming her.

"What about cartridge cases?" West asked.

Detective Brewster was squatting, interested in trash scattered through briars. "Three so far," he answered his boss. "Looks like the same thing."

"Christ," said Dr. Odom.

By now, Dr. Odom was seriously projecting. He continually imagined himself in strange cities at meetings, driving around, maybe lost. He thought of suddenly being yanked out of his car and led to a place like this by a monster who would blow his head off for a watch, a wallet, a ring. Dr. Odom could read the fear the victims had felt as they begged not to die, that huge .45 pointed and ready to fire. Dr. Odom was certain that the soiled undershorts consistent in each case was not postmortem. No goddamn way. The slain businessmen didn't lose control of bowels and bladder as life fled and bled from them. The guys were terrified, trembling violently, pupils dilated, digestion shutting down as blood rushed to extremities for a fight or flight that would never happen. Dr. Odom's pulse pounded in his neck as he unfolded another body bag.

West carefully scanned the interior of the Lincoln as the alert dinged that the driver's door was ajar and the lights were on. She noted the Morton's doggie bag and the contents of the briefcase and an overnight bag that had been dumped out and rummaged through in back. USBank business cards were scattered over the carpet and she leaned close and read the name Blair Mauney III, the same name on the driver's license Detective Brewster had shown her. West pulled plastic gloves out of her back pocket.

She worked them on, so consumed by what she was doing that she was unaware of anyone around her or the tow truck that was slowly rolling up to haul the Lincoln to the police department for processing. West had not worked crime scenes in years, but she had been good at it once. She was meticulous, tireless, and intuitive, and right now she was getting a weird feeling as she looked at the clutter left by the killer. She lifted a USAir ticket by a corner, opening it on the car seat, touching as little of it as possible as her misgivings grew.

Mauney had flown to Charlotte from Asheville today, arriving at Charlotte-Douglas International Airport at five-thirty P.M. The return, for tomorrow afternoon, was not back to Asheville, but to Miami, and from there Mauney was flying to Grand Cayman in the West Indies. West carefully flipped through more tickets, her heart picking up, adrenaline coursing. He was scheduled to fly out of Grand Cayman on Wednesday and stop over in Miami for six hours. Then he would return to Charlotte and, finally, to Asheville. There were more disturbing signs that were likely unrelated to Mauney's murder but pointed to other crime possibly surrounding his life.

This was always the bitter irony in such cases, she couldn't help but think. Death ratted on people who were closet drug abusers, drunks, or having affairs with one and/or the other sex, or those who liked to whip or be whipped or to string themselves up by pulleys and nooses and masturbate. Human creativity was endless, and West had seen it all. She had gotten out a ballpoint pen and was using it to turn pages of other paperwork. Though her forte was not cash and equivalents, treasury and agency securities, derivatives, investment banking, commercial and corporate banking, West knew enough to get a sense of what Mauney might have been intending on his travels.

In the first place, he had an alias, Jack Morgan, whose picture

I.D.s on passport and driver's license showed Mauney's face. There were a total of eight credit cards and two checkbooks in the names of Mauney and Morgan. Both men seemed to have a keen interest in real estate, specifically a number of hotels along Miami Beach. It appeared to West that Mauney was prepared to invest some one hundred million dollars in these old pastel dumps. Why? Who the hell went to Miami Beach these days? West flipped through more paperwork, perspiring in the humid heat. Why was Mauney planning to drop by Grand Cayman, the money-laundering capital of the world?

"My God," West muttered, realizing that Grand Cayman was three syllables.

She stood up, staring at the bright skyline, at the mighty USBank Corporate Center rising above all, its red light slowly blinking a warning to helicopters and low flying planes. She stared at this symbol of economic achievement, of greatness and hard work on the part of many, and she got angry. West, like a lot of citizens, had checking and savings accounts at USBank. She had financed her Ford through it. Tellers were always pleasant and hardworking. They went home at the end of the day and did their best to make ends meet like most folks. Then some carpetbagger comes along and decides to cheat, steal, hoodwink, make out like a bandit, and give an innocent business and its people a bad name. West turned her attention to Hammer and motioned to her.

"Take a look," West said quietly to her chief.

Hammer squatted by the open car door and examined documents without touching them. She had been making investments and saving money most of her life. She knew creative banking when she saw it and was shocked at first, then disgusted as truth began to whisper. As best she could tell, and of course none of it could be proven at this precise moment, it appeared Blair Mauney III was behind hundreds of millions of dollars loaned to Dominion Tobacco that seemed to be linked to a real-estate development group called Southman Corporation in Grand Cayman. Associated with this were multiple bank account numbers not linked by identification numbers. Several of the same Miami telephone numbers showed up repeatedly, with no description other than initials that made no sense. There were references to something called *USChoice.*

"What do you think?" West whispered to Hammer.

"Fraud, for starters. We'll get all this to the FBI, to Squad Four, see what they make of it."

The news helicopter circled low. The cocooned body was loaded into the ambulance.

"What about Cahoon?" West asked.

Hammer took a deep breath, feeling sorry for him. How much bad news did anybody need in one night? "I'll call him, tell him what we suspect," she grimly said.

"Do we release Mauney's I.D. tonight?"

"I'd rather hold out until morning." Hammer was staring beyond bright lights and crime-scene tape. "I believe you have a visitor," she said to West.

Brazil was at the perimeter taking notes. He was not in uniform this night, and his face was hard as his eyes met West's and held. She walked toward him, and they moved some distance away from others and stood on different sides of crime-scene tape.

"We're not releasing any information tonight," she said to him.

"I'll just do my usual," he said, lifting the tape to duck under.

"No." She blocked him. "We can't let anybody in. Not on this one."

"Why not?" he said, stung.

"There are a lot of complications."

"There always are." His eyes flashed.

"I'm sorry," she told him.

"I've been inside before," he protested. "How come now I can't?"

"You've been inside when you've been with me." West began to back away.

"When I've . . . ?" Brazil's pain was almost uncontainable. "I am with you!"

West looked around and wished he would lower his voice. She

could not tell him what she had found inside the victim's car and what it quite likely implied about the not-so-innocent victim Blair Mauney III. She glanced back at Hammer. The chief was still leaning inside the Lincoln, looking through more paperwork, perhaps grateful for the distraction from her own private tragedies. West thought of Brazil's behavior at her house while Raines was watching the videotape. This was a mess, and it could not go on. She made the right decision and could feel the change inside her, the curtain dropping. The end.

"You can't do this to me!" Brazil furiously went on. "I haven't done anything wrong!"

"Please don't make a scene or I'm going to have to ask you to leave," West, the deputy chief, stated.

Enraged and hurt, Brazil realized the truth. "You're not going to let me ride with you anymore."

West hesitated, trying to ease him into this. "Andy," she said, "it couldn't go on forever. You've always known that. Jesus Christ." She blew out in frustration. "I'm old enough to . . . I'm . . ."

Brazil backed up, staring at her, the traitor, the fiend, the hard-hearted tyrant, the worst villain ever to touch his life. She didn't care about him. She never had.

"I don't need you," he cruelly said.

Brazil wheeled around and ran. He ran as fast as he could back to his BMW.

"Oh for God's sake," West exclaimed as Hammer suddenly was at her side.

"Problem?" Hammer stared after Brazil, her hands in her pockets.

"More of the same." West wanted to kill him. "He's going to do something."

"Good deduction." Hammer's eyes were sad and tired, but she was full of courage and support for the living.

"I'd better go after him." West started walking.

Hammer stood where she was, strobing lights washing over her face as she watched West duck reporters and trot off to her car.

Hammer thought about new love, about people crazy for each other and not knowing it as they fought and ran off and chased. The ambulance beeped as it backed up, carrying away what was left of a person whom Hammer, in truth, did not feel especially sorry for at this point. She would never have wished such horrendous violence upon him, but what a piece of shit he was, stealing, hurting, and more than likely perpetuating the drug trade. Hammer was going to take this investigation into her own hands, and if need be, make an example of Blair Mauney III, who had planned to screw the bank and a hooker during the same trip.

"People die the way they lived," she commented to Detective Brewster, patting his back.

"Chief Hammer." He was loading new film in his camera. "I'm sorry about your husband."

"So am I. In more ways than you'll ever know." She ducked under the tape.

Brazil must have been speeding again, or perhaps he was hiding in another alleyway. West cruised West Trade Street, looking for his old BMW. She checked her mirrors, seeing no sign of him, the scanner a staccato of more problems in the city. She picked up the portable phone and dialed the number for Brazil's desk at the *Observer*. After three rings, it rolled over to another desk and West hung up. She fumbled for a cigarette and turned onto Fifth Street, checking cars driven by men checking the late night market. West whelped her siren and flashed her lights, messing with those up to no good. She watched hookers and sh'ims scatter as potential clients sped away.

"Stupid bastards," West muttered, flicking an ash out the window. "Is it worth dying for?" she yelled at them.

Cahoon lived in Myers Park on Cherokee Place, and his splendid brick mansion was only partly lit up because its owner and his wife and youngest daughter had gone to bed. This did not deter Hammer in the least. She was about to do a decent thing for the CEO and great benefactor of the city. Hammer rang the doorbell, her fabric worn in places she had not known she had. She felt an emptiness, a loneliness that was frightening in its intensity. She could not bear to go home and walk past places Seth had sat, lain, walked, or rummaged through. She did not want to see remnants of a life no more. His favorite coffee mug. The Ben & Jerry's Chocolate Chip Cookie Dough ice cream he'd never had a chance to eat. The antique sterling-silver letter opener he had given her the Christmas of 1972, still on the desk in her study.

Cahoon heard the bell from his master suite upstairs, where his view above sculpted boxwoods and old magnolia trees included his building encrusted with jewels and topped by a crown. He threw back fine monogrammed sheets, wondering who on earth would dare to drop by his home at this obscene hour. Cahoon went to the Aiphone on the wall and picked up the receiver. He was startled to see Chief Hammer on the video monitor.

"Judy?" he said.

"I know it's late, Sol." She looked into the camera and spoke over the intercom. "But I need to talk to you."

"Is everything all right?" Alarmed, he thought of his children. He knew Rachael was in bed. But his two older sons could be anywhere.

"I'm afraid not," Hammer told him.

Cahoon grabbed his robe from the bedpost and flung it around himself. His slippers patted along the endless antique Persian runner covering the stairs. His index finger danced over the burglar alarm keypad, turning off glass breakers, motion sensors, contacts in all windows and doors, and bypassing his vault and priceless art collection, which were in separate wings and on separate systems. He let Hammer in. Cahoon squinted in the glare of bright lights that blazed on whenever anything more than a foot tall moved within a six-foot radius of his house. Hammer did not look good.

Cahoon could not imagine why the chief was out so early in the morning so soon after her husband's sudden death.

"Please come in," he said, wide awake now and more gentle than usual. "Can I get you a drink?"

She followed him into the great room, where he repaired to the bar. Hammer had been inside Cahoon's mansion but once, at a splendid party complete with a string quartet and huge silver bowls filled with jumbo shrimp on ice. The CEO liked English antiques and collected old books with beautiful leather covers and marbled pages.

"Bourbon," Hammer decided.

That sounded good to Cahoon, who was on a regimen of no fat, no alcohol, and no fun. He might have a double, straight up, no ice. He pulled the cork out of a bottle of Blanton's Kentucky single barrel and didn't bother with the monogrammed cocktail napkins his wife liked so much. He knew he needed to be medicated because Hammer wasn't here to hand him good news. *Dear Lord, don't let anything bad have happened to either of the boys.* Did a day go by when their father didn't worry about their partying and flying through life in their sports cars or Kawasaki one-hundred horse-power Jet Skis?

Please let them be okay and I promise I'll be a better person, Cahoon silently prayed.

"I heard on the news about your . . ." he started to say.

"Thank you. He had so much amputated, Sol." Hammer cleared her throat. She sipped bourbon and was soothed by its heat. "He wouldn't have had a quality of life, had they been able to clear up the disease. I'm just grateful he didn't suffer any more than he did." She typically looked on the bright side as her heart trembled like something wounded and afraid.

Hammer had not and could not yet accept that when the sun rose this morning and each one after the next, there would be silence in her house. There would be no night sounds of someone rattling in cupboards and turning on the TV. She would have no one to answer or report to, or call when she was late or not going to make it home for dinner, as usual. She had not been a good wife. She had not even been a particularly good friend. Cahoon was struck speechless by the sight of this mighty woman in tears. She was trying hard to muster up that steely control of hers, but her spirit simply could not take it. He got up from his leather wing chair and dimmed the sconces on dark mahogany that he had salvaged from a sixteenth century Tudor manor in England. He went to her and sat on the ottoman, taking one of her hands.

"It's all right, Judy," he kindly said, and he felt like crying, too. "You have every right to feel this way, and you go right on. It's just us, you and me, two human beings in this room right now. Who we are doesn't matter."

"Thanks, Sol," she whispered, and her voice shook as she wiped her eyes and took another swallow of bourbon.

"Get drunk if you want," he suggested. "We have plenty of guest rooms, and you can just stay right here so you don't have to drive."

She patted Cahoon's hand, and crossed her arms and drew a deep breath. "Let's talk about you," she said.

Dejected, he got up and returned to his chair. Cahoon looked at her and braced himself.

"Please don't tell me it's Michael or Jeremy," he said in a barely audible voice. "I know Rachael is all right. She's in her room asleep. I know my wife is fine, sound asleep, too." He paused to compose himself. "My sons are still a bit on the wild side, both working for me and rebellious about it. I know they play hard, too hard, frankly."

Hammer thought of her own sons and was suddenly dismayed that she might have caused this father a moment's concern. "Sol, no, no, no," she quickly reassured him. "This is not about your sons, or about anyone in your family."

"Thank God." He took another swallow of his drink. "Thank you, thank you, God."

He would tithe more than usual to the synagogue next Friday. Maybe he would build another child-care center somewhere, start another scholarship, give to the retirement center and the community school for troubled kids, or an orphanage. Damn it all. Cahoon was sick and tired of unhappiness and people suffering, and he hated crime as if all of it were directed at him.

"What do you want me to do?" he said, leaning forward and ready to mobilize.

"Do?" Hammer was puzzled. "About what?"

"I've had it," he said.

Now she was very confused. Was it possible he already knew what she had come here to tell him? He got up and began to pace in his Gucci leather slippers.

"Enough is enough," he went on with feeling. "I agree with you, see it your way. People being killed, robbed, and raped out there. Houses burglarized, cars stolen, children molested. In this city. Same is true all over the world, except in this country, everybody's got a gun. A gun in every pot. People hurting others and themselves, sometimes not even meaning to. Impulse." He turned around, pacing the other way. "Impaired by drugs and alcohol. Suicides that might not have happened were there not a gun right there. Acci . . ." He caught himself, remembering what had happened to Hammer's husband. "What do you want me—want us at the bank—to do?" He stopped and fixed impassioned eyes on her.

This wasn't what she'd had in mind when she'd rung his doorbell, but Hammer knew when to seize the day. "You certainly could be a crusader, Sol," she thoughtfully replied.

Crusader. Cahoon liked that and thought it time she see he had some substance, too. He sat back down and remembered his bourbon.

"You want to help?" she went on. "Then no more shellacking what really goes on around here. No more bullshit like this one hundred and five percent clearance rate. People need to know the truth. They need someone like you to inspire them to come out swinging."

He nodded, deeply moved. "Well, you know that clearance rate crap wasn't my idea. It was the mayor's."

"Of course." She didn't care.

"By the way," he said, curious now, "what is it really?"

"Not bad." The drink was working. "Around seventy-five percent, which is nowhere near what it ought to be, but substantially
higher than in a lot of cities. Now, if you want to count ten-year-old
cases that are finally cleared or jot down names from the cemetery
or decide that a drug dealer shot dead was the guy responsible for
three uncleared cases . . ."

He held up his hand to stop her. "I get it, Judy," he said. "This
won't happen again. Honestly, I didn't know the details. Mayor
Search is an idiot. Maybe we should get someone else." He started
drumming his fingers on the armrest, plotting.

"Sol." She waited until his eyes focused on her again. "I'm
afraid I do have unpleasant news, and I wanted you to know in person from me before the media gets on it."

He tensed again. He got up and refreshed their drinks as Hammer told him about Blair Mauney III and what had happened this
night. She told him about the paperwork in Mauney's rental car.
Cahoon listened, shocked, the blood draining from his face. He
could not believe that Mauney was dead, murdered, his body
spray-painted and dumped amid trash and brambles. It wasn't that
Cahoon had ever particularly liked the man. Mauney, in Cahoon's
experienced opinion, was a weak weasel with an entitlement attitude and the suggestion of dishonesty did not surprise Cahoon in
the least, the more it sank in. He was chagrined about *USChoice*
cigarettes with their alchemy and little crowns. How could he have
trusted any of it?

"Now it's my turn to ask," Hammer finally said. "What do you
want me to do?"

"Jesus," he said, his tireless brain racing through possibilities,
liabilities, capabilities, impossibilities, and sensibilities. "I'm not
entirely sure. But I know I need time."

"How much?" She swirled her drink.

"Three or four days," he replied. "My guess is most of the
money is still in Grand Cayman in numerous accounts with num-

bers that aren't linked. If this hits the news, I can guarantee that we'll never recover the cash, and no matter what anybody says, a loss like that hurts everybody, every kid with a savings account, every couple needing a loan, every retired citizen with a nest egg."

"Of course it does," said Hammer, who also was a faithful client of Cahoon's bank. "My eternal point, Sol. Everybody gets hurt. A crime victimizes all of us. Not to mention what it will do to your bank's image."

Cahoon looked pained. "That's always the biggest loss. Reputation and whatever charges and fines the federal regulators will decide."

"This isn't your fault."

"Dominion Tobacco and its secret Nobel-potential research always bothered me. I guess I just wanted to believe it was true," he reflected. "But banks have a responsibility not to let something like this happen."

"Then how did it?" she asked.

"You have a senior vice president with access to all commercial loan activities, and trust him. So you don't always follow your own policies and procedures. You make exceptions, circumvent. And then you have trouble." He was getting more depressed. "I should have watched the son of a bitch more closely, damn it."

"Could he have gotten away with it, had he lived?" Hammer asked.

"Sure," Cahoon said. "All he had to do was make sure the loan was repaid. Of course, that would have been from drug money, unbeknownst to us. Meanwhile, he would have been getting maybe ten percent of all money laundered through the hotels, through the bank. And my guess is we would have become more and more of a major cash interstate for whoever these bad people are. Eventually, the truth would have come out. USBank would have been ruined."

Hammer watched him thoughtfully, a new respect forming for this man who, prior to this early morning, she had not understood, and in truth had unfairly judged.

"Just tell me what I can do to help," she said again.

"If you could withhold his identification and everything about this situation so we salvage what we can and get up to speed on exactly what happened," he repeated. "After that, we'll file a Suspicious Activity Report, and the public will know."

Hammer glanced at her watch. It was almost three A.M. "We'll get the FBI on it immediately. It will be in their best interest to buy a little time, too. As for Mauney, as far as I'm concerned, we can't effect a positive identification just yet, and I'm sure Dr. Odom will want to withhold information until he can get hold of dental records, fingerprints, whatever, and you know how overworked he is." She paused, and promised, "It will take a while."

Cahoon thought of Mrs. Mauney III, whom he had met only superficially at parties. "Someone's got to call Polly," he said. "Mauney's wife. I'd like to do that, if you have no objections."

Hammer got up and smiled at him. "You know something, Sol? You're nowhere near as rotten as I thought."

"That works both ways, Judy." He got up.

"It certainly does."

"You hungry?"

"Starved."

"What's open at this hour," he wondered.

"You ever been to the Presto Grill?"

"Is that a club?"

"Yes," she told him. "And guess what, Sol? It's about time you became a member."

Chapter Twenty-six

For the most part, only people up to no good were out at this hour, and as West drove seedy streets looking for Brazil's car, her mood became more grim. In part she was worried. She was also so irritated that she wanted to slug him. What was he, crazy? Where did these irrational, angry fits come from? Were he a woman, she'd wonder about PMS and suggest he go back to the gynecologist. She grabbed the portable phone and dialed again.

"Newsroom," an unfamiliar voice answered.

"Andy Brazil," West said.

"He's not in."

"Has he been in at all the last few hours?" West asked, frustration in her tone. "Have you heard from him?"

"Not that I know of."

West hit the end button and tossed the phone on the seat. She pounded the steering wheel. "Damn you, damn you, Andy!" she exclaimed.

As she cruised, her phone rang, startling her. It was Brazil. She was sure of it as she answered. She was wrong.

"It's Hammer," her chief said. "What in the world are you doing still out?"

"I can't find him."

"You certain he's not home or at the paper?"

"Positive. He's out here courting trouble," West said rather frantically.

"Oh dear," Hammer said. "Cahoon and I are about to have breakfast, Virginia. Here's what I want you to do. No information about this case, and no identification until I tell you otherwise. For now, the case is pending. We need to buy some time here because of this other situation."

"I think that's wise," West said, checking her mirrors, looking everywhere.

She had missed Brazil by no more than two minutes, and in fact, unwittingly had done so a number of times during the past few hours. She would turn onto one street just before he drove past where she had been. Now he was cruising by the Cadillac Grill on West Trade Street and staring out at boarded-up slums haunted by the rulers of the night. He saw the young hooker ahead, leaning inside a Thunderbird, talking to a man looking for a good investment. Brazil wasn't in a shy mood, and he pulled up closer, watching. The car sped off and the hooker turned hostile, glazed eyes on Brazil, not at all happy with the intrusion. Brazil rolled down his window.

"Hey!" he called out.

Poison, the prostitute, stared at the one known on the street as Blondie, mockery in her eyes. She started strolling again. This pretty-boy snitch followed her everywhere, had a thing about her and was still working up his nerve, maybe thought he was going to get something more to leak to the police and the newspaper. She thought it was funny. Brazil unfastened his seatbelt. He reached to roll down the passenger's window. She wasn't going to get away from him this time. No sir, and he tucked the .380 out of sight beneath his seat, as he crept forward, calling out to her.

"Excuse me! Excuse me, ma'am!" he said again and again. "I need to talk to you!"

Hammer was rolling past at this very moment, Cahoon following in his Mercedes 600S V-12 sedan, black with parchment leather interior. He wasn't entirely within his comfort zone in this part of the city, and he checked his locks again as Hammer got on her police radio and told the dispatcher to ten-five Unit 700. Immediately, she and West were on the air.

"The subject you're looking for is at West Trade and Cedar," Hammer said on the radio to West. "You might want to head this way in a hurry."

"Ten-four!"

Officers in the area were perplexed, even a little lost, as they overheard this transmission between their highest leaders. They were still mindful of their chief's feelings about being followed and harassed. Maybe it was wise to sit this one out for a minute or two until they had a better idea about what exactly was going down. West gunned the engine, racing back toward West Trade.

Poison stopped and slowly turned around, seduction smoldering in her eyes as she entertained notions this snitch in the BMW couldn't even begin to imagine.

Hammer wasn't so sure this was the right time to introduce Cahoon to the Presto Grill. Trouble seemed to rise from the street like heat, and she had not gotten where she was in life by ignoring her instincts. Only in her personal life had she looked the other way, turned the volume down low, and denied. She swung off into the All

Right parking lot across from the grill and motioned out her window for Cahoon to follow. He stopped by her unmarked car and his window hummed down.

"What's going on?" he asked.

"Park and get in," she said.

"What?"

She furtively scanned their surroundings. Something bad was out there. She could feel its foulness, detect the scent of the beast. There was no time to waste.

"I can't leave my car here," Cahoon reasonably pointed out, because the Mercedes would be the only car in the lot and possibly the only vehicle within fifty miles that cost roughly one hundred and twenty thousand dollars.

Hammer got the dispatcher on the air. "Send a unit to the All Right parking lot, five hundred block West Trade, to watch a late-model black Mercedes until I give further notice."

Radar, the dispatcher, was none too fond of Hammer, for she, too, was female. But she was the chief, and he, at least, had the good sense to be afraid of the bitch. Radar had no idea what she was doing out on the street, especially at this hour. He sent two units while Poison smiled knowingly and took her time reaching the passenger's window of Brazil's car. She leaned inside like she did all the time and took an inventory of the groomed leather interior. She noted the briefcase, pens, *Charlotte Observer* notepads, old black leather bomber jacket, and most of all, the police scanner and two-way radio.

"You po-lice?" she drawled, a little confused about just who the hell Blondie was.

"A reporter. With the *Observer*," Brazil said, because he was not police anymore. West had made that clear.

Poison appraised him with dangerous flirtation. A reporter's money was as good as any, and now she knew the truth. Blondie wasn't a snitch. He was the one writing those stories that had Punkin Head so cranky and out of control.

"What you trading, little boy?" she asked.

"Information." Brazil's heart was thudding hard. "I'll pay for it."

Poison's eyes gleamed, her lips parting in an amused, gap-toothed smile. She slinked around to his side of the car and leaned in his window. Her fragrance was cloying, like incense.

"What kind you want, little boy?" she asked.

Brazil was wary but intrigued. He'd never dealt with anything like this, and he imagined experienced, worldly men and their secret pleasures. He wondered if they were scared when they let someone like this in their car. Did they ever ask her name or want to know anything about her?

"What's been going on around here," he nervously went on. "The murders. I've seen you around, in the area, I mean. For a while. Maybe you know something."

"Maybe I do. Maybe I don't," she said, trailing a finger down his shoulder.

West was driving fast, passing the same bad places Brazil had moments earlier. Hammer wasn't too far behind her, Cahoon riding shotgun, wide-eyed as he surveyed a reality far removed from his own.

"Will cost you fifty, little boy," Poison said to Brazil.

He didn't have that much in the bank and wasn't about to let her know. "Twenty-five," he negotiated, as if he did it all the time.

Poison backed up, appraising him and thinking about Punkin Head in its van, watching. It had yelled at her and slapped her around this morning. It had hurt her in places no one could see, because of what Blondie had put in the paper. Poison started feeling hateful about it and made a decision that perhaps wasn't very wise, considering she and Punkin Head had already whacked one rich dude tonight, meeting their quota for the week, and cops were all around.

She seemed amused by something Brazil didn't know, and she pointed. "See that corner there, little boy?" she said. "That old apartment building? Nobody in it no more. Meet you back there, 'cause we can't be talking here."

Poison stared into a dark alleyway across the street, where Punkin Head watched from inside its windowless van in dark shadows. It knew what she was up to and was aroused by it and in a mood to murder since it was taking less and less time for it to cool down and get the tension again. Punkin Head felt an insatiable rage toward Blondie that was more exciting than sex. It couldn't wait to watch that fucking snitch soil his fancy jeans and beg on his knees before the almighty Punkin Head. It had never wanted to ruin anything more in its despicable, low, nasty, hate-filled life and its excitement mounted unbearably.

West spotted Brazil's car up ahead. She saw the hooker walking off as Brazil drove to the corner and took a right. She saw the old windowless van slide out of the dark alleyway, like an eel.

"Christ!" West panicked. "Andy, no!"

She grabbed the radio and slammed down the accelerator, flipping on strobing lights. "700 requesting backups!" she screamed on the air. "Two hundred block West Trade. Now!"

Hammer heard the broadcast, too, and sped up. "Shit," she said.

"What the hell's going on?" Cahoon was on red alert, in military mode, ready to take out the enemy.

"Don't know but it's not good." She threw on her lights, whelping her siren as she passed people.

"You got an extra gun handy?" Cahoon asked.

He was in the Marines again, launching grenades at North Koreans, crawling through the blood of his buddies. Nobody went through that and came out the same. Nobody messed with Cahoon, because he knew something they didn't. There were worse things than dying, the fear of it being one of them. He unfastened his seatbelt.

"Put that back on," Hammer told him as they flew.

West was trying to find a place to do a U-turn and finally gave up. She bumped and slammed over the concrete median, rubber squealing as she headed the other way. She had lost sight of Brazil, the hooker, and the van. West was as frantic and frightened as she had ever been.

"Please God, help!" she fervently said. "Oh please God!"

Brazil turned behind haunted ruins of graying old wood and broken windows gaping ragged and black, where there was no sign of life. He stopped and sat in silence. He looked around, increasingly jumpy. Maybe this wasn't such a good idea. He dug in a pocket of his jeans and was taking an inventory of crumpled bills when suddenly the young hooker filled his window, smoking a cigarette, holding a washcloth, and smiling in a way that increased Brazil's misgivings. It was the first time he'd noticed how crazed her eyes were, or maybe something was different now.

"Get out," she said, motioning to him. "I see the money first."

Brazil opened his door and stepped out as an engine roared in from the rear. A dark, old van with no windows bumped toward them at a high rate of speed. Brazil was shocked. He scrambled back inside his BMW, throwing it into reverse. But it was too late. The van blocked him, and there was nothing ahead but a thicket and a deep gully. Trapped, Brazil watched the driver's door open. He took in the big, ugly sh'im with pumpkin-colored hair woven in cornrows close to its skull. It jumped out, its smile serpentine as it walked toward Brazil, a large-caliber pistol in one hand, the other rattling a can of spray paint.

"We got us a sweet one," Punkin Head said to Poison. "Might have some fun. Teach him what we do with snitches."

"I'm not a snitch," Brazil let Punkin Head know.

"He's a reporter," Poison said.

"*A reporter,*" it mocked, its anger raging out of control as memories of Black Widow stories unfurled and flashed and infuriated all over again.

Brazil's stories were the furthest thing from his mind as he thought fast. Poison laughed. She zipped open a switchblade.

"Get out of the car and give me the keys." Punkin Head moved closer to its prey, a .45 caliber pistol pointed between Blondie's eyes.

"All right. All right. Please don't shoot." Brazil knew when to cooperate.

"We got us a beggar." Punkin Head made a harsh, horrid sound that was supposed to be a laugh. "*Please don't shoot,*" it mimicked.

"Let's cut him first." Poison waited outside the BMW's door, knife ready to carve this reporter boy where it hurt.

Brazil turned off the engine. He fumbled with the keys, dropping them to the floor. He groped for them as West squealed around the corner, turning behind the abandoned apartments. Gunshots exploded. BAM-BAM, and BAM-BAM. Her siren screamed and screamed as a gun fired four more times. Hammer turned in four seconds after West, hearing the gunshots, too, flipping on her siren, while backups closed in from all directions of the Queen City, the night a red-and-blue flashing war zone.

West had her gun drawn as she bolted out of her car. Hammer, her partner, was right behind West, pistol racked back and ready. The two women scanned the parked van with running engine. They took in the two bloody bodies not breathing near an open switchblade and a can of spray paint. They locked on Brazil clenching the borrowed .380, as if his victims might hurt him, the gun jumping in his locked hands. Cahoon walked closer to the crime scene, staring at the dead and then all around at the lit-up skyline where his building towered.

West went to Brazil. She carefully took the gun from him and enclosed it in a plastic evidence bag, along with spent cartridge cases.

"It's okay," she said to him.

He blinked, shivering, as his shocked eyes met hers.

"Andy," she said. "This is very traumatic. I've been through it, know all about it, and I'm going to help you every step of the way, okay? I'm here for you now. Got it?"

She took him in her arms. Andy Brazil dug his fingers in her hair. He shut his eyes and held her hard.